D1008349

Also by David Freeman

A Hollywood Education:
Tales of Movie Dreams and Easy Money

The Last Days of Alfred Hitchcock

U. S. Grant in the City

Jesse and the Bandit Queen *(a play)*

Simon & Schuster
New York London Toronto Sydney Tokyo Singapore

A Hollywood Life

by

David Freeman

SIMON & SCHUSTER
SIMON & SCHUSTER BUILDING
ROCKEFELLER CENTER
1230 AVENUE OF THE AMERICAS
NEW YORK, NEW YORK 10020

THIS BOOK IS A WORK OF FICTION. NAMES, CHARACTERS, PLACES AND INCIDENTS ARE EITHER THE PRODUCT OF THE AUTHOR'S IMAGINATION OR ARE USED FICTITIOUSLY. ANY RESEMBLANCE TO ACTUAL EVENTS OR LOCALES OR PERSONS, LIVING OR DEAD, IS ENTIRELY COINCIDENTAL.

DESIGNED BY LEVAVI & LEVAVI
MANUFACTURED IN THE UNITED STATES OF AMERICA

1 3 5 7 9 10 8 6 4 2

LIBRARY OF CONGRESS CATALOGING IN PUBLICATION DATA
FREEMAN, DAVID, DATE.
A HOLLYWOOD LIFE / BY DAVID FREEMAN.
P. CM.
I. TITLE.
PS3556.R3844H65 1991
813'.54—DC20 91-15652
CIP

ISBN 0-671-72738-9

For Sara K. Freeman

Contents

If thou didst ever hold me in thy heart,
Absent thee from felicity a while
And in this harsh world draw thy breath in pain
To tell my story.

—HAMLET, V, II

one

The Magnet of Emotion

1.

When Bobby Shepherd called to tell me that Carla's body had washed up at Rincon Point, a few miles south of Santa Barbara, I didn't believe him. Not that I thought he was joking—just that it was so unlikely. There'd been a yachting accident of some sort; exactly what had happened was still unclear. I don't know who Bobby called before me, or after, but because I was involved in the financing of the picture Carla was shooting, I was high on the list.

It was a Sunday morning and I was still in bed when the call came. When I heard the tension in Bobby's voice, my throat went dry and I got a little dizzy. Then I was still and my mind got very clear. I don't know how much Bobby knew about my personal connection to Carla. Maybe he regarded this as an important but unpleasant business call, but I doubt it. In Hollywood I always proceeded on the assumption that if there's something about yourself that you wonder whether people know, they do. Bobby started telling me all the reasons Carla's death was a calamity. All I could say was "I'm going up to Santa Barbara."

"What for? You think that'll bring her back to life?"

"I'm just going."

"Sidney's ready to bury the picture right along with her. He'll file the claim, so get ready." Sidney Shepherd, Bobby's father, was the chairman of Shepherd-International. Bobby was an executive there. They were financing *Changing Partners,* which would now be her last picture. It's more complicated than that, just as my relationship with Carla was more complicated than the money for the picture, but for the moment I was still trying to get it into my head that she was gone and wasn't coming back. Bobby was going on about direct costs and below-the-line expenses. "Gabe? Gabe, are you still there?"

"Where's the body?"

"Cottage Hospital. It's pointless, but if you want, I'll go with you."

"Is Paul Loeb there?" Loeb was her husband and had presumably been on the yacht.

"I don't know. Gabe, nothing you can do up there affects the bond. So what's the point?" He was referring to the completion bond, a guarantee that the picture would be finished on budget. I had sold him the bond. What Bobby really meant was now he wouldn't be able to get his money out without me.

"I'll call you when I get back."

"Suit yourself," he said, and hung up.

2.

With no one on the Pacific Coast Highway the trip to Santa Barbara took less than two hours. I had last seen Carla two weeks earlier, in Toronto, on the set of *Changing Partners*. Because I held the bond on the picture, I had gone up to look over the production reports. At least that's what I told Bobby and Sidney Shepherd. In fact, I was on more of a personal mission than a professional one. She had been like a narcotic to me, a situation not without its pleasures, but one that always left me feeling led around. The completion bond deal gave me an opportunity to see if I could recapture what Carla and I once had.

She had been promised no more than five weeks in Canada, but now it looked as if she'd have to stay two more. The idea had been to shoot only the interiors there. Then they started doing the exteriors, doubling Toronto for Los Angeles, which is where the story took place. At the time, the American dollar was worth a third more than the Canadian; a lot of movies had gone north.

When I arrived on the set, the gaffer and his crew were

lighting the front of a restaurant. The company had been shooting inside all morning, and now they were getting ready to do a scene on the sidewalk. I crossed the street to watch from there. Several young production assistants were buzzing about self-importantly, walkie-talkies pressed to their ears, barking to one another about crowd control and retiming traffic lights. A crowd had gathered to watch: big-time filmmaking was still enough of a novelty up there that most of the citizenry thought it was just fine to tie up traffic and close off commercial streets in the middle of the day. There had been a lot of publicity about Carla's presence in town—the *Globe* and the local television stations had all been on a Carla watch for weeks. It was that way everywhere. Whenever Carla was around people wanted to see her, and they were willing to wait and even be shoved around for the privilege, mostly so they could tell their friends they had gazed upon Carla Tate.

You can stand around film sets for hours waiting for something to happen, and although I had no intention of doing that, I liked observing the bustle, but being unobserved myself. The director, Frank Wheat, actually Francis A. M. Wheat, known in the trade as the preppy director, was talking to the cinematographer, lining up shots. This was Wheat's third studio picture. The first two had been moderate successes; now he needed a hit if he was going to break into the first rank. He had grown up in New Canaan, gone to Groton and Princeton, and spoke with a boarding-school honk. He looked about as casual as a banker in blue jeans. Carla liked him, probably because he was such an unlikely guy to be making it in the film business.

It was fun to watch the circus from the gallery like this, but when the scene began I realized I wouldn't be able to see much, so I worked my way toward the barricades. I knew if I stepped onto the set, one of those kids with a walkie-talkie would try to have me arrested. I looked around at the crew until I saw a morose face I recognized. It was Dick Schraft, a screenwriter who was here to do a polish on the script. "Once more unto the breach," he said, escorting me into the action.

Screenwriters always complain. It's their normal mode of discourse, but Schraft, who was a well-known guy, celebrated for his ability to fix any script, adjust it to any set of circumstances, seemed gloomier than most. Having spent a few years writing scripts myself, the last thing I wanted to hear was a screenwriter's lament. It always boiled down to the same thing: The director is mangling the script. "Listen to what this clown is doing," Schraft said, glad to have a crony who would understand Wheat's directorial idiocy. He pointed to the restaurant and said, "The scene in there—six full drafts in three days. We go over every beat. I explain it all to him. He's got it, he understands it well enough to think he wrote it himself. Now he's in there playing the whole thing on their hands. He's doing close-ups of fingers. It's a nail polish commercial. I laughed in his face."

"So what happened?" I asked, knowing the answer.

"He threw me out. Why do you think I'm on the street?" Then Schraft told me how smart I was to have gotten out of screenwriting. Just as he was about to launch into a diatribe on the unfairness of the business, there was a murmur from the crowd. It was as if they had turned from several hundred individuals into a single being that moved and breathed all at once. They were behaving like a stage crowd, as if they knew their role was to get excited, playing their parts as supernumeraries in the drama of fame and celebrity.

It was Carla. Her approach made even dour Dick Schraft smile. She was coming out of her trailer, escorted by a production assistant, moving onto the set. The crowd quieted down; there was an unexpected hush. While some stars bring out whistles and catcalls, Carla didn't invite loose chumminess. People tended to hang back and whisper. She was looking down, refusing to acknowledge anyone, concentrating on the scene ahead. It was moments like this that made people think of her as stuck-up or conceited or any of the dumb things Americans ascribe to celebrities who ignore them. I could feel an undercurrent of irritation. People get actors mixed up with politicians all the time. Maybe they expected Carla to trot across the street, shake hands, and kiss a few babies. Despite her concentration, she sensed the crowd's displeasure. She looked up, cocked her head to one side, then tossed her hair. It took only a second or two and she didn't even throw in a smile. But it was an acknowledgment, and they shrieked. The ones in front stretched their hands toward her—she was across the street and the crowd was behind barriers—but they were pressing to be a few inches closer.

She looked tense, high-strung. But even here, under pressure, there was something serene and passive about her. You could see it in her eyes. They were large and dark, set wide apart, and they always seemed to know more than they told. When Carla's mood shifted, she didn't have to use words for you to know it. The changes were in those eyes, dark and malevolent, then radiant and forgiving. Eyes a man could get lost in and never hope to be found. That's how journalists always liked to write about her. Until I saw her eyes, I never really knew what they meant.

Carla was a magnet for the emotions of everyone around her. Part of it came from her fame, but it was also something deeper, a power that was always there. Put her in a village in India where she and her movies were unknown, and the citizens would still follow her, a Pied Piper of the libido.

There've been plenty of gorgeous women on the screen, but no one had ever combined great physical beauty and personal mystery in quite the same way and to such powerful effect. The point at which the inner and outer self intersect, where the flesh and the spirit are joined, is as specific as fingerprints. Carla managed to blend opposite, contradictory qualities. She could be purely intuitive, then logical and rational. When she was younger, feature writers never knew what to make of someone who could be by turns brassy and discreet, incisive then scattered, but always a dominant presence. They dealt with it by calling her spirited or spunky, which is about as useful as describing Albert Einstein as a really smart guy. No matter how well I thought I knew Carla, each time I saw her it was a new experience. I always got a rush that made me feel giddy.

In the picture, Carla played a well-to-do married woman in love with a young carpenter she had hired to remodel her weekend house. Hollywood has been making variations of that one for sixty years. There was no reason to think there wouldn't be room for one more.

Frank Wheat showed Carla the setup for the scene, walking through it, moving his hands around to show her the framing and the camera moves. He didn't particularly want her opinion, and it wasn't likely she would offer it. He was fussing over her because she was bankable, the reason the picture was being made. He would serve as director only as long as he had her confidence and approval. Compared to her, Frank was a novice, and he knew it. As a child star Carla had made a dozen films; as an adult, another twenty-five. He was deferring to her. Because he had those high Groton manners it came easily to him. I couldn't hear what he was saying, but from where I was standing he looked like a duke showing her around his estate. Hovering nearby, waiting to be called, was William Meserve, who played opposite Carla. He was in his late twenties and like Carla had acted professionally as a child. I could tell by the respectful way he stood there, waiting for Frank to finish giving Carla the tour, that he was afraid of her, or at least of crossing her.

Lila Bledsoe, the young actress who played Meserve's girlfriend, stood to one side, waiting to be called. She was from Charleston; twenty-three years old, with spectacular white skin and a sleek figure. She'd been in a couple of pictures, but *Changing Partners* was the first time she'd worked with a star.

After they had rehearsed the scene a few times, Frank called for a take. The scene was brief: Bill Meserve came out of the restaurant, looked around, and a moment later, Carla followed him onto the street. They exchanged angry words, and he walked away. Then Carla looked up and saw that Lila had been watching. Frank was an orthodox director, a conservative guy who had a sketch artist make storyboards of each camera setup. Sometimes Frank would make last-minute changes, usually additions, like the shots of the hands Dick Schraft had been complaining about, but not many. He shot the scene first in master, then moved in for closer angles of each actor going over the same action. First Carla, then Bill Meserve. They were supposed to be arguing, but because they were on a crowded street, they kept their voices low. The spectators were disappointed since the only obvious movement in the scene was the extras, local people who were paid sixty dollars a day and lunch to do three things: walk up and down the block, not look at the principals or the camera, and not, under any circumstances, on penalty of being fired, to act. During the third take, when Carla saw Lila watching her with Bill Meserve, I thought I saw Frank perk up. That should have been my tip-off that something interesting was happening in Carla's performance, but unless you were standing right next to the camera, you couldn't tell what was going on or if it was any good.

I liked watching without her knowing I was there. It was hard enough to have control over Carla. For a few minutes, I at least had the illusion of control. I was going to have dinner that night with her and Cora Cohen, who was nominally her publicist, but really more of a confidante and friend. Carla had plenty of retainers, and Cora was on the payroll, but she was no flunky. When I arrived at Carla's suite, Cora was busy grilling a bodyguard, who had been sent up by the concierge after Cora had notified the hotel that we were going out to dinner. He was a big, dumb-looking kid wearing a tuxedo with a polka-dot tie and wing collar. He looked like a nominee for a Grammy Award. For all I knew he may have been a terrific bodyguard, but one thing was sure: He had never been up against anyone like Cora Cohen. As Carla put it, "The woman accepts no excrement." And she sure didn't accept any from freelance bodyguards. In an attempt to impress Cora with his experience, he announced he had once guarded someone known as Big Willie, when he had passed through Toronto.

"Sonny-Jim," Cora said, looking this guy in the eye, "you can sit on Big Willie's face till the lease runs out, but you can forget about this gig."

After the bodyguard left, Carla emerged from the bedroom, wearing one of the silky jumpsuits that were her trademark. She had them in a dozen colors. They looked comfortable yet still sexy; the silk always moved with her. This one was dark blue, and the zipper that ran up the back was still undone. To see her again, up close, not as part of a crowd, was to know immediately that of course I was still hooked. How could I not be? "Hello, darling," she said, turning her tan and muscled back, asking me to zip her up. As I fumbled, she glanced over her shoulder, amused at my awkwardness, and said, "A real California boy—always a teenager."

Carla gave me a hug and offered her cheek for a kiss. "Still addicted to me, I hope?" she asked, brushing my face with her fingertips.

Without the bodyguard, we decided to eat downstairs in the hotel. The maître d' blocked off a corner table and left the adjacent ones empty. A couple of waiters were assigned to tend to our needs. I knew they were going to be disappointed. It was Cora who always signed the check and she was tight with a tip. I liked Cora but I knew never to cross her. She was about ten years older than Carla and they had been together since Carla was eighteen. Cora was a lesbian, and I always assumed she was in love with her boss. But then, so was I: we had that much in common. In Cora's case it was unrequited in the physical sense. But emotionally, she was one of the few constants in Carla's life.

The waiters made a little show of bringing us silver finger bowls with lemon wedges covered in cheesecloth. Carla's was presented with an extra flourish and bow. Everywhere she went, people hauled out their goofiest pretensions. "Maybe I should ask for Perrier in mine," she said, flicking water at me.

"I think we're the only table with finger bowls," Cora said.

"No, no," Carla said. "If I get one, everybody does. Finger bowls for the house," she announced, gesturing to the room in general. As she raised her hand, the two waiters came hurrying to the table. Rather than trying to explain it, I glanced instead at the wine list and ordered a white burgundy. I managed to suggest we didn't need to hear its history. When the waiters left, Cora noticed a woman standing in the entrance to the dining room. "There's Hello Dolly," she said. "You want to talk to her?" Carla just rolled her eyes.

I glanced over at an intense-looking, overdressed woman of about thirty-five. "Hello Dolly?"

"Her name's Dolly and all she does is work the room." Cora began imitating the woman. "Hello, hello, hello," she said in an unctuous voice. "Don't encourage her, or she'll be over here and never leave."

"She'll ask about my mother. I'm not up to that," Carla said. Cora explained that Hello Dolly was the mother of a child in the picture. She assumed that Carla would pay special attention to a child actress. After a scowl from Cora, Dolly got the idea, waved to us, and left the room. Despite what Carla had said, Dolly's presence set her off about her mother and her own kids—she had two daughters and a stepdaughter. She prided herself on how well she was raising them. "They'll be running wild by the time I get home. Paul just lets them do whatever pops into their heads." Paul Loeb was her third husband.

"Mama Carla, the disciplinarian," I said.

"Damn straight. My mother was the opposite of that. She never knew what hit her."

"Nobody knows how to raise a movie star," Cora said. "Dr. Spock doesn't exactly have a chapter on that one."

"Oh, Christ," Carla snapped. "My mother couldn't raise tomatoes if she had a greenhouse."

We ordered, but before the food arrived, Lila Bledsoe stopped at our table. "I just had to tell you," Lila said, in her honeyed drawl, "in that last shot, when you looked over and saw me, I got goose bumps. I truly did, all up and down my arm. I just learn so much from watching you work."

"Thanks," Carla said, with a coolness in her voice that rattled Lila. She was clearly in awe of Carla. Lila was too young to understand that Carla didn't particularly relish being a mentor to a beautiful actress sixteen years her junior.

Cora introduced me, and I rose when Lila offered her hand.

She held on to mine for an extra beat. I recognized a young actress in action. I'm sure she felt any man dining with a star was formidable. She was determined to be memorable, if only for a second. I was tempted to say, "I'm the insurance man," just to see what she would do. When she was gone, Carla said grudgingly, "She's a good actress. She liked you, Gabe."

"Not my type."

"So which of the girls do you like?" Carla asked.

"I thought you'd make some recommendations. I'm only here overnight," I said.

"Now there's a challenge," she said. "You like 'em dark and slim."

"What else?" I asked. "Aside from dark and slim?" We both knew who we were talking about.

She thought for a long moment. I thought her mind had wandered, but then she said, "Good to her kids, sorry about her parents and hell on her husbands. Sometimes she thinks she peaked around eleven." Then her mood shifted again. "Another week, maybe two, and we're out of here."

"Tired of the picture?" I asked.

"I guess. Tired of the hotel. I want to go home. I'm going to take the kids out on the boat. Up to Santa Barbara."

As we sat there, the dining room was filling up. A couple of above-the-line hotshots—first Dick Schraft, then one of the associate producers—came over to our table, but the others just stared from a distance. Not every second of course, but throughout the evening, everyone in the restaurant would glance over in a proprietary way. The ones not connected to *Changing Partners* seemed to want to record the experience. Carla was aware of the attention, I'm sure, but after a lifetime of it she gave no sign of noticing.

Carla had learned to block out whatever didn't serve her immediate interests. She wasn't always aware she was doing that, but over the years it had become an instinctive, self-protective reaction to the constant stream of supplicants, sycophants and even friends who felt their careers could rise or fall on her mood or whim.

After dinner, I went back to my room, turned on the television, and thought about Carla. Her intensity when she talked about her mother had surprised me. Carla was usually more reactive than reflective. I found myself thinking about the first time I saw her.

As a kid I had seen her movies, of course, but I had never actually seen her. When I was fourteen, I sometimes tagged along with my father, who was a studio musician, when he played scoring sessions. The conductor, who was usually the composer, ran the orchestra while a black-and-white work print of the picture was projected on a big screen. There was a footage counter on the floor, and the musicians played the cues, matching them to the action on the screen. My dad took me along whenever he could. He was playing the trumpet for Bernard Herrmann on a picture at Warner's called *Crescendo*. Because he had been ordered to cut several cues he thought were important, Benny Herrmann was in a foul mood and was taking it out on the musicians. My dad was worried that Benny would yell at him in front of me. So I was nervous, too. Carla played the second lead in the picture, although I wasn't aware of it until I got to the studio. I watched her on the screen—twenty feet tall, the most gorgeous image I had ever seen, starting and stopping, and appearing to walk backward when the film was rewound. Then I felt the air in the room change. I assumed it was my own priapic state, but even from my self-absorbed vantage point, I knew something had happened. The musicians were having trouble concentrating. Carla had turned up at the session. It was too much for my overheated hormones to bear. I positively throbbed. She was three years older than I, a lifetime to an adolescent. She was with the producer and her boyfriend of the moment, an actor who held her hand and stroked her hair.

She was wearing plaid pedal pushers and a tight white angora sweater. I can't say what I actually did, although later my father told me I all but drooled. I don't remember that, but I do recall my eyes darting from the enormous version of her on the screen to the real thing a few feet away. I must have been giving off mating signals, because she glanced over and smiled. It pinned me to my seat. My memory of her outfit is that it was on the trashy side, a style she soon dropped. It sure as hell spoke to me.

Years later, when I told her about it, she kidded me, threatening to have the designer on the picture we were working on duplicate the outfit so she could wear it for me. That was in the early seventies, when I had met her on something more resembling an equal footing. I was back in Los Angeles after roaming around Europe for several years. I had decided to go into a branch of the family business, declaring myself a screenwriter because that seemed as likely a way as any to get started. In addition to a pencil and paper, all I needed was some time. What else does a young man have? If I failed, no one would ever notice.

Because my father had been a music contractor as well as a musician, he knew a lot of producers and agents. I was able to get into offices not usually open to beginners. A script I wrote called *The Confession* was sold for enough money to get me noticed, even though the film was never made. It was enough to make me a screenwriter; I began getting assignments. One of them, the adaptation of a wretched mystery novel about a prison break called *Sing Sing Blues* into an only slightly less wretched movie called *The Joint*, not only got made, but even did some business. I was declared expert at mystery, a form about which I knew almost nothing.

My new reputation led to an assignment to do a production polish on *Desperately Yours*, a picture of Carla's that was about to start shooting in South Dakota. I packed my yellow legal pads and went off to the Black Hills. The company was staying in a motel about sixty miles from Rapid City. The air was clear and the sky huge.

Affairs on location are not unusual. Everyone's away from home and the work is very intense. Location is not like real life. You don't see anybody you know and the one thing you do all the time is the movie. It's so hard to get a movie made that by the time you get up to the starting gate, everyone's emotions are raw. People are vulnerable. *Desperately Yours* was a studio picture with a big star and budget—real imperial Hollywood moviemaking. Under those circumstances people tend to fall in and out of bed.

The director, Felix Hopkins, was gay, and Carla preferred to discuss the movie with me. The idea that the director wasn't even a possible lover put her off. Libidinal energy is one of the major forces that shapes a performance. Not 100 percent and not all the time, but it's a significant component. Felix couldn't stimulate it and there I was. We were both unmarried, far from home, and spending lots of time together.

When we were working, and I touched her or accidentally brushed against her, I would shake. She knew it, of course. How could she not? After the second or third time, she said, "You know what one of the drawbacks to being the star is?"

My throat was too dry for me to answer.

"People think you're unapproachable," she said, locking her eyes to mine.

It was a heady time for me. I felt drunk with the power of love. The opportunity to satisfy an old crush was only part of it. It was also simpler than that. Carla gave me a romantic high that I had never imagined. Just as Carla could lose herself in a performance, she could give herself over to love in a way that made each time feel as if we were inventing sex.

When the picture began shooting, Carla was on the set either all day or all night. But when she came back to the motel, after she'd called her daughter and gone over her phone messages with Cora, she'd call me and ask if I'd like to come to her room for a drink. She had a loose tartan skirt that she wore in the picture and always wore when I came to her room, because it reminded us both of the pedal pushers that had so caught my eye at Warner's, all those years ago. The skirt was wool with a lot of pleats, and it rolled across her legs when she walked.

As soon as the door was closed I would reach underneath the skirt and pull off her tight black underwear, but I would insist that she leave the skirt on. It just drove me crazy to push that rough wool up over her hips and then make love until we couldn't. I think we generated energy and heat enough in that motel in South Dakota to inspire all the scripts the world would ever need.

My work was done well before the movie was completed. Normally I would have gone back to Los Angeles and looked for another job. But Carla wouldn't hear of it. She told Felix she wanted me on the set for script changes. Felix probably knew the truth—news of the star traveled fast. So I stayed on. The idea of being there because Carla demanded it all but made me delirious. It's hard to think of anything quite as powerful as having one of the world's most beautiful and desirable women insist that I be paid thousands of dollars a week to be her consort.

While we were in South Dakota and my head was being turned hard and well, I became aware of Carla's friendship with Jack Markel, a Hollywood lawyer who was thirty years her senior. There were frequent phone messages from him, and the mention of his name always focused her attention. Part of being a star is that it seems absolutely everyone tries to tug at you. It wouldn't have surprised me if Cora had said, "Carla, there are a few people trying to reach you—the Secretary of State, the King of Belgium and the Pope." If that, or something like it, happens to you every day, year in and year out, how much attention do you think you would pay? But whenever Jack's name was mentioned, Carla always listened. When I asked Cora about it, as discreetly as I could, she said, "Don't get in the way of that. You'll get buried." Jack was a lawyer whose considerable position came as much from his perceived power as from his actual influence. When the scene painters local of the stagehands union decided they might do better if they were affiliated with the Teamsters, the studios grew alarmed. Jack had a talk with the head of the scene painters and another with a few officials of the Teamsters. He never threatened anyone, but he told them such a move was shortsighted and in the long run could cause more problems than it would solve. The plan was dropped and nothing more was said about it. Another labor lawyer might have accomplished as much, but no one else could have done it with so few words. What was said of Mao in China was said of Jack in Hollywood: When he spoke, no dog barked.

When the picture was over, our romance was too, although we stayed friends. Given the situation with Jack Markel, and the fact that I was a screenwriter, a position of little dignity and no authority, I thought I was lucky to have had a location dalliance with her, but I knew it could never be more serious. That was the Hollywood line and I bought it. Then she married Paul Loeb. A screenwriter!

The ringing phone jarred me out of my thoughts. She couldn't sleep. "Want to talk for a while?" I asked.

"Come on up."

She was wearing a red silk kimono, loosely wrapped, certainly sexy. But she was also wearing furry, floppy, pink slippers that looked like they should have belonged to her kids. It was an odd combination of a come-on and stay-away look. I had learned long ago with Carla that the best thing was to try to read her mood and then just go with it. Trying to force her in any direction was futile. Just because the very idea of her put me in a fever didn't mean it was mutual. I asked her if she was upset.

"No," she said, meaning yes. "Want some wine?"

Drinking for her was like everything else—when she did it, she did a lot of it. I found a bottle of Pouilly Fuissé in the minibar. By the time I had filled a couple of glasses, Carla had changed her mind about wanting it. She asked me about the sale of the studio. The whole affair was treacherous in the way that movie deals so often are. She knew all about it, and besides, I didn't believe she really cared. I told her what I thought, that it didn't matter who owned the place. She was the reason movies got made, and from her perspective, managements were interchangeable.

We were sitting on the sofa and she snuggled next to me. I kissed her, but she pulled back.

I could sense her mind racing and skipping. After a moment or two, she said, "I don't know if this movie's any good. I can't tell. It's supposed to be set in L.A. Why are we up here? It was interiors only, I thought. I worked on the street today. It's not going to look right. It's like low-budget time or something. It makes me sick. Who cares? Where's my wine?"

"Frank knows how to shoot this stuff," I told her, handing her a glass. "It won't look that bad. No hockey teams."

"Mr. Country Club? Why'd I say yes to that guy? Directors are supposed to be thugs with a vision. He's like from Wall Street."

I could see her winding up to start berating Frank Wheat—even though she liked him. Most of the time. "He make a pass at you?"

"No. The coward. You're the only one who's made a pass at me. Just stay with me for a while." She curled up again, resting her head against my chest. "I'm tired. I don't like it anymore."

"Take some time off. Why not?"

"Maybe we could go away and work on the damn memoirs for a while," she said, knowing that was certain to appeal to me. A few years earlier Carla had gotten talked into signing a contract to write her autobiography. Then she had proceeded to reject everybody the publisher sent to help her. After she had tried to do it herself, and gotten nowhere, she decided I should help. "But I'm already booked into some other stupid thing," she said.

"They'll put it off for you, just like they'll put off the memoirs. They can rewrite the script or something. All it costs is money."

"Maybe. It sounds easy, then it gets crazy. At least the next one's in Paris. It better be. What good is it?" she said suddenly. "The audience is seventeen years old! They go to shopping malls. They don't know who I am. There's no sense of me out there anymore."

"Which polls do you want me to dig out—the ones where you're the most respected woman or one where you're the top woman star?"

"That stuff is such crap. Polls by the studios for the studios. If they want to get a poll that says everybody in America thinks I'm a transvestite, they could do it." She was on her feet, pacing and running her hands through her hair. She meant what she was saying. She was too much of an actress to deliver lines halfheartedly, but I could also see that this was indeed a performance, cathartic for her in some way. "I'm thirty-nine years old," she yelled. "Look what I'm playing in this thing: an older woman trying without much success to hold on to her figure. I'm two steps from doing guest shots on 'Dallas.' If you could see past your prick you'd know it."

"Carla, I believe you believe it. But it's not true. There's a stack of scripts right in this room—whichever ones you say yes to will get made, and you'll earn two million bucks a pop."

"Because the studios are run by idiots. Those guys don't buy the tickets. Kids just want to see movies about kids. I know. I've got daughters. I know what they want. I'm some kind of antique to them and it's going to catch up. Maybe not on this picture. But it's coming. So I'll do exercise tapes or 'Hollywood Squares' and stop putting myself through this. Oh, who cares? Go tell it to little Miss Muffett."

"Who?"

"You know. The bitch you've got a crush on. 'Nice to meet you,' " she said, getting to her feet, doing a perfect imitation of me shaking hands with Lila Bledsoe. "Don't you dare touch her. I'll kill you if you sleep with her. You're probably going to go there right now."

"She admires you," I said, amused to see Carla jealous. "She wants to be like you. It's a compliment."

"Well, she can keep her compliments. The position's taken," she said, sitting next to me on the sofa. "I'm not through being like me yet, thank you very much."

I was rubbing her shoulders, trying to relax her, but also enjoying the feel of her silk kimono over her skin. My hand was on the back of her neck, under her hair. She cooed. That's the only word for it. Then she began stroking my neck, too, digging her fingers under my collar. My head was starting to spin.

Making love to someone who lives so vividly in your imagination, as well as the imagination of others, can be unsettling.

Maybe if this had been the first time for us it would have confused me even more than it did. But Carla made love easily. She never worried if she was doing it right or if it was going well. As a result, it had an ease that I never felt with anyone else. She just slipped down on the sofa and rolled beneath me. At the same time she put her arms around me and wrapped her legs over my back. Her kimono fell away and as she opened my pants we started to breathe together. This was no lengthy, passionate embrace that would last and last, but rather a building cadence, an easy pressing and pulling back. I felt pure, unalloyed pleasure sweep through me. When we relaxed and lay on our sides, she smiled and said, "Didn't things used to be a little livelier?"

"We were younger, I guess. I thought it was pretty great."

"Yeah, for the show-business old-folks home, maybe. You used to make me feel like the dirty girl. We got trashier. Remember?" Did I remember? I often think my entire life is taken up with remembering. But now Carla was taking charge. She pushed aside the coffee table, then rolled the two of us onto the floor.

Carla's libido, an awesome thing, had taken over. I was doing my best not to remind myself that we were about to do this again, with no more than two minutes' rest. She could probably read my thoughts because she smiled at me in a way that seemed to say, "Don't worry, leave it to me. If you're alive, it'll work." She took me in her mouth, which managed to banish all thought and worry. We stayed like that, with her mouth locked around me, until we could both feel me start to revive. Then she moved back, laughing at my recovery and jamming herself down on me, pushing against me, her face turning a soft rosy color. Her whole body was glowing.

I stood and gathered her up. She clung to my neck with her legs around my waist, as we moved against a high-backed wing chair which our unthinking bodies had shoved toward the wall, while I pushed deeper into her, reaching for her center, and perhaps my own. When she began to come, she gripped my shoulders and pushed her fingers into my skin so hard that the marks stayed for weeks, turning a mottled blue, then yellow, until they finally faded. Each time I took off my shirt I would touch them and for the first days it would make me tremble.

The thought of those bruises lingered, as I continued driving up the coast. Just before Montecito, on the outskirts of Santa Barbara, I passed the entrance to Rincon Point. I looked over at the quiet, high suburban houses that line the road down to the rocky beach. As I drove by, a family that might have been the illustration for a greeting card pulled out onto the highway in a Buick station wagon, probably on their way to church. A little boy in the back tugged at his necktie and stared at me. He and his family were surely unaware that Carla Tate had drowned, practically in their backyard, only a few hours earlier.

3.

Santa Barbara doesn't have a morgue. The sheriff, who doubles as the coroner, leases space in Cottage Hospital. One of the pathologists performs the autopsies. At first they wouldn't let me in, but Cora was already there to keep out the reporters and to make sure that no photographs were taken. She assured them I wasn't a body snatcher, or worse, a member of the press.

The place had a lot of tile and stainless steel. It looked like a restaurant kitchen. It was a weekend morning and still early enough that the hordes of journalists who would soon be chasing this story hadn't gotten wind of it yet. Carla's was the only corpse in the place. Not a lot of mysterious deaths in Santa Barbara. I had been in the Los Angeles morgue once, where the stiffs were stacked up on triple-decker gurneys. Here, two hours north, there was only Carla, spread out on a steel table with white plastic clinging to her. As we were standing around and I was starting to feel sick, some dimwit of a hospital orderly, a young guy, maybe twenty, came into the room and tried to take a photograph, probably with a fantasy of selling it for a fortune to one of the supermarket tabloids. Before he could focus, Cora punched him in the mouth, grabbed his camera, and yanked out the film. She moved so fast that none of us realized what was happening until the guy was screaming that Cora had broken his jaw. She threw his camera against the wall and said, "Sue me, asshole." One of the sheriff's men started to say something, but seeing the cold fury on Cora's face, thought better of it.

As the orderly was heading out of the room, he almost collided with Jack Markel. I learned later that Jack and his wife had been in Santa Barbara that weekend and had actually seen Carla the night she died. Jack stood in the doorway, his eyes scanning the room, taking a quick census. No matter what the circumstances, Jack always looked before he made a move. He was a short, barrel-chested, broad-shouldered man, who gave the accurate impression of great physical strength. Despite his age, which was seventy, he looked like a man who, if he could not persuade you with reason, would have no trouble knocking your teeth down your throat to help you see things his way. He was wearing a black-and-white houndstooth-check jacket and a knit tie. There was always a touch of formality about him. Carla used to tease him that he'd been born in a white shirt and business suit.

Carla had married three times and known many lovers, but Jack was her one great, enduring passion. Because of the difference in their ages, he had been father and teacher to her as well as lover. They had been together for more than twenty years in a way that, while hardly traditional, was the fundamental alliance of Carla's life. Whatever happiness Carla had known in this world, she had known with Jack Markel.

Jack walked directly to the body without acknowledging anyone. Like me, he had come to see for himself. When he was standing over the corpse, he hesitated—a rare thing for this very assured man. His face didn't change or betray his thoughts; he just stood there for an instant, as if by putting off uncovering her he might put off her death, or in some way at least delay it. Then Cora pulled back the plastic from Carla's body, which was badly bruised from the rocks. "Take a look," Cora said. "There won't be another."

We all grieve in separate and private ways that are unknowable to others. Jack gave nothing away, certainly not about the state of his soul. I saw a weariness come over him; the muscles in his face seemed to go slack. It lasted only a couple of seconds, but I knew that a turning point every bit as important in his life as in mine had just occurred. I knew how important Jack had been to Carla. What I hadn't known was what she had been to him. I could see now, despite the mask he wore, that a part of Jack had died with Carla. When you're his age, you don't anticipate a lot of new romance. I wanted to stand there for a few moments, staring at her, bearing witness to the obvious, but when Jack finally turned away from her body, he pulled me aside. He retreated into business talk, but I could feel his pain, right along with my own.

"Sidney call yet?" He wanted to know whether Sidney Shepherd had told me that he wanted to shut down the picture and claim the insurance. There was no apparent emotion in Jack's words, just a business question. But there was an intensity in his voice, a sharp quality I had never heard before.

"Bobby did. They'll file tomorrow, start of business."

"Stall him."

"All right."

"We're going to figure out if it can be finished." This was vintage Markel. The "we" included me. What he wanted was to see if *Changing Partners* could be completed without Carla. We both knew it would be a dicey proposition. I didn't know if it could be done in a way that wouldn't look truncated and botched. Since this would be her last picture, finishing it right and getting it into the theaters would be the only memorial Carla would have given a damn about. Sidney Shepherd would be glad to pay tribute to Carla, but he'd balk at eight million dollars' worth of it.

"I'll need your help," he said. I nodded and he turned and left the room. He didn't even glance at her body again; he just walked out. Cora followed him to check about what to do, who should be called before it was on the news and in the papers. As they left, he glanced at Cora as if to say "How could this happen?" It was wildly unfair, but there was a connection there, a moment of shared grief. It was quick and hard to pin down, but it was something like what divorced parents, meeting at the death of a child, must feel.

I walked back to Carla's body, lying on the stainless-steel table. She had already started to turn an awful ash color. Her lips had gone blue. I felt numb enough that it wouldn't have surprised me if I had turned the same gray color just watching her. That didn't happen, of course, but I did stand there for a very long time, looking I'm not sure for what. My mind ranged back over everything she'd ever said to me, all the times we had spent together. A flood of feeling and lost emotion came over me.

She had first asked me about helping with her autobiography over lunch at the old Ma Maison on Melrose, a place Carla adored. She was drinking Napa chardonnay and trying to talk me into doing it. She said I knew as much about her as anyone who could type. But I wanted out of the writing business by then, and besides, she was too young for memoirs. To convince me of how easy it would be, she had said; "If you don't know something about me and I can't remember it, we'll just make it up. Celebrity biographies are all lies anyway." I remember thinking how much I loved this woman, no matter who she was married to, no matter how deeply connected she was to Jack Markel. She could see it in my eyes, I'm sure. She could always read my thoughts, particularly about her. She smiled, held up her glass, and said, "Gabriel Burton, I, Carla Tate, commission you to write my biography. That's an obligation and you can't get out of it."

Cora had punched an orderly, Jack had tried to cut a deal with death, and I retreated into thoughts of the past. Back in Los Angeles that night, the television news shows were an orgy of Carla's film clips. I was so restless that I kept switching channels. One moment I'd be looking at her when she was eight, then I'd switch and she'd be thirty. Another click and she was nineteen. The effect on me was of time fractured, as if the world had lost its moorings and was spinning out of control. Then Jack called. No preliminaries. He just said, "This is Jack Markel." He wanted to screen all the footage from *Changing Partners* at his house. He wanted me to set it up. I had no authority to do any such thing, but it never occurred to me to hesitate. I knew that if Jack hadn't asked Frank Wheat, it was because he didn't trust him. Jack's assumption was probably that Frank would put his own interests above Carla's. He knew the Shepherds certainly would. So I assumed authority. The movie business is always like that—power belongs to those who seize it.

I called Henry Sisto, a lovely, gentle man who was the film's editor, and told him to pack up everything, hire a truck, and bring the equipment to Jack's house in Bel Air the next morning. Cutters are in a unique position on a picture. They have no control, and no participation in the early stages when the decisions that will define the movie are made. But they see the footage more times than anyone, including the director. There are no secrets from an experienced editor, and Henry was certainly that. He was about fifty and he'd been doing this his entire professional life. When I first knew him he still wore the single white cotton glove that was once the badge of his trade.

Because the picture wasn't finished, the sound track was on a separate roll from the image. To show it required a special Siemens projector. I told Henry to borrow or rent one and bring it. "Don't tell anyone about this. Not Frank, not the Shepherds."

"Gabe," he said, nervously, "I work for the Shepherds and for Frank."

"Do you know who Jack Markel is?"

"Yeah, yeah. I could be fired. I'll have to bring a projectionist. Who am I going to get?"

"Why? You can run it yourself."

"But it's a union job. I never ran one."

"Learn. It's just a matter of loading it, right?"

"I don't know . . ." Henry said, sounding frightened.

"Do this the way Jack wants and you could wind up in a better spot than you ever thought possible." I was already sounding like some thug. Jack hadn't told me to say that—it just came out. It must have worked because Henry agreed to meet me at Jack's the next morning at ten.

Jack lived in a big, rambling house that looked like the set of an old Christmas-in-Connecticut picture. The interior was department-store good taste. If there was anything personal about the place, any sign that Jack and his wife Mona had lived and raised two children there over thirty years, I sure couldn't spot it. A maid showed me into a den where Henry was staring uneasily at the projector. He had set up a screen. Jack didn't have a screening room—that was a luxury for people who worked directly with movies. Jack regularly attended private screenings in other people's houses, but he himself lived in a world of deals and maneuvering. Even if he liked movies—movies without Carla in them—he didn't like them enough to run them at home.

A silver coffeepot and croissants had been set out. Jack shook my hand but he seemed a little awkward. I guessed he too was nervous about what we were about to see. Henry explained that he could show the assembly of the film, then the significant footage of Carla that had not been included. "Frank already cut a few scenes," Henry said. "And we have the takes I didn't use in the assembly."

"Were those your choices or Frank's?" I asked.

"Some of each. He gave me notes during dailies. I can show you everything if you want."

"Everything," Jack said. This was going to be one long day.

Looking at assemblies and rough cuts of movies can be an unsettling experience under any circumstances. The image is murky. The sound isn't mixed or balanced and can be tinny or sometimes not there at all. There's no music, and no sound effects.

But even in this unedited, muddy work print, Carla was hypnotic. It was clear that her performance was first-rate: She filled the screen and her face vibrated with hidden emotion—reservoirs of feeling, of meaning implied but unstated. Watching it, I realized again why I loved her. It wasn't just libidinal or glandular, as I often thought. She was astonishing and I was in awe. All thoughts of her capriciousness, her husbands, of the fact that we would never make love again and knock over the furniture in another hotel room, or of Jack, sitting next to me seemingly mesmerized by this footage—it all fell away.

When Carla worked, nothing existed but the moment itself. She merged with it. Playing to the camera never appealed to her. Other than making sure that there was one, she barely paid attention to the camera. She pursued the opposite of that kind of acting. She embodied a character. It wasn't a matter of mimicry or performing, but rather the creation of a person. Her gift was to be able to fully imagine the way a character thought. Carla entered into the dreams and fantasies of a fictional person. From there, the character's inflections and posture followed naturally. It wasn't a simulation or a comment, but the thing itself.

There was one close-up where she said nothing, but her face said it all. It was in the scene I had watched on the street in Toronto, where Carla argued with Bill Meserve, then looked up and saw Lila Bledsoe watching. You could see all the confusion, sorrow and lust of a married woman who had allowed herself to get involved with a younger man. Then she noticed Lila, who looked crushed. That seemed to induce a terrible guilt in Carla. A second wave of emotion rolled through her. You couldn't not watch her. The image kept erupting, and it was all done with her eyes. It was the art that concealed art. When an actor can do that, then the character's actions are almost beyond judgment, and they become reality itself. Actors who play more extreme social types do it. It's rarer for leading players, who are usually working closer to their own personalities.

It's an irrefutable sign of greatness. And Carla had been doing it since she was six.

At one o'clock, Mona came in with a tray of sandwiches. She was a little younger than Jack, with short, silvery hair and the kind of sinewy figure and burnished skin that comes from a lifetime of tennis and outdoor lunches. Her husband looked pale, as if the blood had been drained from him. If Mona ever had any doubts about Jack's relationship with Carla Tate, one look at him at that moment surely cleared them up.

"Ready again," Henry said, as a sequence of Carla and Lila came up. They were in an unfinished room—an addition to Carla's house. At this point in the plot, Lila was unaware of her boyfriend's affair with Carla. What came through in the scene was a sense of guilt that Carla felt toward this younger woman. The more Carla talked to Lila, the worse she seemed to feel. Now that's a no-win situation for an actress. Lila was young and beautiful, the wronged party. It made Carla the villain. Carla knew what the scene was about; she was playing the subtext full tilt. Not many stars would have done that. Almost any other bankable actress would have insisted that Lila's character be rewritten so that she'd be an arsonist or some other damn thing that would make her hateful. Instead of turning Carla into a bitch, her own sense of guilt made it her scene after all.

After Henry had run the assembly, he began to show us the outtakes—the rejected shots of what we had already seen, unnecessary coverage and takes judged inadequate or marred by some technical problem. Jack looked at each one with an intensity I could feel. The enormity of her death began to come over me again. Private grief for a public person is an unusual thing. If someone close to you dies, you may well look through a family scrapbook to try to feel their presence again. But this was a Hollywood movie which ended as abruptly as Carla's life. When Henry turned on the lights after the last reel of outtakes, I was drained. Looking over at Jack, I could see that he had been in tears. The fact that we had both been undone gave me some comfort.

Jack told Henry never to mention to anyone that he had been here or that this screening had taken place. Then he handed him a thousand dollars. "I don't want anything about today in the papers. If there isn't, you've got another thousand coming." Henry couldn't believe it. He just stared at the money—ten one-hundred-dollar bills. It wasn't the amount so much as the idea of cash. Henry was used to payroll checks with deductions and withholding. Jack didn't say when the additional money would be paid or how he would know if Henry had leaked anything.

After Henry had left, Jack looked over at me for a long moment, taking my measure. My stomach was in knots from watching Carla for six hours. I didn't know how much Jack knew about my relationship with her. She had told me he knew everything, but how could he know the part she played in my inner life?

Jack and I were forging a strange alliance. We had each been bound up with her in a different way, but now here we were, about to decide what to do to make the most of her last picture. He wanted to know what I thought of the picture overall—not its commercial chances, which he could judge well enough, but its merits as a movie. No matter how experienced Jack was, and he had been in the picture business longer than I had been alive, he knew that rough assemblies were tough to call. Jack didn't intend to make any mistakes. It was easy enough to say finishing the picture was what Carla would have wanted. Jack wanted to make sure it could be done well and that it would enhance Carla's reputation, and not just be a ghoulish bonanza for the Shepherds.

He had wanted me here because he trusted my discretion in anything that had to do with Carla, but also because he knew that I had once made my living fixing scripts. And although he wouldn't say it, I knew he was going to rely on my judgment about movies because Carla always had.

"What do you think?" he asked, with no apparent emotion, as if he were trying to decide where to have lunch.

"It's a great performance in the making," I answered in as measured a voice as I could manage.

"If that's true, then the only question is whether the picture can be finished in a way that preserves the work that's already been done."

"That's the question, all right."

"Well, can it?"

People on the business end of movies always ask questions like that. They want answers that can't be known. Although I had never been in a story meeting quite like this one, I had been in enough to know that it was up to me to offer a subjective response as if it were objective truth. "The script will have to be rewritten," I said. "More emphasis put on Lila. It'll be a different picture than what Carla had envisioned."

"But still hers?"

"Yes. Because she died in the middle of it, whatever is finally on the screen will have mystery."

"And if the acting is the best she's done," he said, "the public will want to see it, and it'll have the respect of the critics."

When he was talking like that, calm and coolly analytical, I could see how he got his reputation. But still, it sounded so cold—until he stopped, and I realized that he was in tears again. It took him a moment, but then he seemed to summon new strength. "We'll finish the picture," he said. "I'll see to it." After that, I never doubted the picture would be completed, no matter the cost or the problems. Jack had weighed in. Then, as if he had completed the last item on his agenda, he asked, abruptly, "What have you heard?"

"An accident. She was trying to lower a dinghy and she fell in."

He didn't acknowledge what I said, which I took to mean he had heard the same thing. He looked at me hard and said, "Nobody just falls off a boat." It was the first time it had occurred to me that it might have been anything other than an accident. In a flash of unwelcome insight, thoughts of all the people who had accidentally been killed in traffic or had accidentally shot themselves cleaning their guns rushed through my mind. Or did Jack mean something even more sinister? He wasn't someone you could question. "I'll find out," he said, and I didn't doubt for a moment that he would.

Then he turned and left the room, leaving me there in his den with the equipment and my own thoughts. I kept looking at the screen Henry had set up. It was blank now, but fragments of the footage we had been watching seemed to replay there, and then dissolve to Cottage Hospital, where I could see her again, on that steel examining table.

"Nobody just falls off a boat," echoed in my mind as I tried to sort out my thoughts.

I thought back over all our times together, when she had told me about her life, enchanting me like Scheherazade, wanting me to help tell her story. I had teased her about it because I always assumed we'd get around to it when we were both older. Sitting there in Jack Markel's den, I was feeling more tension than I had ever known. I think that terrible pressure forced me to see what would happen. Of course I'd help Jack finish the movie and investigate the circumstances of her death, but I knew just as clearly that it was her life I wanted to pursue. My intention was to honor her request, but it was also, I think, an attempt to come to terms with my own past, so that as I reconstructed her life, my own might finally go forward. The truth would come not only from the accumulation of fact but also from the refuge of what I could recall, facts real and imagined. What couldn't be learned through diligence and investigation, I would trust myself to dream. Completing her memoirs was one of the few things she had ever asked of me. Now it was the only thing I cared about, the only thing I knew I would do.

two

The Mirror of Desire

4.

When Carla and I met for lunch in those days, the idea was that she was going to talk me into helping with her memoirs. Except Carla never tried to persuade anybody. She had no experience at it. She had been a star since childhood. She thought the way you got things was to ask. I don't mean she thought she was the Sun Queen. She knew people might not always do exactly what she wanted. Still, for the most part, they did. So Carla just began telling me her story. She wasn't trying to trick me or seduce me, at least not any more than she already had.

We were at Ma Maison on a sunny spring afternoon, finishing a bottle of chardonnay. Most of the hard-charging lunch crowd, the producers and agents, had left. There were a few other stragglers, but we pretty much had the patio to ourselves.

"My grandfather came out here in the twenties. From Pittsburgh. Well, actually from Hungary. My grandmother had died in the Spanish flu epidemic, around 1918. He put my mother and my aunt in an orphanage and then sort of floated away. She was there twelve years—practically her whole childhood.

When she was sixteen, she graduated. She came out here on a Greyhound bus to live with her father in a boardinghouse in Boyle Heights. It was the Depression by then, but my grandfather always dressed up with a boutonniere and sort of cruised Brooklyn Avenue. He changed his name a lot—Bela Sandor, Bill Sandor, Bill Sanford, Bela Sanhoff. My mother was always Ceil Sanhoff, so when she turned up he went back to Sanhoff for her sake. They worked as extras at the studios whenever they could, which is how Ceil and Milton met."

Carla didn't always stop to explain things. Because I knew some of it, she always assumed I knew all of it. Ceil and Milton were her parents. She spoke so freely and with such a sense of their past that I came to realize that doing these memoirs wasn't at all casual for her, no matter how relaxed she seemed. She was more ready to tell her story than either of us had realized.

"My mother was pretty in those days. Big dark eyes, great figure. She never knew it, though. The thing you have to remember about my mother is she lost her mother when she was four. I never understood till I had kids. It's really awful. It's not that she never recovered or anything as dramatic as that. She liked her childhood. The orphanage, her sister. She thought it was great. But losing her mother was the most important thing in her life. Everybody has something like that. For me it had to be being a star when I was so little. For Ceil it was my grandmother's death. I think it had an influence on me. Maybe even on my kids. A shock like that doesn't go away, it goes down the generations."

Carla wasn't usually so analytical. When she was working on a part, she thought about the character and talked about it with the director. But her real preparation was done within herself, by instinct. Once the movies were released, she rarely thought about them again. But she didn't confuse her parents' lives with the movies. She had thought hard about Ceil and Milton, puzzling her way through all that had happened, using her actor's skills to imagine their lives before she was born.

"By the time you met my father, he was kind of beaten down. But he was a real hustler when he was young. He always worked a couple of jobs at once. Before he knew my mother, he had a job at Universal as an apprentice cutter. They had him in the montage department. I think his job was mostly to carry the footage from one bin to another. I doubt that he ever spliced a frame. Legitimately, I mean. What he did do was make dupes and sell a lot of it on the side. It was fine for a while until a highway montage in a Universal picture turned up in a picture for some other company. In release at the same time! They traced it to Milton and he got fired. He used to claim he was an editor 'before the war.' Like World War Two broke up his career."

She was named Karen, Karen Teitel, and she was born in the spring of 1940 in the public maternity ward of Queen of Angels Hospital, where there were forty women with only screens between their beds. Milton handed out the cigars he had collected from the other fathers in the waiting room.

Three days later, Milton told Ceil that a great opportunity had come up at Paramount, the studio where they'd met. "They're shooting *All Women Have Secrets*," Milton said, standing by his wife's hospital bed. "They need a newborn. For a scene in the picture," Milton said matter-of-factly, trying to make it sound as if there were nothing at all unusual in what he was saying.

"But she's too little," Ceil said, stroking Karen's tiny forehead.

"It shoots Wednesday. Seventy-five bucks a day."

"That's the day we go home."

"Right. Her call's at eleven. We'll go from here to the studio. They'll send a car and driver. They give us a nurse on the set." Ceil just stared at the baby in her arms, unable to find the words to express her fears. "Would I take a chance with my daughter?" Milton asked, sensing his wife's anxiety. "She'll be treated better at the studio than in this hospital."

Despite her mother's misgivings, when Karen was five days old, she was bundled into a studio Packard and driven from Queen of Angels Hospital to Stage 12 at Paramount. A second baby, a six-week-old boy who was the backup, was sleeping in his crib. Milton looked at him, then whispered to Ceil, "He's practically shaving. We're a shoo-in."

The director, Kurt Salzinger, a tall, severe-looking Austrian, walked over to inspect the newest extra. He stared at Karen for a moment, then told Ceil and Milton that he'd need only a few shots. Most of the time they would use a doll, but there were a few over-the-shoulder and cradle shots that would require what he called "the real thing." Milton assumed they would do the shots right away. Instead, Salzinger called for the setup of a different scene.

By five o'clock, when the shooting was over for the day and Karen had slept most of the afternoon, Milton was pleased, because he knew Karen would be paid and called back the next day. Before they left, Milton signed a release and accepted seventy-five dollars in cash. The assistant director asked if Karen could be ready for an eight o'clock call the next morning. Before Ceil could object, Milton told him that would be fine.

Karen and her parents came back the next morning, the morning after that, and a fourth as well before Salzinger got all the shots he needed. There were a lot of jokes on the set about Karen outgrowing the role, but on the fourth day Karen Teitel, aged eight days, was filmed for what would become her debut in *All Women Have Secrets*. Her father collected a total of three hundred dollars.

At lunch one wintry afternoon, when Ma Maison had set up heat lamps on the patio, Carla told me about how her parents had met, working as extras at Paramount with Bela.

"It was *Scarlet Woman*, a Mae West picture. To work extra you had to pay a kickback. Fifty cents, my mother always said it was. You got paid five bucks and lunch, and you had to slip fifty cents to somebody. Bela never had any idea how to do anything. My mother is still like that. So Milton did it for them. It was more than a favor. They would have lost their jobs otherwise. My father might not have been the shrewdest guy in Hollywood, but compared to Ceil and Bela he must have looked like Selznick. Anyway, they started going out. Besides working extra, which was hit-and-miss, my father had a regular job in Santa Monica. He ran a water taxi, taking people from the Santa Monica Pier out to the *Rex*."

"The gambling ship, you mean?"

She just nodded, impatient to continue. She meant that in the thirties there were ships anchored beyond the three-mile limit where people went to gamble. The *Rex* was the biggest.

"Milton always wanted an on-board job. His dream was to be a dealer on the *Rex*. When I think about the two of them dating, it seems sweet. Their first date, he drove her out to the Santa Monica Pier and took her on the water taxi to the *Rex*. They won five bucks playing blackjack. It's the only time my mother ever gambled. They got married because of my Aunt Edna. She got out of the orphanage and came out here. She and my mother spent all their time together. Milton got left out. So he married her."

"And Bela was the best man, I'll bet."

"I don't know. He stayed in Boyle Heights. The three of them got a place in Gower Gardens, a bungalow court in Hollywood. It got torn down for the freeway. My first bedroom, and now you drive right through it going to Burbank. It was the first home my mother ever had, too. Pretty soon she's pregnant."

"That was you?"

"No. I came later."

Milton had gotten his wife a job on the cleaning crew of the *Rex*. She would get up before the sun for the long trip on the Red Car out to the Santa Monica Pier and her early-morning shift cleaning the gambling ship. When she was three months from delivery, Milton insisted she stay home. Their son was born late in 1938. Milton had talked Ceil into naming him for Tony Cornero, the owner of the *Rex*. But the baby's heart was not fully formed. They buried him under a flat stone marker in Home of Peace Cemetery in Boyle Heights, aged six days. No one is prepared for such a loss, and for Ceil and her sister, the death evoked the death of their mother. When Ceil came home from Queen of Angels without her baby, she fell into a depression of a sort she had never known. She stayed indoors and wouldn't come out of her bedroom unless Milton coaxed her. When Tony Cornero heard about the death of his namesake, he pressed five hundred dollars into Milton's hand and told him to forget about being a dealer. "When a war starts," he said, "and believe me, it will, nobody's going to want to play cards in the ocean."

Milton and Ceil never talked of their tragedy, and Milton wondered if Ceil thought about it as much as he did. He was afraid to ask her directly about another child, but one night, when he sensed she might agree, he asked her not to use the pessary that she kept in her bureau. She sat up in bed, very still. He thought he had made a mistake, was moving too quickly, but Ceil embraced him, trying, he thought, not to cry.

The pessary stayed in the drawer and before long, Ceil was pregnant again. She was more cautious and nervous than the first time, but as Milton thought it might, the pregnancy gave her hope. They didn't allow themselves much talk about the baby's future. The reserve they exercised, their hedge against calamity, made them distant, almost as if they were partners who didn't quite trust each other in a risky venture.

After Karen's birth, Milton tried to be attentive to his daughter, but Ceil didn't make it easy. In matters concerning the baby, Ceil felt she had a natural authority. Milton couldn't help thinking she was blaming him for baby Tony's death, as if she weren't going to let him do that to Karen.

By late 1941, Milton may well have been one of the few Americans hoping for war. On Monday morning, December 8, Milton was in line at the courthouse in downtown Los Angeles to enlist in the Navy.

Ceil had learned enough about working extra that she was able to find more work for Karen and sometimes herself. As a toddler Karen had soft, wispy hair that had not yet turned dark. Her features were still only a hint of what was to come, but a sense of the adult was already present. Her eyes were large and dark, giving her tiny face a seductive cast. More important, Karen was no less relaxed on camera than off. That meant she was still ideal for extra work, a rarity among two-year-olds. When directors wanted an adorable child in a scene, they wanted the kid placed on camera, apart from the crowd. That made the child a bit player with a higher fee than the extras.

While she was working extra at Warner Bros. in *The Pacific*, the director, who had been a unit publicist before the war, told the leading man, Roy Tennyson, to chuck Karen under the chin and say, "Hello, cute stuff." Karen smiled at Tennyson and charmed him completely. The director liked it enough to try it from a closer angle. Tennyson repeated, "Hello, cute stuff," and Karen smiled, exactly as she had the first time. The astonished director said, "Print it."

Carla was five when the war ended. By then, she had developed a thick mane of hair that looked more adolescent than childlike. Her face and form were still tiny, but an older, knowing creature lurked not far from the surface. She seemed perfectly formed, but in miniature, like a pony, or a bonsai. Her personality was still passive and serene, as if she were biding her time, gathering power. She kept a framed photograph of Milton in his naval uniform next to her bed. She had no sense of her father, except for the anxiety she knew her mother felt whenever she thought of his return. But Karen knew her mother's thoughts in a way that wasn't clear to either of them. With Ceil, who had trouble knowing what she was thinking herself, the only way Karen could know was to sense it.

Milton had spent four years in the Pacific as deputy radio

operator on a series of picket ships, before being discharged in San Francisco. He had called Ceil from there, and while he hadn't sounded any different, Ceil was jittery as she and Edna set out with Karen to meet his train.

Union Station, a vast Spanish mission–style building on the edge of downtown Los Angeles, was filled with men in uniform and their families who had come to meet them. Edna and Ceil had seen movie versions of the reunion they were about to experience; both had an image of a handsome sailor running next to the tracks toward his beloved—a beautiful young woman with tumbling, flowing, backlit hair.

But the platform was too crowded to permit running, and at a glance Ceil could see that she was not the only nervous woman awaiting the return of a soldier or sailor. There was indeed a touch of the theatrical about the way Milton finally did appear. Ceil had begun to think he had missed the train. Then, like a vision, Milton stepped out from behind the last of the embracing couples. He was in uniform, carrying a duffel bag on his shoulder. He was thinner and his eyes looked darker than Ceil remembered; there were service ribbons on his chest that Ceil mistook for medals. He waved to his wife, who seemed frozen for a moment until she leaned down to Karen and whispered, "That's your daddy. Go on. Give him a hug." Karen knew her part and ran to her father. He dropped the duffel bag and reached out for the daughter he hadn't seen since she was an infant. "Hi, Daddy," Karen said, and kissed him.

Milton wouldn't consider trying to work extra again, but he was eager to hear about Karen's success. If his own plans were uncertain, he had clear ambitions for his daughter. He began checking *Variety* for casting notices for children.

It was Edna who arranged for Karen's first professional interview. Edna had taken a job as a clerk-typist at the University of Southern California School of Dentistry. She had tried for a similar job at the medical school, but too many other young women had the same idea. She was spending as much time as she could with Teddy Soderberg, who was studying dentistry on the GI bill.

One of Teddy's fellow dental students was married to a secretary at Paramount. Teddy was able to get Karen's name on a list of children being interviewed by Claire Berger, the casting director at the studio. The other children under consideration were professionals, with agents and experience in speaking roles. "It's a foot in the door," Milton said, excited at the possibility. "That's all I ask. You take her," he said to Ceil, which surprised his wife.

"You're better at it. I won't know how," Ceil said, turning to Karen, who was listening, interested in the question. "Who do you want to take you, me or Daddy?"

Milton invariably found himself drawn into Ceil's habit of asking for adult decisions from Karen. Both parents watched as their child considered the question, trying to decide to which parent she would award the favor of escorting her to Paramount. Karen looked from one to the other, cocking her head. When no answer came, she shrugged and said, "I don't care."

"I already decided," Milton said. "You're doing it. It'll be all mothers. It's best. Only thing, if it comes up, don't talk money. If we need to make a deal, I'll close."

Claire Berger's office was on the ground floor of the Directors Building facing the main square of the lot. The waiting room was furnished with worn sofas and chairs, like a doctor's office, except that instead of *Look* and *Life*, old copies of *Variety* were piled on the tables. The room was battered from years of actors barging in and out and, in their nervousness, grinding cigarette butts into the carpet.

Ceil and Karen entered to find the room filled with mothers and children. The mothers were gossiping with one another. Their children were sitting on the floor or running around in noisy circles. The din was so intense that Karen gripped her mother's hand in fear.

Behind a desk, in an alcove, a young woman called to Ceil. "Over here," she said, as Ceil, with Karen clinging to her, threaded her way to the desk. The woman found Karen's name on her list, which was a relief to Ceil, but she then asked, "Do you have a composite?" Ceil heard "deposit" and thought she was being asked to pay. "Pictures," the woman said, "of Karen?"

"No," Ceil said, fearing that she had botched the interview. "I didn't know." Ceil wished that Edna had come, too. She always understood situations in which Ceil felt helpless.

"It's okay. Miss Berger's running a little late. Why don't you two sit down."

The boisterousness of the children fascinated Karen. She had already started kindergarten at the Cheremoya Avenue School, but the children there were orderly or were reprimanded. Karen watched two little girls with a coloring book and a box of Crayolas. They had lost interest in the book and were coloring the carpet.

"Excuse me," said a platinum-haired woman in a red Chinese-cut dress, as she waved photographs of her daughter at Ceil. "I heard what you said about the composites," she said, handing Ceil a set of theatrical glossies of her daughter, a child about Karen's age. "I can tell you some photographers."

"Thanks," Ceil said, doubting she could ever afford anything so grand.

"Would you like to have your picture taken like this?" the woman asked, showing the pictures to Karen. Ceil watched as Karen glanced at the pictures, hoping she wouldn't decide she wanted them. "Aren't they pretty?" the woman coaxed. But Karen didn't know what was expected of her so she just smiled and nodded.

"My little brother can take better pictures than that," said another child, whose mother had painted freckles on her nose in what Ceil took to be an attempt to impress Miss Berger with her wholesomeness.

"Shush, Susan. Don't be rude," said her mother. "Not everyone has your advantages."

"They stink," the child said. "I was in more movies than you." She started listing her credits, reciting in a singsong, schoolyard voice. "I was in *And Now Tomorrow* and I was in *Song of Alice* and I was in *Salty O'Rourke*, so shut your mouth."

Ceil had been on movie sets and was aware of stage mothers, but she had never experienced such competitiveness and backbiting. It frightened her, partly because it was offensive, but also because she knew she could never keep up with it. She was relieved when the girl with the photographs was summoned to Miss Berger's office. Ten minutes later Ceil and Karen were called.

Claire Berger was a surprisingly sweet-tempered woman in her mid-forties. She had once been an actress and for a while had even hoped to become a director, an unusual ambition for a woman at the time, and one she was never able to achieve. She had been a casting director for several years. During the interview Karen was her usual quiet self. Ceil didn't try to sell anything; she didn't know how, and it never would have occurred to her to try. To Ceil, whether Karen got the job, which was to say whether she had the appropriate skills and talent, would be based on objective, quantifiable criteria to be assessed by Miss Berger.

Claire had learned that when casting a small role the first impression was the most important. An audience would only get a brief look at the performance and they would have to make up their minds quickly. When Claire looked at Karen for the first time she wanted to touch her, to see if that thick mane of hair was real. When Ceil, who was guileless, spoke, Claire knew there were no tricks. Ceil assumed fairness, and because Claire understood that, she was less hurried than she was with some of the others. The longer she looked at Karen the more fascinated she became with that little face with the big eyes. Claire couldn't remember ever having had such an immediate response to a child. She knew an audience would react no differently. When she asked Karen if she wanted to be an actress when she grew up, Karen just shrugged and said she didn't know. "Then what do you want to be?" she prodded.

"A nurse?" Karen asked, because she knew it was an adult occupation, and one in which other children sometimes claimed interest.

"Really?" Claire said. "Do you know what a nurse does?" Karen, who had no idea what a nurse did, just shrugged, which made Claire smile, surprised to see such equanimity in a child.

"We've never done anything like this before," Ceil said. "We don't have any pictures."

Claire didn't seem to care about the photographs. She looked at Karen and said, "The name of this movie is *My Hometown*. It's about a funny family with lots of children. I want you to pretend you're a little girl named Mazie and you have an older sister who's going out with her friends. She doesn't want to take you along. Do you understand, Mazie?"

"Yes," Karen said, still feeling shy.

"Do you have any questions?" Karen was silent for a moment until Claire reassured her. "Go ahead, ask me."

"Where are they going?"

Claire, who recognized an actorly sensibility, began improvising detail beyond what the script provided. "They're going to the movies. It's a funny one that you would like to see. They won't take you because they say you're too little." Claire whispered the dialogue to Karen and said, "Say it to me first. I'll be your sister. Pretend your mother is your mother." Then in an irritated, slightly exaggerated voice Claire said, "She's too little. She'll mess up everything."

Repeating what Claire had whispered to her, Karen said, "I am not. I know how to go. Why can't I?" Then she turned to Ceil and said, "Mom, make her take me." Karen delivered the lines simply, with some feeling, but without self-conscious inflection. She just said the words in her own voice; the emotions beneath the words, which Karen had made her own, were apparent and appropriate to Mazie's situation. Ceil didn't think anything of it. To her, it just sounded like her daughter. Claire looked up, unsure of what she had just heard. "Let's try it again," she said. "This time be angrier at your sister."

Karen delivered the lines again, a little more harshly. "Try it once more. As if you were disgusted with your sister. Imagine she's done this to you lots of times. Do you know what 'disgusted' means?"

Karen and Claire repeated the exchange; Karen reshaded it, tinging it, as Claire had asked. Each time she spoke the simple lines with understanding, but without theatricality or artifice. She said the words as if the situation were her own.

Claire asked Karen and Ceil to wait while she called Ben Tucker, the producer of *My Hometown*. While they waited for him, Ceil told Claire about Karen's experience, and then because she felt comfortable, Ceil told her about Milton and how he had just come home from the Pacific. As Claire listened, she watched Karen, who sat quietly, ready to do whatever the adults asked. A few minutes later, they heard the noise level in the waiting room well up.

A tall, balding man in a yellow silk jacket let himself into the office. "Bunch of friggin' maniacs out there," he said. Seeing Ceil and Karen, he added, "Pardon my terminology, ladies." When Karen repeated her audition for Mr. Tucker, she did it no less realistically than she had done before. Claire asked her to do it once more, this time as if she didn't really care if she got to go, a subtle distinction for a five-year-old. Claire wanted to show Tucker how easily Karen could shade the meaning and how well she took direction. The performance made Tucker smile with surprised appreciation. "Pretty good, but she's too young. We need a kid who looks at least eight. More established, too." Ceil and Karen accepted the judgment, but Claire looked miffed, which Tucker noticed. "How about the other kid. You have somebody for that?" he asked.

"Not yet," Claire replied. Ceil listened, aware that Karen's employment was being discussed, but she remained detached. Karen sat quietly, not showing any more emotion than her mother.

"So it's not Mazie, but it's in the picture," Tucker said. "There's dialogue. I think it'll work." Then he turned to Karen again and said, "Nice to meet you. If your mother doesn't take stupid pills, I'll see you on the set."

"You understand what happened, don't you?" Miss Berger asked, after Tucker had left.

"I think so," Ceil said. "What did he mean?"

"He meant he hoped you wouldn't be obstructionist about negotiations. Do you have an agent?"

"Well, my husband said he would do that part."

"It's four days work at ninety dollars a day. That's standard. If your husband has any problems with that he should call me."

"Sure. Yes. Thank you."

"Karen, do you understand what we're saying?"

"I'm going to be in the movie."

"Not playing Mazie. Playing another little girl, your own age. It's going to be a lot of fun."

"Okay."

Milton hadn't been on the Paramount lot since before the war. This time there was no question of giving anyone a fifty-cent kickback. He drove up to the high wrought-iron Bronson Gate and said, "Karen and Milton Teitel for the *My Hometown* set." The guard gave Milton parking instructions and passed him through. Milton winked at Karen as they drove onto the lot.

Karen was to play Dulcie, the younger sister of Mazie, the little girl who didn't get to go to the movies. The idea was that when Mazie was denied something, she would take it out on Dulcie. Dulcie said little but was called on to look disappointed several times.

Milton, who knew studio procedures well enough, parked and took Karen to the wardrobe building. As they walked across the lot, Milton pointed out the stages and offices to his daughter and talked to her about what to expect. "Sometimes you have to wait a long time for your scene. But you watch what they're doing. That's the way to learn. The director's the boss. Listen to him, do what he says. If you want to know something, wait till he's not too busy. Don't interrupt if he's talking. You remember his name?"

"I forget."

"Mr. Pressler. Be polite. Are you nervous?"

"Are there going to be other kids?"

"Of course. But they won't be as cute as you or as smart. You're not working extra. You're really in this show, so people'll be watching. Be nice to everybody, only remember you're here to do a job." Milton felt good about being able to instruct Karen in matters he knew were important to her future. He felt that this was the world in which he and Karen belonged, where all things were possible.

At wardrobe, an assistant director hurried Karen through a series of connected rooms filled with racks of clothing and canvas baskets on wheels, stuffed with shoes and belts. As she was pulled along, Karen looked up at the overhead racks where hats of all sorts, more hats than she had ever seen, were stored, and at the shafts of dusty light pouring through the high windows, accepting it all, ready for whatever might come.

While Milton waited, he strolled over to Stage 28 to see if he could meet the director. Lew Pressler was in his chair looking over the scenes he was about to shoot, keeping an eye on the crew rigging lights. A good-looking woman with red hair was standing near him, her hip thrust out provocatively, taking advantage of her opportunity.

"Mr. Pressler? I'm Milt Teitel. My daughter Karen's playing Dulcie. Nice to meet you." Milton tried not to sound frantic, but determined to get it all in before Pressler had a chance to reject him.

But Pressler seemed pleased to meet Milton. He took his hand and said, "Haven't met her. Claire Berger and Ben are high on her."

"It's her first speaking part. She's worked extra and it's sort of the family racket. My wife and I were in the business before the war."

"Well, that's just grand. We'll have a good time." Pressler looked up at the redhead. The woman met his gaze and smiled. Milton knew his moment was over. He walked around the soundstage and introduced himself to the state social worker, the gaffer and anyone else he could corral.

The scene Karen was to shoot was an exterior, done on the American Street—a row of small-town house-fronts with porches and white picket fences. Karen was already on the set, standing near Mazie, while a woman from makeup fussed over them. Milton waved and called out, "Hi, sweetheart. You look nice." Karen waved back and grinned.

The sequence to be shot was of Mazie, looking disgruntled, storming out of her house and encountering Dulcie, playing quietly in the yard, and saying to her "What do you want?" Dulcie was to reply, "What did I do?" Then Mazie was to say, "Kids!" and walk away. Pressler blocked out the action and did a camera rehearsal. He placed Karen on the lawn near the sidewalk at the front of the house. Milton kept moving nervously about the set, trying to catch Karen's eye, to have a word with her. He knew not to disrupt the rehearsal, so he stayed well behind the camera, but he was still frenetic enough that Pressler had the assistant director tell him to sit down.

When Pressler was ready for a take, the makeup woman checked the children's faces, blotting Karen's forehead. The wardrobe supervisor glanced at Karen's dress and nodded. The assistant director yelled "Quiet!" turned to Pressler, and waited. The director glanced once more at his set, then nodded. The assistant yelled "Roll 'em!" and the camera operator threw his switch, simultaneously starting the camera and the sound equipment. "Running!" the operator called out. The soundman watched his dials and when his equipment was running at ninety feet a minute, the speed of the camera, he called "Speed!" The clapper boy held the slate in front of the camera and called out "Scene forty, take one," clapped his board, and got out of the way. Lew Pressler said "Action!"

On the first take Mazie stumbled as she came out of the door and on the second she slammed it so hard that Pressler stopped her again. He went over and had a word with her to calm her. Through it all, Karen played in the grass seemingly unaware of Mazie and her anger. The third take worked well enough, and when Mazie snapped, Karen glanced up with a look of hurt surprise and delivered her line. When Mazie walked away, Karen stuck out her tongue. It was a simple gesture, improvised by a clever child, but it had an additional quality that made Lew Pressler tell the script supervisor to hold that one, but he'd like to do one more. He had seen that Karen had managed to make sticking her tongue out more than an act of childish defiance. It appeared to be the first time Dulcie had done such a thing. The unfairness of Mazie's behavior made Dulcie grow up a little. It made the tiny sequence more complex than the screenwriter had in mind when he wrote, "What did I do?"

Milton could see that Karen had done well, that the director was pleased. Pressler was taking time with Karen; he was going to do another take because he knew he had a real actress on his hands and he wanted to make sure he had taken full advantage of the situation. Lew Pressler might not have been the greatest director on the Paramount lot in 1946, but complete fools don't turn out three pictures a year. Milton could see his future forming and it made him heady. While Pressler was talking to Karen, Milton walked over to hear what they were saying, to offer ideas; this was his daughter, after all, an extension of himself, and he wanted to be near her. "That was great, baby," Milton said. "You feeling okay?" The instant he had spoken, Milton knew he had blundered. Pressler's look told him to stop and he did. Neither man wanted to rattle Karen, so Pressler just said, "We'll do another one," and walked away.

"I'm sorry if I was a little out of line there," Milton started to say, catching up with the director. Pressler ignored him and sat down. A moment later the assistant director whispered to Milton that it would be better if he watched from farther away. Milton started to protest, but the assistant was guiding him away from the set as Pressler was moving the camera closer to Karen. When Milton was so far from the camera that he could barely make out the action, the assistant said, "No closer or you're off the lot." Milton tried to stammer an apology, but the man was hurrying back for the next take. Even from the distance to which he had been banished, Milton knew that moving the camera meant Pressler was going to add a close-up of Karen.

In the parking lot as they were about to leave, as Milton was worrying that he'd made a fool of himself, Claire Berger hurried toward them. Karen seemed pleased to see her, and from the way Claire introduced herself and kissed Karen, Milton knew even if he had annoyed Lew Pressler, it wasn't going to matter. "I didn't see the shot, I just got too busy, but I heard it went real well," she said to Milton. Then she turned her attention to Karen and said, "You're quite a little actress. Do you know that?"

"Thank you," Karen said, more shyly than her father suspected she felt.

"She's got it," Claire said to Milton. "You'll be hearing more from us." She left them there and headed back to her office. Milton beamed at Karen and said, "You were great! You handled yourself just beautiful." He kissed her on the forehead and said, "Baby, if I knew how, I'd stand on my head."

"Want me to teach you, Dad?" Karen asked. Milton laughed

and hugged his daughter, knowing with a newfound certainty that everything was going to work out.

The next morning Milton called Claire Berger with the intention of asking about agents and acting schools for Karen and to nose around about other children's roles that might be coming up at the studio. She was so friendly on the phone that instead of asking his questions, Milton invited her to lunch. When he told Ceil about it, she wanted to know if she should come, too. Milton thought she sounded jealous. "It's not a date," Milton said. "It's a professional thing."

"Where will you take her?" Ceil asked, upset by the idea of her husband taking an attractive woman to lunch.

"I don't know. Wherever she goes."

"It'll be expensive."

"It's an investment."

It might not have been a date, but Milton was still thrilled to be seen with a stylish studio executive. He was waiting inside the door at the Nickodell, a clubby restaurant near Paramount, when Claire hurried in, waving and nodding to the lunch crowd. She was wearing a black-and-white suit, and her gray-streaked hair was pulled into a French twist, setting off her white skin and high cheekbones. Milton wasn't flirtatious and his goals were pretty much as he had told Ceil. But the sight of Claire Berger coming to meet him, apologizing for being a few minutes late, made Milton giddy.

The maître d', who had been cool to Milton until he saw he had been waiting for Claire Berger, took them to a round banquette with dark red leather seats. Claire ordered a Rob Roy, and Milton, who had never heard of a Rob Roy, said, "Make that two."

"I saw the rushes of Karen's scene," Claire said, as she glanced around the room. "She's remarkable. Absolutely real and more energy than I saw in my office."

"She's got energy, all right."

"I mean in an acting sense. It's tough enough to find kids who don't overact, but it takes more than just making it real. She puts oomph into it. She's terrific. To Karen," Claire said, clinking Milton's glass with her own.

"I appreciate your taking the time to talk with me. I want to handle everything the right way. She starts first grade next month. What do you think?"

"About a professional school, you mean?" Milton nodded and sipped his drink, enjoying it, but worried they would be too expensive for him to have another. As he was thinking about it, Claire said, "I limit myself to two of these at lunch." Milton smiled and signaled to the waiter.

"I'm not sure about the schools," Claire told him. "Some kids benefit from them, but not all. It doesn't have much to do with talent."

"But if she were your daughter, you wouldn't just send her to a regular school, would you?"

"I'd probably give a professional school a try and keep an eye on it."

Over steak sandwiches, Claire gave Milton the names of several schools. She told him the tuitions were always negotiable and to mention her name. Milton was grateful for the help and for how seriously Claire was taking Karen's interests. He thought she might be flirting with him. She touched his hand a few times seemingly to emphasize a point. Once he thought her toe brushed his leg, but he couldn't be sure. Milton wasn't the sort of man with whom attractive, worldly women flirted. He was too serious and he gave off an air of anxiety. Now, though, he had a new card to play. It made him feel formidable, at least after two drinks, with Claire Berger. He was trying to stay sober enough to absorb all she had to say, but he couldn't help thinking how different his life would be if he were married to a woman like Claire Berger. Before the check came, Milton tried to calculate how much it would be. When it arrived, Claire reached for it, saying, "We'll let Paramount take us to lunch. That's what they're good for." She signed the bottom of the check before Milton could say a thing.

About ten minutes from Paramount and thirty years later, Carla and I were having lunch at Ma Maison. As usual she wasn't eating much, but the place was so appealing, with its Astroturf patio and goofy porcelain geese, that it always put her in a good mood. The place was thick with the kind of celebrities who are famous only in Hollywood—hot agents, bankable writers and directors with hits. The agents always worked the room, so one after another they came to our table to remind Carla that she knew them. Carla always offered her cheek for a kiss and seemed glad to see the visitor, even if she didn't have any idea who the person was.

Melinda Cummins, a woman who had been a child actress with Carla and now sold real estate, managed to catch Carla's eye from across the patio. Carla smiled at her, which was all the encouragement Melinda needed. She was up and on her way to our table. She was wearing black leather slacks, a turquoise silk blouse and so much gold that she clanked as she walked toward us, saying, "Kisses, kisses."

"She'll try to sell us Brentwood," Carla muttered.

"How are you?" Melinda asked, as if she had been doing nothing but brooding on the question for days. We both knew if we encouraged Melinda she wouldn't leave until we had reviewed the multiple listings for the West Side. Through some miracle of Carla's ability to control everything without appearing to do anything, she managed to be polite to Melinda and still dismiss her with a good-bye kiss on the cheek.

When she was gone, Carla wondered aloud if Melinda was happy with the way her life was working out. Melinda had never been the child star that Carla was, but still this woman once had reason to assume she would be an actress all her life. Carla didn't say that, but I could all but see the thoughts running through her head. "I remember her as a kid," Carla said. "She wasn't bad."

"Talented?"

"We were all talented. So what?"

"Okay. Talent's cheap. What does it take?"

"For an adult—talent, drive and luck. Same for a kid, but also a parent who wants it as much as the kid. That's where the kid gets it. My father wanted it so much for me. And then my mother wound up in charge."

"Maybe that's part of the reason you were the only child star and an adult star."

"That's not true," she said. "Natalie Wood and Liz Taylor were."

"Not in the same way," I answered. "They had careers as kids, but no studio built a picture around them until they were adults. Liz came close, but her stardom began as an adolescent. She was a kid, but men wanted her."

"You mean she was hot."

"Not to put too fine a point on it, but yeah. You're the only one."

"None of the men?"

"Think about it—Mickey Rooney, Jackie Cooper, Roddy McDowall—stars as kids, then big careers, but not really stars again."

"I guess it's true. See, Gabe, you're perfect for this memoirs business. Without you I won't have enough control over it. Even if I have final cut."

"I don't think they call it final cut."

"You know what I mean."

"So don't do it. You're too young for memoirs, anyway."

"Jack says if I don't, somebody else will. Do it with me."

"I'm a screenwriter. I write dialogue and stuff like, 'He pulls a gun, she kicks him in the balls.' "

She laughed and said, "Ever read these things? Maybe we could even do a good one. It'd get you away from scripts. It could be good for both of us. Talk to my parents."

"Your mother's a sweetheart."

"My mother has no known personality. If I hadn't grown up around my Aunt Edna, I sometimes think I wouldn't know how to cross the street. She was the only one who had any sense."

"And Milton?"

"When you talk to Milton, believe about half of what he says."

"Which half?"

"You'll know. I always did."

5.

The Leeper Professional School took up two floors of the Aeolian Hall, a brick building at the corner of Hollywood Boulevard and Vermont Avenue. A wide staircase opened directly from the lobby onto the Leeper School's waiting area, which in turn led to a greenroom where the students horsed around between classes, made calls on the pay phone, and passed rumors.

The headmistress, Mary Louise Leeper, known to her pupils as Ma, had been training children for the screen since the last days of silent pictures. Enough of her alumni were known in the business for Ma and her school to have acquired a reputation as a good training ground. Her pupils, numbering about sixty at any one time, from first grade to high school, spent the mornings studying what Ma called academics and the afternoons on singing, dancing, acting and self-promotion. Ma was a big, raw-boned woman in her late fifties from Bartlesville, Oklahoma, who had come west with her family after the First World War. She had acted in silent films, but had never managed to make the transition to sound.

Ma was in the business of turning out employable actors and

actresses. If the state of California insisted on other courses, then she would uphold the law, but she was not about to spend any more time than she had to on history when her pupils could be at the barre or in elocution class. The tuition was forty dollars a month, and Ma was quite serious when she described her admission policy as selective.

"Sure, I could enroll any little Tom, Dick or Jane who was in the school play," she told Milton, the day after his lunch with Claire Berger. "I could, but I won't. Know why?"

"Suppose you tell me," Milton said.

"It catches up. You don't survive in this business unless you're selective. I don't want my time wasted."

"Well, you were on the list Miss Berger gave me, so I thought I'd come see."

"Claire Berger? Paramount?"

"Yeah," Milton said as casually as he could, watching the name have the desired effect on Ma Leeper. "While we were doing *My Hometown* over there, Claire and I had a little talk about Karen's future."

"How old is she?"

"Going on seven."

"Good age. What else she done?"

"She hasn't had a lot of time."

" 'Course, I'd have to meet her myself, see what I think, but Karen sounds like a Leeper girl."

"Possibly," Milton said, knowing he now had the upper hand. "The tuition is a little steep, though. I'm just back from the war," he said, letting his words drift, managing to suggest that he was not yet on his financial feet.

"Well, scholarships are available in some cases."

"I see. That's a different story."

"For exceptionally qualified pupils we pay half to full tuition. Very rare though. I'd have to have a talk with Claire Berger and meet Karen."

"That's a good idea. Why don't you call Claire, and I'll bring Karen in tomorrow or the next day, to see what she makes of the school. She's the pupil, after all."

When he was telling Ceil about the school and Ma Leeper, Milton said, "I had her eating out of my hand. When Claire gives her the high sign, we're in."

"I don't see how we can afford it, even at half price."

"Ceil," Milton said, exasperated at her inability to see how the world operates. "That was her first offer. If Claire Berger says Karen's got a future, they'll pay to have her in their school."

"Why would they do that?"

"That school is only as good as the kids it turns out. If word gets around that a Karen Teitel went there, every parent whose kid was the star of the school play is going to want to enroll. And they won't argue about the tuition."

The deal Milton cut with Ma called for no tuition for the first three months. If in that time Karen did well and got a job in a movie, she could continue on full scholarship. If she did well, but didn't find work, Milton would pay half tuition for the rest of the year.

In her kindergarten at Cheremoya Avenue, where the most serious competition was over who got to play with which toys, Karen had gotten on well enough with her classmates. At Leeper, she was thrown into a pool of ambition and jealousy, of bragging and lies. The others all knew about her work at Paramount and her scholarship. It made her a target. On the first morning, a ten-year-old girl named Tammy shoved Karen and said, "You think you're so smart." Karen tried to move out of the way and keep her distance, but Tammy wouldn't stop. "Why are you on scholarship?" she wanted to know. "What movies were you ever in?" Karen couldn't remember the name of *My Hometown*, so she didn't answer at all. "Boy, are you a dumbbell," Tammy said, spitting the words.

Tammy was only the beginning. The next day, a fat boy, about twelve, pushed Karen into a corner, butting her with his stomach, until she was backed against the wall. He stood close, pressing his gut against her. Karen tried to stand very still until she could figure out what he wanted.

"You got an agent?" he asked, with a sneer.

"No," she answered.

"Now you do. I'm your agent. Gimme your money."

"I don't have any," Karen answered, truthfully. Other children had gathered to watch, but they kept their distance, apparently afraid of the agent themselves.

"Don't lie. Lemme see." Karen opened her pockets to him and showed that all she carried was a handkerchief and some buttons she had picked up. "I don't want that shit," he said. "You bring in some money. Or else." Then he butted her with his stomach again and walked away. The other kids laughed at Karen and followed the agent.

After school that day, as she was lost in thoughts of Tammy and the agent and how to deal with them, Karen slipped and fell on the doorstep at Gower Gardens and skinned her knee. She went crying to her mother, who put tincture of iodine on the wound and covered it with two Band-Aids. As Ceil was tending her scraped knee, Karen almost told her about the trouble at school, but she wasn't sure how to bring it up without upsetting Ceil. She knew her father would make a big fuss and complain to Ma Leeper, which would only make it worse. Karen decided it would be better if she just tried to stay out of the way of Tammy and the agent.

In the afternoons, along with the others, Karen took basic film technique from Ma Leeper. On Karen's first day, Ma gave her lecture on pratfalls. Most of the other kids had already heard it, but since it involved some physical knockabout, they were glad to listen again.

"There's three kinds of pratfalls and you need to be able to do them all," she began. Ma signaled to Corey, a wiry boy with unruly straw-colored hair, to demonstrate as she spoke. "Now the first, your basic fall, is, say you're walking along the street." As she spoke Corey walked innocently past, whistling to himself, lost in thought. "Then you get hit in the belly with a board," Ma said, pantomiming whacking Corey in the gut. "And over you go onto your keister." As she said it, Corey flopped down onto a gym mat and the children laughed.

"Now, number two is the stiff-back," Ma said, as Corey began his whistling stroll again. "You get hit in the face," she said, miming whacking Corey with a pie. "You keep your feet together and upsy-daisy down you go, heels and shoulders hitting at the same time." When Corey hit the mat, there was a thud and the children cheered him.

"Number three we call the one-eighty and it's the toughest." Corey began his whistling routine again as Ma narrated the action. "You're walking along minding your own business and suppose you step on a bar of soap or a banana peel." Corey pretended to step on something slippery; he rocked back and forth, desperately trying to keep his balance. "You go straight up, lay out flat in the air; hang there, facing the sky, if you can." As she spoke, Corey's legs went straight out and he did indeed seem to hang in the air, facing up, and then he came down hard. "And that, boys and girls, is the one-eighty." The kids whistled and cheered while Corey took several bows. "They're easier to watch than do, but we're going to give it a try. Break into partners."

The kids, who were used to this technique, hesitated for a moment until Corey walked over to Karen and said, "Come on, girlie. I'll show you how."

Karen took Corey's hand. Once he had made his choice, the others paired off.

When the kids had changed back and forth and worked their way through the three pratfalls, Ma concluded the session with the last of her lecture. " 'Course, it's a lot harder with the camera rolling. We'll get to that later, when you've mastered the basics which are the cornerstone of a Leeper Professional School education."

As Ma spoke, Corey moved nearer to Karen, putting his arm behind her; she turned her head toward him slightly, acknowledging his authority. Karen sensed, but didn't fully understand, that Corey was now her protector and she wouldn't have any more trouble with Tammy or the agent.

That night Edna cooked dinner, because her beau was coming to meet her family. Although Teddy had met Ceil briefly, he had never met Milton. She made a pot roast, hoping to show Teddy how easily she could whip up dinner for five. Edna was doing her best to stay calm. Milton was so full of his daughter's acting lessons that Edna hoped if he just stuck to that it would be okay.

Teddy arrived with a cheesecake in a pink bakery box from Langer's Delicatessen. Edna could see he was nervous.

"How does it work, Teddy?" Milton asked, playing the host. "You finish up at USC—then what? Do you go looking for people with toothaches or what?"

"Oh, Milton, don't be silly," Edna said, laughing a little too loudly at the joke.

"We need a dentist for Karen," Milton said. "What do you think?"

"Open wide," Teddy said.

"Now?" Karen asked.

"Sure. Let's have a gander." He leaned across the table and peered into Karen's mouth. "Brush 'em, brush 'em, brush 'em," he said. "Bring her down Tuesday morning for the free clinic. I'll put her in the chair."

"I have school," Karen said, which made the adults laugh.

It didn't seem funny to Karen, but she was pleased with herself for amusing them.

Later, when Karen was in bed, she looked out her window to the street, where she could see Teddy and her Aunt Edna sitting in Teddy's car. Karen knew Edna had hoped the family would make a good impression on her boyfriend. Karen understood the general terms of the relationship—that Edna wanted Teddy to like her and would do whatever she could to be nice to him. Karen understood that cooking a big dinner was part of the campaign, but she also knew there was more to it than that. Looking through the blinds in her bedroom to the street, she could sense that in Teddy's car Edna was waging the rest of the battle. Teddy and Edna were clinched together in a kiss that was more intense than anything Karen had ever seen between her parents. The car was near enough to her window so that she could see what was going on, but far enough away so that she couldn't hear what they were saying. It looked as if Edna was pretending to protest, trying to pull away from Teddy, but not very convincingly. Karen was fascinated as she watched Teddy touch Edna's breasts and put his hands inside her blouse. Karen watched with the clinical detachment of the very young. She could tell something significant was happening just out of her sight. As quietly as she could, she climbed up on her desk to try to look down into the car from a higher angle. Teddy was leaning back in the driver's seat, his mouth open. Karen couldn't see Edna's face. When Karen stood on her toes she could see that her aunt's face was buried in Teddy's lap; he was gripping her head, holding her there. At first the activity in the car was inexplicable to Karen. As she watched, she got a sense of what was going on, but the activity was new to her and she couldn't be sure.

Karen knew that what she had seen in Teddy's car was not something she could ask anyone about. Whatever the details, Karen had no doubt that her aunt was winning her campaign. They were married in his parents' synagogue. Within a month Edna was pregnant. The senior Soderbergs gave the couple the down payment on a house in Sherman Oaks, on a street near an orange grove, where the air was clean and fragrant—just ten minutes from their own house in Van Nuys and at least one generation away from the bungalow courts of North Gower Street.

. . .

After Karen had been at the Leeper School for six weeks, Claire called Milton about a new opportunity. "Do you know the Double Trouble pictures?" she asked.

"Can't say I do," Milton answered.

"They're not great. A step or two above serials, but it might be a situation for Karen. They're westerns."

"I see," Milton said, as Ceil came into the room.

"Juvenile westerns," Claire explained. "Kids as the sheriff, the rustlers. All kids."

"Paramount?"

"Eagle Pictures. They've made six or seven of them. It's Frank Keller's company. I told him about Karen. Give him a call."

The Double Trouble Ranch, in the San Gabriel Mountains above Eagle Rock, enchanted Karen. Here was a western town scaled to her size. Until she saw the ranch she hadn't understood what kid westerns were. But when she saw the herd of Shetland ponies, with their dappled coats and long, soft fringe running down their necks, she knew she wanted to be in this movie. Ceil, who had made the trip with Karen because Milton couldn't get off work, gripped her daughter's hand, afraid Karen would run over to the horses.

"Mrs. Teitel? Glad you could come," Frank Keller called out as he walked across the dusty set to greet his visitors. He was a slender man with a tense expression, dressed in dark working man's pants and cowboy boots. He was speaking to Ceil, but his eyes were on Karen. Before Ceil could introduce her daughter, Frank said, "Hello, Karen, welcome to Double Trouble Ranch. Why don't you come over here with me for a minute." He led them to where the ponies were grazing in the shade, tied to a tree. Keller could see that Karen was smitten, which was exactly what he had hoped would happen. The ponies seemed to grow quiet as Karen approached. Keller knew that some people had an effect like that on animals. It was hard to know who they were or if it would happen every time, but it seemed clear that Karen's presence changed the air around the ponies. As Keller introduced Red Landers, the horse wrangler, Karen walked into the herd, whispering to them. Red, an old ranch hand with a few wisps of white hair, told Karen their names. "That 'un there is Lady and next door you got Prince. There's Billy Boy and Razorback." As Red spoke, Karen pushed her face into the coat of a white-streaked pony named Feather. The pony shook himself but didn't shy away. It was the happiest Ceil had ever seen her daughter.

"Well, I guess you're a little horse-gal," Frank said. "I'll bet Red's got something you'd like to give that pony."

Red fished in the pockets of his dungarees and came up with a lump of sugar. Karen put it in her palm and held it up to Feather's mouth. The pony lapped up the sugar and licked Karen's hand.

Inside the barn that served as a stage, Frank gave Karen a copy of the scene and introduced her to Jocko McCarthy, the director. Jocko had been a cowboy actor and a stunt double until he decided he was too old to fall off horses for a living.

Because Karen couldn't read well enough to get through her pages, Ceil started to read the scene to her.

"Why don't I tell you what goes on, then later you can figure out how to memorize the words," Jocko said, in his Texas drawl. "Dickie Callaghan's been thrown in the hoosegow for shooting up a poker game. Dickie didn't do it, his brother Mickey did, but the law don't know that. You're Mrs. Dickie so the sheriff thinks you've turned up to talk to your brother-in-law, when actually that's your husband in there under the wrong pretenses. You're bringing him lunch in a basket. And a gun in your stocking." Karen didn't really understand the scene, but she sensed the general meaning.

While Karen was being outfitted, Frank Keller offered Ceil some iced tea in his office, in a corner of the barn. "I'm not exactly sure how Karen will fit into the overall," Frank said. "I just figure we need some new blood around here. So many of my kids are getting older. It's darn difficult, I'll tell you. You finally get a kid broken in and running right and they outgrow you, if you know what I mean." He clearly considered puberty in one of his actors a personal insult.

"When this is all played out, I'm going to try to move back a little closer to town and make a series of campus pictures. With kids, I mean. Kid professors, kid homecoming queen, kid fraternity parties." Ceil listened, but she didn't know what to make of Frank Keller. It wasn't until that night when she was thinking about it that she realized Keller had been flirting. It had been like her early dates with Milton, when he would spend the evening telling her about his hopes and plans. Ceil was twenty-nine, an attractive woman, but she had been married so long that she didn't recognize flirting.

Jocko returned with Karen, who was wearing a calico dress and carrying a wicker basket of food. Her face had been subtly made up and her dress padded slightly to give her the suggestion of a bust and hips. Karen adored it and would have been happy to wear the costume forever. Ceil found it unnerving.

When Karen was ready, Jocko walked her through the scene so she could get a feel for the set. "Don't try to act yet, honey," he said. "When you're ready we'll get Dickie in here and do one."

Dickie Callaghan, a few years older than the thirteen Frank had claimed, ambled onto the set, with a Stetson set low on his head. He was wearing tight jeans and cowboy boots. When he wrinkled his face in a smile, the effect was of a miniature Clark Gable. "Hiyah, kid," he said to Karen as he tousled her hair. "Let's make a movie."

"Okay," Jocko said. "Dickie, you're in the can. The girl's bringing you a gun. Play it like the way we did the breakout in *Lost Mine*. You know what I mean?"

"Got it, Chief."

They rehearsed the scene twice before Jocko began to shape it. He put his arm around Karen and told her, "When you take the gun out of your stocking turn toward Dickie so he eyeballs your leg, but the camera don't."

"Okay," Karen said. Ceil, who was listening from behind the camera, thought it was lucky Milton wasn't there.

In the last rehearsal, Karen played the business of taking the gun out of her stocking for Dickie's benefit. When she did, Jocko placed the sheriff in the foreground, keeping an eye on his prisoner. What the sheriff thought he was seeing was a woman showing her legs to her brother-in-law when in fact it was her husband. It was a mix of the priggish and the lowbrow that Karen never quite understood, but her instinct served her well enough to play the scene.

After they had shot a few takes of the master, Jocko told them to take a little break while he moved the camera and set up for the next angle. Dickie wanted to go to his dressing room to relax. "Come on, we can run the dialogue," he said to Karen. Although it made Ceil uneasy, Karen followed Dickie to the other end of the barn and into his dressing room.

Dickie opened two bottles of Coca-Cola and asked, "How old are you?"

"Six and three quarters," she answered.

"Christ, Keller's really robbing the cradle," he said, handing Karen a Coke. "You're pretty good, kid, for six. He'll offer you a part. We have fun around here sometimes."

"I like the horses," Karen said. "Feather's the best one."

"I'm going to be a director in a few years," Dickie said. "I might make Keller let me direct or I walk. Without my brother and me, there's no more Double Troubles. What else you been in?"

Karen told him about *My Hometown* and about working extra. She knew Dickie was showing off for her and she knew he was sort of ridiculous, but they were working together and she understood intuitively that the more time they spent together the better the scene would be. When she was relaxed, Dickie said, "So you like animals, huh?" As Karen nodded, Dickie opened his pants and said, "Then it's time for you to meet Mr. Rabbit." Before Karen could object, he put her hand on his crotch and a pink prong, bouncing on the spring of youth, popped into her fingers. It surprised Karen the way a jack-in-the-box might. "Hey," she said, pulling her hand away as her face turned red.

"Don't let go. Mr. Rabbit likes you. He wants to help you get in the movie." Dickie took her hand by the wrist and shoved it into his pants. It frightened her and she yanked herself free. She was trembling, but all she could think to say was, "Are you crazy?" She knew she didn't want to be here nor did she want to make a scene. She was scared and unsure what to do, when Jocko rapped on the door and told them it was time to start. It had been Ceil, nervous for her daughter, who told Jocko where they were. Jocko, who could well imagine what was going on, walked over to the dressing room, and casually knocked.

"Don't say nothing," Dickie told her, "or else forget the movie." Karen composed her face into a mask of indifference. She walked out and smiled at Jocko, who stood outside the dressing room door until both children appeared.

Ceil asked, "What were you doing in there?"

Karen shrugged and answered, "He was telling me about the movie."

Karen was offered a role in the Double Trouble movies but it came too late. Frank Keller's creditors caught up with him before production could begin. Milton was upset, but Karen was devastated not to see Feather again.

A few classmates took pleasure in the disappointment, but Ma Leeper said, "When you fall off the horse, the only cure is get back on." Neither Ceil nor Karen understood exactly what Ma meant, but they both knew it amounted to keep studying at the Leeper Professional School. Karen's education had become an issue between Ceil and Milton. Ceil had always doubted the wisdom of taking Karen out of public school for what Milton called "the scholarship," as if it were a rare prize instead of a deal he had cut.

Because the marriage was strained, Milton felt doubly pressed to push Karen's career ahead. He himself could find no work that he felt offered him a future. He was working as a salesman at B&R Dry Goods in Boyle Heights, but thoughts of Karen's career consumed him. Claire Berger had given him a list of agents who specialized in children, but none of them seemed particularly impressed by Karen's small role in *My Hometown*. Claire thought that after the movie was released they might have better luck. But that was months away. Milton tried to get a copy of the Double Trouble screen test, but Eagle Pictures' property had been seized by the court as part of Frank Keller's bankruptcy proceedings. It was as if the test had never happened.

When he wasn't working, Milton began hanging around the Paramount lot in the hope of running into Claire, Lew Pressler or Ben Tucker. Lurking near the Bronson Gate made him feel a little unhinged, like one of the autograph hounds who waited there for movie stars. Ceil was relieved that at least Milton had stopped going to Karen's school. She suspected the reason he no longer went there was because he knew it was only a matter of time before Ma Leeper rescinded the scholarship and demanded monthly tuition. Milton couldn't afford it, and the thought of sending Karen back to Cheremoya Avenue was more than he could bear.

While Karen was at school Milton told Ceil, "You call Claire Berger, she'll talk to you. Get her advice."

"She's your friend. You're the one who took her to that fancy lunch."

"Ceil, for God's sake, don't pick a fight. It's for Karen. Claire Berger, I don't know. I came on too hard or something. She don't take my calls. Talk to her. Ask her what we should be doing. She loves Karen. She knows she's got talent."

"Let her alone."

"Claire Berger?"

"No, Karen. Let her alone."

"I thought you meant Claire Berger."

"Let her alone, too."

"Oh, Christ. I don't even know what you're saying anymore. Call up Claire Berger. It's for Karen."

"No it's not. It's for you. You're pushing too hard."

"You think it's for me? You're way off base. I'm not the one going to school. I'm not the one getting in the movies."

"I'm tired of it. You have to back off."

"Of my daughter? Back off my own daughter? Ceil, let me tell you something. Sometimes I think you got your head up your ass." He had never insulted her before, and it made Ceil cry. "Now we get waterworks? Forget it. You're saying all this because you're afraid to help your own daughter. That's the real problem around here. I'm not letting you hold her back. She's getting every chance. To you the whole world is the goddamn orphan home. The hell with it," he said, heading for the door.

"Where are you going?" was all Ceil could manage, but Milton, in rage and frustration, was gone. He moved out of Gower Gardens to a two-room apartment in Boyle Heights, in the building where Bela lived. The two men began spending time together, eating their evening meal at the Famous Restaurant and talking about Karen.

After a full year at Leeper, still on scholarship, thanks to Milton's ability to charm Ma, Karen was cast in a movie. A Poverty Row company called Excalibur Pictures had announced their next production would be directed by Jocko McCarthy. Milton called Jocko and reminded him that he had liked Karen when she had tested at the Double Trouble Ranch. Jocko did indeed remember Karen and he knew she'd be right for a part in his movie. Karen was signed to play the daughter of a country veterinarian in *On the Farm*. It was her first major role. While she was making it, no one had any idea that such a low-rent venture would be the first of an entire series of veterinarian movies. It did modest business. With Excalibur as distributor, the movie would never be seen in first-class theaters, only in what were called "subsequent run houses," which meant dingy firetraps in obscure neighborhoods.

Like *My Hometown* before it, the movie made no dent in the public consciousness. Karen saw it twice in the week that it played—once with her mother and Aunt Edna and once with her father and grandfather. Milton was well behaved and didn't accost members of the audience to point out Karen. But when she was on screen, he couldn't resist whooping and slapping the empty seat in front of him. Karen loved watching herself with the animals. Seeing herself on screen seemed natural to her. She would watch, losing herself in the story, but still keeping an eye on her own performance.

Almost four decades later, in a Hollywood that was very different and yet still the same, Carla and I were at Ma Maison. She was sipping a kir and talking about *On the Farm,* happy to be reminiscing. "We heard Jocko was going to be the director," she said. "We thought that was good news. Jocko made Ceil comfortable when I tested for the kid western. He needed me to cry in a scene. I don't even remember what it was. Maybe the first bird-with-broken-wing crisis. A lot of those guys would have distracted my mother and the social worker and slapped me around."

"Come on, Carla," I said, doubting it. "Actually hit a seven-year-old?"

"Damn right. There were some real maniacs around. Before the scene, Jocko says, 'After we wrap you're going to keep the gray-and-white cat, aren't you? For a pet.' He was talking about this cat in the picture that I sort of liked. All I could think was, Ceil would go crazy if I tried to bring a cat home. 'What's the kitty's name?' 'Ralph,' I said, because it's the first name that popped into my head. Then, when we were about to roll, Jocko says, 'Geez, Karen, a terrible thing, the Chapman crane ran over Ralph. His brains got all crushed out.' "

I laughed at the ghastly predictability of the whole business just as Carla was smiling at the memory. "Did it make you cry?" I asked.

"It was too dumb. I just stood there. 'I thought you loved Ralph,' Jocko said, like I tricked him or something." She was imitating Jocko's beefy voice, giving him a sort of hurt bluster. " 'Not really,' I said. Then Jocko said, 'Why'd you say you were going to keep him?' 'Because you wanted me to.' " Then Carla laughed and laughed. It was one of the few things she learned at Leeper that stuck with her: Never say no to a director.

"So what happened? Did you cry for the scene?"

"I could have. Crying is easy. Jocko was so used to working with kids who couldn't do anything but show off he never even asked me. When the cat business didn't work, Jocko scraped my fingernails on a bar of soap. In the close-up, he told me to touch my eyes. That did it. The shot went in the picture."

Because her thoughts always proceeded with a private logic, or maybe just because she could sense my thoughts, she began talking about her parents again. "You know, around then, just before I went to Metro is when my parents split up. It was hard. I was the reason. I don't know if they understood that. But I was. They both meant well—about me, I mean. Ceil wanted me to work if I wanted to. But to her it was sort of an after-school activity, like band practice or something. She couldn't help being scared of anything bigger than that. Milton never had any doubts. He just pushed and pushed. It must have scared my mother. That's what caused their breakup. I didn't know that in words, not then anyway. But I knew it just the same. Kids always do."

Despite Ceil's accusations, Milton never thought of Karen as his meal ticket, but rather as a sacred trust of which he was the trustee. He knew she could be a star, even if Ceil couldn't see it. He vowed to stay close to her, to sacrifice any opportunity for himself in favor of his daughter. It was his duty and he knew that in the long run it would make him rich. He soon found his first promising job since the war. He was selling cars on Figueroa Street, at Soderberg Ford, owned by Teddy's father. Edna, who was better at getting things from men than Ceil ever was, had arranged it. Because of the war, no new cars had been made in several years. For once, Milton was in the right place.

Perhaps it was Milton's success as a car salesman, or perhaps he had just gotten a little older, but when Claire Berger called him at the Ford dealership to invite him to lunch, he wasn't as nervous as the first time. He told himself that if she was calling, she must have something for Karen.

"Rob Roy, right?" Milton said as he greeted her. Claire nodded and Milton ordered two.

Claire got right to what was on her mind. "The farm picture went nowhere. That's the business. But Karen was terrific and the idea is commercial. I can sell a package of a new script and Karen to a studio."

"Paramount?" Milton asked.

"No."

Milton waited for her to say which studio, but she said nothing more. Milton guessed that meant she had already sold the idea to someone other than her own studio and now wanted to make sure she had Karen's participation. She was starting to play footsie with him again, brushing her foot across his leg, and leaning toward him. Milton remembered those moves from their last lunch. Instead of playing her game, he thought of how Al Soderberg behaved in a tough negotiation: Buddha-like, expressionless. Milton tried to imitate him.

"I need your participation to make the deal happen," Claire said. "If it goes right, it'll make Karen a star."

"I don't get what's so hot about a movie that didn't make a dime."

"The story of a veterinarian and his daughter can become a series of movies—like the Andy Hardys or Our Gang. If they're made by a major, they can run forever."

"If it's not Paramount, what's your angle?"

"I want to represent Karen."

"Be an agent?" Milton asked as calmly as he could. "No more casting work?" he asked, as if his interest in this were Claire's career.

"It's the future," Claire said. "You know what the divestiture decree is?"

"Remind me," Milton said.

"The Supreme Court decision. It's going to shoot holes through everything. The days of the studios are going to be over. The brokers will be king. Whichever agents have the big clients—they'll rule the town."

Milton had no idea what Claire was talking about. He figured she'd heard it all somewhere, or read it in the trades and was spewing it back, putting fancy wrapping on the plain fact that she'd lost her job. He decided the real changes she was talking about were for her. "Very possibly," he said. "So you open an office. Claire Berger, agent. For argument's sake, Karen's on your list. Who else?"

"For a start, only Karen. My focus is to set up the veterinarian movies. When they're moving, I'll have my pick of the talent. Karen will be established. And you will have whatever you want—a lot of money, a role as producer, or just being a proud father. You tell me."

"I still don't get how the movies are going to be such a big hit. The first one flopped."

"Listen to me," Claire said, looking at Milton, hard. "Think of the Andy Hardys. How they're the same each time, with little differences. Very comforting, very successful."

"So?" Milton said.

"There's a vet, same as before. Karen plays his daughter—like she did. In each story the father and daughter team up in the third act to fix up a sick cow or some other thing. We do it at a major, with real production values and a director with an IQ in triple digits."

Milton nodded his general approval and then said, "Well, of course I'd need to think about it. Talk it over with Karen and her mother."

"Oh, bullshit," Claire said. "This is your call and we both know it. In or out, Milton? In or out?"

"We're in," Milton said, trying to appear calm, as if they were playing poker and he had just asked for another card. It didn't fool Claire, but she was excited, too. She leaned over and kissed him on the cheek.

Milton decided not to tell Karen or Ceil about Claire Berger's offer until it was firmer. He knew this could be the turning point for Karen and he didn't want to give Ceil time to think of reasons not to proceed. Milton didn't fully trust Claire. He knew she was up to more than she was saying, but there weren't any other offers and this was a real possibility. When Claire sent him agency representation contracts and informed him that M-G-M was ready to talk, Milton waited for Karen after school, to explain the new opportunity. "It'll be like *On the Farm*, only better. At a major. Metro."

"With a pony?" Karen asked, the excitement in her voice apparent to Milton.

"Sure. All the animals you can name. Are you excited?"

"Oh, yes," she said, hugging her father. "I want it. Oh, please, Daddy. Please, please." She began dancing around him, bubbling over with pleasure at the thought of a pony. Karen started to skip away from her father, repeating to herself, "A pony, a pony."

Milton called to her, "Tell Mommy how excited you are when you get home." Karen sensed she was being used in the ongoing struggle between her parents. But she didn't want to think about that now. Thoughts of her pony filled her head. "You'll go to school on the lot," Milton said. "At Metro."

"Every day?"

"Yeah. You'll be with famous actors. Won't that be something?"

"What about Leeper?" Karen asked, trying to decide if what her father was saying was real or just talk.

"It was okay for a while. But now you're moving up."

Karen just looked at her father, trying to figure what it meant.

Milton had Claire Berger's agency papers examined by a lawyer in Boyle Heights who didn't know much about the movie business, but was willing to wait for payment until Karen was employed. Once Milton signed, things moved fast. An article appeared in *Variety* announcing Claire's departure from Paramount and the opening of the Berger Talent Agency. As her first act as Karen's agent, Claire arranged a meeting with Fred Nugent, the M-G-M executive who would be in charge of the project.

Nugent, who looked to Milton to be about forty, was dressed in a tan linen suit, a blue shirt and a yellow silk tie. Milton could see that Nugent was a very smooth fellow. His large, airy office in the Thalberg Building had signed photographs of M-G-M stars on the walls. Milton tried to read the inscription from Clark Gable, but beyond "To Steady Freddy," he couldn't decipher Gable's scrawl. Claire and Fred seemed to be old friends. After a few minutes of small talk about people Milton didn't know, Fred asked, "Would you like to come to school here, Karen?"

"I think so," she said, which made the adults laugh.

"I hope you can," Nugent said. "May I call you Milt?" he asked, in a deferential voice.

"Oh, sure, Fred," Milton said, glancing down at Nugent's tasseled loafers. The leather was burnished and seemed to glow. Milton watched carefully as Fred rested his feet on the coffee table. It was a grand gesture, one that Milton admired and hoped to emulate. He noticed that Nugent's soles were unscuffed, as if the shoes had just come out of the box and had never touched the ground.

"Here's the situation. I've commissioned a screenplay along the lines Claire told you about. Maury Kelman, one of our top writers, is on it. If the script's as good as I know it can be, we'll move fast. You'll find we do things first cabin, Milt. Right, Claire?"

"Absolutely," Claire said.

"Now, I want to put an if-come deal in place for Karen's services," Nugent said. Milton loved the term. He had never heard it before, but he understood it nonetheless and that made him feel like an insider. "It'd be for Maury's veterinarian script and an option to do sequels. The offer's not firm till we approve the script. When the picture's a go, Karen will start coming to school here, and we'll begin the dance. Okay in principle so far, Milt?"

"Yeah, it is," Milton said in a voice that was starting to get husky. He could feel himself perspiring at the possibility his dream might be coming true.

"One other thing," Nugent said. "There's the matter of Karen's name."

"I know," Milton said. "Teitel is too . . ." Milton stumbled a bit, wondering if Nugent was Jewish.

"Exactly," Claire said.

Karen, who had been sitting quietly looking at the movie-star pictures on the wall, realized that the name they were talking about was hers. It made her grow very still.

"We've been tossing it around," Nugent said. "If the deal goes through, we'll need to change it. Contingent on your approval, of course. We think when she signs, it should be as Carla Tate. What do you think, Milt?"

Before Milton, who would have said yes to changing Karen's name to almost anything short of Tokyo Rose, could answer, Claire turned to Karen and asked, "Would you like that, Karen? To be called Carla?"

Although Karen had little actual say in the matter, even less than Milton, the three adults were quiet for a moment in deference to her views. They were relieved when she broke into a wide grin and started repeating her new name, enchanted with the idea.

"It's beautiful," Milton said, wondering how Ceil would react.

After the meeting, when Milton took Karen home, he tried to think how he could best present the name change. He never got the chance. Karen skipped ahead into the house, shouting "I'm Carla, I'm Carla, I'm Carla!" Karen seemed so pleased with it that Ceil didn't object, although she thought her daughter was as taken with the idea of a name change as with this particular name. Karen wanted to change everybody's name; she began calling her mother Joyce. When she told Edna, calling her Carol, Karen offered to give her new cousin, if it was a girl, the name of Karen, since she wasn't going to use it anymore.

Two days later, when Claire told Milton that Metro's first offer, which she was sure she could improve, was five hundred dollars a week—contingent of course on the studio approving Maury Kelman's script—Milton decided that no matter what happened with the Metro deal, from then on his daughter would always be Carla Tate. Milton reminded Claire that he expected to be cut into the deal as well.

"What did your wife think of the new name?"

As she asked the question, Milton realized that Claire didn't know that he and Ceil had separated. "Fine," he said. "She liked it fine."

"Sometimes name-changing can get a little dicey."

"I want to keep Karen's new name in the family." Then without consciously knowing what he was about to do, he heard himself say, "No more Teitel. From now on, we're Carla and Milton Tate. That's my name, too."

6.

For Carla the studio was a school, but for the adults it was a workplace that looked more like a college campus than the factory to which the newspapers frequently compared it. The studio was populated with beautiful young people looking to take their youth and attractiveness to market, and powerful older ones who could help them get what they sought. It gave the place a lubricious air, thick with hormones and availability. No young actress spoke to a producer, director, executive, agent, writer or an older, more established actor without considering the possibility of sexual commerce. Rapaciousness was always there, hanging in the air along with the heat. The studio was an erotic countinghouse and Carla grew up in it, absorbing its customs and values through her pores. The studio made her as surely as the orphanage had made her mother, and it did the job before she could know it or judge it.

The weeks before her picture began shooting were the last days Carla ever had before she began her lifetime of work. Because she remembered those days the best, she later came to think of them as her childhood, an interlude before the cameras rolled and before she became famous. In preparation for the film, Metro had installed a barnyard menagerie, and Carla was encouraged to get to know the horses, cows, ducks, chickens and pigs. Her teachers and companions were paid to look after her needs. She was seven—an age when a child tends to take the world as she finds it, but also to assume that the world will always be as it is.

While sets were being built and the other roles cast, Claire wanted Carla to get used to the studio, so she persuaded Fred Nugent to enroll her early in Metro's Little Red Schoolhouse, which was neither little nor red, but a white stucco bungalow with a tiled roof and Spanish arches. Because family life was at the center of so many of the studio's films, M-G-M had gone into the child-raising business. Like everything else M-G-M used in quantity, the studio grew its own; for every drama, a child or two was needed—a new crop every year. M-G-M wasn't an organization that made investments without getting a return, so the children were worked as hard as the law permitted.

The principal of the school, Miss Pringle, was a tall, elegant woman in her middle fifties with an upper-class English accent who had taught French and Latin at the Hancock School before the war. She was a woman who took her obligation to the children more seriously than her obligation to her employers. If a child was asked to shoot beyond the legally allotted time, Miss Pringle was the one who drew the line. "Let the sun go down, let the overtime begin, but no child in my charge works more than three hours a day." That was the law of the state of California, and Miss Pringle enforced it.

When Carla started at the Little Red Schoolhouse, the other elementary school contract players were Sarah Milliken and Bobby Dryer. Sarah had been in several musicals and was considered the child with the brightest future. Bobby had the child actor's gift of looking younger than his age. Sarah tolerated him because he was a contract player. Sarah always brought a hamster named Nibbles to class. Although Sarah had a cage for him, Nibbles was usually perched on her shoulder. Carla tried to listen in class, but most of the time she watched Nibbles as he climbed over Sarah's back.

On her first morning at the school, Miss Pringle introduced Carla to the other students and then turned the elementary school children over to Mr. Danzig, their instructor. Sarah whispered, "We're the only girls." Carla could plainly see there were other girls. As Carla was puzzling it through, Mr. Danzig, whom Sarah and Bobby called Skeeter, told the children to divide into groups. The day players broke into three groups while Sarah, Carla and Bobby stayed together, apart from the others. Sarah smiled at Carla, as if to say, "We're the ones who count." Carla knew to appear unassuming and to treat Sarah deferentially, as a wise, older sister. She knew by instinct that Sarah would be a valuable ally only as long as she didn't feel threatened. Carla listened to Sarah and then asked if she could pet Nibbles.

"He bites," Sarah said, turning down the request.

"Not me," Carla said, touching the jumpy hamster. "Hi, Nibbles. Want to play at the barn?"

"Not allowed," Sarah said, putting him in his cage.

After their morning class of reading and arithmetic from nine till noon, the children went to lunch at the commissary. The children ate in a special alcove known as the romper room. It was a safe distance from the raucous, lewd jokes at the writers' table or the sometimes gamy gossip of the publicity table, and far, too, from the exclusive precincts of the directors' table, where actors and producers as well as directors might be found, laughing and making bets on anything from East Coast football games to who might come through the door next.

Skeeter Danzig was a former actor who, having despaired of his ability ever to find steady employment, had gone back to UCLA for a teaching certificate in early childhood education. He started as a "day-by-day" instructor at various studio schools, a roving teacher hired when large batches of noncontract players were at the schools. When the job of permanent elementary teacher opened up at M-G-M, he was hired. He had been married once, but was now divorced, and he devoted himself to the school. Because Skeeter was a man of Hollywood, he gave more attention to Sarah, Bobby and now Carla than to the day players. He didn't mean to be unfair; it was simply an automatic response to the pecking order of which he was a part. In the romper room of the commissary, he sat with the contract players, apart from the others.

Carla ignored the commissary food, the steaks, chops, sandwiches and ice cream sundaes that everyone else ate. She usually had Mr. Mayer's famous chicken soup and some fruit salad. She would stuff her pockets with sugar lumps from the bowl, carrot curls and apple slices from her salad, and pieces of matzoh, a box of which sat on every table, twelve months a year. After lunch, when Sarah and Bobby went off to the soundstages or their locations, Carla loved to visit her animals. No child was supposed to go anywhere unattended, so a studio car, a Packard limousine, waited for her outside the commissary. As she rode through the studio streets, she sat up on her knees to watch for actors in costume. Sometimes she saw a few, but usually it was only grips on bicycles and a few young actors preening for one another or taking the sun. The idea that film studios were crowded with performers comes more from the movies than reality. Hollywood's idea of itself was no more or less accurate than its idea of anything else. When M-G-M, or any studio, was shooting a scene set on a movie lot, the director always called for extras and put them in colorful costumes—witches in conical hats were always popular. There was some truth in it—there were always some actors in costume walking here or there, but most of the people on the lot worked behind the camera, on the crews or in the offices.

The director of animal services was Norman Katano, and he had been told to encourage Carla to play with the animals every day. Norman usually dressed in denim overalls with baggy, grass-stained knees. Even though the studio kept a large crew of greensmen, Norman was frequently on his knees with a hand spade, turning over Mr. Mayer's dirt or pruning Mr. Mayer's rosebushes. When Carla was an adult and Norman Katano long dead, she learned that although he had been born in Pasadena and had never been west of Catalina, he had spent the war years in a Japanese internment camp in Lone Pine. It had been Norman's idea to have Carla name the animals. Ever since her own name change, she had been fascinated by names. She had given most of them human names—there was a duck named Mary Anne and a rooster named Bob; a cow had been Elsie, after the Borden trademark.

In the last weeks of preproduction the studio had acquired a horse, a sweet-looking five-year-old roan that Carla was to ride in the picture. Carla had planned to call him Dobbin, a name Ceil had suggested, but when she saw him, with his reddish flanks, heavy coat and deep, sad eyes, she blurted out, "Hi, Lewis. Want a cracker?" She held out a matzoh that Lewis nibbled. He then lapped up the crumbs in her palm with his gritty tongue.

"He likes you," Norman said, relieved. "That's what you call him? Lewis?"

"And he calls me Carla."

"Want to ride him?" Although Carla seemed reticent, Norman

could see she very much wanted to ride him. He brought over an apple box for a step and helped her up onto Lewis's back. He led them out to the barnyard. Norman walked Lewis in widening circles while Carla sat astride her new friend, her legs spread wide across his flanks. She leaned forward and dropped her arms around Lewis's neck and lay her head against his mane. Norman watched as Carla rubbed herself against Lewis, letting the horse's warmth become part of her. Had she been a little older she might have felt self-conscious, any younger and she might not have felt the pull and physical sensation of the horse.

"You like horses or you just like Lewis?" Norman asked. Carla was too involved with feeling Lewis's muscles against her legs and chest to respond. For that moment she wanted to melt into Lewis.

During those preproduction weeks, Milton took every chance he could to try to talk to Fred Nugent or Claire Berger. He had ideas for new projects for Carla and he felt entitled to an audience. In the mornings, he made it a point to walk Carla to the schoolhouse in order to see her teachers, even if it meant getting to the car lot a little late. Milton had taken to wearing a tan suit with loafers, after his first meeting with Fred Nugent. "So how many teachers do you have again?" he asked Carla.

"Skeeter."

"You call him that? Not Mr. Skeeter?"

"That's his name."

"Who else?"

"Miss Pringle."

"The principal, am I right?" Carla nodded, and waved to Norman Katano, who slowed down in his jeep to say hello. Milton looked up to see an older Japanese man driving what looked like an army surplus jeep.

"Mr. Tate?" Norman asked, offering his hand. Milton stared at him, trying to figure what his daughter had to do with this man. "I'm Norman Katano. Animal services."

Milton still looked baffled until Carla said, "Tell Lewis I have a surprise." The mention of the horse's name made Milton realize that this was Norman from the farm, a man his daughter had mentioned many times. She had not mentioned that he was Japanese.

"Right. Yeah. Sure," Milton said.

Norman, who had been told that Milton had fought in the

Pacific, just smiled and shook hands, told Carla he'd see her later, and drove off.

"That's Norman, huh?" Milton asked.

"Yep."

"So you didn't tell me he was, you know, a Jap—" Then thinking better of it, Milton added "—anese. Japanese."

"Yep."

"It's okay. Live and forget, I say."

At the schoolhouse, still a little rattled from his accidental meeting with Norman Katano, Milton met Miss Pringle. She was wearing a high-necked, long-sleeved black dress that was flattering to her tall, thin figure and contrasted nicely with her silvery hair, but was also as severe and forbidding as she was herself. She was a head taller than Milton, and although there was wit in her face and she had an easy smile, she had a low tolerance for Milton's glad-handed charm. "Good morning," he said with his salesman's cheeriness.

"Good morning, Carla," she answered and then nodded to Milton.

"So how are we proceeding?" he asked, turning slightly formal in reaction to the chill he could feel from Miss Pringle.

"Learning to read and, I hope, to think. It's a long process."

"Yeah, that's very good. Okay, then," he said, feeling clumsy and unsure what to do in the face of her aloofness.

"Am I going to learn to talk French?" Carla asked.

"Not just yet, dear," Miss Pringle said.

"French?" Milton asked. "What's with that?"

"In the afternoons the children have individual lessons. Some of the older ones take languages."

"Important to have that," Milton said. "Be well-rounded. What about acting lessons, though?"

"For now Carla is to spend her elective time with the animals. Perhaps later she can broaden her schedule to include coaching or French."

"That's very good," he said, wanting to get away from Miss Pringle. "Sweetheart," he said to his daughter, "I'll see you later."

"Okay."

Walking back toward the parking lot, Milton caught himself muttering aloud, "Jesus, a Jap in a jeep," when he saw Fred Nugent going into the Thalberg Building. He called to him but Nugent either didn't hear or chose to ignore him.

• • •

Carla was often called away from her afternoons with Lewis for makeup and wardrobe tests and occasionally for screen tests for candidates to play her father. Although Maury Kelman's script, now called *The Veterinarian's Daughter*, still wasn't finished, one scene—with Dr. George, as the veterinarian was to be known, and his daughter in their living room—was declared ready enough for tests. With Maury Kelman's help, Carla learned the dialogue and then shot six versions of the scene in one day.

Each of the actors was experienced, so the purpose of the test wasn't to see if they could act, but how they looked and interacted with Carla. Only Brandon Holt, a character man who had been around Hollywood since the silent days, stood out. Holt was fifty, which was old for the role, but it seemed to give him additional presence, even wisdom. If he and Carla had what Fred Nugent called "chemistry," Brandon Holt would be Dr. George. Brandon looked good because he had improvised a moment in the middle of the test. Even Kelman, who had a screenwriter's distaste for improvisation, liked it. In the scene, after Carla told her father she didn't know where his medical bag was, Brandon walked over to Dr. George's old upright piano, making the camera follow him, played "Twinkle, Twinkle, Little Star," and sang the words known by every piano student: *"Papa Haydn's dead and gone, but his melody lingers on."* It made Carla laugh and for a brief moment the scene came alive.

Fred asked Claire Berger to find out Carla's reaction. "She doesn't have veto power or anything," he told Claire, "But see if she likes the guy. If they'll get along."

The next day, after lunch, Claire went to the barn and while Carla was riding Lewis she walked along next to them, holding the reins.

"Was it fun to make the tests?" she asked.

"It was okay."

"Not as much fun as making a movie, though. Is it?"

"Is Lewis going to be in the movie?"

"Absolutely. You like Lewis, don't you?"

"Hi, Lewis," Carla said, leaning down and speaking directly into the horse's ear. It made Lewis shake his mane.

"Do you remember the last test you did?"

"Which one?"

"With Brandon Holt. For your father. Do you remember?"

"I think."

"It was the scene in the house. Where he can't find his bag and he thinks you know where it is."

"That's the one we do all the time."

"But the last time you did it was with Brandon Holt. The tall man who played the piano."

"He was nice."

"Would you like to be in the movie with him?"

"Okay."

"It's a big decision, Carla. Are you sure?"

"I don't know. Ask my dad."

"I'm asking you."

"Is he going to get the part?"

"Possibly. It's important to know if you're comfortable with him."

"Are we going to start pretty soon?"

"Just as soon as we cast Dr. George. What do you think?"

"I have to ask Lewis." She leaned over again into the horse's mane and said, "Is the piano guy okay to be Dr. George?" Lewis shook his mane again, reacting to her breath in his ear. Carla sat back up on the horse and smiled. "Lewis says okay."

And so Brandon Holt, after two decades of character work, became a star.

When the script was finally approved, put through the typing pool, and bound in red covers, a reading with the cast was held. The director was Bill Brady, a studio staff man, who had worked on other movies with Maury and the technicians assigned to the film.

They sat at a long table set up on Stage 8, where the movie's main interior had been built. It was Dr. George's living room, with beamed ceilings, stone fireplace, and bookshelves filled with leather-bound classics and books about animals. A painting of Dr. George's late wife—serene and saintly, a gentle-looking woman who had been given Carla's features—hung above the fireplace, keeping a benign eye on her family. Bill Brady sat at the head of the table with Maury on his left. Carla sat next to Brandon Holt, and the other actors arranged themselves around the table. Doughnuts, fruit and an urn of coffee had been provided by the commissary. Claire Berger, who had purposely not told Milton about the reading in order to keep him away, sat across from her client. Carla asked Claire if Lewis the horse was going to be at the reading. When one of the other actors laughed, Carla said, "He has a bigger part than you." No one else laughed at Lewis.

Carla could read well enough for her age, but she had always learned her lines with her mother's help. This time she turned to Brandon Holt, who was glad to assist her. At first, when she stumbled, Bill Brady looked nervous, so Claire intervened. "Say it for her, then she'll repeat it." Bill nodded and when Carla had difficulty, she'd listen to Brandon then repeat what he had said. When she had to figure out the words, she spoke in the same singsong voice that all children use when they're learning to read. It terrified the adults until she put down the script and repeated what she had just read in the voice of the veterinarian's daughter. As long as she didn't have to struggle with the reading, her voice was simple and unaffected, direct and always clear. The third time she did it, Maury Kelman muttered, "Damnedest thing I ever saw."

The story Kelman had contrived had to be a tale that was interesting and compelling on its own and that could also serve as the basis for a continuing series. Dr. George was a rural veterinarian, a recent widower, with a little daughter named Georgine. Dr. George had always wanted a son and now that there was just the two of them, little Georgine had to prove to her dad that she was just as good as a boy. In the first story and all the others that would follow, the two would argue about Georgine's ability to assist Dr. George on his rounds of the local farms. Each time, little Georgine would prove her mettle as she worked with her father to help birth a calf or mend a broken wing. At the end of each movie, Dr. George regretted he had ever doubted her. It always seemed to be summer in the Dr. George movies; the sun always shone over the meadow and the brook always ran clear. No one ever said where the farms were, exactly, and the neighboring farmers, the ones with the never-ending supply of sick animals, spoke in a mixture of accents—some seemed to be from New England, flinty Vermonters, maybe; others had soft, Tidewater accents, Virginia gentlemen. Everyone was white and Gentile; every woman was a mom who spent her days making supper and wiping her hands on her apron. Dr. George drove a pickup truck, but in an emergency, when little Georgine had to find her dad, she always rode Lewis the horse.

Unlike most character actors of his era, Brandon Holt had never worked on Broadway or in the West End. Brandon was a man of the movies, his sense of acting purely behavioral. He had never played to a second balcony. Any exaggeration was a mistake to Brandon. Since that style was only a more developed version of Carla's instinctive method, they played well together. Brandon knew as well as anyone at the studio that in the end the success of the movie would come down to the quality of Maury Kelman's script and his own rapport with Carla. He had no children of his own and although he usually got along with those he met, little Carla was a mystery to him. He would look at her, so tiny and opaque with those exquisite features, and think how difficult the movie business was. He tried not to dwell on it, but it was hard to keep it out of his mind: His career, and as Brandon saw it, the rest of his life, depended on his ability to get along with a seven-year-old.

During the last week of preproduction, when Brandon was at the studio every day for wardrobe and lighting tests and for conferences with Bill Brady, he went to the barnyard after lunch, when he knew Carla would be there. He took it very slowly, just watching as Carla rode Lewis. By the time Brandon began coming to the barnyard, Carla could ride Lewis without Norman holding the reins. She wasn't allowed to canter, but could ride at a pace that Lewis found comfortable. As Brandon watched, waiting for an opening, Carla waved and brought the horse over to where he was standing. "Hi, Daddy," she said.

"Hello, Georgine," he answered, feeling a shiver go down his back when she called him Daddy. "How's Lewis today?"

"Ask him."

"Hi, Lewis," Brandon said, speaking softly to the horse and offering a carrot from his pocket. Lewis chewed the carrot, then nuzzled Brandon, sniffing him.

"He likes you," Carla said, delightedly.

"Well, I certainly like him," Brandon said, keeping his eyes on Carla, hoping she would know that they were talking about themselves as much as the horse. "Can we ride him together?"

"Ask him."

"Lewis," Brandon said, cooing to the animal, stroking his flanks, "can I ride with Carla? Is that okay?" Lewis shook his head and whinnied.

"Okay. He said yes," Carla said. Norman brought the apple box and Brandon mounted easily, sitting behind Carla. She leaned back against him as Brandon spoke to the horse, urging him to move a little faster.

As they cantered around the barnyard, Brandon leaned forward to see Carla's face. Her eyes were shining. "Shall we go for a real ride?" he asked. Unsure of how to reply, Carla said nothing, but Brandon pulled the reins to the right and sent Lewis out of the barnyard onto the lot. "We won't be long," he called to Norman, who didn't look pleased with this turn of events.

"Are we going to Lot 4?" Carla asked, assuming they were headed for meadows and open fields.

"Nope. We're going to show him the studio." As Carla realized what he meant, she began to smile. Brandon fanned out his fingers, which almost covered Carla's chest and stomach, and drew her to him. She leaned back, astride Lewis and resting against Dr. George, content and comforted.

They trotted back toward Lot 1, where the main business of the studio was conducted. As they rode past, people on the street stopped to point or wave. At the school, Carla shouted, "Hey, Skeeter, come here. Come on." The loudness and the joy in her voice made Lewis whinny again and as he did, Skeeter, followed by Sarah Milliken and Bobby Dryer, came outside. Skeeter waved and shouted, "You look great!"

Bobby said, "Holy shit!" Sarah just stared and didn't say anything.

"Let's show him our house," Carla said. Brandon laughed and brought Lewis about and set off for Stage 8. Bobby Dryer ran after them, enchanted. Even when Skeeter called to him, Bobby wouldn't come back.

At the soundstage, Brandon headed Lewis straight through the overhead loading door onto the cavernous stage. The painting crew finishing the set for Georgine's bedroom looked up and stopped working; even the guard, who was not paid to have a sense of humor, called out, "Did you change it to a western?"

They waved and trotted over to the living-room set, where Brandon brought Lewis to a gentle halt. "Tell him what this is," he said to Carla.

"This is our house, Lewis. See? You can come in. Just today because it's special."

"Yes, it is," Brandon said, softly, thinking he had set out to woo this child and instead had himself been seduced, entirely. Behind them, standing in the door, Bobby Dryer watched, excited, dancing about, calling, "Hey, Carla. Over here. Hey." But she paid no attention to him, happy to be with her horse in her new house with her new father.

7.

Like other children, Carla lived in a world of perpetual anticipation over events about to unfold. Unlike most children, who look forward to new toys or the next holiday from school, Carla waited in anxious pleasure for the start of photography or for the arrival of new script pages. She accepted it as normal and took it all no more or less seriously than other children accepted their situations.

Each night as Milton drove Carla home to Gower Gardens, he would question her, trying to gauge her progress. She would respond, but it was never enough to give him a clear sense of her life at the studio. Because he thought he might learn something valuable, Milton decided he would try to have lunch with his daughter. "Okay," she said, but he could hear in her voice that she was uncomfortable at the idea.

"Adults are there, right?"

"It's all grown-ups. That's who goes there."

"Then what's the problem? I'll come tomorrow."

Because he wasn't sure if he could get on the lot without her,

Milton decided he'd better hang around all the next morning, waiting for her lunch break.

"So I'll see you later," Milton said as he dropped Carla off at the schoolhouse. He had three hours before the children left for the commissary. He wanted to see the sets for Carla's movie, and he decided that if he just looked as if he knew where he was going, no one would bother him. He tucked a copy of *Variety* under his arm and walked toward Stage 8, imagining that in his tan suit and blue shirt people might assume he was an executive at the studio.

The stage was open so Milton entered. He could see the set Carla had described, the living room, with the high beamed ceiling and bookshelves. A set decorator was spraying dust on the books and Milton decided to stay back where he wouldn't be noticed. When the set was unattended, Milton sat on the big sofa in front of the fireplace and tried to imagine living in a house like this. He put his feet up on the coffee table that was stacked with veterinary magazines and leather-bound books. For a moment he thought of himself not only as the father of a movie star, but as a veterinarian himself, moving from farm to farm with his child, teaching her about animals and life. Milton knew it was just a daydream, but it seemed so untroubled and easy that it gave him comfort, made him feel optimistic.

It was almost twelve-thirty when he got back to the commissary. What he hadn't counted on was that a hostess, who knew all the diners, was seating people. Milton waited until she was busy, and then slipped into the main room. He could see Carla and her friends eating lunch. He knew that her table, with only three children and Skeeter, was for the contract players. As he started to walk toward her, he could feel a buzz, then a hush, come over the room. He thought he'd made a gaffe of some sort and had become the object of derision. His cheeks flushed until he saw that the fuss had nothing to do with him.

Louis B. Mayer had entered the commissary. He was a pale, fleshy man with a prim face and rimless glasses, wearing a dark business suit and attended by two similarly dressed aides. Mr. Mayer was going from table to table, stopping to say hello and shaking hands. Milton had never seen royalty, but surely, he thought, they can't be any different from this. Each time he stopped to say hello to someone, that person would start to rise, and Mr. Mayer would put a gentle hand on the man's shoulder as if to say, "Oh, don't get up." Milton watched him work his way across the room, chatting with his subjects. Milton could hear a few of them calling him L.B. or Chief. Each time Mr. Mayer stopped, Milton saw that every other person in the room noticed to whom he spoke, how long he stayed at the table, and whether he shook hands, or just nodded politely. At what Milton took to be the writers' table, someone made a joke and Mr. Mayer laughed. Milton wondered if the man who had made the boss laugh was Maury Kelman. While he was watching this show, Milton felt frozen, suspended. At first he thought he was the only one, but then he could see the whole room was that way. No one was getting up or moving about; the hostess was holding people at the door. As long as Mr. Mayer was on the floor, all other activity stopped. It seemed to Milton that people had even stopped eating. They just sat there, forks in the air, waiting for Mr. Mayer's next move. The power was palpable; Milton had never seen or felt anything like it.

Then, as Mr. Mayer seemed to be heading for a door that Milton assumed led to an inner sanctum, a private dining room the luxury of which could not even be imagined, Mr. Mayer turned and walked over to the children in the romper room. Skeeter stood up to greet him and told the children to rise. Carla got to her feet with Sarah and Bobby, while behind them the other children rose as well. From where Milton was standing, it was all in a sort of long shot; he could see but not hear what was said. He ached to know what words passed between his daughter and L. B. Mayer. What he saw was Mr. Mayer reaching out and touching Carla's face when Skeeter introduced her. It was a gentle touch but Milton recognized it as a man inspecting his merchandise. It was over in a moment, and Mr. Mayer and his aides were gone. The people in the room relaxed and began to eat again; conversations resumed. Milton felt dizzy and needed to sit down. He lurched across the room toward Carla. She looked up at him and smiled, the same smile she had just smiled at L. B. Mayer. "Hi, Daddy," she said. Skeeter Danzig stood again, just as he had done for L.B., and offered his hand.

"Hello, Mr. Tate, I didn't know you were coming for lunch."

"No, no. I'm not. I was here on some business. I just wanted to say hello to Karen, I mean Carla," he said, as his words, a mixture of lies and truth that he himself could not control, came tumbling out.

"Oh, well, it's nice to see you, even briefly."

Milton leaned over and kissed his daughter. "Eat all your lunch now," he said, offering a bit of fatherly counsel he neither believed nor cared about. He turned and walked back into the room, which was more crowded now than it had been a moment ago. Milton nodded to people he didn't know and as he passed a group of actors he said, "Nice to see you."

Milton saw Claire Berger at a table in the corner with Bill Brady. Claire introduced him and Milton found himself telling the director about his daughter. He knew it was an error, but he couldn't stop himself. "She plays natural," he started, as if he were answering a question. "It's her best thing. She's got a memory for dialogue you wouldn't believe. At Paramount they used to just dolly in on her. Not very cutty, you know? They always thought her left side was better. I don't know." Milton could see Brady's face was frozen into a stiff smile and that Claire was squirming. He knew he was out of line, but he didn't know how to stop. The icier Brady looked, the more compulsively Milton spoke. "You probably know Jocko McCarthy. She did a picture with him. He said, 'The kid owns the lens.' Of course, it's up to you." He would have gone on like that, the words leaking from his face, except that Claire, in an act of mercy, cut him off.

"That's great, Milt," she said. "Glad you stopped by."

As he backed away, feeling light-headed, he bumped into an adjacent table filled with grizzled-looking ranch hands, actors who had been shooting interiors for *Wyoming*.

"Sorry. Excuse me," Milton said, bowing slightly, actions and words that should have been directed to Claire Berger and Bill Brady. As he fussed and apologized, desperate to escape from their table, he knocked over a glass of iced tea, spilling it on one of the ranch hands, who exclaimed, "Christ!" and jumped to his feet.

Before Milton could make it worse by trying to put the glass upright, one of the other ranch hands, apparently still in character, said, "It's okay, partner. No harm done. You just take it slow, now."

As Milton backed away from the tables, feeling as if he were choking, he looked across to the romper room and saw Carla watching it all.

When he was gone, Bill Brady turned to Claire and said, "Who the hell is Jocko McCarthy?"

"I don't know," she said tersely.

Brady nodded and said, "Keep that guy away from me. He'll be out of control by the time we start shooting. I don't want him on the set."

Claire explained the situation to Fred Nugent, who authorized her to speak to Milton. She waited a few days, then called him at Soderberg Ford. She was blunt and told him that it would be in everyone's interest if he didn't come to the studio anymore.

"How's she going to get back and forth?" he asked, more to stall while he considered his position than to argue.

"They'll send a car for her. Back and forth."

"I'm her father," Milton said, trying not to whine. "The ride in is when we have time to talk things over."

"Actually, what Fred wants is to change the nature of your relationship with the studio."

"What does that mean?"

"In addition to the money you've got, he wants you to have another two hundred and fifty a week as long as Carla's under contract."

"To stay away, right?" There was anger in his voice. Claire knew she needed to be diplomatic and firm if she was going to be persuasive.

"Milton, be realistic. They recognize you're her father," she said. "No one wants to change that. But they think things would go smoother if you weren't around. At least for the first picture. Maybe after that, I can get them to renegotiate."

"I have to tell you, I find it offensive. An insult."

"Listen to me. You can do this one of two ways. You can take the money and stay away or you can just stay away. Now what are you going to do?"

There was silence for a long moment. Claire could hear him breathing as he considered. Finally he said, "Don't tell anybody about it. Including my wife."

"No one has to know. The checks'll come through me and I'll send them wherever. I can bank them for you."

When Milton got the first check, he found Claire had deducted 10 percent as his agent. He wanted to complain, but decided he had better just keep his mouth shut. Milton didn't tell Ceil why he didn't want to pick up Carla at Metro, but she figured it out and he didn't deny it. Milton asked her not to tell Carla the reason he wasn't around the studio anymore. Ceil didn't know Milton was being paid to stay away; she just assumed he'd been thrown off the lot for being overbearing.

When production began, Skeeter Danzig built his lesson plans around Carla's schedule. The interiors that involved her were shot in the morning, so Carla could have her instruction uninterrupted. When she had exteriors, which were scheduled around the sunlight, Miss Pringle brought in another day-by-day teacher for the other children while Skeeter went with Carla. They spread a blanket under a tree, and between camera setups would go over reading or arithmetic. The curriculum was determined by the state and it was supposed to be the same as in the public schools. The big difference was that studio kids were never assigned homework. At night they were supposed to rest or memorize their lines. Their instruction, which in Carla's case was a private tutorial, was completed within three hours a day, the minimum the state required.

Skeeter felt an obligation to instruct Carla in matters that went beyond the curriculum. He knew where she was headed and he felt that although arithmetic and reading were important, in her case there were other issues. "The hardest thing to get used to here is the publicity," he told her as they were standing by the pigpen at the barn, while Carla dropped matzoh crumbs from her pockets into the feeding trough. "You know what it is, don't you?"

"With reporters and stuff," she answered, but she seemed more interested in the pigs.

"Pay attention, Carla. You need to know this."

"I am."

"You want the movie to be a success, don't you? A hit? Let's play reporter. For practice."

"You be the reporter," she said, pleased to play a game, preferring a little drama to any discussion.

"If I'm a reporter, that means I want something from you. So I might be a little tricky. What do I want?"

"You want a story."

"That's right. I'll do anything to make you say something I can use. So trust me—but only so far." He changed his voice to an overly friendly manner that in an odd way reminded her of her father. "How'd you get the part in *The Veterinarian's Daughter?*"

"My agent got me the tryout. And I got it."

"Okay," Skeeter said, smiling at the disingenuousness of her answer. "That's true enough, but think how it'll look in the newspaper. You don't want to sound stuck-up."

"I don't know," Carla answered, unsure what he meant.

"Like you're showing off, trying to say you're better than the kids at Cheremoya Avenue or Leeper."

Carla thought for a moment, trying to remember the public school children she had known briefly; she couldn't quite recall them. She could certainly remember her classmates at the Leeper School and her memories weren't pleasant. "Not better," she said, trying to give Skeeter the answer he wanted, but also trying to figure out where she stood. "Different."

"Right. Don't push it."

"What should I say?"

"It's best not to mention agents. When a kid does that, it puts grown-ups off. Most grown-ups don't have agents. The point you want to make is you feel lucky, privileged for the opportunity. You hope you won't disappoint all the people who put their faith in you."

"I can't remember all that."

"Try. Put it in your own words, like an improvisation. Think about the ideas. Make them your own."

Carla was quiet for a moment, considering what Skeeter had asked her to do. She dropped the last of her matzoh on the pigs and said, "It's exciting to play Georgine. I hope I do a good job. It's hard to be in a movie. But it's fun."

Skeeter smiled, gave her a hug, and said, "Let's go see how they're doing at the set."

"Did I do it right?"

"You did just fine."

"Maybe we should get Maury to write it out."

"No. Better this way. Makes it sound spontaneous."

"What's spontaneous?"

"Like the first time you ever thought of it."

"I can do that," Carla said, not boasting, but as certain of her abilities as Skeeter was.

The film shot for forty-two days, and on each one a limousine picked up Carla at Gower Gardens and brought her back at the end of the day. It caused a stir among the neighbors, but they got used to it and even began to feel proprietary about Carla and her big car. Carla spent her evenings with her mother and sometimes her Aunt Edna, who now had two small children of her own, Teddy junior and Cynthia.

Ceil knew she was happier living apart from Milton, but she worried that it was hard on Carla. And she was unsure about Carla's schooling. "I hope we're doing the right thing sending you to that school. You still like it, don't you?"

Carla, who adored the school, had learned that her job was to reassure her mother. "It's great. Skeeter, my best teacher, spends all the time with me. I learn lots of stuff. Everything."

"I never know if you'll blame me for denying you a regular childhood when you grow up or thank me or what."

"No, no. I'm doing a lot. It's fun. The movie's fun."

"But you should be making regular friends. Not just adults. Oh, I don't know, Carla. I just don't know."

"I have friends. Sarah Milliken. She's in my class."

"Maybe you could bring her home sometime."

Carla knew that would never work, but she said, "Okay."

"Your father keeps wanting to come over. I shouldn't mind, but I never want him to. He makes me jumpy." With Carla, Ceil could be herself. She could talk to her daughter and in that way find out what she felt. Carla sometimes got impatient with it, but she was flattered to be her mother's confidante.

When productions are completed, even big studio films where there's a permanent staff, the company scatters, and the intense friendships, romances and alliances formed in the heat of production evaporate. It's difficult for the adults but even harder on a child who has grown attached to the people around her. It wasn't a problem Carla ever had to face. The Dr. George team just took a breather and then started all over again. Lewis the horse was always in his stall, where Carla could visit him every day.

Benny Raskin, the unit publicist, set up daily photo sessions: Carla and Brandon Holt riding Lewis; Carla with the barnyard animals; Carla in class; Carla sitting under a tree looking pensive, then sad, then happy; Carla laughing and Carla pouting. Throughout the dozens of hours of being still under lights or in the sun, Carla sat passively, doing as she was told, always conjuring emotion, always finding a way to smile one more time. Carla's passivity came from her mother. In Ceil it had created a person barely able to maneuver through life. In her daughter, that passivity became serenity. It fed the mystery that even in her childhood made Carla elusive and magical.

At first, Benny's stories were contrived. He sat in his office and typed up imagined interviews with Carla, giving her favorite toys, hobbies and friends. He wrote that she loved Lewis the horse, which was true, and he wrote that she had a large collection of dolls, which was not. Skeeter suggested to Benny that he might actually interview Carla. "You'd be surprised. What she says will be interesting."

"I didn't want to bother her," Benny answered. "She's got school and all."

"As long as she's not shooting, I'll make the time. She'll like it."

Benny took Carla to lunch and sat her down at the publicity table. "So, Carla, what do you want to be when you grow up?" She looked at him, then glanced across the room to Skeeter. Carla and Skeeter had established a shorthand for adult behavior. It had started during the shooting of the movie, when assistant directors were always interrupting their study sessions. If Carla thought the adult was an idiot she would glance at Skeeter, who gave her one of three looks. A stern, no-nonsense look meant this guy's right, do what he says. A faint smile meant he's probably an idiot, but do it anyway. The third look that amounted to rolling his eyes meant this guy has no idea what he's doing, but he's harmless and you're on your own. Watching Benny struggle with his notebook and his lunch, Skeeter could imagine the kinds of questions he was asking. Catching Carla's eye, he sent his own skyward, and Carla relaxed.

"I want to keep on being an actress," she told Benny, careful to avoid saying she wanted to continue being a star.

Across the room, Skeeter could see Benny scribbling furiously. He strolled over to hear what Carla was handing out.

"What adults do you look up to, Carla?" Benny asked.

She was saying, "My dad and mom," when Skeeter arrived at the table. "And Skeeter, too," she added as he sat down.

"Listing your favorite saints?" he asked when he heard his name.

"No, no. We stay away from the religion angle," Benny said. "She was telling me which adults she looks up to. Your name came up. Don't know why," he said, grinning.

"And Mr. Mayer. Put him in too," Carla said.

"Don't forget your parents," Skeeter said.

"She didn't. She got them right off," Benny said.

"Are we going to do any more?"

"What would you say to all the boys and girls in America who want to know what it's like to be in a movie?"

"Fun! I'm really lucky. I wish everybody had a chance."

"Hard work, too. Isn't it?" Skeeter said, prodding her gently. She nodded and Benny wrote it down.

"This stuff is great," Benny said with real admiration.

"You should interview Lewis. He's really smart."

Benny laughed but Skeeter, who knew Carla wasn't joking, said, "Another time. Why don't we call this a success and eat our lunch."

Once each semester Miss Pringle arranged teacher-parent conferences. Skeeter had been told that all dealings with the Tates were to be with Ceil. Skeeter had been around both Milton and M-G-M enough to know not to ask questions. He wasn't aware that Ceil and Milton were separated, but he assumed if he called during the day he would reach Ceil. He made it clear that the invitation was for her alone.

The idea of talking to the teachers didn't worry Ceil as much as did the arrangements. She fretted about it after Skeeter called, and then talked it over with Carla at the end of the day. "How am I going to get to Culver City?"

"Come with me in the car. They'll bring you back."

"How do you know? Did you ask?"

"They will," Carla said.

Ceil and Skeeter met in the classroom, where Ceil sat in one of the tiny chairs while Skeeter perched on the edge of his desk. Skeeter recognized that his relationship with Carla wouldn't be helped much by Ceil, but it could be hurt. Since Skeeter was crazy about his pupil, he was determined to get along with her mother. He didn't have to work hard. Ceil was relieved that he seemed to like her, and comforted by his easy manner. She relaxed enough to talk about what was really on her mind. "Sometimes I worry if I'm doing the right thing."

"You wonder if her pursuing a career is robbing her of a regular childhood?" Skeeter said, smiling.

"Yes. That's right," she said, amazed that he could know her thoughts.

Skeeter, who had heard every variety of parental worry and concern, answered, "It's hard to have a talented child. Nobody quite knows how to handle it. She's getting a good education here. She's performing above grade level. As to the larger question, I tell you frankly, Mrs. Tate, a talent like that won't be denied," Skeeter said, believing it, but also determined to keep his favorite pupil.

Ceil drank in his words, anxious for affirmation of how she was raising her daughter. As Ceil was feeling encouraged, Brandon Holt came into the classroom. "Hi," he said. "Sorry to be so late." He squeezed into a child's desk next to Ceil. Skeeter seemed surprised to see him, but because Ceil never knew what to expect anywhere, nothing surprised her.

"Hi, Brandon," Skeeter said. "We were just talking about Carla and the school." His voice was cautious.

"I know this is a mother's conference," Brandon said. "But I couldn't stay away. That kid's so darned important to me. Hope you don't mind."

"You know Carla's father, don't you?" Skeeter said to Brandon.

"Milt? Sure. I know I'm only her father on screen. But that's an obligation. You can't just turn that stuff on and off with the camera." He turned to Ceil and said, "I want to spend more time with you. Get to know you as a person."

"Well, I guess so . . ."

Then Brandon winked at Ceil, who began to cough.

"Actors use all sorts of techniques to establish their character," Skeeter said, trying to reassure Ceil. "There are wonderful tricks with the imagination." He turned to Brandon and said, "You have to remember that Ceil's the mother of an actress, not an actress herself."

"Absolutely," Brandon said. "Didn't mean to rattle you. If I did, I apologize." As he spoke he caressed Ceil's arm and then patted her hand, which was curled into a tight fist. "Why don't you and I have lunch, Ceil?" When she still looked confused, he said, "It doesn't have to be today. Just sometime."

"Maybe sometime."

"That's all I ask. Now where is the little darling?"

"She's in dance class."

"Maybe I'll go over there and say hi to her." He got up, shook Skeeter's hand, and for a moment looked as if he was about to kiss Ceil on the cheek. When she drew back, he just smiled and left.

"Don't let him get to you," Skeeter said. "He doesn't know he's acting strange. It helps his performance, it really does."

"I'm not used to it."

"No reason you should be. I think Carla likes him. Movie actors can be odd. It's a kind of acting that requires a transformation. You can't tell where the person stops and the actor starts. It's weird. Why don't we call it a day?"

"I think I should go home. The driver's waiting for me." Skeeter shook her hand and found it damp. He thought about trying to reassure her some more, but she looked so confused and tired that he just said good-bye.

At a time when Carla and I had no reason to assume she wouldn't live forever, we were at Two Bunch Palms, a kind of hip resort in the desert near Palm Springs. We had gone there for something called an enzyme bath. Carla had little patience for most of the goofy health cults of our native state, but every now and then she would hear about something that interested her.

We were up to our necks in a hot tub filled with a fermenting concoction of wood shavings, rice bran and enzyme powder. It looked like a giant bowl of oatmeal. It was supposed to revitalize us, whatever that meant.

One of the questions we always came back to—at Ma Maison over duck salad, or here in this tub of bran—was where her skill came from. It was a great mystery, really. She could fill out a character in a fully credible way that completely dominated the action, without seeming to do anything. She delivered lines without a sense of occasion creeping in. Try it. You'll see how difficult it is. Then try it with lights glaring, forty people gawking, and a fortune in money being spent. Carla could do it from the first time she tried.

Although she wouldn't speculate on the sources of her ability, she was always interested in my theories. I had come to believe that it came because she spent her childhood communicating for her parents. There was Ceil, who meant well, but spent her life in a sort of daze. Milton certainly tried to assert himself, but he never got anywhere. Carla was an emissary between them. Subtlety and surface casualness became her strongest weapons. It was an intuitive attempt to create the semblance of a family life out of anger and confusion. It didn't do much for anyone at home, but the same skills, applied to a fictional personality in a movie, created the actress she became. When I told her all that, she just shrugged, then flicked some oatmeal in my face and asked about her memoirs, as if I had already agreed to do them. "How will you know when I've told you enough?"

"That'll never happen. Keep telling me. There's no such thing as enough." As I said it, I recognized this was a gambit on Carla's part, her way of moving me closer to agreeing. My hesitation was a mixture of genuine doubt about my ability and a certain pleasure I took in teasing her, keeping her wondering.

"I know what you'll do," she said, amused at the realization.

"Right. I'll make it up. That was your idea. If I just write down what you and everybody else remembers, it'll be interesting, but not as interesting as you are. To go deeper takes more."

"Then Gabe, I want you to dream it," she said. "Into fullness." She lifted her hand out of the mush, touched my face gently, and added, "Who better?"

Although there was never a moment when I said to her, "Yes, I will do this thing," after Two Bunch Palms, we both knew eventually I would. I didn't completely realize it then, but Carla needed to tell me her story, to enchant me with it, to prove that her life was worthy, and to convince herself it could be fairly told.

Carla's story was played out in modern Los Angeles and, of course, in Hollywood, both of which changed wrenchingly during the four decades of her life. The studios where Carla first discovered her talents were the ones where my father worked. Carla and I both grew up in the movies. She on camera, and I on the sidelines. Of course when I was grown and had an adult relationship with her, things were different. Still, in Hollywood, next to Carla, everyone was an extra.

8.

Metro previewed *The Veterinarian's Daughter* at the Fox-Arlington in Santa Barbara, a theater Fred Nugent liked because he thought he could count on a representative crowd. For a film with family appeal, Nugent knew it was important to watch reactions as well as read cards. Adults filled out cards, but kids either paid attention or they squirmed. When the cards were being tabulated, Nugent had only to flip through a handful to confirm what he already knew, which was there were going to be lots of Dr. George movies in his future. He went to the manager's office and made two phone calls; the first was to the boss. When studio executives called from a preview, it meant good news. If it was bad, they put off the call as long as possible. When his phone rang at nine-thirty, Mr. Mayer knew he had a hit. "It plays beautifully, sir. The cards are ninety percent excellents."

"How'd the girl go over?" It was Mr. Mayer's only question.

"Nobody gets up for popcorn when that kid's on screen."

"Good work, Fred." Then he hung up. Nugent had worked for M-G-M for five years. L.B. usually called him "You" or "Mr.

Nugent." Well, tonight it was Fred. His other call was to Claire Berger, at Romanoff's in Beverly Hills. She had told him if it was bad news to wait till she was at home. When the waiter brought a phone, saying, "Santa Barbara on the line," Claire knew her decision to become an agent was about to pay off. When she hung up, she told her table, "Dr. George is here to stay. Carla's a star."

The premiere was held at the Carthay Circle, the white stucco theater on San Vicente Boulevard. Klieg lights were focused on the theater's faux bell tower—sharp columns of light, slanting up toward the spire. Bleachers had been set up along the red-carpeted entrance for fans who had won tickets in raffles held by the Los Angeles Library Association. For those with seats inside, the studio had sent out gilded tickets, seven inches high.

Outside the theater, a brass band, dressed like the Ruritanian Army, played Sousa marches. One hundred Los Angeles city policemen were on duty to keep a grip on a crowd that the police estimated would be at least six thousand. The studio had built a corral in front of the theater, where Lewis the horse was grazing, indifferent to the throng, the music and the police.

People in the movie business knew M-G-M was high on *The Veterinarian's Daughter*. The publicity campaign had been churning for weeks; pictures of Carla had appeared so often she might have been running for office. If anyone had doubted the studio's intentions, one look at the lavish display was proof enough. Thousands of people without gilded tickets had gathered in the street in the hope of participating in the excitement. They were talking about "the little girl," asking one another what they had heard about her, and had she been seen yet.

Milton was there with Edna and Teddy. Although he would have preferred to escort his daughter in the limousine, that was Ceil's task. Milton was told by the police he would have to wait behind the velvet rope, with everyone else. It made him uneasy, as if he, Edna and Teddy were mere fans. He tried to get Benny Raskin's attention, to demand better treatment, but Benny was busy tending to the reporters.

When the studio Cadillac arrived, Claire got out first and made sure the guards the studio had provided to protect Carla were in place for her walk into the theater. Ceil gave Carla's hair one last brush, gave her a good-luck kiss, and stayed behind until Carla stepped out, onto the red carpet and into the flash-bulbs.

The band played "Stars and Stripes Forever" while the people in the bleachers cheered and stomped their feet. There was no reason for them to be so excited, except that they knew their role and understood that the price of their seats was their enthusiasm. Many of them aspired to work in the movies, so they regarded this as an opportunity to participate in a Hollywood ritual. Perhaps a producer would notice how well they discharged their duties. It's Hollywood, they said, so you never can tell.

The people on the street moved forward, straining at the velvet rope. Milton kept his position at the front and tried to call to his daughter. "Here I am," he cried. "Look over here. It's me, Daddy." But there was too much noise and Carla couldn't hear. She was safe enough with her flying wedge, but the clamor scared her. She was seven, and about to be a star or not, she had never seen such a large crowd, certainly never been the object of so much unearned adulation. The flashbulbs surprised her. She was used to having her picture taken, but by one photographer at a time.

Milton, feeling desperate, tried to scream over the crowd. His yelling just made the others around him yell louder. Edna realized Carla couldn't hear and tried to tell Milton to stop, but he kept calling his daughter's name, trying to will her to notice him.

Carla was too overwhelmed to pick out any one voice or face. She stopped, stilled by fear, in the midst of the triangle formed by her guards. A spotlight was on her, and she froze, a tiny child amid giants, surrounded by thousands of excited people. Claire turned around and asked what was the matter, but Carla couldn't hear her either.

"What is it?" Claire repeated, as she stepped into the triangle. "Come on. We have to go in." Carla just looked down at the red carpet beneath her feet.

"Where's Lewis?" she finally asked, in a whisper that Claire had to strain to hear.

"He's here. In his yard. Do you want to see him?"

The thought of Lewis gave her comfort. "Okay," she said, because she didn't know what else to say.

"After the movie. We'll see him after the movie."

Carla was about to cry, when Ceil, who had been hovering behind, near the car, pushed her way through the guards and picked up her daughter. "What's the matter?"

The only thing Carla knew for certain was that she didn't want to go into the theater. "I want to go home," she said, through her tears. Then added, "Bring Lewis, okay?"

When Milton saw Ceil within the triangle of guards, he ducked under the velvet rope and ran toward them. Before he got more than a few feet, two cops tackled him, bringing him to the pavement. "It's my daughter!" he yelled to the cops, who weren't buying it. "Carla, it's me!" he screamed, flailing his arms, trying to defend himself. One of the cops started to cuff Milton's hands behind his back. Carla was too involved in her tears to see her father's predicament, but the commotion caught Claire's eye. When she realized it was Milton the police were attacking, she yelled, "Stop that! You let him go. Take those things off."

The police tried to apologize, but Milton ignored their attempts and ran to his daughter. "It's okay, honey. I'm here. I'm here."

When Carla saw her father, waving his arms, his eyes flashing wildly, his clothes awry and covered with soot, she began to cry again. "I want Lewis," she said.

"You can see him tomorrow," Ceil said, about to carry Carla into the theater.

"You got to go inside," Milton said, trying to sound calm and reasonable. "Don't you want to see your movie?"

"I don't care," Carla said.

"Not tonight she doesn't," Ceil said, with Carla still in her arms. She turned to go around her husband, back to the car. Milton tried to block her, but she just pushed him out of her way. The guards looked confused for a moment, but since their instruction was to guard the child, they stayed with Ceil and Carla. Claire Berger and Milton followed them to the car, trying to persuade Carla to stay. Claire asked Carla if she was feeling better.

"Sure she is," Milton said. "It just got a little noisy, that's all. We're all going to go in there and see the picture. Right, honey?"

All the adult eyes were on Carla, awaiting a decision. When she didn't answer, Ceil asserted her mother's authority and said, "We're not going in there now." She put Carla in the car, got in herself, and told the driver to take them to Gower Gardens. Carla clung to her mother all the way home.

• • •

Telling me the story at Ma Maison on a warm April afternoon, Carla was in a funny kind of mood, as she talked about that first Dr. George movie. I had been telling her how I had felt when I saw it. She knew I had been taken with little Georgine, and was full of questions about my reactions. Carla was so interested in my memories, I probably embellished a bit. "We lived in Encino then. We all went to see it at a theater in Van Nuys that was actually called the Bijou. It's long gone."

"Did you go in a group—your whole class or something?"

"No. I think it was released in the summer. My parents took me. The part that I was so caught up in was that you seemed so different. You lived on a farm, I lived in a suburb. You had that great horse and you got to ride him through creeks and fields. I had a bicycle that I wasn't allowed to take across our street."

I wasn't sure I was evoking little Georgine and the movie accurately. But it had been thirty-odd years since Carla had seen it, so as long as what I was saying was plausible, it became real for her, too. Usually at those lunches, she was the one who played storyteller, captivating me with tales of her life. We had changed roles. It was still her life we were talking about, but now I had direct memories of it. It's quite possible that as a child Carla had never had a conversation with a civilian kid about her movies. She couldn't remember any, and from the fascination she had with my memories, I suspected that this was the first report from a peer. A little late, but then Carla always operated on her own schedule.

"The big thing for me was that you saved animals. After that movie I wanted animals in my life. My parents weren't about to install a chicken coop, but my dad took me to the pound and I got a funny-looking mutt. I wanted to name him Lewis, but somehow he wound up as Max. He was around till I was in high school."

"I know one thing about that," she said. "Jack told me about it. Starting in the late forties, then for a few years, kids all wanted pets because of the Dr. George movies."

"I think movies were more powerful for kids then. Not so much competition. You must have done wonders for the pet business, Carla."

"And was little Gabe madly in love with Georgine?"

"Absolutely. I was too young to recognize a crush, but no doubt about it, I was bewitched."

She loved hearing that. She laughed her throaty laugh that gave me a very adult shiver.

"See," I said. "If you'd known, you could have driven me nuts all that time."

"But I did, I did. You just said so." Then that laugh came back, rumbling up from her throat, deep and satisfied.

Brandon Holt called Ceil several times asking if he could take Carla and her to dinner. She had said no, but Edna had made her promise that if he asked again, she'd go. So, expecting a quiet dinner in a restaurant, maybe even a place as fancy as the Brown Derby or possibly Chasen's, prospects that made her a little uneasy, she agreed. "Great," Brandon said. "We'll go to Mocambo."

"Oh . . . Oh . . ." Ceil said, all but keening, unable to form words at the thought of Mocambo, the most glamorous of the nightclubs on the Sunset Strip, a place where, at least in Ceil's imagination, movie stars, kings and international beauties danced on diamonds and drank champagne from silver slippers. "We can't go there," she managed to say, feeling short of breath.

"Of course we can. I'm going to take you both. You'll love the place."

Ceil tried to back out, insisting that she had nothing to wear and besides, it was inappropriate for Carla. Brandon offered to buy them both dresses. Ceil wouldn't permit that. Instead, she borrowed a dress from Edna and allowed Brandon to ask the wardrobe department at the studio to find what Ceil called a party dress for Carla.

Mocambo was a place that seemed to feed on its own celebrity. To be there, to have a table and to dance to the orchestra, and most important, to know others there, was to be in the winner's circle. The main room had bright red columns decorated with harlequins, gaudy stripes and elaborate tin flowers. The nightclub was filled with South American music from the orchestra, laughter from the dining room, and the moneyed sounds of crystal, silver, pleasure and indulgence.

Brandon arranged for a table overlooking the dance floor. It was a room filled with the beautiful and the powerful, many of whom fussed over Carla, the first seven-year-old ever to dine there. Errol Flynn was at the club that night, as he often was, and he asked Carla to dance.

"Can I?" she asked Ceil.

"Of course you can," Brandon said, before Ceil could object. "Errol likes them young, but I think you're safe."

Mr. Flynn bowed low to Carla, showed her how to take his arm, and escorted her to the floor. "Do you know how to rumba?" he asked.

"I don't know," Carla said.

"Then climb aboard," he said, as he lifted Carla up so that her feet rested on his shoes. He held on to her, helping her stand as he glided her around the floor. She hung on to his arms and tried to keep her balance. Looking straight up, she could see the underside of his chin, shaved smooth, and smell his cologne; it made her feel a little dizzy. The other couples gave Carla and Errol Flynn plenty of room. They seemed to Carla a sea of chiffon and silk and swirling skirts rushing by her, enveloping her in clouds of perfume and adult pleasure, grazing her arms, making her shiver.

"You're the best-looking girl on the dance floor. Nobody else comes close," he said, looking down into her eyes. It made her face light up and she laughed with a little girl's giggle, clinging to him, as he moved them effortlessly about the floor.

At the table Ceil felt uncomfortable watching Errol Flynn with her daughter, but Brandon loved it. "God, she's a great kid. I guess this evening goes in her memory book," he said, with the pride of a parent who knew he was doing right by his child. Ceil didn't know where to look—at Carla holding on to Errol Flynn, at the fancy people who seemed enchanted to watch them, or at Brandon, now enveloped in another of his parental reveries. It all made her feel unsteady, almost light-headed and even less able than usual to deal with the circumstances of her life. She tried to concentrate on Brandon and his motives, because as strange as he was, it was easier for her to think about him than about Errol Flynn. Ceil wasn't exactly sure what a pass was, but she was sure she'd know it when it came.

After Errol Flynn returned her to the table and bowed low again, Carla sensed something was odd because her mother seemed nervous in a way that was new.

"I'd love for you to come out to my ranch," Brandon was saying. Although he had an apartment in Hollywood where he stayed during the week, his real life was on his ranch, where he kept horses and spent every weekend.

"Oh, yeah. Let's go," Carla said.

"Maybe sometime," Ceil said.

"Can Lewis come?" Carla asked.

"Wouldn't that be grand," Brandon said, smiling at the thought. "We could get Norman to put him in a trailer and drive him out. He'd love it out there. So would you, Georgie-gine."

"I want to go. Oh, please."

Before Ceil had to think of an excuse, Charlie Morrison, who had once been Brandon's agent and was now one of Mocambo's owners, came over to the table and asked if Carla would like to see the birds. Brandon explained that the club had cages with lovebirds, macaws, parakeets and cockatoos. With Charlie leading, Brandon escorted Ceil and Carla to the aviary. Charlie called for the key and when Carla was given a handful of seeds, several of the parakeets fluttered onto her arms and shoulders, chirping and chattering. "The bird girl!" Charlie said. "They love her."

"All creatures do," Brandon said.

"A couple of these guys can talk," Charlie said, then stuck his face up to a parakeet's beak. "Hey, show business," Charlie said in a high-pitched voice.

"Show business, show business, ten percent," the bird crackled back. As Carla was standing with her arms out, heavy with birds, flashbulbs went off as the house photographer recorded every flutter.

The success of *The Veterinarian's Daughter* made Carla the best-known child on the M-G-M lot. As more attention was paid to her, less was paid to Sarah Milliken. Sarah wasn't crazy about the situation. Her fantasies ran to ripping out Carla's eyes and leaving her to wander the desert. Instead, Sarah tried to concentrate on her schoolwork and her hamster. Sarah had been given Nibbles four years ago, which now made him an elderly hamster. He was eating and scrambling about less and generally acting like the old rodent he had become. Sarah began to blame Carla for Nibbles's condition. He had been fine until all this Dr. George stuff, she thought. Now look at him. In Sarah's mind Carla was the source of it all. When Nibbles didn't wake up one morning, Sarah knew it was Carla's fault. She also knew that Skeeter, the biggest Carla-lover of them all, wouldn't see it that way, and neither would anyone else if she wasn't careful.

When Sarah got to school that morning, she left Nibbles in his cage. When Carla opened the cage to play with the hamster, as Sarah knew she would, Carla thought he was sleeping. "Hey, Nibbles. Wake up," Carla said, nudging him with her finger. When she saw that Nibbles wasn't going to wake up, she lifted him out of his cage and peered into his glassy eyes. "Oh, Nibbles," she said.

"What's wrong?" Sarah asked, sounding alarmed. "Be careful with him. What did you do?" Sarah was up, disrupting the class, sounding protective and scared. "Give him to me. Don't hurt him."

"I didn't do anything," Carla started to say. But Sarah snatched the dead hamster away to inspect him. "You hurt him. What did you do to him?" Sarah began to cry. Skeeter tried to console her but she was beyond comfort. Sarah wasn't as good an actress as Carla, but she rose to the occasion, giving a realistic demonstration of sudden grief. Her tears were real and everyone could see that Sarah believed Carla was responsible. "He never hurt anybody. All he ever did was love me, that's all," she sobbed.

Carla was too distraught to defend herself. She began to cry and say she was sorry. As Skeeter tried to calm them both, Bobby Dryer, who would do anything to get out of class, suggested a funeral. Skeeter thought Bobby had a good point. He wrapped Nibbles in a towel and took the children to the yard in front of the schoolhouse, where he dug a hole at the base of a Mexican palm. As Nibbles was being buried, Sarah began to weep again, accusing Carla of murdering her pet. "You killed him. You did! Admit it." Then she turned to the others, as if they were an audience. "She killed Nibbles and she's not even sorry."

As Sarah was carrying on, Bobby Dryer, who wasn't buying any of it, said, "I think it's a suicide. Milliken drove him to it."

"We don't need your sarcasm now, Bobby," Skeeter said. But Sarah heard him and was off on another crying jag.

"Okay, okay," Bobby said. "But it was natural causes. Not murder." He sounded like a movie tough guy. "This could be the start of a rat war."

Sarah turned on more tears and started in on Carla again. "Why did you have to kill him? He never hurt you." Skeeter decided to call the studio hospital for a nurse to look after Sarah for the rest of the day. Carla was inconsolable. Later, she tried to apologize to Sarah, who wouldn't listen.

That afternoon, at the barn, Carla asked Norman Katano what she could have done that would have killed Nibbles.

"Did he feel cold when you picked him up?"

"I don't remember."

Norman took her back to the schoolhouse and found the

carrying cage. He picked through the shredded newspaper that lined the bottom, then said, "No droppings, no food."

"What does that mean?" Carla asked, upset all over again to be looking at the cage.

"He probably died a lot earlier. If he was alive when you touched him, there'd be a sign of it. Something."

"Are you sure?"

"Yes. So don't feel bad."

Carla couldn't tell if Norman was right or just trying to make her feel better. She told Skeeter what Norman had said, asking for guidance. "Well, maybe that's true. But the thing to remember is that Sarah loved Nibbles and we have to be understanding."

"She said I killed him. On purpose."

"When people are upset, they say things they don't really mean. When a little time's gone by, she won't feel that way."

"She hates my guts. I know she does."

"Carla, you're in a situation here. Your picture's a hit. That's good for the studio and for everybody. But it can make people jealous."

"Of me?"

"Yes."

"Why? It's not fair."

"I don't know what Sarah thinks, but look at it from her point of view. She was here first, then you got a bigger part than she ever had. Now this happens. It's hard."

"But why does she have to take it out on me?"

"Part of being a star is everybody wants something from you. Sometimes they want to blame their own failures on you. It's not fair, but it happens." It was the sort of adult counsel Carla never got at home and it made her feel better.

A week later, Sarah Milliken's option was dropped and she was gone from the studio, back to her public school in North Hollywood. Bobby Dryer, who had taken to calling Carla "Killer Tate," explained the facts of life. "You complained to Skeeter about what you and Katano talked about. Skeeter told Nugent. Sarah got canned."

"I didn't complain," Carla said, feeling terrible all over again.

"Bullshit you didn't. Everybody knows Katano says the rat was dead before it ever got to the lot. It's the case of the dead dirty rat," Bobby said in his movie tough-guy voice. "Now there's nobody in your way around here."

After she thought about it Carla decided she wasn't angry at

Skeeter at all. She was glad the movie was a hit because it pleased the grown-ups so much. But the truth was, to Carla, being in a hit didn't feel any different than the flops she had been in; she really didn't think about it much. Mostly she felt bad about Nibbles. Every day, long after she stopped thinking about Sarah Milliken, Carla would stop by the grave under the Mexican palm and say a few words to Nibbles.

9.

All her life Carla had been a beautiful version of whatever age she happened to be. In the Dr. George movies she was an exquisite child. Now, in her mid-thirties, she was an idealized version of an adult woman. Some beautiful women become that way; they grow into their beauty. Those women always retain a memory of their plainness. Carla had no such memory. It might have made others arrogant. Carla often questioned her beauty, but she also accepted it as part of the natural order.

I was certainly consumed by her beauty, even taken over by it. Her beauty had become a part of me, or perhaps I had become part of it. A few years before *Changing Partners*, when we were both in Los Angeles, Cora called to ask if I could escort Carla to the opening of Filmex, the annual Los Angeles film festival. There was to be a screening in Century City and then a dinner at the Century Plaza Hotel.

I left my car at her house and a limousine drove us to the theater, where the paparazzi snapped away at Carla and at my left shoulder. Before the screening dozens of people, each of whom had written out a big check to Filmex, stopped to greet her, kiss her on the cheek, and have a word. A few were pushing one movie or another, but most were just making contact in the hope that she'd remember them for some future scheme. After the screening there was a walk on a red carpet between the theater and the hotel. The path was lined with celebrity watchers, five and six deep. No matter how many times I've seen those crowds, they always surprise me. People line up and stay for hours, all for the privilege of watching someone famous walk past them. When they saw her, they shouted, "Carla, Carla!" as if the word itself had power. The professional photographers bunched up at the doorways, but many in the crowd had cameras. There was a constant click, click of picture-taking. My face froze into an involuntary smile that made me feel, and doubtless look, like an idiot. Carla was aware of it but she'd had a lifetime of gawkers with cameras. The celebrity glow was on her face. It's a sort of serene smile and eyes that seem to look at people without making contact. If she wasn't exactly enjoying it, I thought she was at least enduring it without pain. When we were a few steps from the hotel, she whispered, "I can't bear one more minute of this."

"You want to just split—not go to the dinner?"

"The hell with it," she said. We made straight for the fire exit.

She wanted to go to Carmina's, an unretouched 1950s coffee shop. It was at Pico and Vermont. English was spoken there, but only as a second language. It's safe to say that not too many movie stars wound up at Carmina's. I asked the driver to stay with the car but to keep an eye on us. I didn't anticipate trouble, but if it was lurking around, Carla's presence would stir it up. Our fellow diners were a couple of Chicano families who were quite taken with the limousine, and a few young actors who recognized Carla and grinned in our direction.

We sat in a red Naugahyde booth. The table was Formica with a napkin dispenser and a bowl of salsa. I called to the waitress behind the counter, asking for *"cerveza, por favor."*

The woman opened two long-neck bottles, then broke dried tortillas into a bowl—no packaged chips at Carmina's. When Carla asked for guacamole, the woman cut open an avocado, chopped up some chilies, and mixed it at our table.

Carla curled her legs up under herself and I could see she was ready to settle in for a while. That was fine with me—an evening with Carla alone in a restaurant where it didn't look as if she was going to be hustled or hassled was a treat for us both.

Carla and I always claimed to each other that we were the only true Angelenos in the movie business. It wasn't true, but it did seem everyone we dealt with was from New York. There, in Carmina's, we got to giggling about it. "What always kills me," she said, "is the way they're always saying, 'Well, I'm from New York,' as if that's supposed to excuse them from knowing how to drive or find the beach."

"The screenwriters are the worst," I said. "If I hear one more script-hound in Schwab's talk about the 1954 Giants . . . I mean, who really cares how deep the center field fence in the Polo Grounds was?"

"They're always putting down L.A., 'land of kooks.' "

"I know. L.A. is the most insulted city in America."

" 'No cultural vitality,' " she said in a raspy New York accent. "If Brooklyn's so great, what are they doing here?"

"Tell them," I said.

Then she smiled a sad little smile and said, "No. I can't. You can, maybe."

"Star rules?"

"Yeah. If I put down New York—even as a joke . . ." She let her voice drift off, but I knew what she meant. It would be quoted and requoted until her remarks became legend and she got a harsh letter from the mayor as well as the enmity of eight million people.

As we relaxed we got to talking about acting—not just Carla's, but in general. She was looking back at her childhood performances. "When kids play emotion," she said, "they just imitate adults. That's why it's fake, too broad. Some of them are okay at the big stuff—terror, Shirley Temple cute. I never had an adult who showed any emotion, so I exaggerated less. That's why those old Dr. George performances are still pretty good. That kid was turned inward. You had to watch to figure her out."

" 'That kid'? That's how you think of her?"

"It's not me anymore. It wasn't really me back then."

"Then who was it? Of course it was you. All your performances are you. That's what's so amazing."

"When I watch those pictures, I keep watching little Georgine, trying to remember what I was thinking about."

"And?"

"I'll tell you what I saw. I was playing my mother's fears from the orphanage—humiliation, rejection, shame . . . Oh, listen to me. Theories about everything."

"Why not? It sounds right. Why pretend to be dumb?"

"It was my mother's inner life. I gave it a voice. She sure didn't. But it popped out in my performances."

After the release of *Dr. George's Holiday*, the second in the series, Georgine became the most popular name in the country for baby girls. Benny Raskin claimed it so often that enough newspapers printed it and it became true. Carla's bangs, cut straight across her forehead, became, according to Benny, the most popular girl's haircut in the country. He sent life-sized mounted photographs of Carla-as-Georgine to beauty parlors. He included barber's shears and cutting instructions for the Georgine look.

Metro established a network of fan clubs for Carla. A firm called Fan Mail, financed by the film studios with offices on the Sunset Strip, found high school girls around the country who were enthralled by the Dr. George movies. They were made chapter presidents, and provided with promotional materials and biographies of Carla, Brandon and Lewis the horse. Membership cards and a newsletter were distributed. At first Carla was asked to autograph pictures of herself for the members, but it became too time-consuming, so Fan Mail found a woman who could imitate a child's signature.

By late 1948, when Carla assumed she'd be making Dr. George movies forever, the studio, like all the studios, had a problem: the House Un-American Activities Committee. It meant nothing to Carla. Ceil and Milton had no political views. Maury Kelman, on the other hand, had been a member of the Communist party in Los Angeles during the early thirties. Success had changed all that for him and now he voted straight Republican. At the beginning, the studios all had contacts on the Committee staff so they could get advance warning when any of their personnel were about to be called. Later, when it seemed everyone was being called, that stopped. But Fred Nugent learned of Kelman's subpoena before Kelman did. As far as Nugent was concerned, if the bastard was a Commie, he ought to be hauled in front of the Committee. But not just now—because another Dr. George picture was only a month away from starting, and Kelman was needed to do a last set of revisions. Other writers had worked on the films, but Kelman had been first and he was still the best at it. As a studio veteran, Nugent knew that no matter what anyone said, these things could be negotiated. There was a young California congressman on the Committee who Nugent assumed would not be averse to doing a small favor for a big company in his state. He'd heard the guy was someone you could do business with. Nugent got him on the phone and explained the situation.

"Well, I understand that," Representative Nixon said, in a deep and deliberate voice that Nugent didn't quite trust. "But if the man's a Communist, then he's a danger."

"I agree with you, Congressman, but I think you'll agree he won't be more of a danger in a couple of months."

"Possibly. I understand his Party activity was before the war," Nixon said.

"Yeah, he's a Republican now. Like you and me."

"Possibly. That can be a front, though, you know."

"I want to cooperate with you. We don't want these people around here any more than you do. But he's a key man right now. What about a substitute?"

"Perhaps."

Fred Nugent might have suggested any name that was in front of him at the moment. Almost anything would have been better than losing Kelman. Perhaps because the Dr. George movies were on his mind from the talk about Maury Kelman, and perhaps because there had recently been a large feature story in the *Los Angeles Times* about the studio school, and perhaps because he thought it would be easier to replace a schoolteacher than a screenwriter, Nugent found himself saying to Representative Nixon, "Do you know about our studio school?"

"Why? What about it?" Nixon asked, sensing the kind of information that could get headlines.

Nugent lowered his voice as if he were not taking any chances that the Communists could be listening in. "Well, if you'll permit me to speak in confidence, we've suspected for some time now that one of the teachers there is at least a fellow traveler. He's in charge of some pretty important young minds, and I don't mind telling you, we're concerned."

A few days later a U.S. marshal, a fleshy man in a black suit, was waiting in front of Skeeter's apartment in Hollywood. "Mr. Danzig?" the marshal said in a somber voice.

"Yes?"

"You're being summoned." Everybody in Hollywood knew

those words with their nineteenth-century ring. Skeeter couldn't believe it. The last time he had been involved in politics of any sort was when he lost an election for vice president of his high school student council. When he called to make an appointment with Nugent to tell him what had happened, the secretary put him off. Skeeter just went to the Thalberg Building and waited until Nugent would see him. "It's all crap, Fred. I'm not going."

"What are you making such a fuss about? If you've got nothing to hide, then it's all some kind of mistake and it'll come out. Take it easy."

"The hell with it. This is fascist stuff and I'm not participating. You can fire me. I don't care."

"You got something to hide, Skeeter?"

"Familiar with the Bill of Rights? It even applies to employees of movie studios." Skeeter said good-bye and walked out.

Nugent considered firing him and might have, except he knew Miss Pringle would raise hell. Later that afternoon Nugent was explaining part of the situation to Bill Brady. Fred never told anyone all of anything. He figured if he was the only one who knew all the pieces of a puzzle, he couldn't be replaced. Although Brady was indifferent to politics, like all directors he loved to make scenes, to create drama. He put his feet up on Nugent's desk and said, "Why don't you send Carla to Washington to talk about the school? Think of the ink you'll get."

"How do we know what she'll say?" Nugent asked.

"Who cares? She's so goddamn adorable, they'll forget about Maury. How can we lose?"

Nugent knew he could have a problem with Skeeter, a man perfectly capable of going to the newspapers on his own. He wanted to cut off this business fast. He called Representative Nixon and proposed a trade. "Brightest little girl you'll ever have the privilege of meeting," Nugent said.

The Committee agreed to talk to Carla, to find out, as Representative Nixon put it, "about those teachers and the conditions in the motion picture schools."

Fred told Skeeter he could relax, his subpoena was canceled. "It wasn't easy, Skeeter. I think you owe me one." Then Nugent gave the whole business over to the press department. Not Benny Raskin, who would turn it into a circus, but to Aldo Lane, Benny's boss, who would know how to exploit it without looking as if they were trying to sell tickets. It was leaked selectively to a few papers, which is how Milton heard about it. He called Claire Berger, who for once took his call. She didn't know anything, but she promised to find out. "Is Carla upset?" she asked.

"Not yet," he answered.

An editorial in the *Los Angeles Times* criticized the Committee for subjecting a child to a hearing. Mr. Nixon called the editor. He wanted to remind the press and the public that he had two little daughters himself. "They're precious to me. We would not treat little Carla Tate any differently than I would my own flesh and blood." He explained that the Committee had always intended to talk to Carla in executive session. She was not under subpoena but rather invited because of her expert knowledge. "If her parents object, then of course we would not insist."

Milton was wary of it all, afraid that in some way Carla might wind up blacklisted. Ceil's response was that if the government wanted to talk to her daughter, well, of course she should do it.

Aldo Lane accompanied Ceil and Carla on the trip to Washington on the new TWA Constellation. It was the first flight for either of them and it excited Carla more than the prospect of testifying. Aldo had invited several reporters to see them off. Carla was asked what she intended to say to the Committee. "Depends on what they ask me," she answered.

In Washington Ceil and Carla stayed at the Hay-Adams in a suite overlooking the White House. "It's so beautiful," Ceil kept saying. Aldo Lane, who had stayed in many fine hotels, told her how room service worked and urged her to dial for anything she wanted. He took them to dinner in the Hay-Adams dining room, where he ordered wine in a French accent that awed Ceil. She wondered if the other people in the room thought that the three of them were a family, that this elegant, worldly man was her husband and Carla's father.

The next afternoon, after Aldo had spent the morning showing Ceil and Carla the capital, they met with Representative Nixon in his office. He thanked them for coming all this way to speak to them and complimented Carla on her movies, then suggested they all walk over to the hearing room. Ceil was fascinated by his elaborate manners. He seemed as uncomfortable as she herself usually felt.

Before the session, Representative Nixon spoke to the reporters gathered outside the hearing room. "We will not put pressure on a child," he said. "We are all family men. I think we are doing what all Americans would want us to do, which is simply using good American common sense in these difficult times." The room had dark paneled walls hung with portraits of nineteenth-century members of Congress. The seven members in attendance and Carla sat around a mahogany table with an inlaid leather top. Aldo and Ceil sat a few feet away in soft leather chairs. There were no reporters present. After Representative Nixon explained the workings of the Committee to Carla, he asked if she would like to be sworn in. "It's not mandatory. That means it's not a rule, because you're not of age, that means under twenty-one. You are under twenty-one, aren't you?" he said, with a small awkward laugh that sounded to Carla as if he were reading from a card that said "Tee-hee" on it.

"Okay," Carla said, trying to be polite.

"Let the record show that the witness has been sworn in, *pro forma*, using an *ad hoc* oath." Then he spoke in a deep, formal voice that sounded to Carla like a judge in a movie. "Carla Tate, for the sake and benefit of your fellow countrymen, do you promise to answer truthfully any and all questions put to you today?"

"Okay. Yes."

"Thank you. Let me say, before the questioning begins, and I assure you we won't be asking anything too difficult, but let me first say how much I and my daughters and my wife, Pat, and of course our pets as well, enjoy your movies. My family looks forward to each one. It is our understanding that you attend school at Metro-Goldwyn-Mayer studio in Culver City, California, at a school for children under contract to the film studio. Is that correct, Carla?"

"Yep."

"We are particularly interested in your instructor, Mr. Gerald Arthur Danzig. Do you know who I mean?"

"Mr. Danzig, yes." When Carla called Skeeter "Mr. Danzig," Aldo Lane knew things were going to go just fine.

"Does Mr. Danzig, in addition to your regular lessons, the so-called three Rs, ever talk to you about . . . politics?" Nixon paused for a moment, before saying the final word in an awkward, insinuating voice.

"I'm not sure," she said, vamping for a moment while she tried to figure out just how to handle things.

"Let me clarify," he said, spreading his fingers and glancing at the papers in front of him. "In the curriculum at your school, do you study history?"

"Uh-huh."

"Do you ever study, let us say for instance, the story of Robin Hood?" Nixon said it Robin *Hood* and the strange emphasis confused her for a moment. "The story of robbing the rich to give to the poor?"

"No. We never had any stuff like that." Before the session began Carla had been a little worried that she wouldn't know what to do. She was used to speaking in public, but always with a script. She understood she would be on her own here. There would be no Maury Kelman or Bill Brady to help her. Now she could see it was going to be easier than some of the adults she was up against all the time. She knew Skeeter was in trouble and if she could help him she wanted to. "Does the Pledge of Allegiance count?" she asked, running her hand along the line of her bangs, which was one of Georgine's mannerisms.

"I beg your pardon?" Mr. Nixon said.

"You know, 'I pledge allegiance to the flag of the United States of America . . .' "

When Carla stopped, Nixon jumped in. "Of course. 'And to the Republic, for which it stands . . .' "

Carla began speaking with him. She stood up, faced the flag behind the Committee's table, and put her hand over her heart. Nixon got to his feet and then the other members did, too. Everyone spoke in unison, led by Carla. ". . . One nation, indivisible, with liberty and justice for all." When they sat down again, Carla made her eyes as large as she could and said, "That's how we start every day. Mr. Danzig always has us say that first." If that was true, it was the first Ceil had heard of it. Aldo Lane nudged her. Ceil began to realize that her daughter was in the process of twisting these men around her finger.

After Carla fielded a few gentle questions about the substance of her lessons, Representative Nixon moved in for what he seemed to regard as his big question: "In the course of your lessons, did Mr. Danzig ever say anything like, 'Share and share alike'?"

"No," Carla answered. "My mother says that, though."

"Oh, well," Nixon said, nodding toward Ceil. "Mothers don't count." Then thinking better of it, he added, "That is, in this context."

After the session, which lasted about twenty minutes, Aldo Lane brought Representative Nixon's daughters, Julie and Tricia, his wife, Pat, and a photographer into the room. One of the photos, showing Mr. Nixon carrying Julie in his arms and holding Carla's hand, wound up on the front pages of newspapers all over the country. In addition to saving Skeeter Danzig, Carla's testimony gave Representative Nixon a few days of national coverage and made the Dr. George movies and Carla Tate more famous than ever.

A month later the Committee called Maury Kelman. But Maury really had become a Republican and he told the Committee what they wanted to know, which amounted to the names of other Communists in Los Angeles during the 1930s. Kelman believed that naming the names was his duty. Mr. Nixon and the members of the Committee thanked him and Maury Kelman went back to writing Dr. George scripts.

10.

When I was at UCLA, where I spent two tedious undergraduate years as an English major, writing papers on novels I hadn't actually read, at least not all the way through, the psychology department held a retrospective of the Dr. George movies. It had something to do with what all the shrinks called "Nurturing." It meant they liked the relationship between Carla and Brandon. This was before videocassettes were common, and although the Dr. George movies were often shown on television, those were usually mutilated versions. Because of my adolescent crush, but not yet knowing my life would someday be bound up with hers, I went to see them all.

Carla was adorable as well as vital. Each gesture and word looked natural and spontaneous, without a wasted step. What I sensed, but couldn't yet fully understand, was that Carla brought out the best in Brandon Holt. It wasn't until years later that I understood it. When Brandon played a scene with Carla there was real love between them. Although she made many more movies and played opposite many actors, it wasn't ever quite the same. Brandon was her first pairing, and he was her greatest one. As odd as he sometimes was, what Brandon felt for Carla was pure and even noble. And he had the technique to let that come rolling out. The two of them managed to get it all into their performances. Neither was ever better.

When she was eleven, after six Dr. George movies, a biography of Carla called *America's Golden Girl* was published. Aldo Lane had hired a writer who moonlighted from *Look* magazine to do the job. Aldo provided the information and made Carla available for interviews. When the book didn't sell as well as Aldo had expected, the studio simply bought enough copies to put *America's Golden Girl* on the best-seller list.

About the time of the book's publication, Louis B. Mayer was pushed out of Metro. A studio head losing his position sounds routine by the standards of three decades later. But at the time it was like the falling of the *ancien régime*. Nobody particularly liked Mayer—hell, no ordinary person knew him—but he had always been there, like a mountain or a river. That he could be removed meant the world had no foundation at all.

It was at the time of Mayer's fall that Claire Berger noticed signs of change in Carla, which would mean the end for Dr. George. Claire knew Georgine would never work as an adolescent; her charm was her innocence and when that was gone, so were the movies. Claire realized that Ceil wasn't always aware of her obligations as a mother. "Have you talked to her about it?" Claire asked Ceil one day.

"What do you mean?" Ceil answered, feeling threatened, as usual.

"It's her time. I think you know what I mean." Because Claire wasn't sure that Ceil did know, she added, "There are changes. Have you told her about her period?" Claire tried to keep the exasperation out of her voice.

"No. But I will."

"You ought to do it sooner rather than later."

Ceil called Edna for advice, but Carla was home before she could reach her sister. Ceil needn't have worried. When she tried to broach the subject, Carla told her that one of the older girls at school had already explained it. But Ceil had worked herself up, determined to perform her motherly duties. "Georgine works fine when you're little," she said, "but not if you're getting older."

"I'm not that older," Carla said. "I can do it."

"We could try to get you some older parts."

"What parts?"

"I don't know. You're right in the middle now. The way you're filling out, if you want to do another Georgine, I guess we could tape you down. Your bosom I mean."

Uncomfortable at the thought, Carla reached up and touched her breasts, trying to imagine putting tape on them. "Ecch" was all she said.

"Your father said maybe we should stuff Kleenex in your underwear and do stories about Georgine as a teenager."

"You talked to him about this?" Carla said, embarrassed and angry to think that her sexuality had been the subject of discussion.

"He's your father."

"So?"

"He calls. I have to talk to him. He asks about you."

"Don't do that."

"Well, we have to do something."

Carla thought about talking to Skeeter about the problem of her breasts and what to do with them, but she knew this wasn't an issue to discuss with a man. It was on her mind enough that she didn't feel like staying around the commissary for lunch. She ate a little of her salad, put the rest in her pocket for the animals, and left to go to the barnyard. Bobby Dryer got up and followed her. "I heard the pigs are mating," he said.

"I wouldn't know," she answered as haughtily as she could. She wasn't sure why she did it that way. She actually liked Bobby.

When they got to the barnyard the pigs weren't mating, or if they were, they were being quiet about it. Carla fed them matzoh and watched them nose around in the dirt. After a few minutes, Bobby took her hand and said, "Let's go." He seemed so sure of himself and so relaxed that Carla just went along. They had held hands before and in some way that wasn't entirely clear to her, she guessed Bobby was her boyfriend. When she thought about it, she decided that if God came down from heaven and made everybody pair off right that minute, she would take Bobby. If God gave time for choosing, she'd look around some more. If older men were permitted, she'd have to consider Skeeter. She didn't know many boys her age and Bobby was the one she had known the longest. He had been in three of the Dr. George movies, playing an arrogant rich kid who had thrown a stone at Lewis the horse. The way he was holding her hand now seemed different from the other times.

For one thing, his palm felt sweaty and that was new. Carla was aware by now of her power over older men. When they were around her, they stood close and touched her hair and her arms. But this was the first time a boy her age had done anything like that. She knew he would do something, and she could feel him looking for a way to start. She was afraid he would let the opportunity pass. She didn't want to be too forward; starting things was up to him, she thought. But she was afraid if she didn't take the initiative nothing at all would happen and then, she knew, they'd both be disappointed.

When they had wandered out behind the English Village, on Lot 3, Carla thought that if they stopped walking he'd know what to do. When it looked to her as if Bobby was heading toward the David Copperfield street, she said, "You're walking too fast. I want to rest." They sat under a fir tree by a false-front thatched cottage, relaxing on the pine needles. Carla had spoken to Bobby every day for almost five years but now neither of them knew what to say. Then he leaned over and kissed her. He did it gently, tentatively, a little timidly; brash Bobby had suddenly grown shy. As he was kissing her, she realized she wasn't feeling much more than pressure on her mouth. In her imagination she had thought a boy's kisses would make her feel free and floating above the ground. But instead, contradictory thoughts ran through her mind: I'm not old enough for this yet, that's why it doesn't work, and If I pretend I'm in a movie being kissed, I'll do it right.

So she conjured a vision of a soundstage and saw herself as an adult in a white gown in a passionate embrace, not with Bobby, but with a handsome older man whose face was not clear to her. When she had what she thought was an appropriate romantic response, she began kissing Bobby. The fantasy served as a way to ease into something close to genuine feeling. Her response to him, which he assumed had to do with the quality and intensity of his kisses, made him think he must be doing it right. He put his arms around her and they rolled in the pine needles. But her sense of rightness and romance didn't last. He felt heavy on top of her and that made her feel outside the event, as if she were watching it—not a movie exactly, but not real either. She tried to find her grown-up fantasy again but now it eluded her. She kept waiting for a sensation, for physical or emotional pleasure. But Bobby rolling on top of her and rubbing his lips on hers felt more like wrestling than anything romantic. Still, it seemed to excite him and that gave her a sense of power if not of pleasure. She might have gone on thrashing about, but he jammed his knee between her legs and it hurt her. She decided she'd had enough and pulled away from him.

"Wow!" he said. "That was great."

Carla smiled and nodded.

"Some of the big kids do a lot more than that," he said. "I saw Barbara Ames and some guy behind Stage 9. His hands were all over her."

"I don't care." She meant that kind of talk put her off, but Bobby took it as a sign of encouragement, rolled over on top of her, and slipped his hands inside her white linen blouse.

"That tickles," she said, wriggling away.

"Tickles? Tickles?"

"Well, not exactly."

He kissed her again with his tongue in her mouth until he felt her kissing him back. Bobby was aroused but he was also feeling victorious because he was necking with Carla. The fact of it, as much as his lust, pushed him forward. When she pulled away from him, he accidentally ripped her blouse. "Oh, oh," she said. "My mother'll kill me." Carla knew that wasn't true. Ceil wouldn't notice and if she did, she wouldn't say anything. It just sounded like something a teenager might say and Carla was trying it out. "I don't want to get pregnant," she added, which was another mature-sounding sentence.

Later, when she thought about it, the whole business made her feel older. She enjoyed that, but she would have liked to have had a friend to talk it over with.

As Carla was growing up Milton used his M-G-M money to start businesses. As the ventures came and went he would go back to Soderberg Ford. While he was selling cars, Milton talked Al Soderberg into advertising on television. KTLA, the only local station then, sold inexpensive time during the late show. With Al's doubtful blessing, Milton stood in front of a line of used cars and said, "Hi, I'm Milt Tate. You probably know my daughter, Carla. Transportation runs in our family. Carla knows horses and I know cars." A picture of Carla as Georgine, riding Lewis the horse, flashed on the screen while Milton made his pitch. Carla loved it and insisted on staying up late to watch, but Claire Berger said it was vulgar and it cheapened Carla. She had an M-G-M lawyer send a telegram to Al Soderberg threatening him with a suit if he didn't take the commercial off the air. That was the end of Milton's television career.

Milton saw Carla on the weekends and spoke to her on the phone during the week. He was never sure if Ceil and Carla knew he had been paid the extra two-fifty a week all these years. California law required that most of Carla's considerable income be put in trust for her. Ceil was the trustee and was given a commission which she used for their household expenses. The trust was administered by the Wells Fargo Bank, which invested the principal in stocks, bonds and local real estate. Although she wasn't aware of it, by the time she was twelve, Carla had substantial holdings in the San Fernando Valley.

When she was thirteen and the matter of looking too old to be Georgine had become glaringly obvious, Brandon Holt was found in his Hollywood apartment, beaten to death. Whatever else it might have meant, it was certainly the end of the Dr. George movies. Fred Nugent and Claire Berger knew at once what had happened. The Los Angeles police arrested two young brothers for the murder. They were known hustlers. They were in Brandon's apartment because he had invited them there. Claire, Fred and many others knew of Brandon's secret life. Now they were afraid everyone would know.

"Can't we say it was a robbery?" Nugent asked Aldo Lane.

"Maybe," Aldo said. "They took some stuff. I'll try."

"Just keep the lid on it and get him in the ground," Nugent said. "This is nobody's business."

The murder haunted Carla. She loved Brandon and his paternal feelings had affected her. How could they not? Yet she sensed something more to the circumstances of the death than she had been told. She would have asked Bobby what it was really about, because he always had an instinct for the hidden purposes of adults, but he had been lent out to Warner's for a picture being filmed in Arizona.

Skeeter escorted Carla and Ceil to the funeral, the first Carla had ever attended. It was at the Church of the Good Shepherd in Beverly Hills on a Saturday morning. The front of the church was crowded with photographers and the people who turn out to see bereaved celebrities. Skeeter hurried Carla up the steps and into the church, sparing her the photographers. During the eulogies, while Bill Brady was going on about Brandon's love of animals and life, Skeeter was murmuring under his breath about the hypocrisy of it all. From Skeeter's irritation Carla began to glean what had happened.

After the service they decided not to go to Forest Lawn for

the burial but went instead to Walter's Tea Room on Cañon Drive for lunch. Skeeter knew Carla was upset and the best thing to do would have been simply to offer her comfort. But he was angry and couldn't contain himself.

"Everybody knows what happened," Skeeter said. "Those reporters know. Nobody says. 'To protect his reputation.' What crap."

Ceil, as baffled as Carla, asked, "Knows what?"

"Those characters didn't break in. He brought them there. To do God knows what."

"What?" Carla asked as she played with her tuna sandwich, crumbling the potato chips, finally understanding. "Brandon was a homo? Is that what this is about?"

"Where'd you learn that word?" Ceil asked.

"Oh, Mother. Everybody knows that word. Was he?"

"Brandon was a lot of things."

"Was he or not?"

"What if he was?" Skeeter said. "It was his business."

"Then he was," Carla said, like a prosecutor who had pinned down an evasive witness. "Why didn't you tell me?"

"Carla," Ceil said, "it's not our business."

"I have a right to know stuff like that. You're supposed to tell me everything," she said to Skeeter, ignoring her mother.

"It's all a charade," Skeeter said. "The press knows, the studio knows. Only the public doesn't know. The whole thing is about protecting the studio's film library."

"I don't get it," Carla said.

Skeeter considered for a moment, then said, "The Dr. George movies are worth a lot of money in the future—re-releases, foreign sales, television, all that. But if the public knows Brandon wasn't exactly the noble vet who loved kids and animals in his private life, the whole thing could be shot to hell. It's all about money. The library value of your films. Everything's about money, Carla. Now you know."

"Are you sure?" she asked.

"Yeah. I'm sure."

In the days that followed the funeral, Ceil was confused and a little depressed. She tried to talk about it with Carla, musing aloud about Brandon. "I think he was going to propose to me."

"Really?" Carla said, more surprised than Ceil had expected.

"He always made such a fuss over me."

"If he proposed, would you have?"

"I don't know. Your father would go crazy. But I think that man wanted a family—you for a daughter, me for a wife."

Carla didn't fully understand why her mother was so sad, but it made sense. In her own way, beyond her initial grief, Carla was upset by it, too. She didn't think about the end of the Dr. George movies, or about how she wouldn't see Brandon again. She thought about his sexuality and what it meant. When she did, she thought about herself and Bobby Dryer. She and Bobby had a few more sessions out on Lot 3, always at his instigation. Carla had gone along mostly to see what it would be like. Perhaps if Bobby had been around now, she would have gone to him. But she knew what she really needed was an older person, because the mystery belonged to the world of adults.

In her confusion Carla hung around the school, waiting until she and Skeeter were alone in their classroom. Then she tried to kiss him. Skeeter had been around adolescents for a long time, especially adolescents who worked in the charged atmosphere of a film studio, but this surprised and unnerved him.

"No, no," he said, pulling away from her.

"Why not?" she said, defiantly. "You a homo, too?"

"Carla, Carla. Sit down. What is this?"

"What do you think it is? I want to do it with you."

"Well, I'm certainly flattered. But that's not possible. Let me try to explain something to you."

"It doesn't need explaining or anything. Yes or no?"

"I think it does. A death is very confusing. When it happens, people always want to grab onto life. They do odd things sometimes. This one is so disruptive, but it doesn't mean you should just offer yourself like that. You're years away from that kind of thing. I hope when it happens, it'll be with someone appropriate, someone you love."

Skeeter was doing his best to speak calmly, but Carla knew she had upset him. She had a choice. She could be a good student and ask a few questions, let Skeeter be wise, and then go on her way. Or she could give him a hard time just because she felt like it. She could see his mouth moving and she knew he was saying the right things, but she just didn't care. She nodded as if she were agreeing and then started unbuttoning her blouse.

"Carla, stop that."

"Want to tape them down? I don't," she said, showing him her breasts.

"Shush. Please, don't." He reached across to her and held her blouse together.

"You're so sensible," she said in a bitchy, acid voice. "So mature. I really like that. You a homo, too? Admit it."

"If I were, it would be my business and not yours. And nothing you should make fun of. Brandon loved you in his own way. We have to respect that. And you have to respect yourself. Now button up."

As she put her clothes back together, Carla began to cry. In the past when she had been upset, Skeeter had sometimes held her and she wanted him to do that now, but he kept his distance and handed her a tissue.

She left the school feeling miserable, thinking she might go to the barnyard, but she found herself walking in the other direction. Outside Stage 8 there were several wooden cottages, hardly more than shacks, that served as individual dressing rooms. She usually avoided the cottages because of Sonny Des Barres, an actor who was always hanging around. Sonny liked to flirt and talk to her in a stagy Texas twang. He said things like, "My, my, when you're ready I sure do hope I'm in the vicinity." She hadn't liked it or him, but she knew what he meant. Sonny had been shooting interiors for *The Cattle Drive,* a western that had been, as far as Carla could see, in production forever. Sonny was twenty-two, old to Carla. He was tall and lean and always wore tight jeans over his cowboy boots. She found Sonny sitting in front of his cottage, bare-chested, soaking up the sun. Without wanting to, and without fully knowing what she was doing, Carla said hello, in a curt, I-dare-you voice.

"What are you doin'?" he asked, looking up at her.

"Walking. What are you doing?"

"Studying my scene. That okay with you?"

"Want some help?"

"Yeah. Come on in."

Sonny's cottage had a mirror and makeup table, a chair, and a small chaise longue. On the walls and the mirror, he had taped pictures of real cowboys. Carla walked in with a defiant look that Sonny understood. His face crinkled into a smile. "My, my. You just get hotter-looking every minute. It is a miracle of nature, no doubt about it."

"Shut up, Sonny."

"Then how can I help you out? You grieving for the loss of your homo-dad, like everybody else around here?"

"What he was, was his business," she said, quoting Skeeter without knowing it until the words were in the air.

"Yeah? What's your business?" Sonny dropped his arm around her waist and pulled her to him, kissing her in an easy, grown-up way that was smoother than anything Bobby Dryer had ever come up with. He was so much taller that he easily enveloped her. He ran his hand through her hair and then slid it slowly down her back. He held her like that for a moment. He smiled, caressing her breasts, and then reached up under her skirt and pulled down her underpants. He kept his hands there and massaged her, then kissed her again. "Take my boots off," he said, and sat on the edge of the chaise. He turned her away from him and put his leg between hers, under her skirt. "Pull on 'em," he said. As she slid one boot off and then the other, he brought his foot back and poked his big toe inside her; it made her shudder. Then he turned her around and peeled off his jeans and dropped them on the floor. He lifted her up and sat her down on his lap, straddling him. He spread her legs wide, like a wishbone, then pulled her down, impaling her on him. The fierceness and suddenness of it surprised her and she yelped at the sharp pain. He moved her up and down, bouncing her as if she were a toy, and then rolled her back on the chaise, gripping her tightly and hammering away at her, whispering in her ear that she was "perfect, just perfect."

When they were finished and she wasn't sure if she had liked it or not, he told her she had been wonderful and he wanted to see her that evening and every evening. "I want to do everything with you. There's amazing stuff we could do."

Unmoved by his praise and flattery—after all, Carla was praised and flattered by the entire world, every day—she pointed to the bloody spot on the chaise.

"Does it hurt?" he asked.

"Not really. I have to go." He lay back on the chaise, feeling triumphant, as she put her clothes on and left without looking back.

Carla was reminiscing about Brandon Holt and his death, over one of our Ma Maison lunches. "He almost proposed to my mother. Really. He took us to his ranch, way the hell out in the Valley. He had horses, but it was really an orange grove. I still remember the smell from all the oranges broken open on the ground. Brandon had this picture over his fireplace, from the Dr. George set. It was an early version of the picture of Mrs. George that was in all the movies. It looked like me. Sort of. Anyway, he really thought he was Dr. George. Actors do that, but Brandon really did it. He supposedly started studying veterinary medicine at L.A. City College. Brandon was off into some deep water. Anyway, Ceil and I were out at his ranch. I loved being around all the horses and playing in the orange groves, but Brandon kept staring at us all the time. It really rattled Ceil. I don't think she had a clue about Brandon's sex life. But she knew he might propose. It made her even more nuts than usual. He asked us to stay over. I wanted to, but my mother practically shrieked, 'No!' Like she got stuck with a pin. If he had proposed and talked her into it, he probably would've quit the business so the two of them could open a little dog-and-cat hospital. They were both so flaky, it could have happened," she said, smiling at the thought. She toyed with the label on a bottle of San Pellegrino water for a moment and then said, "It must have been hard to be Brandon. He was such an actor, always trying to play some role. All those secrets."

"I remember when he died. I was a kid, but my parents talked about it. My father probably knew the truth."

"The way it used to be, the studio sent out publicity and that's how people knew what to think about everybody. It's nothing like Brandon, but there are things about me I don't want in the papers."

"Back then, the studios thought if people knew the truth about wholesome Dr. George, they'd avoid his movies. Now if some half-ass actor turns out to be a pederast or a murderer, people line up for tickets. Absolutely everybody is up for grabs."

"See, Gabe. That's exactly right. That's why I want us to do the memoirs. Why I have to. You're not the only one who wants to figure out my life."

"Who else did you have in mind?" I asked, thinking she meant another collaborator.

"Me! You could help sort it all out. You think just because I live it, I understand it?"

Carla read so much praise of herself, she knew she couldn't possibly measure up to that manufactured image. No one could. She felt that if she had a little control over it, it would all be easier to live with. Instead of being gratified by the constant trumpeting of her deeds, she found that all the fuss did the opposite—drained her. The more satisfied she appeared, the emptier she felt, until she finally floated away.

11.

For the first time since she enrolled at the the Little Red Schoolhouse, Carla was out of work. The studio could have dropped her contract when there were no more Dr. George movies to make, but Claire persuaded them to keep the arrangement while they searched for a suitable new vehicle. For Carla it meant more time for school. She was able to stay in class for three consecutive hours each morning. After lunch she took dance, art, music appreciation and gymnastics. Bobby Dryer had returned, ready to take up where he and Carla had left off. She didn't say anything to him about Sonny Des Barres, but she was hesitant when Bobby tried to get her to go out to Lot 3 with him.

She didn't think of herself as different as a result of Sonny, even though she knew what had been done could not be undone. Still, she didn't think about him, and she didn't see why what had happened with Sonny should affect the way she was with Bobby. He was still her boyfriend. She knew Sonny wouldn't tell anyone what had happened because it might get him in trouble. When Bobby asked her nicely, she would still neck with him and let him touch her. She sort of liked it and it seemed so important to him that she went along with it. Once when she and Bobby were eating lunch, she saw Sonny across the room. He looked as if he might come over to their table. She put her arm around Bobby and nuzzled his neck, which kept Sonny in his place. It excited Bobby, who couldn't understand why she wouldn't go off with him afterward. He decided that Carla was too unpredictable and he began looking over the new girls. Because she was only thirteen, she assumed that would be the end of Sonny Des Barres's attentions. But, of course, it wasn't.

Sonny took to cruising North Gower Street in his silver Ford convertible. He'd slow down in front of Gower Gardens and race his engine. The car had a dual exhaust system with noise-making baffles in the mufflers. The rear end had been lowered and the chrome removed. The result was a lot of racket from a streamlined bullet. Carla refused to acknowledge he was there, but Ceil asked, "Is he just a fan? Or do you know him?"

"He's an actor. I know him from the studio."

"How old is he?"

"I don't know."

"He's old enough to drive. That's too old for you."

"I agree. Call the police or something." As they talked, Sonny kept cruising the block. Maybe he was getting as tired of posing as Carla was of pretending not to notice, because he finally parked, and yelled "Come on out, gal!"

"Don't you dare go out there," Ceil said, as Carla headed for the door.

"I can handle him," she said, wondering if she could.

On the street, Sonny had crooked his arm over the side of the car door. He was wearing dark reflecting glasses. A few of the neighbors were looking out their windows. "Well, there she is," Sonny said. "Pretty as ever. How you doing, darling?"

Carla walked over to the car and with more bravado than she felt, said, "Sonny, what is this shit?"

"I come to visit you."

"Ever hear of calling first? Maybe I don't want a visitor now." She could feel herself gaining the upper hand. "Don't come here. You upset my mother."

"I ain't interested in your mother."

"If you don't get out of here I'm telling what you did to me."

"Whew! You are a tough little bitch. I thought you liked me. It was you come knocking on my door."

"Who do you think they're going to believe?"

"Darling, it was a honor and a privilege. There's plenty more we could do, you know."

"Sonny, beat it." She turned and went back into the house, feeling adult. If she could handle Sonny Des Barres, she could do anything. It was the best of feelings, better even than being a movie star.

When Carla came in grinning, it rattled Ceil all the more. "I wrote down his license plate," she said.

"He's gone. It's okay."

"Sometimes I worry. The atmosphere at the studio, it's so . . . mature. Boys like that can get you in trouble."

"He's an idiot. I don't want to talk about it anymore." Ceil continued to worry about the sort of men and boys Carla might be meeting. She knew that Carla went around with Bobby Dryer and although she worried about it sometimes, Bobby seemed manageable to her. When Carla got a television job in New York for the summer, Ceil was relieved.

As a point of the deal, Claire had negotiated a suite at the Volney on the East Side. In the days before rehearsals began, Carla and Ceil shopped and walked around the city, which was new to both of them. They didn't know anyone, so they spent their time together and enjoyed each other's company. Each morning they would order breakfast from room service and then walk down Madison Avenue, going in and out of the shops.

"Kraft Television Theatre" presented original dramas. This one was called *Tomorrow's Hope*. It was a family saga by Sherwin Lesser. The play was a combination of *King Lear* and *Volpone* set in a Brooklyn tenement. The grandfather of the family was near death and everyone was squabbling over his will. Carla played Rachel, the one granddaughter who cared more for her grandfather than her inheritance. It was an ambitious script and the big switch was that by the time the dust had settled and all the relatives had shrieked and wept, the grandfather revived, but little Rachel died, either of heartache at her family's venality or of meningitis; Sherwin kept changing his mind. Because Carla didn't know how to play either, she just worked on an unnamed illness. It was her first chance to play a death scene. The other cast members kidded her about dying before she'd even been kissed.

During rehearsals Carla had the beginnings of a romance with Tom Ross, a young actor who played a cousin who tried to get the grandfather to include him in the will. He was sixteen and a student at the High School of the Performing Arts, which Carla took to be an East Coast version of her own Little Red Schoolhouse. They would sit in the greenroom and drink black coffee because it seemed grown-up, although Carla disliked the taste. They had long, earnest conversations, consisting mainly of Tom's theories of acting. Tom lived with his family in Queens and took the subway to rehearsals every day, so there wasn't a lot of time and rarely any privacy, but they held hands and kissed when they could. Ceil noticed them together and it worried her.

"Mother, he's in high school," Carla said, shrugging it off. "We're friends. Okay?"

"He might be after something."

"You can't get pregnant from holding hands."

"I didn't mean that. I trust you with that. He could be looking for a Hollywood connection."

"That's ridiculous," she said, but the talk of pregnancy made her think of Sonny Des Barres. That was her secret and although she felt it made a charade of her chaste romance with Tom, she certainly wasn't going to tell him about Sonny. She worried about how she would handle the Sonny question when there really was somebody she wanted to sleep with. She decided she would just wait till it happened, then figure out what to do. In the meantime, she would go back to being a virgin, at least in her mind, and she'd tell her mother as little as possible about her boyfriends.

Carla tried to be polite to Sherwin but he made her uneasy. He seemed to disapprove of her in some way she couldn't understand. He was a tall, broad-shouldered man with a full silver beard who always wore black shirts and trousers. Carla found him remote and too intense. He always wanted to talk about her character and the subtext, a term Tom used all the time, too. The truth about Carla's acting technique was that she would read the script, think about the character she was to play, and then she did it. She didn't analyze anything—at least, not consciously. She knew what subtext meant, because her acting coaches at the studio had talked about it. But Carla had never been on the legitimate stage; her school play had been an M-G-M movie. She assumed live television wouldn't be all that different from films. What she found was that for *Tomorrow's Hope* entire scenes had to be done in what she thought of as one take. "Why can't we stop and start till we get it right?"

she asked Sherwin as they were reading over some new dialogue.

"What are you talking about?" he said, making no attempt to mask his irritation.

"Stop and start comes out better. I can concentrate more."

"This is a play, young lady."

"But we're shooting it with a camera."

"It's going to be live. You can't hide."

"I don't want to hide. I want to do it the best I can."

Sherwin walked away, infuriated by his inability to make Carla see the difference between film and live television. The writers Carla was used to, men like Maury Kelman, were easygoing, accommodating sorts always ready to change dialogue or do whatever she needed to make her performance better. Wasn't that the point of it? she thought. Later, she resolved to compliment Sherwin on the script. As the rehearsal was breaking up she asked him if he had any ideas for movies they might do together.

"I don't write to order, young lady," he said, as if he had been waiting in ambush for her. "I wouldn't do it for Gertrude Lawrence and I won't do it for you."

Carla had no idea who Gertrude Lawrence was but she knew not to ask. "I just mean I admire your writing so much. I hope I can do some more." She was old enough to sense that Sherwin was either going to snarl at her again or make a pass; neither prospect was pleasant. All in all, she decided New York writers were difficult and she'd stick to West Coast screenwriters.

The critics praised Carla's work and she was offered more television, but it would have meant going to school in New York and in her mind that meant teachers who were more like Sherwin Lesser than Skeeter. She was getting bored with Tom Ross. He was very nice, certainly sincere, and it was better to have a boyfriend than not, but he was starting to get serious. She didn't want to sleep with him, and she didn't know if she would know how to say no. Carla and Tom promised to write to each other, and he sent her a few long letters, but his handwriting was so awkward she couldn't read them. She meant to write back, but she never did.

After a summer of room service at the Volney and the pleasures of New York, Ceil and Carla felt cramped and uncomfortable at Gower Gardens. Jim Spencer, the officer at the Wells Fargo Bank in charge of investing Carla's money, had been advising Ceil to buy a house. "You'd be more comfortable," he said. "And there are tax advantages. The soundest counsel I can give you is buy a house and live in it." Ceil had grown comfortable with Jim. He was English, in his mid-fifties, and seemed wise to her. Although he had never met Carla, he always asked about her and followed her career. Ceil appreciated his interest, but what she really liked about Jim were the framed photos of his wife and children that he kept on his desk. The family looked so happy and normal that Ceil knew Jim would give only good advice.

The houses they were shown looked grand to Ceil. She couldn't imagine herself the mistress of any of them. Besides, she reasoned, it was Carla's money, so Carla should decide. Carla liked the second house they saw. It was a low-slung ranch house in Trousdale Estates, on Loma Vista Drive, where the houses tended to the ersatz Greco-Roman. The house Carla picked was simpler than some of its more extreme neighbors. It had a swimming pool with a view of the city, and Carla could imagine herself swimming there and inviting boys over to visit. Because the house was empty, Ceil and Carla were able to move in right away. "You mean it's closed?" Milton asked when he heard about it.

"Yes," Ceil said. "In my name as guardian."

Milton knew that if Wells Fargo had handled it, it was within the law. He had no objection; it was a sound financial decision. It was that he felt more left out of his daughter's life than ever. "Can I visit?" he asked.

"As far as I'm concerned, sure," Ceil said.

Ceil and Carla didn't argue about the house until it came time to furnish it. Carla wanted the whole thing to be pink and fluffy and she wanted to pick out all the furniture. Ceil wanted to hire a decorator. She asked Jim Spencer what they should do. He said that his services and expertise didn't extend that far, but he would be willing to make a suggestion. He recommended that Carla be allowed to decorate her room and bath and the pool cabana as she liked. The decorator would do the rest.

When Carla was sixteen she began to date. Aldo Lane arranged evenings for her with young men he felt the public would accept. Since adults did everything else for her, Carla didn't think there was anything odd about it. Aldo's office would send a car for the young man of the moment, who arrived at the house on Loma Vista with a photographer. The three of them would go to movie premieres and restaurants. The next day pictures of the date would go out over the wire services and appear in newspapers with captions like "Out on a Date" or "All Grown Up." If the young man in question was what Aldo termed "on the mature side," he would go along, because the photographers were inclined to shoot a roll or two, then leave the young people to themselves. Once in a while Carla would get into a wrestling match in the front seat of a car or the banquette of a restaurant.

If the boy was attractive and Carla was in the mood, she'd neck for a while. Terry Seaver, an actor who was twenty-one, called her after their studio date and asked her to go on a real date. Terry was well known as a pursuer of young women, so Aldo Lane had been present during their studio date. Terry had played a small part in Carla's most recent Metro film, *A Funny Feeling*. He had been attentive, getting positively moony when she was around.

He took her to the Unicorn, a coffeehouse on the Sunset Strip. It was an unusual evening for Carla because for once in public she didn't look oddly out of place. She was still younger than most of the crowd, but this was where young people came to hear folk music. She was with a date instead of an entourage, accepted as a famous peer of the regular crowd. Carla and Terry cuddled and wore paper hats and fed each other french fries while Terry told her his life story. He had grown up in St. Louis, where he played football on the high school team, and then gone to a local college for a year before he took his looks to Hollywood.

As they were enjoying each other, the columnist Sam Lipsky came to their table. "Hiya, kids," he said. "Having a good time?" Mr. Lipsky was a short, round man with thick glasses. His syndicated column, "The Unbuttoned Lip," was always datelined the Polo Lounge.

"Hi, Sam," Carla said, happy enough to greet him, because if he wrote about seeing her, for once the date was a real one. "You know Terry, don't you?"

"Sure. Sure. Weren't you two kids in *Funny Feeling?*"

"Yes sir, we were," Terry said, sounding like the friendliest boy in the class. As he spoke to Sam Lipsky, Terry dropped his hand below the table and ran it along Carla's thigh.

"So then what's this? The cast party?"

Carla smiled and said, "I guess you could say that. We're just having dinner, though."

"Put in your column that Terry Seaver is madly in love with Carla Tate. Then everybody'll be jealous and they'll know I have great taste in women."

Sam Lipsky smiled at them, interested in what looked like a budding romance. Carla could sense a little sadness in Sam. He always had a touch of melancholy about him, but this seemed different. She realized Sam had a crush on her. She gave him a kiss on the cheek and vowed to herself to call him soon and be friendly.

After they'd listened to music and been the object of a lot of admiring glances and gossip, they sat in Terry's red Jaguar roadster in the restaurant's parking lot. He kissed her and then said, "You are the most beautiful thing there ever was on this earth. No doubt about it."

"Where are you taking me now?"

"For a drive," he said, then drove up into the Hollywood Hills. Terry had a small house in Laurel Canyon, on Wonderland Avenue.

Carla walked through the house, taking the measure of it, inspecting his furniture and records. "Did you pick all this stuff out?" she asked. But Terry wasn't answering questions. He lit a fire in the fireplace, poured brandy, and put on a Billie Holiday record.

Carla was excited and nervous, but determined to keep a cool mask in place. "What is this, the perfect seduction?"

"I'm just trying to make it nice. If you don't like it, I'll stop."

"No. I like watching your moves."

"Don't be like that. I want to make love. Why deny it? If you don't, I mean really don't, well . . ." He shrugged and then added, "Takes two or what good is it? You know?"

"I don't get you."

"I want to be with you. That's all."

Carla had stayed away from anything that looked as though it might turn serious since Sonny Des Barres. That one was easy. She had been in a mood to do something, so she'd done it. But this was different. Terry was so earnest and so respectful of her that she knew that no matter what happened she wouldn't be able to ignore him afterward. When she had said yes to the date, she knew this was a possibility. Now, with the brandy warming in her and the fire going, she didn't want to make any decisions. If Terry wanted to do anything, he could start it. Seduction was Terry's principal skill and he could sense her mood, knew she was relaxing. He began to kiss her, covering her face and eyes with soft, gentle kisses. She didn't kiss back because she was enjoying it just as it was. He began kissing the back of her neck, licking her earlobes and making her shiver. As she was feeling that she could put up with this forever, he pulled away, kissed her on the forehead, and changed the record, then sat next to her on the sofa, stretching his legs out, holding her hand. "Do you want a joint? Would you like some?" he said, leaning over to hunt in a drawer.

"Marijuana, you mean?"

"Yeah. That's what I mean," he said. "That shock you?"

"I've never had it," she said, scared and fascinated.

"Try a little. See if you like it," he said, as he found the joint, lit it, and drew in a long hit.

"You'll turn me into a dope fiend."

"That this stuff is against the law is the biggest crime I know." He took another hit and handed it to her. "Careful or you'll cough." Carla held the smoke in her lungs as Terry had done, then exhaled, suppressing the strong urge to cough very hard. "Do you have an undeniable craving for anything now?" he said, laughing.

"Name some categories."

He took another drag and gave her the joint while he got up to go to the bathroom. She stayed on the sofa feeling comfortable and relaxed. If this was a real seduction she liked it. Terry was the first boy she had been with who didn't feel compelled to try to tear her clothes off the minute they were alone. She thought about telling him about Sonny but decided because he was so sensitive and careful, the information could have an unpredictable effect. She decided not to take the chance for fear he might not go through with it. She smoked more of the joint and studied the things in Terry's living room, a basket of firewood, the pictures on the walls, the walls. She began to giggle when she realized she was high on marijuana. Guess I'm a drug addict now, she thought. I'll have to hang around with dangerous musicians. Into a life of badness . . .

Terry came back with a bag of chocolate-chip cookies and two bottles of beer. "Hungry?" He fed her a cookie and then began to kiss her face and neck; he opened her blouse and kissed her breasts. When she sighed he carried her to the fireplace, where they burrowed into the pillows stacked in front of it. Terry began to kiss her arms and her stomach until she could feel her head whirling. She closed her eyes as he lifted up her skirt, pulling it away from her legs. He tugged on her underpants and she twisted about to help him pull them off. Then she could feel his tongue curling inside her. The intensity of his tongue swirling into her was a new sensation. She knew from the moment it started it was what had been missing up till now. When she felt him draw back, she opened her eyes long enough to see that he was taking off his pants. When he knelt over her she knew just what he wanted and reached out for him and pulled him into her mouth, sliding her tongue over him and holding him in her hand. She could feel him breathing hard; it gave her a sense of power. He drew himself out of her and lay next to her, putting his mouth on her again and swinging his leg over her face until they were locked together, trying to swallow each other whole.

In the morning, when Carla arrived home to change and go to the studio, Ceil looked as if she hadn't slept much. "Why didn't you call?" she said, trying to contain her anxiety.

"I don't want to talk about it right now."

"I was worried. You could have been dead."

"I'm fine. I'm sorry I didn't call. I didn't think of it. I have to hurry up."

"Will you be home tonight?"

"Of course." Carla kissed her mother on the cheek and patted her shoulder to reassure her, the way a mother might comfort a daughter. Later that morning at the studio as Carla was daydreaming about Terry and the night before, she was shown the gossip column in *Variety*: "Chummy Chewsome at the Unicorn. Li'l Carla Tate, not so li'l anymore, and dreamboat Terry Seaver."

At the end of the term, the children who attended studio schools full-time had to take graded achievement tests administered by public school examiners. "They're worried that you get a free ride," Skeeter explained to the older children. "That classes here aren't as tough as public schools." The kids laughed and booed at that. "What do they know?" Bobby Dryer yelled.

"That's the point," Skeeter said. "They're worried that they know a lot more than you do."

Carla had taken these tests for years and had always done well. This year they were to be held at John Marshall High School. Carla and Bobby, along with Megan Maxwell, Bobby's latest crush, a fifteen-year-old beauty who had just started working at the studio, and Toby Sheridan, an overweight boy who had been signed to play a teenage killer in *The Evil Within*, climbed into a studio Packard for the drive to Marshall High. Carla's first glimpse of the red-brick school was from the back of the limousine. When she saw the school's green and leafy lawn with an American flag flying, she felt a twinge of nostalgia for something she had never had. For a brief moment she wanted to have gone to this school, for this place to be in her past, to have known what it was like in a world of people her own age, where celebrity and fame didn't extend beyond the schoolyard. Now she was about to graduate, and it made her sad to know she would never meet boys who played at sports or tinkered with cars or were in the science club, instead of boys like Bobby and Toby who thought only about their careers and their agents. She was lost in thoughts of missed opportunity, aware that no matter how fine and enviable a hand life had dealt her, there would always be something missing.

Carla's reverie was interrupted by the gawking crowd that had gathered in front of the school. Carla could see that the windows of the school were filled with students and teachers, awaiting the arrival of the actors. Bobby loved the idea of being stared at. He smiled and waved up at the windows. Carla was certainly accustomed to being stared at and had long ago learned how to ignore it or bask in it as she chose, but this seemed different. For a moment she felt the opposite of what these people thought she was. The idea that she was glamorous and sophisticated was in their minds, not in hers. It made her self-conscious, in no mood to take an examination.

They were met by an assistant principal, who gushed a greeting and introduced himself as Mr. Miller. Carla recognized a fan. Mr. Miller, although he dealt with adolescents all day long, was excited by the presence of the actors. He led them to the Advisory Services office where they were to take their tests. The M-G-M kids were being tested along with children from 20th Century-Fox, including Sarah Milliken. Carla had heard Sarah had landed a contract at Fox. It was the first time Carla had seen her since the death of Nibbles. "Hi, you guys," Sarah said. "How's Metro?"

"Hey, Milliken," Bobby said. "Your tits are growing."

"Shut up, Bobby," she said and turned to Carla. "You look really good. How's it going?"

"I'm okay, Sarah," Carla said, unable to think what else to say.

"Fox is great. I'm already shooting one picture, *About Mrs. Smith*, and I'm reading scripts all the time. I love it," she said, keeping her eye on Carla, looking for signs of doubt. "Do you have a picture now?" Sarah asked, certain that if Carla did, she'd know about it.

"No," Carla said, reporting the fact, neither ashamed nor worried.

"You'll get one. Eventually. You always do."

"Trying to spook her, Milliken? Can't be done." Bobby said, laughing and holding Megan's hand.

Mercifully, Mr. Miller interrupted and told them all to take their seats so the tests could begin.

The examinations took most of the morning. There was a reading comprehension section in which they were to read an account of the American Revolution and then had to answer essay questions about it. Since there was a question like that every year, Skeeter had prepared them by giving them sample tests. Skeeter had left the current crop of younger kids in the hands of a day-by-day teacher, while he helped the older ones cram. He had given them practice questions about the Civil War and the Louisiana Purchase. The science and math sections were true-or-false questions. It never occurred to Carla that she wouldn't do well, but seeing the high school, Sarah's bitchiness, and probably even Bobby Dryer's attention to Megan all rattled her. She knew she wasn't getting the answers right and although she wanted to care, she just didn't. She could see Bobby was struggling. She knew it wouldn't be long before he tried to copy from her. A lot of good it'll do him, she thought. Let him copy from Megan. Sure enough, Bobby coughed and tried to catch her eye. She glanced up and he gave her a silent pleading look. She didn't think much of Bobby, but she didn't want him to fail. She knew without a little extra help, he would. She tilted her paper slightly so he could see what she had written. Maybe if she had felt better, or more in control, she would have tilted the page more. As it was, Bobby had to crane to see. Bobby was so cavalier about everything, so unaware of the consequences of his actions, that he all but stood up and leaned over her desk. It frightened Carla and she pulled back from him. Then Mr. Miller came striding down the aisle. He had seen them cheating. Carla was certain they were about to be thrown out. An image of a montage of swirling newspapers with headlines about her disgrace flashed through her mind. But Mr. Miller wasn't about to create difficulty if he could avoid it. "Sit up straight, young man," he said. Then he scowled at Carla and walked back to the front of the class. Bobby grinned and winked. It made Carla feel sick; if they had been regular students they would have been in big trouble. She was glad to be out of it, but the unfairness of it made it hard for her to concentrate on the test.

Afterward, Bobby wanted to hang around and "look over the local talent," he said. But Carla only wanted to get away. She called to Mr. Miller and said, "Could you please get me a cab?"

"What?" he sputtered, still angry at the cheating and not pleased to be asked to perform what he considered a menial chore.

Carla knew immediately she had made a mistake. "Or let me use a phone. I'll do it."

"Young lady, you must stay with your group. You can't be calling cabs. You're not a movie star here."

"I'm sorry," she said, trying to figure a way to calm Mr. Miller down.

"You will leave together, exactly as you came."

"I want to stick around," Bobby said.

"There are no arrangements for you to stay. You're to go back to your studio schools after the tests."

"Come on, Mr. Miller, show me where the commissary is. I'll buy you lunch."

"Shut up, young man. I've had quite enough of you."

"Right. Sorry."

Carla knew she had caused this last flare-up. She hadn't meant anything rude by asking Mr. Miller about the cab. She knew it was the sort of thing that led to people calling child actors stuck-up. All she wanted was to get away from this place, from school tests, Sarah Milliken, Bobby Dryer and weak adults who let them get away with murder.

Carla was right; she had failed the tests. It meant that the school couldn't graduate her. It surprised Skeeter, of course, but it wasn't the first time he had faced such a problem. After talking it over with Miss Pringle, Skeeter suggested to Carla that she enroll in summer school. "You don't really have a home school, so you'd be assigned to Beverly. They're tough. No telling what would happen. A private school is a little more under our control."

"I feel so dumb," she said.

"What happened?" Skeeter asked.

Rather than try to explain the whole business about Bobby and her own confused feelings about John Marshall High, Carla said, "It was a hard day. I screwed it all up."

Skeeter suggested the summer session at the Hancock School, which was for the daughters of Hancock Park, an enclave of expensive houses a few miles from downtown. At Hancock Carla took courses in expository writing, American history and something called Study Habits. The girls wore white blouses, tartan skirts and green knee socks. Carla decided to regard the whole thing as sort of a location shoot and make the best of it. She bought a loose-leaf notebook and book covers with the school's name, put on her uniform and turned up for class. The other girls knew who she was, but they were a smoother lot than the gawkers at John Marshall. Most of them were nice enough, but by the third time one of her classmates asked if she had really met Montgomery Clift, Carla knew this place was not for her. These girls lived in a tony Hancock Park world of boys, deb parties and clothes. Carla went for a few days and then just refused to go back. She called Skeeter and said, "If there's anything really important that you learn in high school, would you please just tell me about it?"

"You don't like it there?"

"I am in hell, Skeeter." He laughed and suggested that perhaps she was exaggerating. "If you're busy, we could do it on the phone," she said.

"Tell you what, if you go once a week, and don't make a fuss about it, I think we can work something out."

So Carla turned up once a week for the next six weeks at the Hancock School for Girls. The rest of the time she swam in her pool, read scripts, and went out with Terry Seaver. Sometimes they'd go to restaurants and clubs, and then back up to his house in Laurel Canyon. During the day, if he wasn't working, he'd drive up to Loma Vista in his red Jaguar and they would lie in the sun by the pool and talk or hold hands. At first Ceil would glance out, in an attempt to keep an eye on them, but it made her uncomfortable when she saw them kissing. If Carla and Terry saw her watching, they'd go into the cabana where Terry would peel off Carla's bathing suit and look at her, delirious at the sight of her body. "You're my church and temple," he would say as he kissed and caressed her. Sometimes they would make love in the water, standing at the shallow end of the pool. Carla would wrap herself around him and they would float together to the deep end, in each other's grip, until both were dizzy and finally sated. Once, when Ceil was away on an errand, they made love sitting on the end of the diving board, while the board bounced up and down until they fell into the water.

At the end of the summer Carla was pronounced educated, rehabilitated and a high school graduate. Because she didn't go to the graduation, the school mailed her the diploma. Ceil framed it and hung it on the wall of the cabana.

12.

Carla was a veteran movie star but she no longer had an immediately perceived identity. Articles were still written about her, but they were fewer, and she had stopped appearing on magazine covers. While she waited for a vehicle that would catch the public's imagination the way the Dr. George movies had done, she went out on Aldo Lane's studio dates, which confused the press. They loved to chart the progress of her romance with Terry. Sam Lipsky was always interested, reporting every restaurant and movie premiere they attended. When Carla was seen with someone else, Sam would pose rhetorical questions to readers of "The Unbuttoned Lip": "Has Carla Tate dumped Terry Seaver?" Then he'd describe how she had been seen with another date. Carla thought it was funny, but Terry had a low tolerance for stories of that sort.

Aldo arranged an evening at the Hollywood Bowl. He escorted Claire Berger; Carla was with Peter Rhinehart, a young client of Claire's the studio was considering. Peter confided that his girlfriend had a fit when she heard he was going with Carla.

"Terry wasn't crazy about it either," Carla said, trying to reassure him.

"Yeah, but he's in the business. My girl works at Bullocks."

Carla found that funny; it seemed to relax her. "As long as Terry doesn't start calling her," she said.

"Would he?" Peter asked, alarmed.

"Not if he wants to live."

The studio had a box at the Bowl; that meant an elegant picnic before the concert. Woody Herman was going to play "Ebony," the concerto written for him by Stravinsky. As the four of them arrived, Aldo was explaining who Igor Stravinsky was. "He'll be there, you know. I'll introduce you."

"Great," Carla said, taking Peter's hand. "If they're going to be jealous, let's at least have a good time." The boxes at the Bowl were small, fenced-off areas with folding tables and deck chairs. They were much sought after and people held on to them for years, fighting over them in will contests and divorce settlements. To have one in the first few rows and on the keyboard side was a mark of social position. M-G-M had one of the best. Claire had arranged a picnic hamper of champagne, pâté, cold beef, and chocolate mousse. Concerts like this reminded Carla of Hollywood restaurants. Everyone knew everyone else and they paraded from box to box to say hello, as though it were a remarkable coincidence that they had run into people they knew. Carla's status was such that she didn't have to get up and work the room the way Claire Berger was doing. She could just sit and sip champagne, and people would come by to say hello and be seen with her. She was surprised when Aldo asked her to come with him. "There are some people you should meet." Because she was in an accommodating mood, she threaded her way with Aldo, while his photographer—the only one allowed near the boxes—recorded the event.

"Mr. Stravinsky," Aldo said. "I'd like to present Carla Tate." A small European gentleman wearing a beret and rimless glasses that reminded Carla of the ones L. B. Mayer sometimes wore stood up.

"Ah, yes," Stravinsky said, taking her hand. "Little Georgine."

When Carla and Stravinsky shook hands, the photographer swooped down. Stravinsky touched her arm and her hair. Vera Stravinsky muttered, "Stop it. She could be your granddaughter."

He ignored his wife and said, "You are a very beautiful young woman. I suppose you know that."

"Thank you," she said.

"It's quite true that every woman has a physical peak. Seven or eight months it lasts. In more obviously primitive societies, it's the mating time. Breasts are higher, firmer, the flesh glows—"

"You're embarrassing the child," Vera said, embarrassed herself. But Carla was interested in Stravinsky's praise and only a little self-conscious about it. She had received many compliments in her life, but this was surely the most elaborate, and on that ground alone it fascinated her.

"It's all relative, you know. The beautiful are more beautiful. The dumpy, less dumpy. After that, entropy begins to win the long battle. My dear, this is your moment."

As they all laughed, Aldo turned to the others with the Stravinskys and reminded Carla that she knew Bob and Ann Holleran.

"Yes, of course," Carla said. "It's nice to see you."

Aldo quickly added, "Bob's at Fox. In fact, he's the biggest fox of all."

"I know," Carla lied.

"And this is Mr. and Mrs. Markel," Aldo said, introducing the third couple.

Carla turned to greet Jack Markel, a man in his late-forties who took her hand in greeting and held it a little longer than necessary. Carla had adapted a man's handshake for everyone she met. She used it for men and women. It was firm and direct. She felt it made her worldly and sophisticated. But the way Jack held her hand while she was trying to shake his put him in control. As Carla said hello to him and his wife Mona, she sensed something beyond the casual introduction, a spark of interest that went beyond the social. She knew she was having a different effect on Mr. Markel than on Mr. Stravinsky. It wasn't unusual for men to light up around her, as Stravinsky had done. But that wasn't quite it. Markel wasn't staring at her breasts or her hips, as so many of them did. It seemed to Carla that Markel was trying, and for all she knew succeeding, to see inside her head. Maybe it was his gaze, direct and as lingering as his handshake, or maybe it was his smile. Part of what Carla was reacting to, although she couldn't yet put it in words, was that Jack had the musk of power and possibility about him. It was a distinctly Hollywood air. It said, "When I'm here, magic can happen." She knew when this evening was over, despite Stravinsky's unexpected extravagance, Jack Markel's was the one face and voice from the dozens she met that she would remember. She wondered if he was a musician, but Carla had learned when she was around men and women who were either famous or used to fame—and anyone who went to concerts with the Stravinskys qualified—never to ask what they did, since the answer was likely to be something like the governor of California or the discoverer of uranium.

"I'm an admirer of yours, Miss Tate," Markel said. "I've followed your career."

"Thank you," she said, trying to place him in the Hollywood firmament.

"There's no reason you should know who I am," he said, reading her mind. "I'm a lawyer."

Aldo laughed and said, "For Jack to describe himself as a lawyer is like Mr. Stravinsky saying he's a songwriter."

Carla enjoyed Woody Herman and his Herdsmen—twenty-six men in white dinner jackets—but even as the music played she found herself glancing over at Jack Markel's box. Many people were doing that, but the others were looking at Stravinsky, watching to see how he was reacting. Carla had already forgotten that she had met the composer. She found herself glancing at the composer's friend.

The next day Aldo called to ask if she had enjoyed the concert and meeting Stravinsky. "Sure," she said. "Who were those other people again?"

Aldo sensed that she meant Jack Markel, but pretended not to. "Bob Holleran from Fox you know. Jack Markel's a very big lawyer. Shall I tell you about him?"

"Okay," Carla said, as though she didn't care if he did or didn't.

"That's the guy you want if there's labor trouble. He's settled a lot of Hollywood strikes. He's plugged into big labor, the studios and, supposedly, the mob."

"You mean gangsters?"

"He's represented some of them. He's called the fixer."

"Sounds like a tough boy."

"Never raises his voice. Doesn't have to."

"Does he always go around with Mr. Stravinsky?"

"Nothing Jack does and nobody he turns up with ever surprises me. He is king of the markers."

"The what?"

"Think about it. You'll get the idea. You might enjoy knowing him. He could be helpful to you."

"How?"

"A lot of people in the business have never heard of him. But he knows everybody who counts and most of them owe him. He doesn't exactly have clients, but it couldn't hurt. We could get together if you think it'd be interesting."

"Okay. I guess. Sometime," she said casually, as if it didn't matter one way or the other.

Jack and Carla met at the Vine Street Brown Derby, where the walls were covered with caricatures of prominent people in the movie business. They were seated in a leather booth with dark wood, beneath a drawing of Carla as Georgine. "They'll put that thing on my tombstone," she said of the picture.

"I think that's a long way off," Jack said. Carla ordered a Cobb salad, and the waiter asked Jack if he wanted his usual, which was corned beef hash. He was wearing a dark gray suit and a white shirt that made him look like the lawyer he said he was. "You rattled me the other night, and you rattle me now," he said. "I think I'd better give you my career counsel while I still can."

"I think I like to rattle you. It'll be my new hobby."

"As you no doubt know, you need a vehicle," he said.

"Oh, I see. We're being adults now. This is the serious part, right? You have more experience, but I'll try."

"If you don't come up with one," he said, masking the desire he felt, "you'll find yourself having an interesting career, but not a great one. You will fade from the public's mind and become someone who used to be famous."

"I'm looking, you know," she said, having no difficulty taking the subject seriously. "I read scripts all the time."

"You are opening the mail."

"What?"

"You wait to see what scripts are offered. It's reactive. You have to seize the reins. Either commission a script to be built around you, or buy the rights to a novel and have it adapted for you. The way you're doing it depends on luck and the enterprise of others." Carla saw him looking at her and thought, He's right, but that's not why we're here. She knew what it was this man wanted. No matter what he was saying, how serious the subject. He's way too old for me, she thought, but still she couldn't stop flirting with him. She smiled and all but batted her eyelashes. Stop it, she thought, and then reached across the table to touch his hand. Finally she blurted, "I'm really flirting with you. I don't do that."

"No. I suppose you don't. You're somebody people flirt with. Isn't that so?"

"I guess. Is the serious part over?"

"Yes. Mr. Stravinsky certainly did."

"What was that all about?"

"I think you know."

"About the peak, you mean?"

"May I ask how old you are?"

"Eighteen. Almost. May I ask how old you are?" she said, imitating his formality.

"I'm forty-seven." What went through her mind was that he was older than her father. But instead of putting her off, it had just the opposite effect; it made her shiver with the rush of a secret thrill. He seemed to understand, because he said, "Your father's age, probably."

"He's a little younger."

"Well, I have kids your age. So there we are."

"Is this a date?"

"It's lunch. Two people who have mutual interests, who met casually. And here they are." As he spoke he gazed at her, and she recognized the actor's trick of fixing on the other person's forehead as a way of looking soulful without having to worry about blinking. It should have put her off, but instead it endeared him to her.

In an intuitive flash she knew they would become lovers. It's usually difficult to identify the precise moment a passion is born. Years later she came to understand that this was the moment of her transition into adulthood. She talked about it a great deal, trying to measure it exactly. Part of her attempt to identify it was the actress's need to calibrate emotion. It was also the more tender response of a young woman who was captivated entirely.

She could never explain to me, or even herself, exactly why she was so attracted—he was short and compact with broad shoulders, more like a bull than the long, lanky boys she favored. Still, she was drawn. It was undeniable. She hadn't bantered quite like this before, at least not with someone she was attracted to. She might joke and toy with Peter Rhinehart, who wasn't a romantic possibility, but with men who really interested her she just waited in the certain knowledge that the less she said and did, the sooner they'd come around. She found herself able to voice her thoughts directly, without subterfuge; his presence was the cause of it. She could feel herself rising to his level and it made her feel heady. This careful, guarded man made her unguarded. She knew he was in heat over her. Instead of making her cautious, as it usually did, she felt alive. She loved watching him squirm with his fear about her age while he lectured about her career.

"What did Aldo mean, king of the markers?"

"That's Aldo exaggerating. He's talking about favors people do. What they owe and how they collect. Markers."

"And you have them?"

"If people like Aldo think so, it becomes true."

"Where do the gangsters come in?"

"No gangsters. Would you like something other than your salad?" he asked, changing the subject.

"No. It's fine. Are you afraid of my age?"

"I am in awe of your age."

"Then what's going on here? Tell me."

Jack thought for a moment, considering. He was not a rash man and he didn't like to say things he could later come to regret. "We're both concerned about the difference in our ages. We've both flirted before, but never across so many years."

"You're married."

"And you go with Terry Seaver. I'd like to propose something. That we get to know each other, spend time together. Like this. I believe I can be of some help to you in your career. Not replacing your agents or anything like that. But trying to see why you're not as big a star as you ought to be, can be. Will be."

"That'd be great. But I know what you really mean."

"What's that?"

"That you want to go out with me but you're afraid."

Jack laughed, and said, "How do you know that?"

"I just know. The other night at the Bowl? Your friend, Mr. Stravinsky—what he wanted was to be charming and outrageous. His dream would be that I would get excited and call him up and he could turn me down. Not that I would."

"And me?"

"You're just going to try to wait. Don't do anything dumb about Terry, okay? Don't get any gangsters after him or anything. I would like some grapefruit cake."

"You're quite something."

"I'm not always like this. You bring it out."

"I'm flattered."

"One last thing, then the cake. About being a minor."

"Yes?"

"Twenty-one's a long way off."

"When will you be eighteen?" he asked, smiling.

"Real soon," she said, smiling back.

A few days after her lunch with Jack Markel, Terry Seaver was offered a picture that began shooting almost immediately in Rio. He was heartbroken at the thought of being separated from Carla, but the role was a good one, a break for him, and he couldn't say no. Carla called Jack and accused him of engineering the job for Terry.

They met at the Polo Lounge and sat in a large round banquette in the dark front room. Jack swore he had nothing to do with Terry's job. "You're going away for two months—give me credit for a better sense of tactics than that."

"How do you know I'm going away?"

"New York and Paris. *Natural Affection*. Baron Mellenkamph's picture. You'll like him."

"Did you have something to do with that?"

"Your career might not be what it could, but you're a long way from needing help getting jobs. Why'd you say yes?"

"To go to Europe. I've never been there," she said with a shrug. "It's about rich people, so I get to wear great clothes. Why not?"

"When this one's over, I'm not resting till you set up your own company. You can't say yes just because there's airplane tickets and pretty clothes."

"Just 'opening the mail'?"

"That's it. You'll get a kick out of the Baron. He's full of shit, but he's a high roller."

"Is a baron better than a duke?"

"To him, it's better than God. He's a hustler. An Algerian Jew who made a lot of money, some of it honestly. He declared himself a baron—an aristocrat by preference. He's been called portly and courtly. Don't lend him money."

"Is that the same suit you had on the other day?"

"No. I have a number of them."

"All that color?"

"Some are gray, some blue."

"Always a white shirt and a dark tie?"

"Carla, I'm a businessman, not an actor. This is considered normal."

"I want to try your suit on sometime. Will you let me?"

"It would be one of the high points of my life." Jack wrote a phone number on his business card. "This is a private number. If there's any trouble, you call me."

"What's going to be different from what always happens?"

"The Baron isn't Metro. If he doesn't pay you on time or if you think he's cutting too many corners and the picture's going to suffer, you tell Claire Berger, but then you let me know."

"Then what?"

"Then I'll reason with him." Jack reached across the table, took her hand and kissed it.

"Is that to get me ready for Europe?"

"That's because I already miss you."

Carla had a theory that her acting changed after she met Jack, or at least after their affair began. Her theory was that after Jack she had adult emotions, so she gave fuller performances, as if somehow her adult work were better than what she had done as a child. It wasn't true. She gave good performances all her life. The mystery of it wasn't how old she was, but rather where it came from at any age. She always seemed to have a reservoir of feeling and knowledge that was an accumulation of all that had ever happened to her or to the people she knew and cared about—everyone from her parents to Jack, who was the polar opposite of Ceil and Milton. It all lay dormant when she wasn't working, then burst forth when the cameras rolled.

13.

The birthday that had so interested Jack, Carla's eighteenth, was celebrated in New York. To honor the occasion, Baron Mellenkamph took her and Ceil to dinner at "21." The Baron was about ten years older than Ceil. He had a puffy face that seemed to be melting or just collapsing under the weight of all the expensive food and wine he pushed into it. He had thick gray hair combed straight back and dense eyebrows that spiraled out in wiry gray corkscrews. His mouth was so fleshy and sensual that even Ceil recognized she was dining with a man of the senses. "Zo-oe, darling," he said, exaggerating his own accent, toasting Carla with a flute of Dom Pérignon, "I wish you *joyeux anniversaire*."

"Thank you," Carla said, sipping the champagne and wondering if he expected her to make a speech.

"It is my honor to produce your first love scene: 'Little Georgine, not so little anymore,' " he said, conjuring an advertisement. "You approve?"

"Sure."

"If you're excited, I'm excited."

Throughout the evening people stopped at their table to meet Carla and say hello to the Baron, who seemed to know everyone. For most of them Carla slipped into her studio date mode, smiled, shook hands, but didn't even try to let the names and faces register. It seemed like a blurry parade of the well-to-do, the well-known and the well-spoken. A father and son, introduced by the Baron as "the Messieurs James Jay Van Osburgh III and IV," caught Carla's attention. At first it was because the younger Van Osburgh, who was a junior at Yale, was the first person her age she had seen all evening who wasn't a busboy. "We call them Three and Four. *Père et fils,*" the Baron said.

Four couldn't take his eyes off Carla. "I've seen your movies," he said, as if that gave him proprietary rights to her. Carla rewarded him with a smile that almost made him lose his balance. "I've been in Europe all summer," Four said. "If you're going, I wish I were still there."

"You're going back to school," his father said, then turned to Ceil. "Will you go to Paris, Mrs. Tate?"

"Yes. I'm the most excited of all."

"I doubt it," the Baron muttered, looking at Four.

When the Van Osburghs were gone, the Baron said, "*Trois* is in finance and *Quatre* is usually in trouble."

"I liked them," Ceil said. The Baron, who had an instinct for these matters, understood that Ceil wanted to ask if Three was married. The Baron had made it his business to learn a bit about Milton, and he recognized Ceil's casual interest as the start of a fantasy of being rescued by a wealthy older man. He wondered if her daughter shared that fantasy, particularly in regard to himself. "It will be a race to see which one calls which of you first," he said in order to flatter Ceil.

The next day Four called Carla at the St. Regis, where they were staying, but she was in rehearsal all day and too tired to return the call that night. He was persistent and caught up with her on the set a few days later. The picture was shooting in Grand Central Station, which was only available to them at night. It never occurred to Four that she wouldn't remember who he was or might not care to go out with him. "They must give you some time off," he said. "I could come to the set and take you to lunch."

"My schedule's kind of brutal. During the break I study my scenes. They keep changing." But he wouldn't take no and finally Carla agreed to see him on Saturday, the evening before her day off.

Four picked her up at the hotel, was polite to Ceil, and then took Carla downstairs for a drink in the King Cole Room. He ordered martinis without asking what she would like, and offered a toast, "Welcome to New York and I hope I'm welcome to your life. Or a little bit of it." Carla lifted her glass and thought he was very cute, even if his idea of a toast to her involved him. Four pointed to the mural behind the bar. "Old King Cole. The nursery rhyme? It was painted by Maxfield Parrish. My grandmother knew him. They sort of went out together or something. Great, huh?"

"Yeah," Carla said, with more enthusiasm than she felt. Actually, it looked like a big magazine illustration to her, but she decided to play the good date, so she praised the mural.

"I thought we might meet some friends of mine for dinner. At the Bird. I mean, if that's all right with you. There's a party later if you feel like it."

"Okay." Carla didn't know what the Bird was, but she knew that part of the good-date mentality was to let the boy organize everything.

Outside the St. Regis, Four had a hansom cab waiting. Carla loved it, even as she recognized it for the tourist attraction it was. He had the driver take them up to Central Park for a canter along the East Drive. Carla lay back in the seat, looking up at the starry night, feeling dreamy and happier than she had expected. "When I was little," Four said, "this was the biggest treat there was."

"It's not so bad right now," Carla said, taking his hand. "I love horses."

"Do you ride?"

"In my movies when I was little. Lewis the horse."

"I remember. Do you ride show horses or anything now? In Hollywood?"

"No. People play polo all the time, but not girls." Four leaned over and kissed her. She thought she could feel his heart pounding as he pressed against her. "They also do that in Hollywood. A lot," she said.

Four kept her hand and spoke to the driver. "Stork Club, please. Take the transverse and go down Fifth. Just in on Fifty-third."

Four's friends, who were already at the Stork, were Nicholas Foy and Maia Howard. As Carla and Four were joining them, Nick Foy, who had been Four's classmate at Trinity, was going on about their table. "They were going to put us on the left side," he said. "But I had a word with Mr. B and here we are." Maia nodded her approval and began to ask Carla about the problems of getting up early to be on a movie set. "You have to be up at six in the morning, I heard," Maia said. "I could never do that."

"I'd like to dance," Carla said. As Four led her onto the floor, he whispered, "Want to go to the party? Without them?"

"Right this minute."

Four and Carla walked the ten blocks to his parents' apartment building. "Sixty-third and Fifth," Four said. "God's country."

"Is the party there?"

"The car's there. Party's in Connecticut."

In the building's garage, the attendant was polite to Four, and respectful, but he wasn't about to give him a car without a senior Van Osburgh's permission. "I'm sorry, sir. That's my orders. Should I call upstairs for you?"

"I'll do it," Four said, as he took the phone from the man. He didn't seem upset or put out and Carla liked that. Four spoke for a moment, then said, "Let's go up. He wants to say hello."

The Van Osburgh apartment was an enormous duplex filled with furniture that Carla knew had not been assembled by a decorator. There were chintz-covered sofas, wing chairs, and a lot of odd-looking Orientalia—Japanese prints and large porcelain vases. Over the fireplace was an oil portrait of a beautiful woman in a riding habit, her hand resting on a white wolfhound. Carla thought the two of them resembled each other. Four saw her looking at the picture and said, "My grandmother." Carla was aware that the Van Osburghs were rich and she knew vaguely that a Dutch name in New York, which the Baron had told her Van Osburgh was, meant old money, but it hadn't seemed real to her until this portrait. She thought of her own grandfather, with his accent, and for a brief moment felt less certain of herself than usual. It was a new feeling and although it wasn't at all pleasant, she could feel herself filing it away for future use. As Carla followed Four through the living room, she noticed *Fortune* and *Holiday* on the coffee table. She wondered if they read *Life,* which had put her picture on the cover twice.

Mr. Van Osburgh III was sitting in his den having a drink, which Carla thought was not his first. "Come in, come in," he said, struggling to get to his feet. Carla shook his hand and he plopped back down in his chair. "Please, have a cocktail with me. There's a shaker," he said, pointing toward the bar. "Do the honors, Jimmy." As Four poured the drinks, which turned out to be martinis again, Carla could feel the senior Van Osburgh's eyes on her. He seemed to approve but his glance was as probing and unforgiving as any camera. "Where were you?" he asked.

"Bird. We went with Nick and Maia. They bored her."

"It wasn't as bad as that," Carla said, trying not to sound rude.

"Doesn't surprise me," Three said. "They bore me, too. Anybody else there?"

Four began to tell his father about friends he had seen at the Stork Club. As Carla listened, she was thinking, These people don't keep secrets, at least not the way she and Ceil do. Father and son had mutual interests and acquaintances. It was a matter of casual routine to ask where the other had been. They assumed what interested one would interest the other. Carla's life and romances were a matter of public record, written about all the time, but still, a self-preserving instinct kept her from telling any real news to Ceil. Of course Ceil wouldn't be interested in who was at a restaurant. If she did ask about an evening, Carla would censor her answers, giving information that wouldn't alarm her mother—generalities and lies. The Van Osburghs, or at least these two Van Osburghs, were a different kind of family altogether.

"Enjoying our town?" Three asked, looking her over again.

"I like New York," she said, looking him in the eye, not about to be intimidated by a drunk.

"Maybe we can have an evening while you're here. If you get tired of my son, or if he can't keep up with you, I'll be around."

"Seven?" she said. "Sounds like too much for me." Four and Three laughed at her joke. It wasn't much of one, but then Carla rarely made jokes, certainly not around strangers. Jokes were made for her. But here, in front of all this old money, some busker's impulse to entertain the patron came out. As she said it, she knew it was odd and in a moment of insight she realized that here in this Fifth Avenue gin haze, under the portraits of dead Jays and Van Osburghs, she had cast herself as the outsider, the strolling player, ever ready to accommodate.

As they drove to Darien on the Merritt Parkway in the Van Osburghs' station wagon, Four told Carla about Yale. He was about to start his junior year. After college he intended to go on to law school. "You'd like New Haven," he said. "Maybe you could come up sometime."

"Okay," she said, trying to imagine what it would be like to go to college.

The party was at an estate in Tokeneke, in Darien, on the shore of Long Island Sound. The main house, a vast Georgian brick affair with a circular drive and an enormous, well-tended lawn, looked to Carla like a place Cary Grant and Katharine Hepburn might live. The party was in the pool house, next to the apple orchard.

The guests, who had been drinking most of the day, were college students, Carla's age, but it was a different world from the one she was used to. Some of the girls wore ruffled, white strapless dresses and a lot of the boys were in white dinner jackets with madras cummerbunds. "This the prom?" Carla asked, wondering if the black dress she had worn for dinner would be appropriate.

"They were somewhere," Four said, with a shrug, explaining nothing. He was wearing a jacket and tie, but he was so assured in this crowd that Carla thought he'd probably feel at home here in overalls. She noticed some of the girls were in Liberty sleeveless dresses and pink backless pumps. Carla guessed they hadn't been "somewhere." She glanced at the band, six young men in badly fitted tuxedos, playing "Bony Moroni." It was like a movie set for a story about rich kids.

Four began greeting people and introducing Carla. Within moments she could see her presence was a social coup for him. She was certainly used to being the center of attention, and she knew how to handle it with grace, but still it was a disappointment. She wasn't sure what she had expected at a party in Connecticut—if not Grant and Hepburn, something more sophisticated than a lot of drunken, noisy college students repeating minor variations of "Glad to meet you. I never met a movie star before." As she looked around, her relaxed smile in place, she realized she had misread it slightly. She was part of a larger drama. A good-looking, coltish young woman was glaring at her. "What's her problem?" Carla asked Four.

"That's Tina," he said.

"You must go out with her or something," Carla said, aware from the look on Tina's face that she might be one step from committing murder.

"Yeah. Don't worry about her." As they worked their way

to the bar and the gin and tonic that seemed to be the drink of choice, Carla could see the other girls crowding around to comfort Tina.

"Two G and Ts," Four said to the bartender. Carla was glad to get hers. Behind her she heard a slightly drunken voice make a remark about "an Aryan from Darien," which was a popular line at the time from *Auntie Mame*. It was followed by someone else saying, "Yeah, and a Deke from Tokeneke," and then laughter. Carla lived in a world that was certainly aware of anti-Semitism, but it didn't affect her. In the studios Jews were the ruling majority, although everyone pretended that wasn't the case. Carla certainly knew she was Jewish, although she had never practiced the religion and took little interest in it. Since this was an evening of references she didn't get, she decided to ignore it. "Let's dance," she said to Four, and they moved onto the crowded floor.

They had a few more G and Ts and got a little drunk. Some of the kids were necking on the sofas and others were going for walks down to the beach. The band was playing slower music now and the lights were dimmed. Carla and Four were hugging and dancing close.

"I hope you'll excuse me for a moment," he said. "I'm sorry, but I have to speak to Tina. I won't be long." She didn't much care if he ran off with Tina. When Four and Tina were engaged in their little chat, other boys swarmed around Carla, asking her to dance. The suddenness of it made her realize they had been waiting till Four left her unguarded. They're so earnest, so sincere about their manners. All this opening of doors and lighting of cigarettes. They make politeness the occasion, she thought. And yet, Four barely listens to anything I say that isn't about him.

As those thoughts were floating through her mind, she realized that two boys, one who looked like a darker version of Four and another, a big, blond, athletic-looking sort, were waiting for her to choose. She didn't know why, but she turned to the Four look-alike and stepped into his arms. The blond jock didn't look pleased. Her new partner told Carla his name, which sounded like Pug or Tug, and moved very close to her as they danced. Pug or Tug began complimenting her, saying what a great actress she was, and mentioning names of people he knew in Los Angeles. Carla leaned on him and nodded at his questions, too drunk to care what they were. He was a good dancer; that was enough.

Over his shoulder she could see Tina and Four in a deep discussion. Tina had been crying. Carla just moved a little closer to her partner and kept dancing. He was still talking, whispering in her ear now. "Why don't we?" he was saying. "Come on." She hadn't been listening to him at all, but she understood his tone. She wasn't sure of the specifics, but it seemed to add up to going for a walk on the beach. Before she could think of an excuse that wouldn't insult him, the blond jock tapped him on the shoulder and cut in. Pug or Tug didn't seem crazy about the interruption, but manners prevailed and he backed away.

Carla's new partner wasn't quite as concerned with decorum. He yanked her toward him and began pawing. "That's enough of that," she said, and pulled away and danced with the first unattached boy she found. Before they had taken a step, the spurned jock punched Carla's latest partner and knocked him down. When he grabbed Carla by the waist, she knew she was in trouble. Then Four came running onto the floor to rescue her. He yelled something at Carla's abductor that she couldn't understand, and the jock howled, just screamed. Then, in quick succession, he punched Four and a boy who happened to be standing there. That was all this bunch of raging, late adolescents needed. As if by spontaneous combustion, a brawl broke out. Fists started flying about; people were pushed into the pool. Carla didn't know if she should laugh or run for cover. She couldn't see Four in the confusion, but when she realized the band had stopped playing and were protecting their instruments, heading for safety, she knew things had turned serious.

She felt herself spinning, partly from the G and Ts, but also from the intensity of the brawl. Food and drink were being hurled back and forth, like a cafeteria food fight, with lawn furniture and bottles of S. S. Pierce gin adding to the pandemonium. The kids who had wandered down to the beach were coming back, looking unbuttoned and disheveled, to join in the fun. When she saw a few boys picking up girls and carrying them off, she decided the party was close to being dangerous. She knew her presence had served to heat it up.

Then she saw Tina eyeing her across the room. She'd knife me if she got the chance, Carla thought. She wanted Four to protect her. The jock who had started it all loomed into view. He grabbed Carla and lifted her into the air, hoisting her onto his shoulder. As he began swinging her around, she yelled in genuine fear and at the same time twisted herself about, and from her precarious position kicked him in the crotch. It was his turn to scream. He dropped Carla to the floor. Four, his jacket torn and nose bleeding, scooped her up. "We'd better leave. This is getting crazy," he said, in a voice Carla found astonishingly calm.

In front of the house their station wagon was blocked by other cars. "Gee," Four said, perplexed for the first time all evening. "I know. Come on." While the brawl continued on the other side of the house, they went back to the garage where Four commandeered a bicycle. They walked it out to the road and Carla got on the crossbar and Four pedaled toward town. Four didn't seem concerned about the station wagon or the chaos, assuming someone who was paid to do so would take care of it in the morning.

"Is that typical?" she asked.

"Nice party," he said with a grin. "We'll have to take the train. Hope that's okay." For the trip into the village of Darien, which was a few miles from Tokeneke, Carla leaned back against Four as he pedaled. She dropped her hands down onto his legs, feeling them pump.

In Darien they left the bike at a gas station near the depot. It was an hour before the next train, a milk run, the last of the night. "Let's have a drink," Four suggested. "There's a place by the station where they'll serve us."

"No, thanks," Carla said. "Bars can be hard for me."

"Yeah, I guess so," Four said, understanding what she meant. They wandered through the village, which was quiet at that hour even though it was Saturday night. Four took her to a parking lot behind the hardware store, where it was dark and certainly private. They stood amidst the packing crates and the litter, their adrenaline surging. Four pressed her up against the store wall and began kissing her. She pushed herself into him and he lifted her leg, wrapping it around his waist. As she teetered on one leg, he fumbled with her clothes. He held her there, pinned against the wall. When he entered her, with the urgency of youth, she bit his cheek, still flecked with congealed blood from the brawl. They finished in time to make the last train back to New York.

Carla had two more weeks of filming before the company left for Paris. She managed to see Four whenever she could. He would come out to the set and wait in her trailer until they could make love. Once, when his parents were out, and she had an afternoon off, he took her to the Van Osburgh apartment and into his own bedroom.

Terry Seaver called from Rio every night, but after a few days of trying to call him back, given the state of Brazilian phones, she gave up. As the New York location work was ending, Four was about to leave for New Haven. He begged her to visit him at Yale when she came back from France. "I'll take you to a game at the Bowl," he said, as if it were the greatest of all possible enticements.

She knew he was talking about a football game, but it made her think of the Hollywood Bowl, which made her think of Jack Markel. It was funny, she thought, the way one man made her think of another. She had been happy with Terry, but he was in Rio and now she was with Four. She wasn't sure how she felt about him. Maybe it was the lovemaking that kept her interested, or maybe it was just that she didn't know anyone like him. She had convinced herself it was fun to be with him, although every time he talked about his college she knew their affair would be over by the time she left New York. She imagined Yale to be a larger version of the Darien party, with a lot of noisy rich boys pawing at her. Maybe it was better than that, she thought, maybe she was being unfair. It was a famous college and it must have something besides drunks, but she didn't think she'd find out, at least not with Four.

Jack Markel was something different. She had never slept with him, never even kissed him, but still he lingered in her mind. Maybe it was his age. Forty-seven. She said it to herself a few times. While Four went on about Yale and something called "the Fence," Carla subtracted eighteen from forty-seven. Instead of putting her off, it heightened her interest. She wondered if Jack knew about Four. He'd been around the set so much that everyone on the picture knew. She thought she might call Jack just to talk to him. Maybe from Paris.

"Is it okay? When you come back from France?" Four was asking her a question. "For the Fence party. Can you?"

"Sounds like fun," she said, with no idea what he was talking about and no intention of going.

In Paris Carla and Ceil stayed at the Crillon. In the days before her work began, as they had done in New York, they explored the city together. The Baron, who kept an apartment on the Rue Poulletier in the Île Saint-Louis, was their escort. Ceil wanted to see the Eiffel Tower, the Arc de Triomphe and the Mona Lisa; they walked across the Pont Neuf and wandered up and down the Champs Élysées. Throughout it all, Carla knew something was wrong and that Four was responsible.

As the Baron suggested that he take them to lunch at a bistro in the Marais that he favored, Carla was thinking about Terry, who hadn't been on her mind at all. He always took responsibility for things like that, she thought. That's how it should be. Then she realized she didn't think of Four as a man at all, but a boy, and a spoiled one at that, with all his endless talk about Yale.

The Baron and Ceil seemed to be getting along famously. Every now and then, Carla would come out of her private thoughts and glance up at them. They were in the Baron's restaurant now; Carla only vaguely remembered getting in a car to come here. She knew she had a problem, aside from the obvious one. She couldn't let this thing consume her thoughts or she'd make a mess of the picture. As the Baron was ordering wine, something he seemed to do frequently, Carla tried to calculate the time. They'd be in Paris for two weeks. Figuring backward to the night in Darien, the first time she had been with Four, was three weeks ago. He certainly didn't take any precautions that time. Her period was a week late, the first time it had ever been more than a day late. If that was the night, she thought, then I could be as much as six weeks before I get back to Los Angeles. Was that too much time to wait? How was she going to find out? She certainly wasn't going to ask Ceil, who probably wouldn't know anyhow. She had to find a book. In English. And she had to be able to concentrate on her work. When she got home, she knew who she could turn to for help. Damn that Four, she thought.

"Have a bit of this, dear," the Baron said, filling her glass. "Haut Brion. It is to wine what you are to acting. Which is to say, very fine indeed."

"Oh, thanks," she said.

"Not hungry?" he asked.

"She never eats anything," Ceil said.

"I'm fine," Carla said, sipping the wine to prove it. "It's delicious." She couldn't stop thinking about her pregnancy. In her mind's eye she saw herself bloated and heavy. She tried to imagine having a baby, an actual infant, but no matter how hard she tried to focus on it, no picture would come into view, only an image of herself, swollen and unattractive. She tried to imagine that what was in her stomach was life, but all she could see was Four's face. Carla knew there was a complex question at issue here, but try as she might to fathom it, all that would come to her was a picture of herself, fat, splay-footed, no longer pretty, unable to work in a movie. And that, she realized, was the only thing she knew how to do. It frightened her terribly. There might be a Five in the Van Osburgh future, but Carla certainly wasn't going to have anything to do with producing it.

Carla found that having the movie to think about helped keep her mind off her condition. As she lost herself in her role, she found that the work improved. The Baron was thrilled, and kept repeating that Paris was her city. They would make many movies here. Sure, Carla thought. Me and my baby. But she smiled at the Baron and said, "I hope so. I hope you're the producer of all of them."

As they prepared to fly back to California, Ceil asked if Carla wouldn't like to spend a few days in New York. "I'm sure the Baron would say okay. You could see your friends and we could go to a show."

"No. I just want to go home."

"I thought it might be fun."

"L.A.," Carla said, refusing to discuss it further.

14.

In Los Angeles, Carla's first order of business was to call Jack Markel, who was in San Francisco at the Mark Hopkins. She told him she wanted to talk to him but not on the phone.

"If you need me, I'll be on the next plane."

"Can you?"

"Be at Chasen's at seven. We can have dinner and talk."

"Thank you," she said, finally starting to feel safe.

Chasen's had begun as little more than a roadside barbecue and chili stand and had grown into a venerable Hollywood restaurant, where movie stars and studio heads turned up every night. Jack always sat in a round booth in the front room, a small area reserved only for big names. He was sipping a ginger ale when Carla arrived. He rose to greet her, gave her a peck on the cheek, and told her she looked wonderful.

"I doubt it," she said, assuming she looked as tense as she felt.

If he had a sense of what was wrong, he didn't show it. He told the waiter to bring them the seafood-on-ice, because he thought it might amuse her to look at the mound of shaved ice with shrimp and lobster claws stuck in it. After the waiter left, he said as gently as he could, "Just tell me. It's unlikely I haven't heard it before."

"Could I do this my way?" she said, sounding irritated.

"Sorry."

"I'm pregnant."

"How long?" he asked, without betraying any emotion or seeming to give out any reaction at all.

"Six weeks, I think. Maybe less."

"Been to a doctor?"

"I need a doctor to undo it, not tell me what I already know." She knew she was being rude, that her voice was sharp, but she couldn't stop herself.

He reached across the table and took her hand. "Six weeks is okay. It can be taken care of."

"I'm not going to Tijuana or anything," she said, knowing Jack would be able to reassure her.

"No farther than Beverly Hills," he said. "Terry Seaver? If I may ask?"

"I don't want to talk about it. I just want it fixed." Then she dissolved into tears. Jack moved around the banquette and put his arms around her while she cried. He stroked her and helped her dry her eyes with a napkin. Carla knew her attraction to an older man had to do with her own father's ineptitude. Now, while Jack was acting like a father who could take care of everything and a lover who wanted to touch and hold her, she knew this was what she needed; all the amateur psychiatrists could think what they wanted. "I feel so stupid," she said, unable to stop her tears.

"Were you worried all the time you were in Paris?"

"What do you think?"

"Call me. Whenever anything's wrong, call me. I can help. With anything. I know what to do." He said it calmly, without emotion or emphasis. She knew it was true.

"There's somebody at Metro I heard about. Is that who?"

"No. Too public. The medical procedure is simple. It's discretion we need. A studio guy is for starlets and secretaries. Not for you. I'll speak to the Baron. You'll have tomorrow off. You'll be picked up at home in the morning. Don't have breakfast."

"Aren't you going to take me?" she said, sounding more like a child than she wanted to.

"Too risky. I'll have Cora Cohen pick you up. She's a friend of mine who knows how to keep things out of the papers, which in your case is a hell of a lot harder than getting them in. Your mother know?"

"No."

"Probably best that way. It's going to be okay."

"Promise?"

"Tomorrow this time, it'll be over and done. I promise."

Cora Cohen, driving a dark Cadillac sedan, arrived at the Loma Vista house the next morning. Cora was in her late twenties, a publicist, and one of the people Jack Markel felt he could count on to handle difficult situations. He didn't pay her—the public relations firm she worked for did that. Jack knew her discretion was absolute and that whatever might come up, Cora would anticipate and solve. Jack knew there was a possible complication with Cora, but his instinct told him she was the one to look after Carla, not only this morning, but in the future. If things went well, he was going to recommend that Carla hire Cora's firm to represent her; then he'd see that Carla was Cora's only account. The complication was that Cora wasn't attracted to men; or maybe it was that men weren't attracted to her. Jack knew that eventually Cora would fall in love with Carla and that could have unpredictable consequences.

When Cora arrived, Ceil knew something was unusual. This woman wasn't a studio driver. Besides, it was late for a morning call. Ceil offered Cora a cup of coffee and went to rouse her daughter. When Carla was ready to leave, Ceil asked what time she would be back, but Carla didn't answer. Ceil couldn't find the words to question her daughter further.

In the car, Cora was comforting and easygoing. "I had one of these. I have an idea what you're going through."

"This same doctor?"

"No. But I know him. Lumsford. He has a regular practice. We're going to a normal doctor's office. He's not doing this entirely for the money. He believes the laws are wrong. He knows people take dangerous risks and he doesn't like that. His nurse is his wife. There's one thing."

"There's about a hundred things."

"Right. I want to be in the room."

"Why?"

"You're a very famous young lady. I want to see with my own eyes that nobody else is in there."

"Cameras?"

"I trust him. But I always cut the cards."

"Some trust," Carla said, feeling nauseated at the thought of photographs.

Lumsford's office was on Cañon Drive in Beverly Hills, on the second floor of a medical building. Carla and Cora used a staff entrance and never saw the waiting room. Lumsford was in his mid-forties; he seemed relaxed and very direct. He asked Carla about her medical history and gave her a brief physical. He explained that what he would do was called a D and C. It made Carla think about the way Four had called a gin and tonic a G and T.

As the doctor was saying reassuring things, all Carla could see was the brawl in Darien. She heard something about a local anesthetic and then she was on the table, her bare feet in the cold stirrups. A sheet was draped over her knees and she couldn't see what was going on at the foot of the table, but she closed her eyes and tried to think about cool, iced G and Ts.

When Cora got Carla home, she made her a cup of tea, helped her undress, and put her into bed. Cora told Ceil her daughter hadn't been feeling well. Nothing serious, but it'd be best if she rested for a while. If Ceil suspected the truth, she didn't know how to talk about it or even what to ask. She decided to let Cora, who certainly seemed to know what she was doing, handle everything. Carla dozed while Cora sat in a chair near her bed and read a magazine, making sure Carla wasn't disturbed. When Jack called, Cora told him Carla would be fine, but it was best if she slept. It irritated Jack to be told he couldn't speak to Carla, but he deferred to Cora's judgment.

Because she had to go right back to the set the next day, Carla thought she would be able to push thoughts of what she and Cora called "the operation" from her mind. But at night, when Carla was alone, it came back to her. Carla had never had to wrestle with large questions of right and wrong; philosophical issues seemed by their nature abstract and impersonal. She knew she had done the best thing, the only thing, but still she couldn't help seeing a little ghost. The image would come to her of a tiny, idealized baby in a long, lacy white gown floating through the air. The child had no name, no gender and usually no face, but there it was, troubling and insistent. When she couldn't sleep, Carla would remind herself of all the reasons she could think of that made what she had done right: There was no choice, it hadn't been a baby at all, only an embryo without form or feature, the laws were unrealistic. When she had run through everything, and convinced herself anew, she would doze. A few hours later, on bad nights, she'd wake, still troubled by the little ghost hovering above her.

One night, when the little ghost wouldn't leave her, and she couldn't find comfort, Carla got up and drove into Hollywood. She took her mother's Buick, even though she wasn't used to it, because it was in the driveway. She had a sort of half-formed fantasy of picking up a sailor, some rough trade, down on the waterfront, someone who would hurt her and punish her in the way that in her secret heart she thought she deserved. But she didn't know where the waterfront was, and it was so late that not even the seamy bars of Hollywood were still open.

She drove around for a while thinking about Lewis the horse, wondering where he was and if he was still alive. She didn't think Metro kept a whole menagerie anymore, but she decided she would find out what particular pasture Lewis had been assigned to and visit him there, take him some matzoh. She knew she was thinking about Lewis in order to go back in her mind to a time when there were no little ghosts. As she drove along Franklin Avenue, toward Ivar Street, the thoughts of Lewis made her start to cry. She remembered the day she and Brandon had ridden into Stage 8 at Metro to show Lewis the set and how excited it made Bobby Dryer. The thoughts were sweet and sad. Her past, her own childhood, seemed distant and yet somehow immediate. She saw herself as little Georgine playing in a green field that she knew to be Lot 3 at Metro but was for this moment a green pasture unconnected to the movies. Then the vision began to dissolve, as if on a screen, into an image of the little ghost. They seemed to run together, Georgine, the little ghost and Lewis the horse. It made her tremble and her eyes well up. As always the floating child made no sound, gave no sign, remaining passive and serene, an object of elusive fascination. Only Carla could see into its heart and know the pain that was there. It was a glimpse into the heart of the mystery and of the generations, how she herself was to Ceil and she supposed as Ceil once must have been to Sophie, her own mother. As she was lost in shifting, treacherous thoughts of her past, the car drifted up onto the sidewalk and bounced sideways off the Four Star Army Surplus Store on Ivar Street. When the Buick's fender scraped against the bricks, she came out of her reverie in time to stop the car as it banged through Four Star's window, knocking over a display of camouflage outfits—the green-and-black pants that supposedly disguise soldiers. As what? Carla wondered, as she sat there in the Buick realizing she wasn't hurt. Green-and-black trees, maybe.

Hollywood was such a different place then. It was late at night and no one was around. Breaking the window hadn't set off an alarm and no one had come running out to see what had happened. She wasn't sure how long she sat there in Ceil's Buick, half in the Four Star window and half on the sidewalk. Probably just a few minutes. There was a pay phone on the corner of Ivar and Hollywood Boulevard. Although Carla wasn't carrying any money, she rooted around in Ceil's glove compartment and found a coin for the phone. Cora was there fifteen minutes later, reassuring Carla that as long as she was unhurt everything would be okay. They waited until a tow truck arrived and with it a man to guard the broken window. Four Star was paid for the damage, the police were never called, and nothing appeared in the papers.

Cora took Carla home and helped her into bed. On the drive back to Loma Vista, Carla had been near tears again. Now, in her own bedroom, she was no longer crying. She seemed to bounce between shivering and laughing at the dumbness of the whole thing. The swings seemed manic to Cora, and more incomprehensible than the accident itself. She gave Carla a chloral hydrate tablet and once again waited until she fell asleep.

In the days and weeks after the surgery and then the accident, Cora attached herself to Carla, becoming a secretary-companion, making herself indispensable. Carla never questioned the arrangement, never asked how Cora was paid or just what she considered her duties. She needed someone like Cora and couldn't imagine how she had done without her.

The Baron had rented a stage at the Goldwyn studio in West Hollywood to shoot the remaining interiors. Between setups of *Natural Affection* Carla and Cora would wait and talk in Carla's dressing room. At the end of the day they'd go across the street to the Formosa Cafe, a rickety Chinese restaurant and saloon that serviced the studio. They'd sit in a booth by the bar and unwind. It was to Cora, in the Formosa, that Carla unburdened herself. "I know what I did was the right thing," Carla said more emphatically than she felt, trying to convince herself.

"That's for somebody else to figure out. What counts is how you feel about it."

"I don't know what to do," Carla said.

Cora could hear the despair. She thought about it for a few

moments, well aware that Carla needed the wisest possible counsel, advice free of platitudes and received wisdom. Finally she said, "You should think about having a baby. I think that's what you want."

"You mean get married?"

"A lot of people do."

"Who? I'm too young, anyway."

"Terry Seaver calls all the time."

"What do you tell him?"

"To wait, not to press it. That it's not a good time. He always asks why you won't tell him yourself. He's very sweet."

"He's not a husband," she said, smiling at the thought of Terry.

"You don't have to decide a thing like that right now. Just if you think when there's the right person, you might. It'll make you feel better. If there's even the thought of a baby, I think it'll help."

"I don't know," she said, feeling bleak and empty.

"The next time you see that thing, like you said, the ghost or whatever it is, think of it as the future. A possibility. Not what happened already." Carla was quiet for a moment as she thought about what Cora had said. She didn't mean to, but tears came. Cora handed her one of the Formosa's scratchy red napkins and tried to comfort her. Carla wasn't sure if the tears were because of what she had done, or because she thought she might have found a friend with a clear head who could listen and help her. The idea appealed to her—a child, an adorable, loving baby of her own and a cute husband, a man to wake up with each morning. She knew it was more complicated than that, and Cora was only suggesting a possible course of action. It wasn't something she should rush into, but still the thought of having a family made her feel better.

Jack had sent her the manuscript of a novel called *Barbara Farrell*. Carla had no interest in reading it, but Jack kept after Cora to keep it in front of her. When Carla finally managed to look at it, she saw that the part was rich and diverse. She wanted the role. It was the story of a young woman's political and sexual awakening as she moved from humble beginnings to great wealth. Carla called Jack to tell him she had read it and wanted to talk. Carla and Jack had met only in restaurants and public places. Carla thought she had made it clear to Jack she was interested in him. Still, he didn't do anything about it. Maybe that's what happens with older men, she thought. Then she found herself laughing at the idea that Jack's hesitation was because of his age. "What's funny?" Cora asked, as they were sitting by the pool at the Loma Vista house, going over Carla's mail.

"Nothing. You know Jack pretty well, don't you?"

"Nobody knows him well."

"But you sort of do."

"He's secretive."

"No kidding. What's his wife like?"

"The fabulous Mona? She's all right. She plays golf, she plays tennis, she has lunch. Not bad."

"Does he fool around?"

"Not with me."

"Come on, Cora, tell me what you know."

"If you mean when is he going to make a pass, then the answer is, if it's like everything else he does, when you least expect it."

"No bad effects?" Jack asked, over lunch at the Derby. "Depression or anything?"

Carla assumed he knew about her late-night encounter with the window at the Four Star Army Surplus. "Nope. I'm fine," she said, not mentioning her little ghost. "Are you going to have corned beef hash again?"

"I suppose. Why?"

"We're going to be like this old couple where we always eat the same thing at the same time in the same place."

"I'll try not to bore you."

"Good. Me too."

In light of their last meal together, Carla expected this lunch to be more personal than it turned out to be. "I think you should rethink your representation," he said, a few minutes after they were seated.

"My agent? That's what you want to talk about?"

"Claire Berger was good for you when you were a child. But she's putting you in the wrong things."

"*Natural Affection?*"

"It'll be okay but it won't be a hit. Claire's always going to be putting you with marginal charmers like the Baron. He'll never get the distribution a studio can."

"Fire Claire? After all these years?"

"It's a business decision. It won't come as a complete surprise."

"And do what?"

"MCA. There's a young fellow there I think you could do business with. Freddy Durslag. You've met him."

"What would I say to Claire?"

"Nothing. I'll handle it for you."

"Just like that?" She was fascinated by the cool way he proposed major changes in her life and in Claire's.

"We have to extract something from MCA first. Did you read the manuscript?"

"Yeah. It's great."

"We tell Freddy you'll sign if they acquire it and give you script and director approval." Carla looked baffled, so Jack added, "MCA is in the agency business and the production business. They're the only ones of any size who can do that."

"How?"

"MCA has a waiver from the Screen Actors Guild."

"Is that one of Ronnie Reagan's stunts?"

"Yes. When he was president of the Guild, Ronnie worked MCA's street as much as the membership's. It won't last forever, but for now they can deal you in both ways."

"How do you know all this stuff?" she asked, not so much expecting an answer as acknowledging his acumen and skill about how the movie business worked.

"It's not a secret. You just have to pay attention to it. I think this book could be the big one for you."

"Could be."

"Well?"

"I've been with Claire a long time."

"You can't worry about her. She can take care of herself. Freddy's got moves Claire Berger's never seen. How're you getting on with Cora?"

"She's great. Do you pay her?"

"Here's how that works. You've hired her publicity firm. They've assigned her to you full-time. After a while, if you still like her, she'll quit and work directly for you. You'll pay her what she's getting now. It'll cost about three hundred a week with fringes."

"What are fringes?"

"About fifty dollars a week."

She smiled, impressed with his methodical approach to the mysteries of her business life. She decided to leave it at a smile, enigmatic and uncommitted.

Carla invited Freddy Durslag to come for a drink at the Loma

Vista house. She asked Cora to be there. Freddy didn't look at all like the agents she had grown up around. Carla guessed he was about thirty-five. He was wearing a dark business suit, of the sort Jack wore. Freddy was polite and well-spoken, with an easy, genuine smile. He let her know he was a married man with children, the implication being that he wouldn't make a pass or do anything unexpected. "We can't promise you things, Carla. But we are the biggest talent agency and we have a collective clout that can be effective. We've all read *Barbara Farrell*. I don't see any reason that things can't happen along the lines Jack indicated. Jack is a real fan of yours. And so am I, if I may say so."

Carla heard him, but mostly she watched him, interested in his calm manner, his obvious stability. "No pinky rings?" she asked.

"We put them in storage. I could learn to shoot my cuffs."

"No," she said, smiling.

"I'm a businessman, and I hope not a glad-hander."

"It's a big change for me. Can I think about it?"

"Of course. May I make a bit of a sales pitch? Not long."

"Sure. Pitch away."

"To go from what you've been to what you can become is treacherous. Easy to lose your public. If I may be blunt, you are in the process of letting that happen. We can change your course and see to it that your career as a child was only a prelude. You have the talent and the skill. We have the know-how. Together we can go to unparalleled heights."

When they were alone, Cora asked, "So what do you think?"

"I don't know. He seems like such a grown-up. Am I the only one who worries about Claire?"

"Because of you, Claire has a going business. You think you owe her so much that you should let your career suffer?"

Since that question didn't require an answer, Carla just said what was really on her mind. "Jack's sort of reorganizing my life. I mean, first you, now a new agent. What next?"

"I think Jack's next," Cora said. "This is a power broker's idea of foreplay."

Carla laughed, but it made her realize that the likeliest way to give Jack a push was to accept his recommendation of Freddy Durslag.

Carla was at home, reading scripts, which was what she always did when she couldn't sleep. As she was finally starting to doze,

Jack called from Las Vegas and asked if she wouldn't like to join him. "It's a lot of fun here," he said. "The dice are hot."

"Okay. How long are you there for?"

"Come. We'll decide."

"When?"

"Now. Come now."

"This minute?" she asked, knowing that's what he meant, but still finding it hard to believe.

"Yeah. That's what I mean."

"I can't do that."

"Sure you can. You can do whatever you want."

Carla wasn't sure what she should tell her mother, who was already asleep. She didn't want to frighten Ceil by disappearing, but she also didn't want to explain the situation. Being old enough to embark on this adventure but young enough to worry about her mother's reaction amused Carla for a moment, but didn't stop her. She called Cora and told her what she planned to do. "I'm going to the airport. There's a plane waiting."

"I'll take you out there," Cora said. "Did you tell Ceil?"

"She's already asleep."

"Don't wake her. I'll think of something to tell her."

Without so much as a toothbrush, still wearing the tight pedal pushers, white sweater and espadrilles she had worn all evening, Carla boarded what turned out to be the Warner Bros. jet for the forty-minute flight to Las Vegas.

As she flew over the San Gabriel Mountains she found herself thinking about her lack of luggage. It had amused her to accept the invitation without a thought and to leave with no preparations. As she flew, she realized what she was doing was saying to Jack, "I'm in your hands completely. You take charge of everything. I'll do as you say." Those thoughts, as much as this spur-of-the-moment adventure, thrilled her, made her shiver with anticipation.

At the airport, a car was waiting to take her to the Thunderbird Hotel. The Las Vegas strip was about ten years old then, and, although it was a booming place, there was less of it. There were a dozen hotels growing out of the sand, each with a huge neon sign straining to be gaudier and brighter than the next. Instead of driving up to the hotel's front entrance, the car drove around to the back and Carla was let in through what seemed to be a private door. It reminded her of the way she got into Dr. Lumsford's Beverly Hills office. With Jack, there's always a private way, she thought.

She was ushered into a penthouse elevator by a hotel flunky. For all Carla knew he might even have been the owner. Mr. Thunderbird. He said nothing. He admitted her into a suite at the end of the corridor on the top floor. When she turned around, he was gone. "Jack?" she called, but no one answered. She wandered about, exploring, expecting to find Jack Markel. In the style the world would come to know as high Vegas, the suite was larger than any useful purpose would require. She was particularly amused by a dining room that seemed to evoke an English manor house. The bedroom featured a red leather headboard built into the wall. The bed itself was at least four times the size of any Carla had ever seen. She found herself giggling at the gilt-edged mirrors on the walls and even the ceiling.

When the doorbell rang she called out, "Jack? Are you there?" Instead of Markel, a middle-aged woman carrying several dresses entered. "I brought some cocktail dresses for you to look at, dear," she said, as if it were a routine matter. "I think I've got your size."

"Sure," Carla said, unconsciously touching her pedal pushers. Carla pointed to an ice blue satin number with a sheath skirt that she thought might fit her. The woman, adept as any studio dresser, helped Carla try it on. Within minutes, the woman was pinning the hem, then stitching it quickly. She had a pair of shoes that matched the dress. "Makeup's in the powder room," the woman said. "Want some help?"

"No makeup," Carla said, with the confidence of youth. "This dress is plenty." She looked at herself in a mirror, adjusting the scooped neckline, thinking, This is the sort of dress Audrey Hepburn would wear.

"Now what?" she asked.

"I'll take you down to the casino if you're ready."

In the elevator, Carla tried to get comfortable in her dress. She tugged on it, trying to get it to hang more comfortably over her hips. It doesn't matter how elegant this *shmata* is, she thought, slipping into her father's Yiddish, I feel like a hooker. The thought made her smile.

Carla had never been in a casino before. She had a rough idea of what to expect, and when she saw it was true that there were no clocks and no windows, she felt reassured, as if the casino knew its role. It was a vast, shadowy room with the gambling tables in pools of light. At a glance, Carla could see that the people were trying very hard to have a good time, in an effort to convince themselves and those around them that they were gamblers, high rollers. It was her audience. She wasn't sure how she felt about walking among them.

Jack was at the craps table with chips of different colors in front of him. Carla could see he was concentrating on the dice. She remembered that Cora had once told her that Jack's only vice, if that's what it was, was gambling. All Carla knew about gambling came from Milton's stories. She pushed thoughts of her father from her mind and concentrated on watching Jack, unobserved. She could see that unlike the other gamblers, Jack played without histrionics—no blowing on the dice, no murmuring little prayers. His chips were in neat stacks; he placed his bet and threw the dice. He seemed to win more often than not, but his expression was the same either way. As Carla was enjoying watching him, she realized that something unusual was going on. Very few people were staring at her. Oh, the occasional gambler's woman or dealer looked up at her, noting that she had walked into the room, but mostly these people were like Jack in that the only thing that interested them was the action. A less secure actress might have been unnerved.

When he saw her, he handed off the dice and walked toward her, for the moment ignoring his stack of chips. He kissed her lightly on the cheek and said, "Hello, my dear," as if this were a studio commissary and they had run into each other as they were waiting for a table. "Get here all right?"

"I guess so. Here I am."

"Ever play roulette? Classier game for a classy dame."

"Show me how," she said, ready for whatever might come.

He took her to a roulette table in a private room. Jack nodded to the croupier and said, "We'll play for a while if we get hot. If we don't, to hell with it." Before Carla could answer, Jack began putting his chips down on the various numbers and watched while the wheel turned. After she had watched Jack a few times, she said, "Let me try."

"My pleasure," he answered, handing her a stack of chips.

Carla put one down, then another and another. She lost a few before she won. When her number came up, Carla laughed and collected a stack of chips. "Do you know what you just won?" he asked, knowing she didn't.

"Nope."

"You put twenty dollars down at thirty-six to one. You're

seven hundred dollars richer than you were a few minutes ago."

"Then it's good enough to quit," she said, losing interest in roulette.

"Marlene's at the Sands," he said. "Ever seen her show?"

"No," she answered, unsure who Marlene was, but certain if she needed to know, Jack would tell her.

At the Sands, there was a crowd milling around the entrance to the main room, maybe a hundred people, all dressed in their fancy, flashy clothes, waiting to get in, despite the "Performance Sold Out" sign. This group, less intent on gambling, noticed Carla as she and Jack approached. The buzz of "Look . . . Carla . . . Carla Tate . . ." began, and then she heard the insistent click-click-click of cameras as people snapped her picture.

The big, simian-looking guy at the door raised his hand when he saw Jack. Two of his assistants, men even larger than their boss, parted a way through the crowd for Jack and Carla. They were shown to a large table near the stage where several couples, apparently friends of Jack's, were already seated. Carla nodded to them all as Jack said their names.

One of the women at the table—Carla never got any of their names straight—told Carla how much she admired her. Carla guessed the woman was about thirty-five, rich-looking, but not particularly attractive. The thing that caught Carla's eye was her dress. It was a rose-colored version of the one Carla was wearing. As the woman gushed, Carla was thinking that every woman in here must have arrived as she had—in pedal pushers and sweater—and then had been given one of these dresses.

When Dietrich made her entrance, the crowd at the Sands stood to applaud her. Dietrich was wearing one of her beaded see-through gowns. The backlighting showed her long trim figure to advantage. She thanked everyone in her thick accent, then as her eyes scanned the ringside tables, she seemed to stop at Carla, pleased to see her there. Carla thought she nodded at her before she began to sing. Jack saw it too, leaned toward her, and whispered, "I think you've got a German admirer."

When Dietrich began to sing, it was clear that she was singing to Carla. She glanced at the rest of the audience, but her eyes returned to the table down front and Carla Tate as she began to sing in her dark, husky voice:

> Falleeeg een luff a-gane
> Never vanted to

Vot am I to do?
Can't help eet . . .

In their suite, after midnight, Jack finally kissed her. It was more of a relief than anything else. Carla was a little drunk, so she didn't fully formulate her thoughts, but at least, she decided, she was attractive to him, she wasn't doing anything wrong. Usually with men, Carla let them kiss her. She made them work at it to earn the privilege. It tended to make them ardent and hopeful that they were doing it well enough that she would allow them to continue. She never planned it that way, but her beauty and her position made it so. Jack, who always arranged things to his advantage, had turned that around completely. She was the uneasy one, hoping to please. Instead of making her unhappy, she found it stimulating and she wanted to work at it, to make him want her.

After the first kiss, she kissed him back and waited for the feel of his hands running up and down the cool satin of her dress. She could feel her slightly contrived emotion becoming more real. Jack seemed to sense it too and he stopped—pulled back from her and held her head in his hands. She was flushed, ready to follow his lead, to do whatever he wanted. "Want some champagne?" he asked. When he went to the bar to open the bottle, she undid the zipper of her dress. She watched his back and saw him tense slightly when he heard the zipper opening, but he didn't turn around. She stepped out of her clothes and, wearing only her underwear and the blue high-heeled shoes, walked to him, pressed herself against his back, and whispered that she didn't want any champagne just now.

He turned to her, smiled, and said, "Finish what you started." She locked her eyes to his, undid her bra, stepped out of her underpants, and then, wearing only the ice blue pumps, began kissing him, whispering his name. He lifted her in his arms and carried her into the bedroom.

The mirrors on the walls and ceiling reflected the two of them into infinity; the idea of it, of so many Jacks and Carlas, made her feel light-headed. They stood like that in the middle of the room, Carla naked in Jack's arms; he turned in a small circle until their reflected images began to blur. She pushed her hands inside his shirt and ran her fingers through the thick black hair on his chest. Without meaning to, she tore at his shirt, popping the buttons and pushing his jacket back off his shoulders. He put her down on the bed and dropped his jacket to the floor.

Carla could feel herself trembling as she watched him. She reached out and put her hands on his legs, pulling him to her. She opened his pants and dug her hands inside, finding him hard and erect. She lay back, legs apart, saying, "Come on . . . please . . . now . . ." But instead of joining her he brought her upright again, on the edge of the bed, and pushed himself into her mouth. She was so glad to have him ask for something, to want her in any way, that she took him as fully as she could. Her enthusiasm made him ecstatic and he clutched her head, pulling back and running his hands through her hair. Then he shoved himself back into her mouth again, suddenly, brutally, until she almost gagged. Instead of pulling away, she tried to encircle him with her tongue, wanting to consume him completely.

When he was breathing hard it made her feel better and that allowed her to move her mouth away and try to pull him onto the bed with her.

"Now what?" he asked, teasing and watching her.

"Come on, Jack. Please," she said, impatiently.

"Say it."

"Fuck me. I want you to fuck me. Do it," she said, ashamed of the word, but unable to think of another. Still, he said nothing, but finally got on the bed with her. He put his hands on her waist and turned her over on her stomach. He pushed her face into the pillows and raised her rump high in the air. When he entered her, she felt an abiding sense of pleasure and triumph. His hand was on the back of her neck, keeping her head down, buried in the pillows, as he pushed into her, again and again until she could feel herself starting to float, head spinning as the waves of her orgasm began. When he heard her crying out his name, he pulled himself out suddenly and spread her cheeks with his hand and before she realized what he was doing, he was forcing himself inside her again, this time differently. It brought a flash of pain and her pleasure dissolved into fear that he might rip her apart. She tried to say no, to wriggle away, but he held her there, by the back of the neck, as he pushed in deeper. Her thoughts were jumbled but she gave herself over to it; at that moment she realized he was doing this to dominate her as much as out of lust or desire. Instead of resisting it, she was thrilled and wanted him to hurt her like that and never stop. It was a part of him she had never guessed existed. Hurting her was a part of his pleasure and, to her amazement, her pleasure too. Those thoughts—confusing and difficult, mixed with the pure physical sensation of something she had never experienced before, and in fact had hardly ever thought of—eroticized her all the more. When he stopped for a moment, she wriggled away and rolled onto her back and pulled him to her, grabbing him, hard, squeezing him, wanting to hurt him back, then jamming him inside her, putting her heel on his shoulder, making him thrust again. She ran her fingers over his back, digging her nails into his flesh, scratching him until she drew blood and hurt him so much that he pulled out, about to slap her. Before he could, she grabbed his hand, pushed him off her, and got atop him, enveloping him. As she pushed herself down onto him like that she saw him smiling, a superior air on his face. She began to slap his face, hitting him with her open palm each time she plunged down on him, making red welts on his jaw. When she felt Jack coming, she lost control of herself; felt her orgasm roll through her, making her shudder until she felt light and detached from herself and from him. She fell down onto his stomach, weeping, laughing, and finally sleeping.

A few days later, while Carla was at home waiting for Cora to arrive so they could do the mail and read scripts together, she heard a car horn in the driveway. It was Cora, in a new white Thunderbird. "When did you get that?" Carla asked.

"I didn't," Cora said. "You did. It's from Jack."

Carla began to giggle as she walked around her new car, amused at the idea that this was the way Jack would memorialize their first time together. "It's fabulous," she said, and went to call Jack to thank him. She kept that sleek little car for years, almost as attached to it as she was to Jack. The only one who didn't like it was Milton. He couldn't understand why she didn't get it at Soderberg, where he could have gotten her a discount.

Because Jack and MCA wanted *Barbara Farrell* to happen, it did. The picture had a good possibility of success no matter who produced or starred in it, but the person who benefited the most was Carla; that was what Jack had intended. "Movies succeed because of their merits," he told her. "But they get made because of someone's ability to maneuver." Carla didn't doubt him and she never forgot it.

When Carla wasn't shooting, and her time was her own, she saw Jack, usually on his terms. He didn't call at the last minute and tell her to get on a plane again, but he did say when they could have time together. Jack lived at home with his family in Bel Air, but he kept a bungalow at the Beverly Hills Hotel, which he used as an office and now as a trysting place with Carla. The bungalows, the most expensive suites at the hotel, were little cottages that afforded privacy. You could come and go from a bungalow without ever going through the lobby.

Sometimes Carla just parked the Thunderbird on Crescent Drive and walked across the hotel's lawn. Because any number of people might recognize the car, Cora thought it unwise to display it so prominently. Since Cora usually made the arrangements anyway, she tried to drive Carla to the hotel herself. She would stop on the north end of Crescent, far enough from the main part of the hotel so that Carla could get out unobserved and close enough to the bungalow that she could be inside in seconds. Sometimes Cora would come back to pick her up in an hour or two; other times she'd just sit out in the car until Carla reappeared.

Carla rarely asked about money, since from before she could count it, there was always enough, but she was curious about the price of a bungalow at the Beverly Hills Hotel, which even she knew cost a fortune if taken by the year. Howard Hughes was famous for keeping two or three, but Carla knew that even Jack didn't have as much money as Hughes. Jack never gave her a straight answer about it, usually telling her not to worry about money—such concerns were beneath her. As they were driving to the hotel one afternoon, Cora explained it. "Jack doesn't pay a penny for the place. He picks up his room service bills and that sort of thing, but I'd bet anything the hotel comps him on the rent or at least gives him such a big discount that it's practically a gift."

"Why?" Carla asked, fascinated.

"He's Jack. It's like a retainer. The hotel's like the studios or anything else you can think of. They're not exactly sure what they're going to need him for or when—but they'll need him. Maybe a labor problem, maybe getting business from the studios. If you're a big deal in Hollywood the way that hotel is, eventually you're going to need Jack."

"I'm not sure I get it, exactly."

"Think of it this way," Cora said. "You're a big deal in Hollywood. Has he helped you?"

"Sure."

"He can be a good friend and a bad enemy. That hotel's glad to let him use the place."

Some days Carla and Jack would spend the afternoon in the bungalow making love. Other times they would sit and hold hands and just talk. At first Carla thought, This is because of his age. Younger guys just want to screw. But she came to see this was a ridiculous oversimplification. Jack's libido was active enough. It was, she eventually realized, that he really wanted to talk to her. Carla wasn't sure why—when they were together, it was Jack who said interesting things, rarely Carla. He liked to instruct her about the ways of the business, but that didn't explain the intensity he felt for her. She came to realize that having a student of sorts was important to Jack, but really it was simpler—her beauty enchanted him, bewitched him even, certainly gave him pleasure and drew him to her. Since for as long as she could remember, men had been attracted to her for just that reason, she accepted it as her due. As the mixture of his lust and his need to instruct her grew, their love deepened. But it was always Jack who dominated; Carla received his attentions and was moved to love by his growing need to be with her. He wanted to know how she was, what she was doing, and even about her past. He asked her questions about the Dr. George movies. Well, not exactly about the movies, but about the deals and how they had come to pass. He was interested in Milton and tried to explain to Carla that her father just wasn't very good at operating in the world. "There shouldn't be any shame in that," Jack told her. "But we both know there is. Nothing sadder than a guy who wants to be a *gonif* and can't quite cut it." No one had ever explained her father to her so succinctly. It moved her, made her feel closer than ever to Jack. He often told her she was beautiful but rarely said he loved her. She knew he did, she could see it and feel it. She knew she loved him, yet because they didn't say it, there was a barrier between them that Carla didn't know how to cross.

Jack wanted the world to know about their business connection, that he was her adviser and mentor. He knew that would make the studios think twice before they tried to cut corners in their dealings with her. He was frank and not boastful about it. "If they know I'm behind you, they'll be wary. That's just what we want." Carla also understood that if they were seen in public, it would justify some of their private time together.

They often had lunch in the Brown Derby or Lucey's across from Paramount, where they talked about agents, producers and deals. Once, when they were at the Villa Capri on Yucca Street, supposedly a place where Mafiosi hung out and where

James Dean used to come in the evenings, Jack was telling her about the ins and outs of one deal or another. Carla kept a serious, earnest look on her face, while under the table she opened his fly and fondled him. "Tell me again," she said, as Jack was trying to appear calm. "Do the profits come off the net or the gross?" Those were favorite terms of his. They both knew Carla could never remember the difference between them. She continued to ask disingenuous questions while her hand was in his pants, hidden from the room by the long white tablecloth that reached to the floor. Jack's eyes bulged as she asked, "Does break-even mean from all the box-office money, or just what the studio keeps?"

"I can't seem to remember just at the moment," he said, managing to keep his voice reasonably steady despite the fact that he was coming. He mumbled something about having to ask a specialist for the answer to that one. It was all Jack could do not to shout out. She cleaned him up with a linen napkin and then pulled his zipper shut.

Carla would have been happy to continue like that—as mistress to a man who had no intention of giving up his wife and who gave her professional counsel and passion as a form of love. She had come to depend on him. It was Jack, one sunny afternoon at the bungalow while they were sitting on the sofa, who told her she ought to get married.

"You proposing?"

"Not to me. Getting married would wreck what we've got."

"What does that mean?" she said, a bit of irritation creeping into her voice.

"We have secrecy and that's what we both want. I want you to have children. It's what you want. If you don't lead a normal life, you'll resent me. Then I'll really lose you."

"Is everything strategy? Don't you ever just do something?"

"Yeah, everything's strategy. If I only teach you one thing, that's what it should be."

"So I marry Mr. Husband, then maybe I won't want you around anymore."

"You'll want me." He said it with such certainty that Carla knew he was right. She also knew it came from his vantage point of middle age. It still annoyed her.

"You think you know. But you'll have to see what happens," she said, picking up a fork from their lunch plates and jabbing at his arm.

He grabbed her wrist and squeezed it till the fork fell. "I'll only be in trouble if you marry somebody my age. I won't let that happen."

"Then that's what I'll do. Only not as old as you. Somebody only twice my age."

"You're mad now, but when you think about it, you'll know I'm right. I want to be part of your life, but I don't want to hold it up. You want to have children. You told me that yourself. That's not going to happen with me. And in the end you'll blame me if you don't."

"Jack, you're so full of shit. This is some trick. I don't even know what, but it's a stunt."

"I'll never let you go," he said as patiently as he could. "But if you don't find a regular life because of me, you'll resent me. You know that's true. Pick one of the actors who chase after you. Surprise him. Then when you have a kid or two, do whatever you want with him."

"Real romantic, aren't you?"

"Carla, I'm the most realistic man you're ever going to meet. That's where real romance comes from. Not from moonbeams in your hair. People who marry for what they think are romantic reasons are usually disappointed. Marriage for somebody like you is an economic decision and a cultural one. You're never going to be somebody's little wifey at home baking bread. You're too famous, too rich and too much of a bitch."

"How do you know I want kids?"

"Hey. Remember me? I'm the guy who made the arrangements with Lumsford. I know what you went through."

"Cora told you what I said, didn't she?"

"Cora says nothing. I have eyes. Why shouldn't you? It's normal enough." He said it with finality. She knew it was silly to deny it. "If you find one you like, keep him around. If you change your mind when he's done his job, I'll help you dump him."

"You are one cold son of a bitch."

"Probably. But not with you. You make me feel alive."

"Do you sleep with your wife? The fabulous Mona?"

"Yes."

"How often?"

"We've been married twenty-two years. The fires bank a little bit at that point."

"You're lying."

"I lie in my business and sometimes in my personal life. Never about this. You know what kind of passion I have for you. And

I know what you feel for me. I'm making a gamble to protect that, so it never goes away."

As she began to cry, he put his arms around her and kissed her face and her eyes, kissing her tears, trying to comfort her. Maybe because she knew that what he said was true and it frightened her, or maybe because she thought she might lose him, or maybe just because the libido is a mysterious thing, she responded to his kisses. She pushed him down on the sofa, on his back, while she unbuttoned her skirt. When she was sitting on his belly, wearing only her blouse, she put her hands on his throat and threatened to choke him. "*Now* what are you going to do?" she asked. "What's your strategy, General?" She squeezed his throat, starting to hurt him. She moved forward, feeling the hair on his stomach and chest rub on her legs, until her knees were locked on the sides of his face. She held his arms still and tight by his side. When his tongue was inside her she eased the pressure on his face and arms. But instead of stopping, he reached behind her and pulled her even closer to him, digging his tongue deeper, biting her until she thought she would bleed. When she had come and come again, she pulled back from him with a contented sigh. Then she punched him in the stomach, hard, and said, "But you're still a cold son of a bitch."

That night when she was at home, after she had thought about everything Jack had said, she called Terry Seaver and asked him how he was, as if there were nothing unusual in her calling him. It astonished him and he asked if he could come over. Two days later, they eloped. He wanted to go to Las Vegas but Carla didn't care to do that. Cora made the arrangements for them to get married in Santa Barbara. They drove up in the white Thunderbird.

After Carla called each of her parents, Cora informed the press, and the marriage was reported all over the world. Carla and Terry spent their honeymoon at the San Ysidro Ranch. Then she moved him into her house on Loma Vista Drive.

15.

Carla liked marriage more than she had expected. Terry was nothing if not attentive. She always had an attractive man around as an escort, for meals or talk. The real talking she did about questions of marriage was with Cora, who, if she wasn't exactly expert in these matters, knew more than Carla did. And Carla could trust her. Terry was certainly trustworthy, but he wasn't as wise as Cora or as experienced in the world. And he was a man and, although men had their uses and value, they couldn't be compared to women in questions of friendship.

Terry's career benefited from his marriage. Carla had asked Jack to see that MCA signed her husband and got him work. If that made him Mr. Carla Tate, he was able to make his peace with it. MCA gave him regular work on television. The rest of the time, he reminded himself that his wife loved him. He took pleasure in her success, which was far greater than his own. He knew people gossiped, but Terry delivered the goods. He believed until that stopped, the jobs would be there, no matter who his wife was. It might even have been true.

Carla and Terry tried for a baby from the start of their marriage. Before they were married their lovemaking had been passionate, explosive and constant. Carla was still enthusiastic and she had always found Terry attractive. But now, probably because she continued to see Jack, things were calmer at home. If Terry missed the athletic enthusiasm of their earlier times together, he too wanted a child and was happy to go with her to doctors who recommended calendar-watching, temperature-taking, and certain unimaginative positions. Since Carla had once gotten pregnant more easily than she had wanted, she assumed it was only a matter of time. But each month her period would come and go.

She talked it over with Cora, who knew exactly what questions to ask. "Before you were married, did you take precautions?"

"Yeah, of course. I wasn't going to go through that again."

"But that was your idea. Was it ever his idea?"

"I guess. It was romantic. I wasn't keeping score."

"Think about it, Carla," she said, trying not to sound as exasperated as she felt. "If it was his idea, that means he was worried you'd get pregnant. In other words, he assumed he could make a baby. We know you can."

"I see," Carla said, feeling a terrible sadness coming over her. "What should I do?"

"Be very careful with Jack. If you get pregnant, Terry'll assume it's his. Then all hell'll break loose when the kid turns out like a killer bulldog movie business *macher* instead of an ex-football player from St. Louis. And have a doctor test you both. Like you don't have a clue."

When they found out the truth, Terry was devastated. He insisted on going to a second doctor and then a third. He began looking into experimental treatments. Nothing worked. Years later, when she thought about it, Carla was proud of the way she had reacted. She was sympathetic and generous to her husband, doing all she could to comfort and encourage him. They were both young enough to believe they could make their peace with it. Carla tried to convince herself that there were all sorts of medical progress being made, and it was just a matter of time before a solution would be found. If it was hard on her, it was worse for Terry. His sexuality was his center. Before his marriage, he had pursued and caught a string of beautiful actresses. He was an ardent and expressive lover and now his self-esteem was damaged. It put a damper on his libido.

. . .

Maybe it was her marriage, or maybe it was her affair with Jack, but in *Barbara Farrell*, her first fully realized adult role, Carla was able to play complex adult emotions before she ever experienced them. Unlike in her childhood performances, where she seemed to be playing Ceil's emotions when her own weren't there, as Barbara she was playing things that neither she nor Ceil had ever experienced. It had to have been the result of what she felt about Jack; the aspect of art that defies rational understanding. In a scene at the beginning of the picture, Carla, as Barbara, a young girl from the wrong side of the tracks, goes to a pool hall to find her brother. Her brother isn't there, but she meets a tough, troubled boy, played by John Mauldin, who becomes her lover. There's a shot of Carla standing under a hanging light, through the smoky haze of the pool hall, when Mauldin first sees her. He's smitten by that vision of her, and so was the rest of the country. Carla looked startlingly alive and sexual. Her eyes had a mixture of innocence and knowledge that was indelible. The image of Carla in that smoky light was the precise beginning of her adult stardom. It became an icon of the time, as famous in the late fifties as the shot of Rita Hayworth in a nightgown had been in the forties. It was before movie-star posters were common, but the picture ran in magazines, and boys all over the country clipped it and kept it on their bedroom walls and inside their locker doors. It was the most famous still photo ever made of her. It was shot just after her nineteenth birthday.

The critics liked the movie, but mostly they liked Carla. She knew her work had been good, but she also knew her triumph was possible because she had a dense, complex role to play. She had risen to the occasion. Jack told Freddy Durslag just what to do. "Get her nominated," he said. "Then get her a gold friend."

In those days Academy Award nominations in the major categories were voted on by all the guilds—the actors, writers and directors—fifteen thousand people. The Oscar voting itself was done only by Academy members—fewer than two thousand. A nomination was a matter of a good, popular performance and a lot of publicity. Carla's was a likely bet, but there was a problem.

The studio had another possibility for best actress. Letitia Allen, who had starred with Anthony Delano in *The Outback*, was the competition. Letitia was also represented by MCA and appeared in their pictures. Her performance was a fine one, as eligible and as likely as Carla's. Jack and Tom Sullivan, Letitia's lawyer, met for lunch at the Vine Street Brown Derby, where Jack told Tom that this just wasn't Letitia's year to be best actress.

"Why not?" he asked, not needing an answer. Tom Sullivan had been expecting this conversation. He recognized Jack's power, but he didn't get to be a lawyer to movie stars by backing down easily. Tom was only thirty-five and although he knew his first responsibility was to his client, he also recognized a chance to audition for Jack Markel. If he handled himself well, fought hard but knew when to compromise, he would be able to call on Jack in the future, which for an ambitious young lawyer was certainly as valuable as Letitia's business.

They sat in Jack's regular booth, beneath the caricature of Carla as Georgine. Jack made a point of introducing Tom to all the people who stopped to say hello. "I hope you know Tom Sullivan," he would say, managing to suggest that Tom was his protégé. Jack knew if he gave away enough, he could win. Since what he had to give belonged to MCA and the winner would be Carla, Jack was ready to deal. He suggested that if Letitia didn't make a serious run for the nomination, her contract would be renewed and her salary bumped up to whatever reasonable figure Tom might suggest.

"Take a dive, in other words."

"That kind of talk isn't productive."

"That's exactly what Letitia will say. I know her. What if she gets nominated anyway? It's possible, you know. Then God knows what happens to the MCA vote—they could split it and somebody else could win," Tom said, keeping his voice calm and steady, subtly imitating Markel's style, suggesting admiration for the older man. "Maybe there's a better way out."

"What do you propose?" Jack asked.

"I think Letitia would be a shoo-in as best supporting actress."

"Interesting idea," Jack said, his respect for Tom Sullivan growing. He knew they had a deal; now he wanted to see how well Sullivan had thought this out. "She was the lead," Jack said.

"I thought Tony Delano was the lead. He got the billing. He's an established star," Tom said. "Not even her mother would suggest Letitia has Tony Delano's kind of weight."

"The question is, can that be sold to the Academy?"

"If the studio gets behind a best supporting campaign for

Letitia with the same vigor I know they'll give to Carla—then everybody can win."

"What will your client say?" Jack asked, not because he wanted an answer, but to hear how Sullivan would respond to one of the key issues in this discussion.

"We both know," Tom said, a tiny smile on his face, "no lawyer can say with certainty what a client will do, but I think if I present it to her with the news of her new contract and point out she can win this Oscar and not the other, she'll play."

Jack nodded, thinking, This guy has his head screwed on right. "Shall we order?" Jack said. "I usually have the hash."

"I want to be clear on one thing," Tom said, not quite ready to move on to food. "Once nominated, Letitia will require a campaign of the same size, duration and cost as Carla's."

"I'm sure MCA will go along with that."

"Good. The hash sounds fine."

For weeks MCA bought full-page ads in *Variety* and the *Hollywood Reporter*, showing Carla as a child in her Georgine costume and as Barbara Farrell. Each day the copy line on the ad would change—quote after quote from reviews, and when those ran out, from distinguished writers and producers, all saying Carla Tate ought to be nominated for an Oscar. It was a clear signal that the company line was to vote for Carla Tate. Letitia's ads, not quite as imaginatively done, appeared every day as well. There was grumbling from the other likely candidates for best supporting actress, but at the time the ploy was new and the complaints were seen as sour grapes. In the end, Letitia loved seeing her name and face in the trade papers every day for weeks. It made her think the studio really cared about her.

Once she was nominated, Jack knew, Carla's performance could win as long as MCA did its job, which amounted to arranging a series of private screenings so that each Academy member could see the picture. The Academy voters probably couldn't be bribed, but they could be influenced and persuaded in an aboveboard way. Most of them were rich anyway, so if it smelled at all corrupt, they'd run the other way. An MCA executive invited each member to a screening and then made a low-keyed pitch for Carla's candidacy. When it was possible, the call was made by someone in a position to help the voter. The phone call was followed up with a selection of favorable reviews, sent by messenger. There was nothing particularly imaginative about it, but no other candidate in any category was pushed quite as hard.

When Jack told Carla about the campaign he compared it to running a candidate for Congress. "You figure out who the voters are, and you persuade them. That's it." Because Jack didn't treat it as a big deal, Carla didn't either. She never quite understood the expensive, time-consuming lengths to which MCA was going in the campaign to get her an Academy Award.

On Oscar night, Carla was escorted by her husband, her mother and Cora to the Pantages Theater, a cavernous, wildly ornate movie house on Hollywood Boulevard. As they stepped out of the MCA limousine, Terry said, "You're going to win. I can feel it."

Before Carla could answer, the fans in the bleachers next to the theater began shouting her name. She waved as the reporters gathered at the curb to ask the questions reporters at the Academy Awards always ask: "How do you feel?" "Are you excited?" Carla recognized they were playing their part in the comedy, the elements of which were only slightly less rigid than the rules of the well-made play. She answered each question as if it had never been posed before. "Oh, yes. I have butterflies in my stomach."

"You think you'll win?"

"That would be wonderful, but just to be nominated is a thrill. No matter what happens, I feel like I won."

Across the street from the Pantages, the Leeper School had put up a placard with pictures of Carla—as a six-year-old, labeled Karen Teitel, and the pool-hall shot of Barbara Farrell, unnecessarily identified as Carla Tate. In prominent letters, it said, "We Trained Her, MGM Named Her."

The Oscar show was the country's first look at Carla as a sophisticate. The wardrobe department at the studio decided not to compete directly with the plunging necklines and ballooning mammaries so much in vogue at the time, or the billowing gowns worn by older, more established figures of glamour.

Carla's dress was a Chinese gown—a red silk version of the traditional cheongsam, with a slit up the leg and a high collar. Her hair, with a gardenia in it, was fashioned in an elegant chignon. Some of the press was critical, calling the gown more appropriate for a Chinese New Year party, but everyone talked about it. It made her stand apart, hovering between young girl and adult.

In those days the important nominees also served as the presenters. That way the country got a look at them whether they won or not. The Academy hadn't yet hit on the idea of two presenters for each category, so the star presenters trotted out alone to give someone else an Oscar and maybe, if they were lucky, a second time to collect one. Before the show, Carla was escorted backstage to wait in the wings with Letitia Allen. Carla knew Letitia, who was in her early thirties, from the studio. If Letitia felt jealous or angry at Carla, it didn't show. "Are you scared?" Letitia asked. "I sure am."

"I'm scared I won't pronounce the name right. I've been practicing all day," Carla said.

"Not of being a presenter," Letitia said, exasperated at Carla's cool.

This was the era of "The envelope, please," because after the presenters had been introduced, had bantered for a moment with the host, they would ask the representative from Price Waterhouse, the accountants who tabulated the votes and guarded the envelopes, to hand it over. The presenter opened it and read the winner's name. That was it. No recap of the nominees; a minimum of manufactured drama. Carla's presentation came early in the evening. When Bob Hope, who was the host, brought her out to present the award for black-and-white cinematography, he said, "And here she is, America's favorite daughter, Carla Tate. Right here, ladies and gentlemen, Carla Tate."

The orchestra played entrance music for each presenter—usually a song associated with them. There wasn't an obvious choice for Carla, so the orchestra came up with "Farmer in the Dell," as if she were still eleven. Carla stepped out of the wings, entering to that ill-chosen music. It was patronizing, and Jack Markel, who was sitting with his wife and one of the officers of MCA, was not pleased.

When Hope saw the Chinese outfit, he cracked, "Did we get you out of bed, dear?" It was an ad-lib and it threw Carla a little. She glanced over at him with a cool look on her face that seemed to say, You and I will never have anything to do with beds. It was subtle, but the meaning—which was don't be smart with me—was unmistakable. Since absolutely nothing ever fazed Bob Hope, he just laughed and said, "It's been exciting watching you grow up. And you sure have!" That was the line they had rehearsed, so Carla smiled and said, "The envelope, please."

The winner for best black-and-white cinematography, one Dragoljub Djekovich, a name Carla pronounced perfectly, bounded up to the stage, bowed to Carla, and proceeded to mangle his remarks. His accent was so thick Carla started to laugh and that gave the audience permission to laugh, too. Mr. Djekovich was so intent on thanking the technicians at Eastman Kodak and the lab, he didn't notice.

When the show had cut to a commercial, Jack used the break to go backstage. He grabbed the producer of the show by the collar—actually pushed him against a wall—and said, "She wins best actress, don't play that music."

"Who the hell are you?" the terrified producer asked.

"Play that kid crap again and you'll find out." Jack shoved his card in the producer's pocket, assuming the gentleman would recognize his name, if not his face.

Carla's seat, since she was a nominee, was near the front, on the aisle. Terry was next to her, then Ceil and Cora. "They love you," Terry said to her as she sat down.

"Was it all right?" she asked.

Cora leaned across Ceil and Terry and said, "You were fabulous."

"He made fun of my dress," Carla said. "Is there a way to change—if I have to go back up?"

"Don't be silly," Cora said. "Your dress is as great as you. Bob Hope is a putz." But Carla kept glancing down at her Chinese dress, wondering if it had been a mistake. It made her nervous and gave her a taste of stage fright, something she had never before experienced.

Carla expected to win. Not because she thought she was the best or anything like that. She knew as well as anyone that "best" was an absurd idea and couldn't be assessed. She thought she was going to win because Jack thought so, and in her experience, Jack was never wrong.

When her name was announced, the orchestra played "A Pretty Girl Is Like a Melody." In those days, acceptance speeches were shorter and less list-like. Jack had told her when she won to thank her husband and her parents for their support. "Leave me out of it," he had said.

"You're the one I want to thank."

"It won't do either of us any good. I'm not being shy here, or coy. No surprises. Is that clear?"

Carla knew Jack was dead serious, so she said, "Clear, Chief."

On the stage, behind the podium, there was a globe on top

of an enormous reel of film, a set designer's idea of film as international medium. Carla took a moment to glance at it. The world was waiting for her to speak, but she saw no reason to hurry. A hint of a smile traced across her face and lingered. It implied, "Silly, but amusing." She might have meant the stage set or she might have meant the entire evening. Whichever, it kept her separate from her audience—a figure of glamour, certainly, but apart from the surroundings. It had helped make her not only the best actress in the world, but a woman of mystery, a sensibility both elusive and knowing. And she was beautiful, radiant really, the unobtainable source of erotic fantasy and dreams for men and boys. Standing there, on the stage of the Pantages with her statuette, offering her genuine thanks, moved by the honor, Carla was what America wanted to see and hear. In that moment she seized the attention of the world.

After the ceremony Terry wanted to stop at Romanoff's, where Baron Mellenkamph was giving an Oscar night party. Carla would have been just as happy to skip it because she had to go to the Governors Ball later that evening. She was certainly in a good mood after winning, so when her husband urged her, she agreed.

Romanoff's, in Beverly Hills, was the classiest of the famous restaurants. Prince Mike, the proprietor—who was no more a prince than the Baron was a baron—ran his restaurant as if it were his home. The host himself always sat in one of the front booths, across from the bar.

The crowd that had watched the show on a pair of television sets applauded as Carla walked in. The Baron extricated himself from a woman in a backless, form-fitting gold lamé dress and hurried over to Carla. He kissed her hand, got down on one knee, and said in his accent that was already a little slurred, "My one darling. You are my winner, my princess. I bow down to you." He tried to drop his forehead to the floor, but since the Baron was pushing two hundred fifty pounds, that wasn't quite possible.

For a moment, Carla thought he might try to kiss her foot. "Hi, Baron," she said, grinning. "Don't get your pants dirty."

"Champagne!" the Baron crooned, struggling to his feet. "Champagne forever." Then the Baron kissed Ceil's hand, hugged Cora, and shook Terry's hand. Since on any night the customers in Romanoff's were all in the movie business, the party didn't seem to change things much, except that the Baron was picking up the tab. He had brought along a few of his outré friends. Carla looked around the crowded restaurant at the collection of beautiful young women who always seemed to be around when champagne was poured. She saw pink mink, plunging necklines, gown straps sliding down arms, and one statuesque blonde who seemed to be dressed as a mermaid. Carla was kissed and congratulated by waves of people, all of whom wanted to get close to her, to touch her, to be near the winner, as if something—that part that was luck and not talent—might be seen and understood.

"I have plans for you, my darling," the Baron cooed, pulling her away from her husband and the crowd that surrounded her. Carla knew, if not exactly in words, then by long experience, that having her turn up at his party on this night was victory enough for the Baron. They both knew it was unlikely that MCA would let her do another picture with him, but her friendship—evidenced by her arrival on the night she won an Oscar—would impress everyone else who was here and give him leverage in some other project. Because he had been attentive to Ceil when they were in Paris, Carla was willing to participate. "Plans, big plans for us," he repeated, hugging her again.

"I'll bet you do, Baron," Carla said, amused by him, but already nodding to Cora, which meant let's get out of here.

The Governors Ball, given by the governors of the Academy, was held at the new Beverly Hilton Hotel, in the Bali Room, which was decorated like the set for a South Seas picture. There was a thatched, dropped ceiling and colored lights that were meant to suggest a tropical sunset. The dinner, like almost every other Hollywood dinner of the time, was prime rib and baked potatoes. Most of the men drank Scotch, right through the meal. Throughout the evening a line of grandees trekked over to Carla's table. She shook hands with each one and thanked them for their good wishes. Terry was in awe of her ability to say essentially the same thing to two hundred people and sound genuine each time. When Jack came to the table to offer his congratulations, Carla asked him to dance with her. He tried to beg off, saying he didn't know how. "Why, I'd love to. How sweet of you to ask," Carla answered. Everyone else, the silky, expensive-looking members of the Academy, the other nominees and winners, gave them plenty of room. The orchestra played "Ole Buttermilk Sky" while Jack and Carla moved around the floor, dancing in a sweeping circle, as if they owned the night. Terry Seaver watched with a proud smile frozen in place. Ceil asked, "Who is that man Carla's dancing with?"

"I can't place him," Terry said and had another drink, his sarcasm lost on Ceil.

No one ever knew just how much Terry Seaver knew about his wife and Jack Markel. It was easier for him not to know, but he might well have guessed part of it. Maybe it was the bad medical news, or maybe Terry sensed that the center of Carla's emotional life was elsewhere, but he began fooling around. He certainly had plenty of opportunity. He was good-looking, with a career of his own; he was frequently on movie lots around attractive, available women. Perhaps because she felt guilty about Jack, Carla didn't notice, or chose not to. Cora Cohen, on the other hand, saw everything.

In the weeks after Carla won the Oscar, when her mail increased, Cora hired a young woman to help with the secretarial chores. Unsolicited fan letters, most of which came to the studio, were handled by MCA. They sent out signed photos and kept a mailing list of everyone who wrote. But there was always correspondence that required Carla's attention, or at least Cora's, acting as her representative. Nancy Beeman, the woman Cora hired to help with the typing, came to the Loma Vista house and worked in the study. Nancy was a little mousy but she had a nice figure and was quite competent. Later, when Carla thought about the whole messy business, she wondered if Cora had unconsciously, or maybe even purposely, put temptation in Terry's way. But as Cora told her, if she was going to set a trap, she would have hired a hotter number than poor Nancy Beeman. When it was over, Cora's view—which Carla came to accept—was that Terry was ready for trouble and nearly anyone would have served.

They were looking at scripts, out by the pool, when Cora said, "Your husband is in the typist's pants."

Carla was quiet for a moment. She knew Cora wouldn't say it if she weren't certain. "Does my mother know?"

"She's the only one who doesn't."

"Is it Nancy's fault?"

"Probably not. On the other hand, she didn't say no."

"How'd you find out? Never mind, I don't want to know."

"I'll tell you. All of a sudden the typing wasn't getting done. She was very efficient. So I checked with Adela—"

"Adela?"

"The maid. She does the laundry. The sheets have stains. The sofa in the study has spots. The maid always knows."

Carla was quick and deadly about it. "You fire her," she said, "I'll talk to him." When Terry came home that evening from the studio, where he had been shooting an episode of "The Virginian," Carla told him she wanted a word. She didn't raise her voice or sound angry at first. "I know what you're doing with Nancy. I want you out of here. I'll send your clothes tomorrow."

"Carla, whoa. What are you talking about?"

"Don't make it worse. If you're not gone in a half hour, I'll have police detectives throw you out. Don't think I won't."

"Wait a minute here."

"You don't go around screwing the help in my house under my nose and expect to get away with it. How could you do that to me? How?" She was working herself up into a state, calling forth the tears and agony she thought she ought to feel.

Terry got out, but he never quite got over Carla's coldness. "I couldn't believe it," he said later. "It was like she was doing a first reading of a script. Boom. Over and out. Adios."

What Terry didn't know was that what upset Carla most was she had used a double standard. She could have Jack but he couldn't have Nancy. "Look, maybe you don't win any medals for marriage, but that doesn't make what he did right," Cora told her, as they sat in the study drinking Chivas Regal.

"I used it all for an excuse to get rid of him. You know I did. I mean, think about the way I did it. There's ice water in my veins, there has to be. I was horrible to him. Hateful," she said, feeling sick at her behavior.

"He did it. Not you."

"I tell him nine hundred times I want a baby. Then I'm going off with Jack all the time." She picked up her Oscar and said, "It's this thing." The statuette had come back from the engraver, still in its box, packed with wood shavings and tissue paper. "All that sperm count stuff. Then this," she said, poking an accusing finger at the little statue. "It had to make him nuts."

"Maybe," Cora said, considering. "What are you going to do, not be successful because your husband isn't?"

"Why her?" Carla yelled, meaning Nancy Beeman. "She's a nothing."

"That's why. Men like to strut. You know. Around you that's not so easy. Around her . . ." Cora shrugged. "She doesn't give him any shit. She was probably thrilled at the attention. He says, 'Take off your clothes,' she says, 'Yes sir.' "

As Cora was talking, making good sense, not trying to paper

over anything, Carla took the Oscar out of the box and examined it. "At least they spelled my name right," she said. Cora laughed and poured more Scotch.

"It was me. I forced him. Don't try to tell me different," Carla said, starting to cry again.

Cora put her arms around Carla, comforting her. "Don't blame yourself because he couldn't keep his zipper up."

"I can't help it. I was so mean to him," Carla said, resting her head on Cora's shoulder.

"You weren't fair," Cora said. "You're going to have to live with that. But keep it in proportion. It's over."

"I had to fake getting angry. I was even acting that," Carla said, sick at heart all over again. "Is that the only way I can ever feel anything? To act it? If I pretend I'm mad or passionate or any goddamn thing, then it gets real. But if I try to say something for real, it comes out fake. I was the coldest bitch in the world to him. What's wrong with me?"

"No, no," Cora whispered, putting her hand in Carla's hair.

"It was ugly and hateful and I want to die," Carla said, refusing to be comforted. "What good am I to anybody?" She was unwilling, or maybe unable, to listen to Cora's reasonable voice. "Hate, hate, hate," Carla screamed. They were both overwrought—Carla for the way she had treated her husband, and Cora because her own sexual frustrations were immense. Maybe it was because they were both a little drunk, but Cora began to kiss Carla on the forehead and face; sisterly kisses meant to soothe, not arouse. It comforted Carla for a moment, but had a different effect on Cora. She wasn't able to control herself completely and she kissed Carla on the mouth. She did it lightly and Carla might have seen it as one kiss of many, but the kiss had a questioning, tentative quality. The nature of the question was unmistakable. Carla recoiled. It made Cora feel terrible. She pulled back and began to make an apology. "I didn't mean . . . I'm sorry . . ."

Carla pulled away and her emotions boiled over. She was trembling and crying at once. Cora didn't think she was the only cause of it, but she stammered her apology. Carla wasn't listening. "Oh, I don't care about anything," she said, as she picked up the Oscar, wielding it like a weapon. For a moment Cora thought Carla might hit her with it. Because she was drunk, Carla's eyes had gone hazy and she wasn't in complete control. She began smashing the wooden packing crate, scattering splinters and wood shavings. Perhaps if it hadn't broken so easily, she would have been satisfied, but one blow demolished the box. Instead of stopping, Carla began banging the desk, then the telephone, screaming "I hate myself, I hate myself! I'm horrible, horrible. He loved me. I cheated him out of it." Cora wanted to hold her, to comfort her, which might have stilled her anger, but she was afraid she'd be misunderstood. When the phone was in pieces, Carla threw the Oscar across the room at the wall. She threw it hard—it weighed, as the Academy loved to point out, eight and a half pounds. It made a crashing noise as it broke the plaster. It had to have awakened Ceil. Maybe the noise was enough, or maybe her energy was spent, but Carla collapsed against Cora, crying again. "Now it's over," Cora said.

"It is not. It's all I think about. How did I get so hideous? Why?"

"You're not hideous. You're protecting yourself. It took courage to tell him you won't put up with that. He did it right in your own house."

"It's me," she cried, clinging to Cora, spasms of agony rolling out of her. "When we couldn't have a baby, in my heart I wanted him gone. I wanted an excuse."

"Well, then you've got a good sense of tactics and we both know where you learned."

"No matter what you say to make me feel better, I feel horrible. I hate what I'm turning into. Hate it!" This time there was no mistaking Cora's motives. She comforted Carla, put her on the sofa, took off her shoes, and stroked her forehead until Carla finally slept.

The next day, when Carla told Jack what had happened—sparing neither Terry nor herself—he said, "Try not to blame yourself."

"I can't help it."

"Don't. I'll get somebody to handle the divorce. You'll give him a settlement. A lot of money."

"Good," Carla said, thinking money might assuage her guilt.

"Not all at once. The deal is, if he writes his memoirs, or talks about you to the press, the money stops. If he keeps his mouth shut, regular checks forever. Cora can police it."

"I thought I was cold, but you are the one. You really are."

"It'll keep him in line."

As always, Carla listened to him, and as always, he was absolutely right.

16.

At the time Carla's marriage was coming apart, Milton got it in his head that he wanted to open a restaurant. He had a vision of himself dressed in a tuxedo, greeting people at the door, seeing to it that his favorites got good tables, giving credit to old friends who were down on their luck, and generally being thought of as a shrewd man who knew how to operate. He had his eye on a vacant place on Beverly Boulevard in Hollywood. It had room for thirty tables and fifteen booths. Milton had begun to dream of ways to make it his. It would be called Milt's Place, a spot where a man could get a good steak or a little conversation. There would be a bar, where the regulars would hang out, come to relax, and have a word with Milt Tate, restaurateur.

Milton was very direct about it with his daughter. He needed her to co-sign the lease and help him with the bank loan. "I want you to be as proud of me as I am of you," he told Carla when he asked for the help. He chose his words well. If it had been up to Carla she would have done it. Cora was the first to hear about it. "He'll call it Carla Tate's Father's Place before he's through. Better to give him money *not* to open a restaurant."

"Come on, Cora. It's harmless. If it doesn't work out, so it'll cost some money. Big deal."

"If he gets it open, and I wouldn't count on it, you'll have to turn up every night just to keep it alive. It's really dumb."

It was Jack, of course, who straightened it out. He understood that it was important for Carla to do something for her father. It didn't have to be this ill-conceived restaurant idea, but it had to be something that gave Milton a sense of dignity. Jack admired her for wanting to do it. They were together in the bungalow, which had become more than a trysting place for them, more like their household. No matter how luxe this place was, it was still a hotel room, but it belonged to them and no one else. Carla kept only a few personal things in the bungalow, but her mark was on the place, and she and Jack were comfortable there. They had spent a lazy afternoon in each other's arms while she told him about Milton's restaurant idea.

"Cora's right," Jack said. "He'll botch it and one way or another, your name will be cheapened. That'll be the price."

"He's my father. I should be able to help him," Carla said, with pain on her face.

"Now you're doing good deeds?" Jack said, teasing her.

"What good is my money if I can't do what I want with it? I don't care if it's wasted. I want to do something for him."

"Let me get him a job. Something interesting that won't harm either one of you."

"What?"

"I'm not sure yet. Don't do anything for a day or two. Let me think about it."

Jack's solution was to get Milton a position as a sort of official greeter at the Friars Club in Beverly Hills. The Friars was a New York club that had opened a West Coast branch after the war. It was a fraternal group that met for lunch, drinks and cards. They raised a lot of money for charity. A typical member was someone who either worked in show business or wished he did. Carla had never heard of it.

Milton learned all the members' names and all the club rules. He learned to call the president the Abbot and remember which officer was the Dean, which the Prior, the Proctor and the Herald. He began dressing like the members, with suits from Sy Devore's, cut to show a lot of cuff. He couldn't make jokes the way some of the professional comics did, but he could laugh at their stories and, when he had the chance, he could swap tales—telling about his famous daughter and the way she had danced with Errol Flynn when she was only seven. The job made Milton happy and that gave Carla satisfaction.

Jack knew that with a divorce about to be final, it would be better for Carla if she was out of town for a while. She was in demand, but that didn't mean she could just glance up and there would be an appropriate movie for her. Star players were no longer under long-term contract to the studios. Carla read scripts daily and after the success of *Barbara Farrell* she did as Jack had suggested—commissioned her own. But as anyone who has ever worked in Hollywood will tell you, script development moves at its own inconvenient pace.

Sidney Shepherd, of Shepherd-International, had a western called *Dark Sky* that was about to shoot in Mexico. It had already been cast—that is, until Jack called to suggest Carla might be available. The story was about a young Mexican woman; although Carla was the right age, she was hardly Mexican. If Jack had a fault, it was that he never really understood that scripts and roles weren't interchangeable. The whole point, as Jack saw it, was that Carla was an actress and could play any role. That this role had already been cast with a Mexican actress was of no importance to Jack. He considered such matters details to be worked out by screenwriters and directors. Jack told Freddy Durslag to make it happen, to get Carla into *Dark Sky*. Sidney was glad to put a big name into his picture. For doing it at the last minute, which meant paying off the Mexican actress who had finally gotten a break, Sidney was promised another picture, to be named later. *Dark Sky* was to shoot in Mexico for five weeks—far enough from Terry Seaver to ensure that when Carla's divorce became final, she would be far from unpleasant publicity.

The studios shot exteriors for their westerns in Durango—Hollywood production had become an important local industry. A few miles out of Durango, at Chuperdoso, there were standing western sets booked so heavily that producers were constantly feuding over the scheduling of the dance hall, the swinging-door saloon, or the blacksmith shop. Durango's dusty locales were certainly authentic, with the kind of luminous, blue Mexican skies that directors loved. Extras, horses and white-faced cattle were plentiful and cheap; life and the unions were relaxed.

The picture that Carla had come to make was about poor

peasants, *campesinos*, exploited by a cavalier local government. In an early draft, the villains had been mine owners, but that was too far to the left for Sidney Shepherd who, although he hadn't been tarred by the blacklist, certainly remembered it and had no desire to court trouble. Sidney would have been just as happy to make musicals on soundstages about boys and girls on dates, but since even studio owners didn't have complete control of the juggernaut of production, he found himself financing *Dark Sky*. The director was Leo Davidson, a man in his early fifties, who a decade earlier had indeed been blacklisted. He'd gone to live in England, where he'd worked in advertising. Now he was back, trying to make up for lost time. Leo, who had started out a screenwriter, was a tall, dour man with a high forehead. Although he tried to appear relaxed, he was as angry and bitter as he had every reason to be.

The company was staying at the Posada Duran where Carla had a big corner suite and Cora an adjacent room. On her first morning, Carla was covered in dark body makeup, her hair dyed black, and she affected a Mexican accent, or tried to. Carla was a fine realistic actress. She had proved that over and over again. She was not, however, possessed of any theatrical or stage technique. Her Mexican accent, according to both Cora and Carla herself, sounded like a comic on "The Ed Sullivan Show." After one glimpse at the makeup tests and hearing her read about thirty pages, Leo knew it too. If it had been a lesser star than Carla, he would have canned her or walked off himself. Instead, he put everything on hold and rewrote the script. Carla's character, who had been called Conchita, now became Lucy Jarvis, who just happened to be living among the *campesinos*. The critics might laugh, the screenwriter might tear his hair out, but Carla would look good, sound right, and her performance and her presence would make the picture.

Sidney Shepherd's son, Bobby, who had taken a year off from Stanford to work for his father, was on the picture as an associate producer. Cora knew that Carla was in a fragile emotional state and likely to fall in bed with someone. She was concerned about Bobby. He was an attractive rich kid, heir to this company—and his father's eyes on the set. Cora could see that those eyes were mostly turned to Carla.

On the third night the company was in Durango, Bobby gave a cocktail party to welcome everyone. He had the hotel set up a bar and asked them to serve what he called Mexican snacks, as if they might have been planning a New England clambake.

Carla was glad to meet the actors and the production crew. She knew that since she was the star, they would look to her to set the tone for the party and ultimately the atmosphere on the set. Leo Davidson might be in charge of the movie, but Carla's mood and attitude would define the working and living conditions. She was aware that someone had been fired to make room for her. She acted on the assumption that some of the people in this room were friends of the fired actress. She was younger than almost everyone, but still, she was the senior person. She took the obligation seriously. She shook every hand and had a word with each person, saying again and again that she was excited about the picture and looking forward to starting. Bobby stayed close, introducing her to the cast and crew. He'd put his hand on the small of Carla's back in a proprietary way and steer her from the camera operator to the makeup woman. After he'd had a few drinks, he started to tell her his life story. As Cora remarked later, "The kid's nineteen. How long could it take?" When he got to the part about dropping out of Stanford "to make my move in pictures," Carla knew she'd heard enough. She excused herself from the party, saying she wanted to get some rest, waved good-bye, and went upstairs with Cora to giggle about Bobby Shepherd.

Cora felt that if Carla was going to climb into somebody's bed, it ought to be someone who could do her some good. She went for older men anyway, and Leo was certainly available. He'd be likely to favor her in the shooting and the cut. Also, unlike younger men, he'd be discreet and unlikely to get her pregnant. Most important, Cora knew Leo would take it in stride. Carla wouldn't be the first, nor the last, actress on a set with whom he'd slept. It was a kind of *droit du seigneur*. Leo knew the rules. Cora doubted that Bobby Shepherd did. Cora made a point of not letting Bobby near Carla when she was alone. Once the rewrites were done, romance blossomed. At dinner, after the first day of shooting, Leo asked Carla to come up to his suite to discuss the script.

What Carla hadn't counted on with Leo was that he was angry at the movie business, which was understandable, and she represented Hollywood to him. It wasn't that Leo hated Carla—he knew her presence in his movie meant it would have a chance at the box office. He was the one who knew that rewriting to accommodate her was the right course of action. But that didn't mean he didn't resent her for having a career untouched by politics and for living what he thought was a charmed life. When he took her in his arms, that first night in the Posada Duran, he told her, "You're going to be great in this picture because I know how to shoot you."

"I believe you, Leo," she said.

When Leo kissed her and put his hands on her, it made her smile. Perhaps it was the smile that infuriated him. Had she looked nervous or scared he might have behaved differently. But she was twenty-one years old and he wasn't. He took her smile to be a smirk. He thought she was saying, "You might be in charge on the set, but I'm in charge now." In fact, Carla was smiling because she was pleased to have found a new lover—it was no more complicated than that.

He pulled her close to him and held her jaw in his hand, squeezing her mouth, distorting it. "If you do exactly as I say, you will give a great performance on screen and a memorable one right here." Her mouth was beginning to hurt. She certainly couldn't speak, but she looked at him, and with her eyes, told him, yes, she would try. She could see she was in for a bumpy ride. She was in his hands, figuratively as well as literally. It was the only way she knew to behave. Leo could see it and intended to take full advantage. He let go of her jaw and picked up his silk dressing gown. It was from Sulka, a sign that his time in London hadn't been quite the hard-luck story that he often liked to suggest. He took the sash from it, tied one end around Carla's wrist and the other to the bedstead.

"What is this?" she asked, starting to feel embarrassed.

Leo didn't answer, but pulled the drawstring from his pajamas, tied her other wrist to the bedpost, and pushed her onto the bed.

"I don't know if I like this so much," she said, feeling a little scared, but also fascinated to see what would come next, how Leo's sense of drama might play itself out.

"I didn't ask if you liked it," he said, and then ripped a pillowcase, tearing off strips of the linen, which he wrapped around her mouth as a loose gag, and around her eyes as a blindfold. He didn't want her yelling out, but on the other hand, he didn't want to seriously hurt her, since they did have a movie to shoot. She was kneeling now, on the bed, her arms attached to the bedposts, her mouth and eyes covered. Leo took off her blouse, letting it hang back over her shoulders, caught on the knots at her wrists. She could sense him admiring her breasts.

The idea of being held like this, at his command, unable to

object, or to see what was happening, began to appeal to her. There was no denying there was something dark, fierce and definitely erotic going on. She was wearing loose linen trousers. Leo pulled them off, and then her underpants, too. She began to tremble with a mixture of excitement and fear—each feeding the other—as he stood near her. She could hear him undressing. Then she felt his weight on the bed as he knelt next to her. She felt him push himself against her neck, getting hard, pressing himself against her. He began tracing patterns on her stomach and back. She could feel the electricity in them both, and even though she would have preferred a more traditional approach, the fact was that it was exciting her and Leo knew it. She could feel him move around to face her. He pulled her legs out and shoved a pillow under her. He jammed his hand between her legs and felt her wetness. It made him breathe harder, audibly. She spread her legs and he pulled off her gag, but not the blindfold, and kissed her. She wrapped her legs around him as he entered her, hard.

Her arms, stretched above her head, felt odd to her, as if they weren't hers. She was only to clasp him with her legs. She squeezed them along his back and tried to press herself closer to him. She felt herself about to come when the blindfold slipped from one eye. The first thing she saw was Leo's face, twisted in a hateful snarl. She thought he was about to spit at her, but instead he came, with hard, bucking snorts. His face was so unpleasant that her own orgasm evaporated. When she thought about it later, she couldn't understand why she had found it so exciting. When she told Cora about it, because she told Cora everything, Carla asked, "Why was that so hot? What was it?"

Cora thought about it, then said, "You learn things about yourself that way—in bed—that you can't find out any other way."

"Does it mean I want to be hurt? Punished or something?"

Cora paused, trying to frame her answer. "I think it means that's what you wanted last night. With that man. It doesn't mean you're a masochist all the time."

"But he's a sadist, isn't he?"

"He's a director."

They spent a month in Durango shooting all the exteriors. Two or three nights a week, Leo would come to Carla's room and spend an hour or two. Once, early on, she wanted to turn the tables and tie him up, but Leo wouldn't permit it. He never upped the ante of the first night—he never wanted to hit her or really hurt her, but he loved binding her, making her helpless.

Everyone on the set knew that Carla and Leo were sleeping together—they didn't know more than that, and they accepted it as a normal part of location life. It was well known that Carla was separated from her husband—the papers were full of news of the divorce, and Leo was single, so other than the normal amount of gossip, people didn't think much of it. Only Bobby Shepherd seemed to be in the dark. He continued to be courtly toward her, conducting a one-sided flirtation. Carla claimed to be unaware of it until Cora reminded her. "He has a crush on you."

"Is that what all that fussing is about?" Carla asked. "I thought it was because of Sidney."

"No. Don't get in a situation where you turn him down. He's the boss's son. He's going to be around for a long time."

Carla took Cora at her word on this, as on most things. She was always nice to Bobby, listened to what he had to say and smiled whenever he was around. It was enough for him. If he had any idea that she spent her nights being tied up and fucked silly by the director of the picture, a man he thought of as a family employee, he never let on.

The staff at the Posada certainly knew Carla was a film star. They had been instructed not to bother her, and since even menial jobs at the hotel were like family capital, the staff tried not to gawk. It wasn't quite like a civilian's holiday, but for Carla it was pretty relaxed. She didn't have to deal with the constant clicking of cameras and requests for autographs.

Carla's call wasn't until afternoon, so she and Cora were having a late, outdoor breakfast on the hotel patio—dark Mexican coffee and *huevos rancheros*, seasoned with fresh lime—when Carla said, "I'm a creature of everyone else's fantasy."

"Leo, you mean?"

"For sure, Leo. But everybody. That's what I am."

"Every star is. Maybe even every actress."

"No. Not like me. With the others, it's only people they don't know. With me it's people I know, too."

"I think that's probably true," Cora said, amused at Carla's speculations.

"What I need is to keep control of it with people I know and have some control over the others."

"Leo set this off?"

"Sort of. His ideas aren't really about me. Once I knew that—really felt it, like it was a part I was ready to play—I lost interest. At first, though, it was pretty great."

"That's it for Leo?"

"I guess. How much longer are we here?"

"A week. Just enjoy yourself."

Carla nodded, thinking that a corner of some sort had been turned; her ruminations were the thoughts of a grown woman and not a girl. Those thoughts had been unloosed by Leo Davidson's tastes and notions of sexuality; they had given her a new avenue of access into her own mind.

At night when she couldn't sleep, she'd want to call Jack. If he was out of town, she would do it no matter what the hour. When he was away, his calls were screened by hotel switchboards. Carla never gave her name. She identified herself as Miss Mulligan. Jack always left word that Miss Mulligan's calls should be put through. If he was at home, she couldn't call him at odd hours. That didn't bother her when she was in L.A., because she knew that in a few hours she could see him or talk to him at the bungalow. But at times like this, in Mexico, where she was shooting all day and sometimes lonely at night, it made her sad.

She knew that what she and Jack had together was more intimate and more deeply felt than her marriage had been, or than Jack's marriage was. She didn't know if he saw other women when she was away. She supposed he did sometimes—the calls from Miss Mulligan at very odd hours were partly a test of that, but she never sensed him anxious to get off the phone, or awkward because someone else was there. Despite their obvious differences they had such temperamental similarities that Carla knew if she fooled around, the way she had been doing with Leo, that probably meant that Jack was doing something similar. Carla was realistic about these things. She knew there would be other Leo Davidsons in her life on other locations. It was hard to think about it. She tried to push such thoughts from her mind.

On the nights when they were able to talk, he would ask her all about the picture she was working on, about the dailies and the working conditions. She always kidded him about it by saying, "How was your day, dear?" as if they were a suburban couple sitting by the television set after the kids had gone to sleep. Her biggest treat when she was on location was to talk with Jack until she got drowsy enough to drift off. At first he claimed to be insulted that he had put her to sleep, but it gave her such comfort he was glad to do it. He would talk softly, lovingly, to her and when she could finally doze, she would just drop the phone, leaving it off the hook till morning.

Dark Sky wasn't much of a movie but the public turned out anyway to see Carla. The critics, however, weren't kind at all. There had been so much praise for her in *Barbara Farrell* they seemed to feel they had gone overboard and now had to balance the scales. It bothered Jack more than Carla, who usually thought all reviews missed the point—good ones or bad. Jack knew that critics, at least the substantial ones, couldn't be bought. At least not directly. Carla's harshest critic, one Perry Dawson of *Style*, a man who seemed to take pleasure in calling attention to Carla's many imagined flaws, was positively on the warpath over *Dark Sky*: "A farrago of western clichés unredeemed by an awkward performance by Carla Tate that has no observable connection to the script, such as it is, or to life as it has ever been lived. Oscar or not, Tate was overrated in *Barbara Farrell* but at least that was a tale worth telling. Here, she meanders her way through a hat dance of mediocrity, as if she were looking for the Sunset Boulevard exit on the Hollywood Freeway."

Carla was upset by it, but willing to put it behind her. Not Jack Markel, who said to Freddy, "Find out if this guy has a script or a book or something."

"Then what?"

"Get him to start taking your checks." As it turned out, Dawson did have an unpublished novel that had been circulating without much luck among New York publishers. It wasn't a bad book and eventually it might have found a home. Instead, MCA bought the film rights and hired Dawson to turn it into a film script. "After all," Freddy Durslag pointed out to Dawson's agent, "the man's a film critic. He writes cinematically. It's a natural transition." Dawson was paid generously for his efforts. Each year he was sent an option renewal check. As long as he was taking MCA's money, he felt it would be unethical to review their movies. *Dark Sky* was the last Carla Tate movie he covered. Once a year, Freddy would take him to lunch in New York and solicit his opinions about casting and directors for his script. He had lots of ideas that Freddy dutifully wrote down in a little notebook. This, along with the annual check, seemed enough to satisfy Perry Dawson.

17.

Carla had always ignored politics. In a vague way she thought of herself as a Democrat, because that's what Jack was. I always thought she had political affiliation mixed up with religion. Her parents were Jewish, so she was. But she took only a casual interest in it. It was pretty much that way with the Democratic party. For the first years she was eligible to vote she never quite got around to it. She tried once. But when she found out that she had to go to a public polling place, and that they wouldn't send the ballot to her house, even if she sent a messenger, she lost interest. In those days there was no limit to how much money an individual could contribute to a political campaign. The idea of fundraising parties as egalitarian events was still years away. Larger sums were raised from fewer people; it was all a quiet business. When it was done in Southern California, Jack Markel was usually involved. His view of electoral politics was to cover every base. He wrote out personal checks to all the candidates and helped raise serious money for the ones he thought might win. Jack knew some very rich people who wanted to be certain that the major office-holders in California owed them one.

The handwritten note Carla received from Sidney and Ruth Shepherd had asked her to "Come have a drink with Dick Nixon." Jack asked her to accept and turn up at the Shepherds' house for the Sunday afternoon poolside bash for their old friend. After he'd lost to Kennedy, he'd moved back to California, and now he was running for governor. When Carla and Cora arrived at the Shepherds' house, an enormous Tudor pile on Stone Canyon Road in Bel Air, there were eighty people, including Jack and Mona, standing around the pool making small talk while Sidney ushered Nixon from one group to another. In recent years, with the success of his studio, Sidney had put on weight, but he continued to dress like a younger man. For the party he wore a knit golfing shirt that was a little snug for a man with a belly and breasts pronounced enough to wobble. Sidney usually had a cigar in his mouth that he rolled from one side of his mouth to the other when he got nervous. The men were wearing jackets or pastel sweaters. The women were in sundresses or slacks. Nixon was dressed for the office, but with a tiny nod to his native state—he was in a lightweight tan suit, a change from the heavy, dark business clothes he habitually wore. He was attended by a silent aide, a tall, serious young man who jotted down the names of everyone Nixon met.

This was a money crowd, skewed toward the business side of the movies—producers, agents and studio executives. Some of them were even Republicans. They were there because Sidney or Jack had asked them and they wanted a look at the former Vice President.

When Carla, with Cora in tow, stepped toward the pool, Sidney hurried over to her and kissed her on the cheek. "Thank you for coming, darling. Ever meet him?"

"Yes," Carla answered. "But it was a long time ago."

"I'll get you a drink," Cora said. "You go say hello to the government."

Before Sidney could take Carla to Nixon's side, they were intercepted by Dick Brewer, a production executive at M-G-M. "Carla, great to see you," he said, stepping between them. Carla thought she detected a predatory note in his voice, and in that moment she realized why Jack had wanted her to come. She was as much the draw as the candidate. She groaned to herself at the thought of half the people at the party trying to pitch her stories. "Hi," she said to Dick Brewer, trying to place him.

Sidney moved away as Brewer took Carla's hand, said his name, and went to work. "We miss you at Metro. It was your home. I can't believe you don't want to come back. I had this great idea of turning the schoolhouse into a dressing room for you."

"Now that would be fun," she said, amused at the thought.

"Consider it done," he said, pressing the tiny opening. "Have you read *Morocco Dawn*—that script I sent you? Love story about the woman explorer. North Africa and Paris?"

"No. I haven't, yet."

"Fabulous character. Woman leaves her husband, heads out for the desert. Looking for her father. That's only the emotional pretext. Really, she feels drawn by a primeval instinct to seek a more intense life than she's been raised to want. Set before the war. Great clothes." Carla was listening politely when Nixon saw her and excused himself from a conversation with the chief financial officer of Paramount. Nixon's arms seemed to flap up and down as though he were trying to fly, while he hurried around the pool.

Carla wondered if Nixon remembered their time together during the hearings. She assumed he would do as she did in those circumstances, which was to claim he remembered whether he did or not. But the smile on Nixon's face, and the goofy way his arms were waving, told her he hadn't forgotten.

"Well, hello," he said with a nutty cheeriness, as he took her hand in both of his. "Little Carla," he announced, as if it were the answer to a hard question. The others near them stepped back. It wasn't necessary. They were both public people and knew without thinking how to shut out the crowd so they could talk.

"Hello, Mr. Vice President," Carla said, which is what Jack had told her to call him, at least at first. She offered her cheek for a kiss. He puckered his lips and leaned toward her. But he kissed before his mouth got to her face. It made a funny sound that seemed to hang in the warm air. "It's been a long time," Carla said, trying to ignore the missed kiss.

"Yes. That's correct. Nineteen forty-eight. I've followed all your motion pictures. I and my family, my wife and daughters, have. Congratulations on your Academy Award, the Oscar," he said, as if he were reading from a briefing memo. "I appreciate your coming today," he added, in a voice that sounded more genuine.

"I can finally vote. The least I can do is vote for you," she said, vowing to herself to do just that.

"This is a difficult election, but important to the people of our state," he said, slipping right into his canned speech. Carla nodded, but she wasn't sure what to say next. He had looked happy to see her, but small talk didn't come easily to him. She could see his mind racing backward looking for some fact about the two of them, something he wanted to say to her. Because she knew Jack was watching, she felt too ornery to help him. Then Nixon's face brightened. "Do you know the photograph we all took? Was taken of us? My girls, and you and me. In Washington?"

"Sure. It ran everywhere."

"Well, we still have it. All these years. I'll bet you don't have a copy."

"No, I don't think so."

"I'm going to send you one. Mrs. Nixon always said it's adorable. You'll like it." As the silent aide was jotting down notes about the conversation, Jack strolled over to them. "Hello, Jack," Nixon said. "Do you know little Carla Tate?" He said "little" with what he must have thought was a hint of lasciviousness, because he followed it with a quick, breathy laugh to let everyone know it was a joke. "I have to stop calling you that. Miss Tate."

"Yeah, Dick, I do," Jack answered quietly. "We're friends."

"Oh, I see. Well, good. We go back a ways."

"I know. Carla told me about it." Jack put his hand under Nixon's elbow to guide him away. When Nixon's back was to her she glanced at Jack and rolled her eyes. Cora, who had been standing a step away, handed Carla a gin and tonic and said, "There're some people who want to meet you."

"I'm first in line," said a lanky man with a ruddy, creased face and thick, silvery hair, offering his hand. He wore a blue blazer and a tie that had been loosened. Carla noticed his shoes were scuffed and run-down at the heels. The effect was more intellectual than impoverished. "Dennis Catton," he said. "How do you do?"

"How do I do what?" Carla answered, and then it was Cora's turn to roll her eyes.

Mr. Catton looked at Carla, amused to think, So that's how it is, is it? Not only is she famous and beautiful, but she likes to spar. "How do you manage to talk to Mr. Nixon without getting the giggles?" he asked.

"Well, I'll tell you about that. There was a time when he was very nice to me and my mother. He was careful. In his own way. Not everybody was. I was little."

"HUAC? When you gave testimony?"

"Yes."

"Do you know who I am?" he asked, because he could see she didn't. It wasn't boastful, more as though he had some information that might be useful to her. As he spoke, he gazed directly at her in a way Carla knew was practiced, and no doubt had worked wonders on women before. She could feel its effect, even as she recognized it as a performance.

"I appreciate your reminding me," she said, finding herself staring back at him, as if it were a contest to see which of them would blink.

"I'm a reporter. A political columnist, actually. I'm covering Mr. Nixon. I'm not here as a guest."

"I see. So I should be careful what I say?"

"I hope not too careful. But you should know I might quote you."

"Are you the first fair reporter in the world? You warn your victims?"

"Nah. I'm an Irish thug. I just don't want to get on your wrong side, in the hope that maybe I'll get a chance to be on your right side."

"Cora," Carla said, nodding to her to come a little closer. "Put this man down in the book of flirts. He might be world-class. This is Cora Cohen. She keeps score."

Cora nodded at Dennis and said, "Anything Carla says is absolutely off the record. If that's not clear, you can flirt on out of here."

Dennis laughed and said, "Deal." His smile was so grand, his teeth so wide and white, even Cora was charmed.

"I know you," Cora said. "The reporters we run into are usually more the gossip-column type."

"Well, believe me, a lot of what I do isn't much different—spreading rumors, claiming I know the difference between a truth and a lie." He was speaking to Cora, but his eyes never left Carla.

"Is Mr. Catton a big deal?" Carla asked. "And he's being modest?"

"Yeah," Cora said. "I'd say he's a big deal." Cora had been a publicist in Hollywood, not a political beat in the generally accepted sense, but she read the major papers and knew that world better than Carla did. "Syndicated. Everybody in New York and Washington reads this man."

As they stood there, with possibility in the air, Carla knew Jack was watching. He was never easy to read, but if anyone knew what was going on behind that poker face it was Carla. When she talked to someone attractive while Jack was around, he barely deigned to acknowledge it. Usually the men were in the movie business and Jack knew he could control them. But Dennis wasn't in his orbit. Carla knew he didn't like it one bit. She was still a little angry with him for dragging her here as bait, so she made a point of looking at Mr. Catton so intensely that she could feel him swallow and work to maintain his balance. She was attracted to him, and if being friendly might make Jack a little uncomfortable, then it pleased her to be standing and talking with Dennis Catton.

For his part, he couldn't believe his good luck. He was an accomplished, famous man. But he knew his fame didn't extend to the world of Carla Tate. If he was going to interest her in himself it would have to be by force of personality. He had noticed her when she arrived—everyone had—but Dennis had also noticed that when the movie producer, as he thought of Dick Brewer and all the men here, had been trying to sell her something, she had looked restless. When Nixon was talking about her movies, the air was strained. He thought that if he talked about himself in a self-effacing way, it might appeal to her. "I've been chasing Mr. Nixon up and down your state. You're the first person he seemed glad to see."

"That was his idea of a reunion?"

"Well, he's not always so great at small talk."

"What are you going to write about him?"

"I'm not sure. It is intriguing, you know. Former Vice President. Loses the big one. Doesn't give up. Now this. Unusual in American history."

"Sounds like the movie business to me."

"You mean not giving up?"

"That's right."

"People in the movie business don't give up?"

"Not the winners."

Sidney came and pulled Carla away from Dennis, saying, "Just have a word with a couple of people before they go."

"Good-bye, Miss Tate," Dennis said. She gave him one more smile as she left. It made Cora roll her eyes again.

Later that night while she and Cora were having a drink at

the Loma Vista house, Carla asked, "Okay, so what's Mr. Reporter's story? A little bit higher up than Sam Lipsky?"

"He's the big political reporter on the New York *Herald-Tribune*. It's a terrific paper. He wrote a couple books."

"How old, do you think?"

"Forty-two or -three. In there."

"Single, right?"

"Yep. Never married. But he gets around."

"I'll bet. How do you know all this?"

"I knew you'd ask. I made some calls after the party. Should I invite him over for a drink?"

"No. He'll call or something."

Sure enough, Dennis began calling from around the state. One night from San Francisco, the next from Sacramento. She never asked how he got her phone number, which was certainly not listed and was known to only a few. He would tell her about Nixon and ask about her life. They eased their way into a friendship in a way which Dennis declared "an electronic version of an old-fashioned courtship."

"What do you mean?"

"I'm two hundred miles away. There's no question of me yanking on your knickers, uninvited. There's a sweet, nineteenth-century air about it. We spend our time together on the phone—the twentieth century."

"What makes you think I'd invite you to yank on my knickers if you were here?"

"I simply mean it would be an issue—presumptuous, perhaps. Maybe it would only be an issue in my mind, but then my mind would soon involve your knickers."

"Should I read your books?"

"I'd be flattered, but I can think of more pleasurable ways to put you to sleep. They're about old political campaigns. 'Writ on water.' I'll send you what I'm doing about Nixon. You might get a kick out of it."

"Is he going to win?"

"If he doesn't, he's through. He knows it. He's a little odd, but very smart. Shrewd."

"But will he?"

"Too early to tell. As others have pointed out, this state is capable of absolutely anything."

"Oh, no," she said. "You're not going to start putting down California. Health nuts and all that stuff?"

"You kidding? I know the promised land when I see it."

She wasn't sure if he meant it or was just ingratiating himself with her. The sentences seemed to roll out of him in a way she wasn't used to. He didn't know much about the movie business, which made her realize how few people like that she knew. She remembered how it had irritated Jack to see her talking with Dennis. He must be formidable if Jack noticed. Once again she realized how much she counted on Jack's reactions to formulate her own views. Maybe Mr. Catton really wants to be a producer, she thought. Another one of Ceil's meal tickets. The ridiculousness of that made her laugh. No, she thought. I know what he wants. And it's not a new career.

18.

Carla was about to start a picture that would take her to New York and Connecticut for a month. She and Dennis would both be on the East Coast and Carla was looking forward to seeing how they'd get on once they were in the same room.

After the debacle of *Dark Sky* Jack had pressed MCA to come up with a commercial venture, a big love story, the sort of thing that might put Carla in line for another Oscar. *Red Roses*, a tearjerker about a concert pianist who goes blind and triumphs over her affliction, was the answer.

The film was to be shot in Carnegie Hall, on midtown streets, and at an estate in Greenwich. Carla hadn't been to Connecticut since the party with Four. As she stretched out on the big bed at the St. Regis to shake off her jet lag, she found herself thinking about the various men in her life. Maybe it was because Greenwich was only a few minutes from Darien, or maybe it was because she missed Jack, but all their faces, including Four's and her ex-husband's, came back to her. She watched them float in and out of her mind, like a movie that refused to stay in focus. She knew when men had reveries like that they tended to think in terms of conquests and body parts. That seemed rude, almost ugly. Much nicer just to see their faces, like a really good photograph of each one—not idealized, just looking their best. Her mind lingered longest over Jack and his intense eyes that always seemed to see into the heart of everything. She thought about the way his hair was thinning, and although he claimed not to notice or care, he sometimes touched his scalp—unaware he was doing it. As far as she knew, he only did it when they were alone. It had a funny kind of intimacy about it that she liked.

As easily as she had slipped into thoughts of Jack, precious Jack, who loved her and guided her through the difficulties of life, she realized why lovers—old and present—were on her mind. She was about to take on a new one. There was a certainty about it that was new. She remembered the reasons she was attracted to Dennis and ran them down in her mind, like a checklist: He spoke in those wonderful, complicated sentences that always surprised her. He was gorgeous in just the long, lean way she liked. He knew everything about politics and the government and she knew nothing about that, so she would learn new things. He wasn't in the movie business. He made Jack jealous. She dozed with her mind a blur of lovers past, present and future.

They both had difficult schedules—Carla was shooting every day and Dennis was turning out two columns a week, and he was always working on long pieces like the one on Nixon. Despite the difficulty, they managed to meet for a late supper at the end of the first week she was in New York. He took her to Orsini's on East Sixty-third Street, where Paolo, the maître d', who had seen budding romances among the celebrated before, put them at a quiet table where they could sit close, alone in a public place. "Do you know about this joint?" Dennis asked, wondering if she was aware of Orsini's position in the New York pantheon.

"That means it's probably the most famous restaurant in New York and I never heard of it."

"Well, let's just say a lot of fancy people come here and it's not in the guidebooks."

"You mean your friend the headwaiter there won't call the columns to say we were here."

"He might, but he'd only call a better class of column. And he probably wouldn't be crazy about being called a waiter."

"What is he?"

"I think he considers himself a social arbiter and global taste-meister."

Carla laughed at that, a genuine laugh that had nothing to do with being polite. He took it as encouragement.

Most of the room was either New York Social Register or international society, so no one was obvious about their glances. Dennis was used to being pointed out, at least in sophisticated places, but it was nothing like what Carla went through. She gave no sign the crowd was bothering her or pleasing her or that she was even aware of it. The odd thing about the evening was that Carla turned unexpectedly shy. It wasn't that she had trouble talking to Dennis, but that she felt awkward when he put his hand on hers. When they touched knees under the table, she backed away. "What's the matter?" he asked, concerned he had done something to displease her.

"Nothing. I mean, I don't know. I can't explain it."

"Is it me?"

"Probably. Probably me, too."

"We don't have to rush things. We can just have dinner and talk."

"Okay. I don't know. I feel like I'm playing a scene about the shy virgin or something."

"Want to go somewhere else?"

"No. When I think of some of the stunts I've pulled in restaurants . . . Oh, I don't know."

"I've been thinking about you so much, maybe in my mind things are more advanced than in yours. Know what I mean?"

"I guess. This picture's hard. That might be it. For about half of it I'm blind. I don't do any of the blind stuff till next week. After I get a day or two under my belt, maybe I'll be in better shape."

Dennis looked uncharacteristically puzzled. "In all my life I have never heard anything quite like that. I've certainly had women turn me down—but never because they had to be blind for a couple days first." He signaled to the waiter and tapped on the empty bottle of Barolo. "That calls for more wine."

It had seemed perfectly understandable to Carla. She realized that was because she was seeing it through a Hollywood filter. From Dennis's vantage point it must have sounded absurd. "I'm not turning you down," she said.

"Asking for a rain check?"

"Yeah. I guess."

"Do you practice being blind?"

"Of course. I try everything sightless."

"Everything, huh?"

"Come on, Dennis. Not tonight."

"Just a thought."

"I go blind during the picture. I can't be used to it. It has to be happening for the first time when it happens."

"Can I come to the set? To watch?"

"Sure. It gets boring though. I'm either working or in my trailer getting ready. Did you grow up here?" she asked, wanting to hear about him and not think about herself.

"I did indeed. On Sickles Street in Inwood—up at the top of Man-a-hat-a, where the cops come from. My father was one. I went to Fordham where all the smart little Catholic boys went to get their fangs sharpened."

"You liked it though, didn't you? Fordham, I mean."

"Too complicated for like or not like. We're talking Jesuits here. They specialized in taking the sons of nobody in particular and turning them into precision instruments for the promulgation of the law—God's and man's."

"You liked it. I can hear it. That's how you reward things—with those elaborate sentences."

"Oh, they would have loved you," he said, taken with her ability to see him whole. "Of course I liked it—in retrospect. At the time I thought I'd go mad. They told us God was our weapon. But a mind like a razor was the ticket out."

"Are you still a Catholic?"

"Spoken like an infidel. It's a life sentence. The question is, do I practice it?"

"Well?"

"I'm a Catholic, alas; alas, I am lapsed." He poured more wine and, perhaps to change the subject, added, "I live in Washington part of the week and in a grand apartment on Sutton Place. I hope you'll come visit."

"I guess you like New York, huh?"

"My dear, New York is the only city I ever loved that loved me back."

She knew she was asking him date questions, but she enjoyed interviewing the interviewer and for once talking about personal matters that had nothing to do with movies or Hollywood. "Your family must be proud of you."

"Oh, come on, Carla. We both have careers that are bigger than our parents. You know how nuts that gets."

"I thought it was only me."

"Yeah, right. My whole family says, 'Dennis has gone high hat on us.' " He said it in an Irish brogue that was more theatrical than accurate.

"What would they make of me?"

"First they'd fuss over how famous and beautiful you are. Then one of them would call you a Jewess."

"They're bigots?"

"Not really. They don't think so. Sooner or later they define everybody by race or religion or nationality. They're congenitally incapable of seeing beyond that. Mostly they're against anybody who isn't Irish and from Inwood." He seemed sad when he said it—not because he was ashamed, Carla thought, but because they were so limited and denied themselves so much of the world. "I'll tell you the best thing and the worst thing about my father. He lived and died broke—a New York city cop who never took more than a cup of coffee. An honest man."

"What's the worst thing?"

"The same."

When Carla looked up, it was one o'clock and they were the only ones left in Orsini's. The waiters were waiting for them to leave. Dennis signed the check and they walked back to the St. Regis, where he leaned over to kiss her good night. She whispered, "Come upstairs with me."

"No. I think you should just sleep tonight."

"All I meant was I don't like to take elevators by myself. People are around."

"Oh," he said, blushing. "Guard duty." He took her through the lobby, where she picked up her key and a fistful of phone messages which she handed back to the clerk. "For Miss Cohen, please," she said, leaving them for Cora to deal with tomorrow.

Upstairs, when Carla walked into the room, Dennis stood in the door, uncertain of himself. "Well, come in or don't. Or something."

"I don't want to force myself."

"Then you're the first man in history."

He took that for the challenge it was and kissed her. She certainly kissed him back, but she could feel his nervousness. When men kissed her for the first time she could usually sense their strategy building. They were like generals planning their attack. But Dennis didn't seem to have any scheme other than getting out of there with her honor intact.

She turned to go into her bedroom and leave him to let himself out, when he put his arms around her from behind. He kissed the back of her neck and whispered, "You're going to get the wrong idea about me. Why hurry? You probably have to get up at dawn or something."

She turned around in his arms and kissed him, letting her tongue graze across his lips. She slipped her hands into the pockets of his jacket and pulled it around her.

He stammered her name, too dazzled to form a sentence.

"Shh . . . Talking's for restaurants," she said, taking off his jacket and loosening his tie.

They fell back onto the sofa and rolled themselves into a tangle of arms and legs. She kissed his face and neck. It made him smile and when her skirt was pushed up, Carla pressed herself against him, pushing and relaxing. She concentrated on the sensation of it, but in a corner of her mind she marveled at how making love was always different. Like fingerprints or snowflakes. She could see he was about to come; his face had a pink tinge and he was rising up, above her, his mouth open in a sort of astonishment that she found endearing. She knew there would be no orgasm for her, not this time anyway, but it didn't bother her—letting him go without this, that would have bothered her. When they were through, she pulled her legs free of him and said, "Now you can go home."

While she was shooting *Red Roses* Carla was able to see Dennis only occasionally and then only for an evening. The truth was they were happier talking on the phone. Because she also talked to Jack regularly, Carla seemed to be spending all her spare time on the phone.

Jack asked if she was seeing Dennis. She wouldn't lie about something like that to Jack. He knew she wanted children and would eventually marry again, but she wondered how he knew. An unsettling thought that it must be Cora who had told him went through her mind. If it was true—and Cora was the likeliest bet—then in one brief flash of insight, her sense of the two people who mattered most to her was changed. It made her shudder and she put it out of her mind.

Carla liked having Dennis in her life. But she wasn't about to do without Jack. She knew that she probably should feel conflicted or at least confused, but she didn't. Of course she would never mention Jack to Dennis, but she knew she could always talk about Dennis to Jack. It was as if Jack were her husband and the others—the ones from whom she would pick her next actual husband—were the lovers. As she contemplated it, she decided, why not? Men did a version of that all the time—and they were admired for it. What was it Jack had once told her? She'd never be somebody's bread-baking wifey. Well, he was right. What was the good of being a movie star if she couldn't do exactly what she wanted, the way she wanted? Who the hell cared what the good-manners crowd thought, anyway?

After the picture wrapped, Dennis invited her down to Washington for a few days. "For a dinner in Georgetown. There'll be people from State there. Real D.C. stuff. You'll get a kick out of it."

She agreed to go, wondering what it would be like, but in her heart a little fearful that she wouldn't know how to talk to the people there or that they would ask her stupid questions about Hollywood. Still, the prospect of an adventure excited her. What to wear was a problem. Carla had a lot of clothes, but she didn't have any idea what was appropriate for a dinner of this sort. "I'll ask Marta," Cora said. Marta was the costume designer on *Red Roses*. Carla suspected Cora had a crush on her.

Marta thought it a wonderful challenge. She called Mrs. Swanson, an elegant *vendeuse* at Brooks Costume, told her what was required, and asked that a dress be built overnight.

The next afternoon Carla, Marta and Cora went to the Brooks workroom on West Forty-fourth Street for a fitting. Carla kept her eye on Marta and Cora, trying to see if there was anything there. Marta was about forty, Carla guessed, and although she wasn't particularly mannish, this woman wasn't a candidate for wifey and bread-baking either.

Mrs. Swanson, a middle-aged woman with black hair pulled into a bun and half-spectacles that dangled from a chain, took them back into the workroom, a long dusty space with a central cutting table thirty feet long. Beyond it there were a dozen sewing machines, each with a seamstress working on costumes of some sort—trousers or ball gowns, military uniforms and tweed jackets.

Carla slipped off her slacks, and tried on a blue-and-aquamarine chiffon skirt. "Bianchini, the best Italian chiffon," Marta said, examining the fabric. It hung on Carla's hips in an easy, sensual way. The top, a chemise with a fitted bodice, had been beaded and sequined and sewn with gold thread. Marta pulled it tighter in back and asked that it be adjusted.

"Isn't the skirt too short?" Carla asked. It fell a few inches below her knees.

"It'll be shorter than the others, but you've got the legs," Marta said, tugging on the skirt. "The brocade is Swiss. For a thing like this you want better materials than we use on a show. The dames where you're going will recognize it. They'll be in their little Hattie Carnegies and their Mainbochers."

"I think it's elegant and I'm grateful to you all."

"What about a jacket?" Marta said. "There was a little chinchilla number here last week."

Mrs. Swanson nodded to an assistant, who went off to hunt down the jacket. Carla looked at herself in a mirror, turning around, unable to see the flaws Marta had asked be corrected. Despite the harsh light, the effect was smashing. She knew that even if she didn't look like the other women who would be at this dinner, Dennis would approve. When she tried on the chinchilla jacket, Marta marked the sleeves.

Mrs. Swanson pinned the marks herself and said, "It'll be at the St. Regis by four."

As they were leaving, Marta told Carla she'd pick up shoes, stockings and a purse at Bendel's.

Dennis, who was already in Washington, asked Carla how she felt about flying or taking the train.

"Not unless I get plastic surgery first."

"Right. I thought it might be a problem."

"You bet it is. How long does it take to drive?"

"Four, five hours."

"That's what I'll do." She asked Cora to arrange a car and driver—someone who could take her down on Friday morning, stay overnight, and bring her back on Saturday.

"You want me to come with you—make sure it all goes right?" Cora asked. "Then we could fly?"

"You don't have to," Carla said, thinking that Cora might like some time to herself. Carla sometimes worried about Cora. She had seen too many stars turn their servants into friends and their friends into servants. In the end everybody suffered. She and Cora were devoted to each other. Carla knew she couldn't manage without her. She was concerned Cora would have no other life. Carla didn't care who Cora slept with, or what sex they were, but she didn't want her to be alone. Somewhere deeper, she didn't want Cora feeling unrequited and,

Carla was sure, unrequitable love. "Get me a car. I'll read scripts."

A Carey Cadillac limousine picked her up at the hotel. George, the driver, was a middle-aged man with a round, pink face, who Cora had been assured had driven big stars before. George could see Carla wasn't in a chatty mood so he closed the window between them and Carla napped, looked out the window, and dipped into the scripts Freddy Durslag had been after her to read.

For the two or three days a week he was in Washington, Dennis kept a small apartment near Dupont Circle. He thought Carla might be happier at a hotel, where he could join her. "There's nothing in my flat but books and me," he told her.

"Let me look it over, then I'll decide," she said, pleased with the idea of making him audition his apartment.

They were late leaving New York and by the time George found Dennis's apartment, there wasn't a lot of time for Carla to inspect the real estate. He was wearing a dinner jacket, which surprised her. Dennis loved her outfit; he kept touching the gold threads on the bodice.

As Dennis navigated the way to Georgetown, he recognized a fellow New York Irishman in George and asked his last name and where he was from.

"Cooney from Bay Ridge, Mr. Catton. Sacred Heart." Carla could hear in George's voice that Dennis was a greater star in Mr. Cooney's world than she was.

"Glad to hear it," Dennis said. "And what paper do you read?"

George sounded a little sheepish as he answered, *"Daily News."* When Dennis laughed, George added, "But when I look at the *Trib*, I always read your column."

"Stay away from the *Times*, George Cooney—it'll turn you gray as it is."

"Yes sir," George answered. "We don't take the *Times* in our house."

Dennis rolled the divider window back up and said to Carla, "Sacred Heart's his parish, in case you were wondering. New York Irish. God bless us all."

Carla was fascinated by the streak of chauvinism. "Who's going to be at the dinner?" she asked.

"It's for Skip Whitney—"

"That's his name? Skip?"

"Yeah. I wouldn't mind skipping him, thank you. This town is WASP heaven and State is their nest."

"Get a little more basic. What state are we talking about?"

"State Department. As in Secretary of. Skip just got made Assistant Secretary for East Asian Affairs. The dinner's at Nancy Bryant's. She's the widow of an ambassador. Horsey *in excelsis*. She's more fun than she sounds. You know what F.F.V. is?"

"Why do I think I should come up with a punch line?"

"Not necessary. First Families of Virginia."

"It's a different universe," Carla said, wondering if she'd get through the evening without feeling stupid.

"Hey. Remember me? The Cattons think lace curtains are fancy. We're not even a first family of Sickles Street. They'll be in awe of you. What you don't know, ignore. Believe me, that's what they do."

Mrs. Bryant lived in a Federal house on Thirtieth Street near R. "Definitely the high-rent district," Dennis said, as George parked. Carla admired the white columns in front, and Dennis added, "It'll be tiny. Around here, the older the money, the smaller the rooms."

The door was opened by a dignified black man in his late seventies. As he smiled and bowed slightly, Mrs. Bryant came forward. Carla thought she was about sixty. She absolutely beamed when she saw Dennis. He kissed her on the cheek and said, "Nancy, this is Carla Tate."

"How lovely you look and how grand of you to come," Mrs. Bryant said, taking Carla's hand in hers. She was wearing a billowing green-and-black plaid taffeta skirt and black silk shoes that peeped from under the hem. With it, she wore a long-sleeved white silk blouse, with a high neck, but the part Carla liked most was her hair. She wore a bow with an enameled pin with a tiny painting of a horse. Behind the bow, her hair was gathered in a net.

Mrs. Bryant, who insisted that Carla call her Nancy, took them into the library where the other guests were gathered for drinks. As Carla was introduced, she could see that everyone here knew who she was. Mr. Whitney might be the guest of honor, but she was the draw. Over the next few days all these people would drop her name. It was a comfort.

Scotch and bourbon were the only drinks in sight. There was a silver bowl of salted nuts on a little table. The names of the other guests seemed to bounce off her, but she enjoyed cataloguing their clothes. The men wore dinner jackets like Dennis, or pin-striped business suits. Some of the women were wearing what Carla assumed were indeed Hattie Carnegie and Mainbocher clothes, gray and garnet; one woman was in a sari. Carla knew her own outfit was perfect—different from the others and ideal for her. God bless Marta.

When they went into the dining room, which was in fact small, Carla saw a sea of crystal, porcelain and silver. Four wineglasses were at each plate and as many forks. There were monogrammed linen place mats on the long mahogany table and a white Wedgwood bowl of daffodils at each end. The plates were decorated with a band of cobalt and gold. It was quite beautiful, certainly graceful, and, Carla assumed, none of it either manufactured or purchased during the lifetime of anyone at the party.

She was seated between the new Assistant Secretary and a lawyer whose place card was pointed away from her. Dennis was on Nancy Bryant's right—the charmer's spot, Carla thought. The first of the wines, a white, was poured—each bottle was covered with a napkin, but her palate and common sense told her they were French and very good. Nancy Bryant asked Dennis to make a toast, which made Carla wonder just how well these two knew each other.

Dennis stood, lifted his glass, and said, "The first thing people who don't know him ask about is his name. Whitney, I mean, not Skip—they ask about that, too, but that's another story. Whitney is a name that carries weight in the life of our country. It can be a burden to its bearer and it can be a challenge, but it is always an obligation. Skip is a man who has never pretended to false humility about his name, nor has he ever backed away from the duty it demands. Those of us who have known him longest know what the country is about to learn: Skip Whitney is as capable a man as this country has produced. They know it at State, and if I have anything to say about it, the world at large is going to know. Ten years from now will be an election year and I wish to be the first to put forth your name for 1600 Pennsylvania Avenue, 1972. I drink to you, Skip, and to the possibilities." People cheered, then drank. Carla heard someone at the other end of the table say, "Hear, hear." She knew Dennis believed very little of his toast. It was all ritual. God only knows to what purpose. Before she could consider it further, Skip rose to respond. He was tall but a little fleshy, with flat blond hair that fell over his forehead. Carla guessed he was about forty.

"Thank you, Dennis. Well. The only thing I can say to that is, you are wildly optimistic." He waited for the laughter he knew would come, then said, "Seriously. My only plans are for my new job at State, trying to help our country get a grip on Southeast Asia before it's too late. That's the truth, no matter what fantasies are running through Mr. Catton's wonderfully imaginative head. I thank you all."

The butler who had greeted them at the door, now pressed into table service, came around with bowls of consommé with fingers of crustless white toast. Since the soup spoon was the easiest to identify, Carla picked it up, and waited for the next wine. Skip turned to her, about to speak. Carla wondered if he knew just how full of shit Dennis's toast had been. "I've seen all your movies," he said. Carla groaned to herself. Not another one who wants to hear about Dr. George. Before he could pursue it, she said, "Tell me about your job. Will you go to Asia a lot?"

"Yes, as a matter of fact. Tomorrow. To Saigon. Vietnam. Forgive me if I ask if you know where it is—about half the time people don't."

"I'm terrible at geography."

"It's a peninsula that juts out of China. The French have been going at it there for years. Fighting I mean." Then he added, "War," in case Carla had missed the point. "It's all about the rubber plantations. We could get sucked into it."

"And you're going to see that doesn't happen?"

"Well, I'm going to look over the factions and make some recommendations. The President is concerned." When he said "the President" his voice seemed to Carla to drop a bit. She nodded demurely, as if she too respected the very word, let alone the man. Dennis had told her that social life in Georgetown had been affected by the young President and his gorgeous wife, but she hadn't known till now quite what he had meant. "There are several important factions," Skip said, starting what clearly was his standard lecture. "In the North there are the Vietminh, Communist insurgents. Then there are the South Vietnamese regulars and the Vietcong. But you probably know about all this."

Before Carla had to answer, a young black woman in a uniform with a lace apron and cap removed her soup, at which she had poked in a pantomime of interest, managing to stir the slivers of carrot and celery. Then the butler appeared holding a silver tray with a crown roast of lamb. The chops, with little paper frills, had already been cut and they had fallen back on the tray—as if they had fainted. In the center was a mound of stuffing—bread crumbs and herbs. As the guests were serving themselves a chop or two, Carla looked up to smile at Dennis and saw Mrs. Bryant turning away from him, to the gentleman on her left. Skip turned away as well and the guest without a name turned to her. Their knees touched under the table. First current events, now Don Juan, Carla thought.

"Have you been to Washington much, Miss Tate?" the mystery neighbor asked.

"Not since I was a child."

"Oh, yes," he said. She could see him trying to remember what she had done as a child in Washington. Since she didn't know how these people felt about giving testimony to HUAC, even at seven, she didn't refresh his memory. "My children were crazy about the Dr. George movies. Our daughter loved the horse."

"Tell her I'll say hello to Lewis for her."

"You mean he's still alive?"

"Actually, I'm not sure. But your daughter probably doesn't know that."

"Well, she knows a good deal about horses. Certainly how long they live." There seemed to be tension between them about the horse. As the irritation in his voice grew, he pushed his knees against hers a little harder. "Is Dennis turning you into a flaming radical?" he asked. She thought his tongue was in his cheek, but she couldn't be sure because she didn't really know what Dennis's politics were. It made her feel stupid to realize that she was going out with a political analyst of some distinction and she was unable to characterize his views. He knows my pictures, she thought, chastising herself. "No," she answered. "Not yet, anyway. I take it you don't approve."

"His heart's in the right place on most things. The trouble with your Mr. Catton is he only has to deal in the theoretical. The task facing those of us who actually have to spend the money is figuring out which excessive ventures are least likely to run up the national debt."

"I see," she said. "That makes sense."

"Then there's hope yet that you won't become a complete Cattonite." He bowed his head to her and turned away. Her instinct made her look up at Nancy Bryant, who was turning her head again, back to Dennis.

By ten, when a molded *bombe* was served—two flavors of ice

cream—Carla was restless, anxious either to leave or to get drunk. Chocolate sauce, in a silver creamer, had been served with the dessert. After the sauce had been walked around the table, the butler left it, so it might be passed from guest to guest as it was needed. Carla noticed Nancy Bryant staring at it. Clearly, Carla thought, the hostess didn't approve of leaving the chocolate sauce on the table. She'll probably have a word with the butler about that. When Skip Whitney offered it to Carla she reached out and took it from him. She could feel the air around Nancy Bryant change; a coolness was unmistakable, a judgment made. She realized when the others passed it they put it down and let the next person pick it up. No one else had grabbed it out of the air as if it were a football. One more obscure refinement I don't know and hardly care about, she thought. When a few of the men talked about adjourning to the library for cigars, Carla caught Dennis's eye, letting him know she was ready to go.

Back at his apartment, Dennis was exhilarated, high from the evening, certain that Carla's presence was a great success. She wasn't so sure. Dennis could see it—he was sensitive to her moods, a good sign. "I'm sorry if it was hard," he said. "There's a lot to get used to. All the glasses and silverware and stuff."

"Fuck the forks," she said, realizing he hadn't seen what was upsetting her at all. "It's the world I don't know anything about."

"You know more than you think," he said and then kissed her. Their lovemaking didn't feel quite right to her that night, although Dennis seemed transported. When he fell asleep, she got out of bed and went into the living room. She stood in front of his bookcase, naked, looking at the titles. He had a mixture of college textbooks, new titles that hadn't been opened, and paperback mysteries he probably used as sleeping pills. She ran a finger over the spines and thought about her own reading—mostly scripts and novels that might make scripts. Her life had been easy, charmed, others often said. She knew it was true as long as she stayed in the cocoon of the movie business. It had made her a star—but, as she was painfully aware tonight, an uneducated one.

"Can't sleep?" he asked. She turned around to see Dennis standing, watching her. She wondered how long he had been there. He was wearing his robe, but it was open.

"I want some books," she said. It was a simple enough request but the intensity in her voice told him all he needed to know.

Dennis scanned his bookcase, considering. "Not a lot here," he said, then started pulling down titles. He handed her a copy of Samuelson's *Economics*. "This unhappy thing is part of every college education in America—good or bad. It's a digest of Keynes."

"What's that?"

"John Maynard Keynes. A Cambridge economist and the main guy these days. The shortest possible form is, debts, called deficits, are good for governments, bad for individuals. You owe any money? Besides a mortgage?"

"I don't think so."

"Then, according to Maynard, you're a better person than you would be a government."

As Carla was leafing through the thick green volume, she saw it was Dennis's own college copy, with his notes in the margins in a youthful hand.

"Read this," he said, handing her a paperback copy of *Decline of the West*. "It's hard and it's short. It won't exactly get you through a Georgetown dinner, but it'll give you an intellectual anchor. And these," he said. "*The Theory of the Leisure Class*—Thorstein Veblen—because everybody in Washington's read it or claims they have. And *Making of the President*. Teddy White on the election. It's fun and it'll teach you what there is to know about electoral politics."

"Will you help me?"

"We can talk about each one chapter by chapter. This is just what's here. There's more to read."

"Thank you," she whispered, pressing herself to him.

"Let's do something you're already good at." He kissed her and took the books away. When they dropped to the floor, Dennis pushed the copy of Veblen under her, saying he liked the angle and it was very much to the point of the leisure class. She wasn't about to enroll in college, but rather embark on some reading. Dennis would be her teacher. She knew how Hollywood worked, or at least she knew more than most twenty-two-year-old actresses, stars or not, because Jack had taught her. Now she would learn about history, politics, the economy and foreign affairs. She reached down, stroking his leg, then took him in her hand and guided him inside her.

Over the next months Carla embarked on what Dennis called

her tutorials. She read with a ferocity she hadn't known she had, demanding that he give her tests to prove she was absorbing the reading. "Like college, just like college," she insisted. She used any excuse to go to New York. When she began making the trips alone, Cora was hurt. She couldn't imagine how Carla managed. "I'm not an invalid," Carla said. "You take me to the airport, I get on last and off first. A car meets me."

"Yeah, but on the plane? Don't people bother you?"

"Sometimes. I deal with it. Okay?"

"How do you know who's going to sit next to you?" Cora asked, refusing to let it go.

"We can buy the other seat," she said, sounding like an adolescent rebelling against her family.

Dennis's apartment on Sutton Place was vast, with high ceilings and wooden moldings. The apartment seemed to Carla like a college—Four's Yale, a place she never got to see, or Dennis's Fordham. In the evenings they would go to the theater or to dinner with journalists. Dennis liked to show her off. She was used to being on display and considered it ordinary behavior. But the lure of his books, of having him to herself to ask questions and to explain what she had been reading, was what she really liked. After dinner Carla would read and Dennis would walk around the apartment, naked, strutting from room to room, reciting poetry from memory:

> I ranted to the knave and fool,
> But outgrew that school,
> Would transform the part,
> Fit audience found, but cannot rule
> My fanatic heart.

"More William Butler Yeats, right?" she asked.

"Bravo. Just call him Yeats. Like '21.' The name is the '21' Club but only tourists say that. Yeats."

"Is it me?" she asked, refusing to be deflected. "Being transformed?"

"Do you want to be?"

"I know what that poem means," she said, irritated at what she took to be a patronizing quality in his voice. "It pretends to be about acting, but it's about more—trying to change, I guess, but then not being sure you want to."

"You've interpreted it."

"Yeah, I interpreted it," she said, the irritation mounting in her voice. "That's what I do. Maybe only screenplays, but I can follow a poem. What else is it supposed to be about?"

"Ireland, Ireland and Ireland."

"I might be being transformed, but you're the one with the fanatic heart."

"God, what have I done?" he said with the kind of mock seriousness that they both knew wasn't mock at all. "The great beauty of the world and I'm turning her into just one more smart girl. A bookist. God forgive me."

Later, while she was trying to penetrate Parkman's *History of France and England in North America,* she fell asleep on the sofa with the book open on her lap. Dennis found her there and carried her into the bedroom. As he put her into bed, she told him to test her on the book, to ask questions about the French and Indian wars. She wanted to know about the notes he made in the margins, and about the professor who had taught him. "Was it a priest?" she asked.

"I can't remember who taught that. Some mother's son who wanted to love God enough that God might love him back. It's about the eighteenth century, written in the nineteenth. American history before 1776."

"I'm going to read every damn word."

He took her face in his hands and said, "You are the greatest *tabula rasa* since the stones for the Commandments." He got into bed with her but she wouldn't make love until he explained what *tabula rasa* meant.

19.

Jack could make his peace with the fact of other men in Carla's life, but he didn't like her being three thousand miles away. The hardest time for him was when he was also in New York, but, because of Dennis, not able to see her. When he called, Dennis answered. Jack introduced himself and the two men made a moment's worth of small talk before Carla came to the phone. Dennis was a reporter, a trade that tends to make its practitioners suspicious, and since in his heart he doubted a woman as glamorous and beautiful as Carla could really love him, he was always on the lookout for competition. "Who is that guy, again? One of your agents?"

"He's a lawyer. He advises me. He found *Barbara Farrell*."

"He's in love with you, isn't he?"

"A lot of people are in love with me. If they know me or not. It comes with the job."

"But he's not a stranger. He's somebody you deal with. You in love with him?"

"I don't like being interviewed."

"Okay, sorry," Dennis said, as sure of her answer as if a senator had said, "No comment."

Although Jack had certainly expected to see her and was not pleased to be refused, he was calling about business. MCA's free ride as combined agents and studio was coming to an end. After eight years of being able to cut deals that benefited them more than their clients, the Justice Department was putting a stop to it. MCA had decided to remain in the production business and continue building Universal Pictures, their studio. The agency business would be sold off. The issue was Freddy Durslag. He wanted to use the breakup to start his own agency. He had asked Jack how Carla would respond.

Freddy had hinted that if it worked, Jack would be in line for a piece of the business—silent equity in his new agency. Jack wasn't above it; kickbacks and under-the-table payments were the staple of his business. How else could he settle labor disputes before they got out of hand except by buying off the opposition? But he was offended that Freddy would assume he would do such a thing with Carla's career. He told Freddy that he was duty bound to explain to Carla that if she signed, she would be putting Freddy in business. Her presence would attract other clients. He offered to represent Carla for 8 percent instead of the usual 10. Jack knew he was talking to a desperate man. Because he felt the kickback scheme had insulted his loyalty to Carla, he toyed with Freddy. "Be a *mensch*, Freddy. Call it at five. You know that's your bottom."

"I'll take it at five. But it's our secret."

"And a piece goes to Carla. Cash payments."

"Jack, please," Freddy said, trying not to whine. "How am I going to do that?"

"I'll let you know," Jack said. Neither he nor Carla ever spoke to Freddy again.

Carla refused to get involved in the selection of a new agent. Jack suggested a guy at William Morris named Jimmy Chase. Carla was ready to sign without even talking to him. Jack made Jimmy fly to New York and audition, in case she changed her mind after meeting him. To Carla, he seemed interchangeable with Freddy—same diminutive nickname, same modest, unassuming, corporate style. She talked to him for twenty minutes and said he'd be fine.

It appeared that Carla was going to burrow into Dennis's library and not come out until she'd read every book on his shelves. No script was enticing enough to lure her away. She would look at the ones she was sent and declare them empty.

"Of course they are," Cora said. "They're movie scripts."

Jack took her at her word about why she was going to New York and what she did there. He knew she wouldn't bother to lie—that was for people who had to scramble for advantage. Occasionally Carla fibbed, but if she preferred not to tell the truth, she just remained silent. Cora, who was usually perceptive about Carla, felt she was up to something more than an education. Jack read it correctly. "Of course she's having an affair with him," he told Cora. "But that's not why she's there."

"She never studied anything except scripts," Cora said, exasperated by the gulf that was growing between them.

"That's why she's doing it. You and I never read all those books, but we had more traditional educations. We were at least exposed to people who had read them. The library at Metro was strictly false fronts. Don't look for a motive beyond that. You won't find one."

While his daughter was in New York, Milton was busy at the Friars Club. He'd arrive early each morning and patrol the clubhouse. He'd examine the staff uniforms and make sure no trash had been left out. When the members began arriving for lunch, Milton would station himself in the lobby. He loved to shake their hands and act as if he were only sorry he couldn't join them for lunch or a couple hands of gin rummy.

Jack got word of the calamity before anyone else. He moved quickly to separate Milton from the worst of it, calling the district attorney, Cora Cohen, and then the tough one, Carla, in New York. Jack was quite direct, lawyerly, about it, not trying to make it sound better or worse than it was. "Your father has gotten himself in a jam," Jack said. "At the Friars." She was three thousand miles away, but Jack could sense her tension. "Are you alone?" he asked.

"Yes. Dennis is at the paper. What did he do?"

"You know they play a lot of cards there. Gin rummy, poker, pinochle. Several of the members have been losing large sums of money."

"What did he do?"

"Some of the biggest games were cooked. They play on the second floor, in the card room. The heavy games are in an alcove with a dropped ceiling. Somebody was in the crawl space looking through a hole, sending signals to the table."

"What was my father's part?"

"He had the keys. He let them in."

"Oh my God," Carla said. "What do we do?"

"The complications are that some bottom-level hoods are mixed up in it. I don't know how high this goes, but if the mob's in, it could get difficult. The big loser so far is Ted Berg-hold. He's a grocery wholesaler. It looks like he lost about sixty grand."

"Let's write him a check," Carla said.

"I've offered. The problem is Ted's dignity. He's been made a fool. That's also our advantage—he won't want his foolishness in the papers. Ted can be reached. The problem is I don't know yet who else got taken."

"Jesus . . ."

"There are going to be indictments. I think I can keep him out of jail, but if he's indicted, I can't keep him out of the papers."

"Should I come home?"

"Yes. Don't tell your Mr. Catton about this. Not yet."

"I trust him, Jack. I have to tell him."

"He's the press. Don't do it."

"Does my mother know?"

"As far as I know, you, Cora and I know. That's it. Just get out here. Tell Cora what flight you're on."

She told Dennis she had to go to Los Angeles on an emergency business matter, a meeting about a movie. It was the first time she had lied to him and she wondered if it was necessary, or a way for Jack to drive a wedge between her and Dennis. It made her smile to think of Jack being jealous. It was her only pleasant thought during the flight.

When the scandal broke, it quickly became an international story. The idea of the Friars fleeced in their own clubhouse was irresistible. The papers went wild with it, running pictures of various Friars going in and out of the clubhouse, regardless of whether those particular Friars had anything to do with the scandal.

The second day Carla was back in Los Angeles, she had Cora call her father and tell him to come to the Loma Vista house that night. Carla didn't trust herself to talk to him on the phone. She wanted to speak to him face-to-face.

Carla watched through a window as Milton got out of his car. She could see his chest heave as he tried to get a grip on himself. He was biting his lower lip as if he were trying to stop more words from spilling out of his mouth. As an actress Carla knew all about private moments and private terrors. She could see, unobserved, her father's true condition, no matter what face he would put on when he got inside.

He was waiting for her in the living room. When he kissed her on the cheek, she could smell his sweat. "Honey, I want you to hear my side of all this," he said, in what Carla took to be an attempt to control the discussion.

"Your side is you could wind up in jail before this is over." Without really knowing she was doing it, Carla took her initial tone and attitude from Jack. The more serious the issue, the lower-keyed Jack became. Carla did the same.

"I know that. I'm not trying to deny it. It was stupid. I want you to know it wasn't my idea. These guys came to me with it. I got talked into it."

"Milton," she said, cutting him off. "Do me the favor of allowing me not to know the details so no matter what happens, I won't have anything to testify about."

"Yeah, sure," he said. It hadn't occurred to him that he wouldn't have to tell his story to his daughter. He had assumed that's what this visit would be, a trip to the woodshed, in which he would have to come clean. He'd spent the last few days trying to think of ways to tell it that made him look the least bad. It hadn't been easy.

"I'm doing what can be done to keep you out of this."

"I know. I appreciate that." He looked as if he was about to cry.

She wanted to ease her tone, and comfort him, but she couldn't. The more scared he became, the more she wanted to stop, put her arms around him and tell him she loved him no matter what, but those words wouldn't come. "Do you have any idea what you put at risk?" she said, again using Jack's words, making them her own. "Do you think if the papers get hold of your name, they're going to leave me out of it?"

"Can you keep me out of the papers?" he asked, barely able to form the words. No matter how stupid he'd been, Milton knew full well that publicity was the thing that would harm his daughter. If he could have accepted a jail term right then and had Carla left out of it, he would have gone to prison. He wanted to tell her that, but her anger, which was mounting and had no end that he could see, was too great and his own fear too deep. It was the lowest he had felt since the police had arrived at the Friars.

"I will do what I can do to keep a lid on it, but don't you

kid yourself for one minute that I'm doing it for you. You might benefit, but it's strictly a side issue. I think what you did was scummy and disgusting. You can't have done it for money. If you needed money you know you could get it from me. I think you did it because some thug fussed over you, made you feel like a big shot, so you took a chance. God knows what else you did that hasn't come out. I'm telling you right now, I don't care who you are. I'm not going to be dragged through the mud with you."

Carla's diatribe was rolling out, beyond her control, and, it felt to her, beyond her making. It was like a performance, except she was speaking without a script. She believed what she was saying. Still, it was a performance—of what she thought she ought to say, or what Jack had said to her, filtered through her own anger.

When Carla paused, Milton thought he had come through it. But then, feeling the power of what she was learning from Dennis, Carla became furious at what her father had done in the past, as she saw it at that moment, for denying her an education.

"You did this to me!" she shouted. "You were the only one who could have done it differently. You made me grow up feeling stupid because all I know about is the goddamn movie business!"

"No, no," he said, shaking his head in confusion at the turn things had taken. "You had the greatest childhood ever. You did great."

"I was a kid. What did I know? You didn't have enough sense to send me to school. Your idea of school was those idiot places where they don't even know about what they're supposed to—let alone anything important. I should have been reading history—not learning how to play make-believe. My whole life, year in and year out, it was like summer camp. I was studying crap when other kids were reading, learning, becoming whole people instead of distorted little acting machines."

All the things Milton had always thought of as his triumph, the clear, irrefutable signs that he alone had raised her properly, had prepared her for the life she now led, were being attacked.

She would have continued, but his face had turned an awful ash color. She thought he might be about to have a heart attack. He was suffering the worst of fates for him—the daughter who was his whole life, the only thing he had ever done that had turned out exactly as he had wanted, had hoped for, was practically disowning him. That Carla, his own Karen, could turn on him like this was more than Milton could bear. The only thought that kept him from collapsing was his belief that she was wrong and would someday come to know it. The way he had raised his daughter was the one heroic thing he had done in his life. That knowledge allowed him the tiny comfort that eventually her fury would pass and she would come back to him.

When Carla realized the power of her anger, that she was speaking more viciously than she wanted to, that she might shatter him, she went to him to try to hug him, to say in actions if not words that he was still her father. But they were both too upset for it to work. The embrace was awkward and contrived. It made Milton feel a little better—any sign from her that she didn't hate him completely and irrevocably was a godsend and probably the only reason he was able to walk out and not crawl. But it didn't help Carla at all. She felt worse than ever—awful that he had done this ghastly thing, worried that her career would be damaged by it, and shaken that she had such cruelty in her. When Milton had left, Cora came to her to hold and comfort her. "Did you hear any of it?" Carla asked.

"Hard not to," Cora said. "You have to put that part out of your mind. Now Jack and I have to do what we can." Carla leaned her head on Cora's shoulder, wanting Cora to be mother, father and friend.

When the grand jury handed up the indictments, Milton was not named. Most of the club members knew of his part in the crime. They assumed that Jack Markel had persuaded the district attorney not to go after Milton. They were such a gambling bunch that they liked the idea of the chicanery that went into keeping Carla's name clear. If anything, it made it all worth it to them, a sign that the world was indeed as corrupt as they all knew it to be. Milton could no longer serve as official greeter; for a long time he was afraid to go anywhere near Beverly Hills for fear he'd run into a Friar. Eventually, Al Soderberg took him back, but he was subdued, without the sparkle he once had. He changed from a man with a sort of bargain-basement raffishness to one beaten down by little mistakes that had grown into a pattern of failure that lined his face and gave him the kind of permanent smile suggesting not happiness but rather a hope that he might please.

After the Friars episode, Carla decided she didn't want to live in the Loma Vista house anymore. It was fine for a teenage girl, but she was twenty-four, an established international star. She wanted to live like one. She found a house she liked not far away, on Schuyler Road, a large stone place that looked more like Connecticut than Beverly Hills. After one walk through its six bedrooms, five bathrooms, and library, and a glimpse at the pool and tennis court, she bought it. The year was 1964 and the price was $145,000.

Carla put Cora in charge of finding a decorator and hiring gardeners and maids. Ceil was given a sunny suite. Carla knew she was treating her mother particularly well because she felt bad about how she had treated her father.

She began going back to the bungalow in the afternoons. Dennis had gone to France for a month to interview political leaders and get a feel for European politics. He called frequently, suggesting books to her and telling her he missed her. When he returned, she went to New York to meet him for a weekend at Sutton Place. She felt comfortable there, making love with him among his books, listening to his stories about the French elections. She stayed two weeks instead of a weekend.

As they were sitting up in bed, in a gentle mood, their legs entwined, the television flickering, Dennis asked if she thought all the reading she had been doing helped her as an actress. "In *Red Roses*, were you a better blind person than if you hadn't read, say, Saint Augustine?"

"Not really," she said, thinking about the question. Neither Carla nor the critics had thought much of *Red Roses*, but the public had loved seeing Carla stumble around in dark glasses, and the picture had been a hit. "What the tutorials do is help me think in a different way." When she said "tutorials" she imitated his voice. It was one of his favorite words and it amused her to throw it back to him. "They help me as a person. As an actress, I work on instinct. We all do. It's sort of magic."

"If I were going to write about you—"

"You wouldn't dare."

"I might. I would say, 'If Miss Tate believes in anything larger than herself, it is in using her considerable psychic energies for the clear portrayal of emotion.' "

"That's right. Make it clear that acting with psychological accuracy is her one true goal."

He smiled at her and said, "Nobody's going to call you Monroe again." When Carla was first going out with Dennis, a number of reporters compared them to Arthur Miller and Marilyn Monroe. At first Carla had laughed, but as she thought it over, she realized that in their ludicrous, reductionist way they were saying she was stupid, or at least uneducated. To complain about that, however, would be to imply she believed Monroe had been a dummy. Carla neither thought that was the case nor cared to insult Monroe's memory in public. It was one of the reasons she read so much so fast. She also did it for herself, to make up for lost time, as well as in reaction to clumsy public characterizations of her.

When she missed her period she knew she had done it on purpose. She didn't want to see a doctor she couldn't control, so without telling Dennis what it was about, she went back to Los Angeles. "You want to see Lumsford again?" Cora asked, knowing she didn't.

"No. I want a regular doctor."

"You want the baby?"

"Yes," she said, not trying to disguise the excitement she felt.

"Are you going to marry him?"

"Why not?"

"Well," Cora said, choosing her words, "I think he'll make a better father than he will a husband."

"I should have time to do one picture before I get fat. Let's find one that shoots here, so I can live at home." When Cora went off to start the hunt for a suitable script, and Carla was alone, she called Dennis and told him. He was even more exhilarated than she had expected, as happy at the prospect as she was. It made her love him, or at least think she loved him.

Before her marriage, Carla flew back to Los Angeles to tell Jack. She met him at the bungalow and when he was in her arms, she told him gently, with protestations of love. As she stroked his forehead, he grew still and his mouth got tight. She thought he might cry. Instead, she did. Jack kissed her tears and told her that no matter whom she lived with or was married to, no one would ever know her better than he did or love her more. She knew it was true.

Carla and Dennis were married in his apartment on Sutton Place, in a ceremony conducted by a U.S. Court of Appeals judge. Cora wanted to send telegrams to a handful of reporters and friends. "Not before we tell the *Trib*," Dennis said, hugging his bride. "The *Trib* can tell the world."

. . .

In Los Angeles, Jack was the one who dealt with Jimmy Chase and the Morris office, demanding that they find a script Carla liked, that the money be big, and the schedule such that she could live at home. Jimmy knew if he didn't deliver on her first request, no matter how outrageous, he could be the agent who signed and lost Carla Tate in the same year. He studied old coverage—brief synopses of scripts that had long since been abandoned—searching for anything with a bravura role for a woman. In the end it was his secretary who turned up *Balancing Act*, a thriller about a woman trapped in her house while three vicious intruders run wild, pursuing her from room to room. The script was several years old, but it had a strong, sympathetic role for a woman. When Jimmy reported his find to Jack, he said, "There's a lot of interest. If we move fast, we can get it."

"If you like this thing," Jack told Carla when he gave her the script, "we can get it going. Jimmy gave me the usual lies about how hot it is. He's nervous and working hard. Just what we need."

Carla barely read it before she said yes. As preproduction started, Dennis flew back and forth to be with his wife during her pregnancy. Ceil, who was always nervous when there was a new man in her daughter's life, found Dennis charming. The idea of being a grandmother appealed to her enormously. Just before Carla began to shoot *Balancing Act*, Ceil called Milton to tell him he was going to be a grandfather. She had spoken to her husband over the years, but only when he initiated it. He was pleased at the news, of course, but also because he assumed Carla had asked Ceil to make the call, a sign that if he wasn't quite forgiven, he soon might be. It wasn't true—Ceil had done it on her own, out of a sense of fairness and generosity of spirit.

Ceil's happiness was tempered a bit when Bela, in his mid-seventies, now about to become a great-grandfather, fell ill. He thought it was an ulcer, but the doctors believed it was cancer. Edna had been taking care of him. Now it was a question of a nursing home, an expensive undertaking. Edna called Carla directly, rather than talking it over with Ceil. Edna was ready to pay part of the cost, but she wanted help from her niece. It took Edna a while to get through—between *Balancing Act*, the pregnancy, and Dennis flying in and out, Carla wasn't taking many calls. When she did hear about her grandfather's condition, she said of course she'd pay whatever was required, but she didn't think a nursing home was quite right. Knowing it would give her mother a sense of purpose, Carla suggested instead that Bela be moved into the Schuyler Road house. The last time Carla had tried to help a relative had been to get her father a job. She felt more optimistic about taking care of Bela. Ceil was thrilled and Carla asked Cora to supervise the construction that would turn a part of the house into a little hospital.

Carla could see that her grandfather was failing, but that it might be a slow disintegration. She was determined to get to know him. She got a kick out of having him around—even if he didn't pray or do the odd things Carla associated with old Jewish men. Dennis, who was used to the suspiciousness of his own relatives in these matters, assumed Bela would disapprove of him. But Bela was fascinated by his granddaughter's second husband, the famous reporter. In what Bela seemed to know was his last illness, he began to talk about Sophie, his wife dead so long. When Carla and Dennis weren't around, Ceil would sit by her father's bedside, stroking his hand, listening to stories of Budapest she had first heard as a teenager.

After *Balancing Act* was finished, when Carla was seven months pregnant, she went to New York to be with Dennis for a week. She wanted her child born in Los Angeles, although she knew Dennis preferred New York. They sparred about it from time to time, but it never became an issue between them, because Dennis knew she would win.

When they were home, on Sutton Place, Carla told her husband she wanted to get involved in political issues.

"Any particular issues?" he asked. "Or did you just have in mind running down the list of Republican editorials in the *Trib* and declaring yourself in opposition?"

"I'm talking about politics at home," which was the way Carla always referred to California. "Sidney Shepherd's got it in his head that Ronnie Reagan should run for governor."

"God help us all," Dennis said. "Does he want you to give money?"

"Of course. But he wants me to get involved in the campaign. I think it's nuts."

"That's a relief."

"I wouldn't mind talking in public about something. Not for some actor trying to hold his career together, but maybe conservation. The way we're ruining the forests."

"Ecology."

"What?" she asked, unfamiliar with the word.

"The study of the natural environment. I'll get you the literature. Read it, then we'll find the right candidate, some guy who will get behind ecological reform as the price of your public support. Why the hell not?"

"What if that turns out to be Ronnie Reagan?"

"Then we scrap the whole idea and let the trees take care of themselves."

Left to her own devices, Carla would have put a soapbox down in Central Park and announced her opinions to the crowd that surely would have gathered. Jack, who supported the idea of her making public statements, made sure that didn't happen. Before she would go out in public, Jack would review what she planned to say. He made sure she didn't overdo it, or sound like a zealot. When she spoke, on television news shows and to environmental groups, the sight of a famous, very pregnant actress talking about the future of the earth was very effective.

Carla and Dennis had become part of New York's hip café society. They were both fond of the back room at Max's Kansas City. When their uptown friends would ask them if they'd like to go to Pavillon for dinner, or to "21," Dennis would be tempted, but Carla would always urge him to say no so they could go down to Union Square. Carla always watched the waitresses, fascinated by those girls juggling dishes, rushing back and forth to the kitchen, fending off randy customers, all to support the opportunity to be an out-of-work actress. She looked at them all, trying to see in their eyes the spark of compulsive desire that might make it possible for one of those young women to have a career in the theater or the movies. Carla always urged Dennis to leave big tips at Max's.

The back room was Andy's room. He was often there in the evening, along with other celebrities and journalists. Carla was charmed by the patron of Max's. Mr. Warhol always stopped at their table to say hello or invite them to a private party at the Factory, as his studio was known.

One night at the Factory, after dinner, with everyone sitting on the ratty sofas, one of Andy's minions began shooting 8-millimeter film of Carla talking with one of the resident so-called superstars, a pale young woman with delicate, aristocratic features, called Chaillot. Talking might be too strong a word for it, because Chaillot was too high to make any sense. Dennis soon got restless, but he stayed because Carla seemed content. Then a couple of Factory denizens—a well-muscled young boy and a supple girl—began to make love behind Chaillot and Carla. Chaillot was ready to join in—but that sort of thing didn't interest Carla no matter what her physical condition, and certainly not now. "I'm playing the audience," she said.

Dennis, who had a better sense of what the press might do with the footage, pulled his wife out of frame, grabbed the camera, and yanked the film out. As he was doing that, Andy turned up with his own camera, filming Dennis ripping the film out of the first camera. "It's a happening!" one of the others yelled. As if that were their cue, the other boys and girls, sullen, poetic and posturing young people who looked to Dennis to be middle-class kids in Halloween costumes, danced into Andy's frame, taking off one another's black leather, consuming drugs and either fucking in unusual combinations or nodding off. Dennis decided that was quite enough for himself, his wife and his unborn child.

As they left, Carla told him, "Cora Cohen couldn't have done it better."

Dennis, who was already irritated at her blasé view, stopped in the street and said, "Carla, I don't work for you. Do you understand that? I'm not on the payroll. What I do for you, I do out of love and for our marriage and our child. Don't get me confused with the help. Got it?"

"I got it," she said, chastened. Then, remembering Cora's words, she said, "You'll make a very good father."

True to her plan, Carla was in Los Angeles when her time was near. The day she went into labor, Cora checked her into a suite in the celebrity wing of Cedars of Lebanon Hospital. On July 19, 1966, Carla's daughter was born. When the doctor placed the baby on Carla's breast, he gave the scissors to Dennis, who cut the cord. When Carla nursed her, the baby made a tiny fist and tapped on her mother as if she were asking, "Who are you?" or perhaps, "Who am I?" The act of nursing made Carla think, I have what I need, now I can be happy. The child was named in honor of Carla's grandmother. Sophie Catton was born forty-eight years after the death of Sophie Sanhoff, her maternal great-grandmother. When Bela was told of it, he wept.

20.

Before Sophie was six months old, her father's thoughts and journalistic ambitions were drawn to Vietnam, the international drama that more than any other would define the decade of his daughter's birth. Dennis wanted to report from the front, even to be under fire if necessary. Although it was Dennis who talked to Carla about the details of the war, it was Jack's view that shaped her own. He saw the war as misguided and badly conducted. He did not, however, see it as a moral issue. Carla knew it was wrong. She wanted to make public statements, giving voice to the outrage she felt. Her husband counseled patience and quiet. For himself, he said, "I want to go. I want to be there."

"Fine," Carla said. "We'll both go." She knew him well enough to know that wasn't what he wanted. What concerned him was that she would become notorious for her views on the war and his own objective journalistic voice would be lost. Or, equally troubling, she would make such a public fuss that his paper would use it as an excuse to keep him away from the only story that mattered.

The *Trib* was in the midst of financial problems. What was left of it was now called *The World-Journal-Tribune*. Between his wife's newfound political views and the paper's shaky finances, Dennis was afraid he would never get an overseas assignment.

While Dennis was trying to find the most effective way to persuade the publisher that he should be in Southeast Asia, Carla suggested that he consult Jack Markel.

"What for? What does he know about it?"

"He's the best guy for strategy in Hollywood."

"This isn't a movie deal," Dennis said, annoyed at what he took to be an insult to his ability to navigate his way around a profession in which he had been operating for twenty-five years. Carla knew he was wrong, that anyone who could master Hollywood would have an idea or two about how to maneuver at a newspaper. It was partly the hubris of an old Hollywood hand, which, at twenty-six, Carla was. No matter what the situation or the problem, according to veterans of the movie business, Hollywood had already seen it. Carla recognized it was Dennis's suspicion of Jack and not of Hollywood that made him bridle at her suggestion.

The next day when she went to visit Jack at the bungalow, he told her what Dennis ought to do, then told her to say she had thought of it herself.

As a result, Dennis asked for an appointment with the publisher, where he laid out what he assumed was his wife's approach to the problem. It amounted to telling the paper that if they didn't send him to Vietnam he would quit and sign on with *My Weekly Reader* or any damn paper that would print his dispatches. The publisher argued that he was a columnist who couldn't go back to reporting. It was, he insisted, a demotion, a step backward. Dennis listened, then said he was going, no matter what the *Trib* did. They could either get in on the action, or suffer the consequences of the story he would write about how mismanaged the paper was and why it was about to go under. He would document the extravagance and foolishness that was the paper's specialty. Let the advertisers read that! It was a vintage Markel approach, a mixture of the noble—I'm going to get the story with or without you—and the scabrous—a threat to drag the paper through the public mud. When the *Trib* agreed to send him, Dennis was too elated to question the source of his wife's strategic abilities.

Carla still hoped to go with him. She had been reading about the war, thinking about it and talking to Dennis about it. She was sure this was a significant opportunity in her life. She didn't want it to pass by.

"What about Sophie?" Dennis asked. "You can't take her to the front."

"Why not? All it costs is money. I'll hire a nurse to stay with her when I can't."

"Carla, no. It's crazy."

"You can't tell me what I can or can't do."

"You're my wife. You're Sophie's mother."

"I have as much right to go as you do."

"That's positively delusional. I'm a journalist. You're an actress. Do you have any idea what the press will do if you're photographed in the jungle with your baby, speaking against the war? Ask Cora. She knows all about the press."

"You could do it," Cora told her. "But you'd have to be very careful. Not go where you're going to want to go. And not say the kinds of things you're thinking."

"Because of Sophie?"

"That's part of it, but that can be controlled. Lots of pictures of you and Sophie at orphanages and hospitals. Exactly the kind of Lady Bountiful crap you won't want to do. Start making speeches, you'll get in trouble and you'll screw up Dennis. That's just the truth, Carla."

Carla didn't see it as part of a larger cultural issue; the women's movement was forming, but Carla wasn't yet aware of it. She saw it as an argument with her husband that she was losing. It was natural that she would blame someone. The likely candidates were her husband and daughter. She loved Sophie. It constantly amazed her how much, how devoted and protective of her she felt. Sophie had taken over a portion of Carla—she was always there, if not in Carla's arms, then curled into her thoughts. She wasn't about to blame her daughter for her disappointment.

Carla and Sophie saw Dennis off at the airport. Carla tried to put a good face on it, but she resented that he could do what she could not. Dennis recognized her resentment, but he was so excited about going that he put it out of his mind. He swore he would call when the phones worked and write long letters when they didn't. Carla embraced her husband, but her instinct was to hold the baby up to her father so his face would be imprinted on her mind.

In her husband's absence, Carla went back to Jack and the bungalow. He was crazy about Sophie and sometimes urged

Carla to bring the child with her. "I'm too old for you," Carla would joke. "You just want to see the baby."

"There's some truth in that," Jack said, laughing.

Carla thought Dennis's dispatches were slanted toward the government's point of view. In fact, they were dispassionate, written by a man who was in pursuit of an elusive truth. Dennis was among the first to question the Army's optimistic statistics. He reported on the indomitability of the Vietcong, who burrowed into tunnels and stayed there, seemingly for years. Then the Left hailed him as one of their own—until he wrote about the furious spirit and will to win of the American boys. Then the Left would call him an apologist for a corrupt government. Carla knew Dennis would say that if everything he wrote angered someone, then he was doing his job. The problem was that the *Trib* folded, and Dennis was told to report back to New York. When Carla heard that's what he was expected to do, she told Cora, "He'll file freelance if he has to. Somebody'll hire him." She was right. The Associated Press grabbed him and he went right on filing stories.

For Jack's fifty-sixth birthday, Carla wanted to give a small party. Jack, who never liked to have the personal details of his life known, wouldn't allow it. Instead he suggested they go away for a quiet weekend together. Carla had wanted to go back to the Thunderbird, where they had spent their first night together. She had been famous then, but not as famous as now, and she hadn't had a celebrated marriage or an infant daughter. By the time they had sorted out the problem of privacy, they decided not to leave Los Angeles. In the end, they stayed in the bungalow, making love and talking. Jack always said that in many ways their love affair paralleled a marriage. Sex was still a cornerstone of their relationship, but it was not the only one. Like a marriage in which sex gets lost to the urgencies of finances and children, Jack and Carla no longer spent as much time in bed as at the beginning. Part of the reason, Carla knew, was that her husband was thousands of miles away, and that reduced the danger, and the edge of mystery.

Another part of it, a part she didn't like to think about, was that Jack was getting older. In his aging she could sense her own. When she first met Jack, when she was seventeen, the world had no end. At twenty-seven, it shouldn't either, but Carla shared in Jack's age. His calendar was hers. Looking at him as he dozed, her eyes rested on the paunch that was now a permanent part of him, rather than the "few pounds I'm going to take off." She looked at his balding scalp, tempted to run her fingers over it. He no longer made an attempt to comb his remaining hair over the bald spot. That had always looked like a silly vanity to her, and she much preferred that he just accept what could not be changed. She watched him breathing evenly, resting next to her, his left leg curled over hers, while she sat upright in the bed that had become theirs. She couldn't help thinking about his death, about the day when he would no longer be there, when she would be alone, no matter who her husband was. She liked looking at him like this, unobserved. She sometimes looked at Sophie in a similar way, examining, probing, detached but enjoying the fact that while they slept, her stare could not make them uncomfortable—Jack, if he were awake, and Sophie, if she were older. She couldn't help but think that this was how the public looked at her. They sat in the dark and watched her, always on display but never acknowledging their eyes. As she thought about all Jack had done for her and all he might still do, she wondered if that was what made her love him. What if I met him right now? she thought. Would I love him? Would I even notice him? She suspected she might not. It was a painful and difficult thought, but she didn't try to avoid it as she contemplated Jack's life. She thought about his marriage to Mona and wondered if they had ever, even for a short time, been as happy together or felt the intensity that she and Jack had known. It seemed impossible to her, but she knew that was probably just wishful thinking on her part. They must have had something. He married her. He must have loved her, she mused. Instead of making her sad, it pleased her. She preferred that Jack was once happy with Mona. That was certainly better than his having been unhappy. She felt no competition with Mona, only a sense that Mona was lucky to have had any good years with this man. Carla's mind roamed to Jack's professional life. That, too, was a mystery to her. She knew that everyone in the movie business was careful of him, that he knew everyone and seemingly everything. But that still didn't answer what he did all day, or at least what he did when he wasn't with her in the bungalow.

It was hard to ask him about his marriage. She knew any question about that would make him uncomfortable. So that evening, while they were sitting on the bungalow's patio talking, she decided to ask him about his business. "What is it exactly that you really do?"

"After ten years? *Now* you want to know?"

"I know some," she said, refusing to be deflected by laughter. "Explain it."

"For years, you thought what I did was help guide your career."

"You know what I mean. I know you know everybody and you tell them how to do things. But who pays you? Do you send out bills?"

"Carla," he said, avoiding the substance of her question, "this is your husband's doing. That man has absolutely kick-started your mind. Good."

"So tell me."

Jack thought about it. He knew he couldn't answer glibly, in a way that was clever but not informative. His oldest son, who was only a few years younger than Carla, had asked him a similar question when he was in high school. Jack had been evasive then. He didn't want to do that now. "It's not something you can see. Not a performance, at least not one like yours, or a script that I write."

Carla watched him, realizing that he was really trying to answer her; he was assessing himself, considering his life. He was not by nature a reflective man, or a self-absorbed one. He was doing this for her, looking into himself because she had asked and felt entitled to an answer. She knew he was making an effort that wasn't easy for him; it ran against his secretive grain. It touched her and made her realize anew how much he loved her.

"In a way it is like those things—scripts and performances. I know a lot of people. They listen to me. I have a certain perceived authority because of that. When I was a lot younger, before I even had an active interest in the picture business, I did legal work for labor unions. This was during the Depression when I was still in Chicago, right out of law school. It didn't pay much, but I was lucky to get any kind of work. Contracts, calculating the so-called benefits, formulating demand patterns. I went up against gangsters. Some in the union, some outside of it. Not all the time, but enough. I didn't flinch. I don't know why, but I didn't. I got a reputation for toughness. Then the mob wanted me, too. If I had done it—taken their money, gone with them—God knows what would have become of me. Instead, I managed to stay with the unions and keep the other side open. I brokered contracts—labor, management, government regulators and the mob. We called it the syndicate in those days. Nobody else could do it. Here in the picture business I do a version of that. Every picture is a collection of deals. Access to the dealmakers is everything. If you don't have that access—relationships on every side of the big questions—forget it. In a way it comes down to my telephone directory. The truth is, it's mostly in my head."

"Do you know gangsters? Mob guys?"

"If I need to, I can get to them. Keep something like a lid on them."

"How?" she asked, fascinated and aware that she was hearing things no one got to hear—not agents or lawyers or reporters, and certainly not actors.

"By promising them something new, on the come. A rich deal on another picture, or sometimes a little more of a personal gift to an individual, to cool things off. You'd be surprised how cheap some of those guys can be had."

"Girls?"

"Not exactly. But glamour. To be around a movie star. You've met them. God help me, but I've introduced you and bought a little time. Hard to believe, but anybody who's ever been around it wouldn't doubt it."

"I wish I'd known. I would have flirted with them."

"That's why I didn't tell you," he said, laughing. "That's not a significant part. The real problem in Hollywood isn't the price of the talent, or the audience going over to TV. The brutal below-the-line costs on a picture go to the Teamsters. That's the money that doesn't show on the screen."

"The Teamsters are the mob?"

"They're not exactly the same, but they're connected."

"But why do the studios keep paying them?"

"To keep labor peace. The Teamsters don't control the craft unions—painters, carpenters, electricians—but they can stir up trouble when they're not happy. That can shut down production and that costs more than the Teamsters."

"And you keep them happy?"

"In the long run, only money keeps them happy. But I can deal with them and with the studios. And with Washington, where they can change our rules whenever they want to. I don't break any laws and I try not to promise what can't be delivered. But I work with people who sometimes do. When I work on a specific problem, I send a bill, very large. Never to a union, only to management. When I advise people on both sides about general strategy, I usually do it for nothing."

"That way everybody always owe you one, right?"

"And when it comes time, I call the debt."

"King of the markers," she said, nodding her understanding.

"Yes, king of the markers," he said, smiling and sharing the unspoken memory.

That was very likely the most he had ever told anyone, but still Carla knew there was more. She believed, for that moment at least, if he didn't tell her more, it was because he had never given it a voice. She couldn't help but think that it was indeed a lot like her own performances—in the end, done on instinct.

Although Carla became a familiar celebrity at the rallies and marches against the war, her real focus, as always, was her work. With Dennis away, she had more time to think about roles. The Morris office and Jimmy Chase kept the scripts and offers coming, but now, from her new perspective, she wasn't as quick to say yes to a script, often puzzling over the decision for weeks on end. To the agents, that made her difficult, not the team player she had been for MCA and Freddy Durslag. No one said that to her, of course, but Cora, who always kept Carla informed, heard the rumors. There was a time when that might have bothered Carla, but not now. She was past caring what agents thought and focused her professional worries on finding scripts she thought of as significant.

One film, *Coaltown*, she accepted only on ideological grounds. In it she played a mineworker's wife who turns into a radical because of the government's reaction to a strike. It wasn't a hit and when it was over Jack gave Carla a lecture about political involvement. "Give them money, give them your name, give them your time. But for God's sake don't try to make commercial movies about subjects that are better suited to documentaries. You make Hollywood pictures. You're famous for it. Deservedly. But you'll blow it all with this kind of stuff."

"What should I do? The world's coming apart. It's out of control," she said, feeling heated and angry at Jack for not seeing it as she did. For a brief, agonizing moment he seemed old to her, of another generation. The thought of it, as much as the thought of the world spinning loose, upset her and made her shudder. "I'm not going to just sit by the pool. I can't make movies that don't pay any attention. This is not a time for business as usual."

"No. That's right," he said, speaking calmly, realizing the degree if not the specific causes of her anger. "But the solution for you is to push the ball a little way down the field. Not redesign the game. Don't ignore who you are. Use it to make studio productions a little more alive. They'll do it. They have to be leaned on, but if it's a story with a commercial hook and you're in it, they'll give you control over the content. Don't confuse yourself with some kid at the barricades."

It made her sad not to be a kid at the barricades. She felt that was the most interesting thing you could be. When she realized it wasn't available to her, she could feel her life narrowing down. No matter what she did have, she missed the options that other people had—people not as rich, not as famous, and not as old.

After Dennis had been in Vietnam for six months, Carla and Sophie flew to Honolulu to meet him for a week's holiday. Carla had rented a house above Kahala, in the flatlands beyond Diamond Head. They spent serene days lazing under the Hawaiian sun, taking Sophie for walks on the beach.

"Do you see people get killed?" she asked him.

"Mostly I try to finagle my way to the front. Then I scream at the foreign desk to run my copy, which is usually hell to get out."

"Do you?" she asked, refusing to let him deflect the question.

"When I get to the front, I see the bodies."

"Could you get hurt?" She asked it simply, but they were both looking at Sophie, thinking about their daughter and what her life would be if her father got hurt, which they both knew was a euphemism for getting his brains blown out in a rice paddy.

"I'm careful as I can be."

"Do you have a gun?"

"I wouldn't know how to use it."

"Learn."

Dennis could see Carla meant exactly what she said. He said that he would.

Dennis made two more trips to the States during the two years he was in Vietnam. For the first, after he had been in Vietnam for eleven months, Carla took Sophie and went east to spend a few days with him. Sutton Place had been sublet, so they took a suite at the St. Regis, which had romantic memories for them. Although they tried to take advantage of every moment, Carla couldn't help thinking that Dennis wanted to get back to Asia.

For the second trip, a few months before he returned home for good, Carla was shooting in Los Angeles, and although Dennis said he was trying to arrange a quick trip to the West Coast, she didn't think he was trying very hard. He went back without seeing his family. It upset Carla. She told Cora, "It has to mean he's got a girl. What else?"

Cora looked into it. There weren't so many prominent reporters based in Saigon that it couldn't be checked. It appeared that although Dennis had taken advantage of the brothels while he was there, no one had reports of a serious relationship. Cora was told, "He's in the grip of Asia."

When Carla asked what the hell that meant, Cora told her, "I think it means he's obsessed with the story he's there to get—taking crazy chances, going anywhere, not caring about anything else."

"To tell you the truth," Carla said, "that's easier to believe than a girlfriend."

The picture Carla was making when Dennis made his second trip home to New York turned out to be one of her most celebrated performances. *Second Front* was the story of a working-class woman whose husband was killed in Vietnam, leaving her with two small children. Despite the unpopularity of the war, the woman still loved her husband and honored his memory. She kept the memory alive even when she fell in love with a conscientious objector and turned against the war. It was a little advanced for the late sixties, and it wasn't a commercial success in its initial release. Jack called it an honorable failure, but Carla was prouder of it than anything she had done since *Barbara Farrell*. She didn't think of *Second Front* as a feminist story, at least not then. When it was revived, all through the next decade, the years of feminism, the picture became a sort of anthem, a rallying point for women.

After months of rumors that Dennis wasn't well, the A.P. brought him back to the States. At first he didn't want to come home at all. He had a scheme for going to Hanoi. But the A.P. insisted. In 1969 Dennis left Asia. Carla had suggested that she and Sophie meet him in Honolulu for a few days, as they had done a year and a half earlier. Dennis said he'd rather "go from one hellhole to another, nonstop." Carla hadn't exactly understood what he meant, but it was a bad connection, so when he said he'd be in Los Angeles in a few days, she didn't press it.

Seeing him upset her. He had lost weight—not a great deal, but he hadn't bothered to have his clothes altered. His trousers hung on him and were gathered beneath his belt. His khaki bush jacket drooped off his shoulders. But it was his eyes that troubled her the most. They looked sunken, haunted. Sophie was a toddler and Dennis enjoyed sitting on the grass and watching her walk to him or play with the dogs. He was polite to Ceil, but Carla had to remind him of her mother's name. Dennis started to walk down to the other end of the house to visit his grandfather-in-law, but as he neared Bela's wing, he remembered that it had been made over into a virtual hospital. He'd seen enough of hospitals, and he turned around without seeing Bela. The next day he announced he was leaving for New York.

"When?" Carla asked.

"Now."

"This minute?"

"TWA has a flight at four. Gives me an hour. Could someone drive me?"

Carla's worry wasn't for her marriage but rather her husband's health. Was this depression? Something worse? Jack advised her to do nothing at first. "Keep Sophie with you. If he asks if she can visit him in New York, say no or say you'll both come."

"Why? He wouldn't hurt her. I know he wouldn't."

"Custody belongs to the parent who's got the child. Don't tempt him to take her off somewhere."

"Like Vietnam?" Carla asked, alarmed at the idea.

Jack didn't deny that was what he had meant. "The A.P. will send him to a psychiatrist. I promise you that. You might not hear about it, but they will."

"What should I do, though?"

"The hardest thing of all, which is nothing. Let events unfold. He's in rough shape. Be easy on him for Sophie's sake, if not his."

"I'm scared for him. He looked nuts." Carla started to cry. Jack held her, comforting her.

"God, can you imagine?" he said. "If that's what a reporter looks like after two years, what are the troops going to be like?"

Carla called Dennis every night. He always said the same thing. "I'm fine. How's Sophie? Put her on the phone."

When Carla would ask what he had done that day, he would say something bland like, "I don't know. Walked around."

"Do you want to file?" she asked, trying to get him to talk about himself. "Get a new beat? Politics, maybe?"

"I wouldn't mind going back, but they seem to want me to stay around here for a while."

"How do you feel?"

"Well, if everybody asks you that all day long, I guess the answer must be different than how I think I feel."

"Have you seen a doctor?"

"You mean a shrink?"

"Well?"

"Yeah, I did. He was some Talmudic crank. I'd do better going to confession and there's no chance of that."

"Why not? It helps a lot of people."

"Forgive me, Father, for I have sinned." He said it in his old mock-Irish brogue. But Carla could hear bitterness in it instead of wry humor. " 'And when was your last holy confession, my son?' 'Father, it was 1936 and at the time it was all lies. Sin everlasting, Father. Will you show me the hope of bliss eternal?' "

Carla was quiet for a moment. "Why don't you come out here for a while?" she said, finally. "You could have all the privacy you want. See Sophie. She'd like it."

"Privacy means separate bedrooms?"

"Whatever you want."

"I'll think about it," he said.

Carla said that was fine, but she knew he would never come back to Los Angeles.

After he'd been in New York for a few weeks, Dennis seemed to be getting better, or at least a little more talkative. He was thinking about writing a book about the war, a sign that he felt he had a future. When Carla told Jack about it, asking for his opinion, he said, "Time is healing him, I guess. You know, we always think these things are going to be more dramatic than they turn out to be, that they'll have flamboyant conclusions or big consequences—like a movie."

"I guess Dennis is more resilient than I thought."

"Most people are resilient, Carla."

"You think the marriage is over?"

"I'm probably not the best judge. If you're married to him and he's three thousand miles away, that's the best situation I could hope for. Does he need money?"

"I don't know. He didn't say."

"Would he be insulted if you sent him some?"

"Dennis doesn't care about money."

"It'll help. It always has, it always will. Not just Dennis. Everybody."

His easy solution to what she saw as a far more complex problem irritated Carla. "Just because you think the world revolves around money doesn't mean everybody does. Dennis doesn't give a shit about it." The tension she felt made her snap at Jack. He didn't like it one bit.

"I'm not the only one who holds this view. You'll find that significant sums of money arriving, unexpected and unasked for, tends to please people—makes them fucking overjoyed."

"Sorry," she said.

Carla had Cora send Dennis a check. Even after she assumed he had gotten it, he didn't mention it when they spoke. He still seemed so fragile to her that she didn't say anything about it. Then, as if they had been talking about it all along, he asked, "Do you want a divorce?"

"What brought that up?"

"I'm in no shape to be married. I have no interest in it. I would want to be able to see Sophie. You wouldn't deny me that, would you?"

"Of course not. You're her father. She loves you."

"But you don't anymore, do you?"

"Dennis, I'm not sure this is a conversation we should be having on the phone."

"You kidding? On the phone I can talk. It's face-to-face I have trouble. I know you, Carla. You want out, but don't want to do it. Get one of your lawyers. Uncontested as long as I can see Sophie. Oh, thanks for the dough."

It was such an odd conversation that Carla felt more baffled than saddened. In her heart she was convinced that in some way she couldn't quite grasp, sending Dennis money had pushed him into ending the marriage. The thought she couldn't get out of her mind was that Jack had known that would happen and that was the real reason he had told her to do it. Unlike her first husband, whom Jack could control, Dennis was independent of Jack's power. Dennis had made him nervous in a way that no man in the movie business ever could. It made Carla angry to think Jack had manipulated the situation. Then, as she thought about it more, she came to see that it was also a sign of his love. In his own way, Jack was protecting them both. It still confused her, but it also helped her make peace with the end of her second marriage.

21.

Paul Loeb, a screenwriter, met Carla the same way I had—over a script. He had his chance with Carla when they made a picture called *The Third Circle*. It was a romantic thriller shot in London and Paris. He pursued her on the set and when the picture wrapped Paul didn't behave like a screenwriter and go away. He took her to Venice in the reasonable belief that if romance was ever going to deepen, that was the place for it.

Paul and Carla went to Europe separately and came back a couple. When they were back in Los Angeles, he devoted himself to her. He did it so relentlessly, it brought out her passivity. He became her third husband. I couldn't help thinking that she'd now made three marriages—none of them quite right. She'd made the decisions casually because her real marriage was to Jack—no matter who else either of them was married to, or who the father of her children might be.

Paul was good-looking, I suppose, but other than that he wasn't much different from other screenwriters—smart, cynical, charming, with an eye for the main chance. What he did have was flamboyance, with an instinct, or maybe just a lust, for the best—wine, clothes, paintings, cars, real estate and, it's fair to say, wives. I don't mean he was a fortune hunter. He made a lot of money and he spent it freely. Carla had more, of course, but when Paul had the chance, he didn't spend hers any more recklessly than he had spent his own. He had a nine-year-old daughter by his first wife, an actress who had gone back to New York. Although they had joint custody, his ex-wife was undependable. The child, named Susan, spent most of her time with her father. She was an exquisite little girl with enormous black eyes.

Carla was crazy about Susan and was as devoted a stepmother as she was a mother to Sophie, who was three years younger than her new sister. Ceil took her cue from Carla and embraced her stepgranddaughter with genuine enthusiasm. The child took to her new life as easily as her father had. Even Dennis, who was doing better, thought Paul was good for Carla. When he called to talk to his daughter, he and Paul would have polite chats; both men recognized that civility between them would benefit their children. For Jack, Paul was just the right kind of husband for Carla—ambitious and in the business, which meant that eventually Paul would need a favor. Jack knew it would keep him in line. I was certainly envious of Paul; I've had to make my peace with that. Carla loved Paul, at least for a while, and he was in awe of her.

Paul had grown up in the suburbs of New York, Mount Vernon, mostly. He'd gone to film school at NYU for a year and then come west. He saw screenwriting as a way to make money while positioning himself to become a director or producer. He looked enough like a leading man to have once been given a screen test. In the years he'd been in Hollywood he'd cut a wide social swath—going out with beautiful women, turning up at parties and screenings. He was the sort of man who was easy to understand too quickly. He could be mistaken for a lounge lizard—and there was a bit of that in him. But he was more complicated. He probably loved hustling and deal-making more than he loved movies, but that never hurt anybody in the picture business. He was a combination of the relaxed—laid back, as people said then—and ambitious; hungry, for anything that might come his way. Despite an avaricious edge, Paul was a man of some charm who saw the world for what it was and wanted to make sure he got a piece of it.

After their marriage two things happened fast. Carla got pregnant again and she sold the Schuyler Road house. Paul might have liked Dennis Catton but he wasn't about to sleep in his bedroom—no matter how rarely Dennis had used it. They bought an enormous place in Bel Air, on Chalon Road. It had been designed in the twenties by Wallace Neff. After movies, real estate has always been the favorite pursuit among the recently rich of Southern California. The Chalon Road house was on three hillside acres that looked out across the estates of Bel Air toward the city beyond. Like most of Neff's houses, it was Spanish; a long, low structure of flowing white stucco broken up by arches and iron grilles. The windows were deep-set and the roof was made of red tiles. At one end there was a four-story tower, rounded, like a turret. Outside there were tiled fountains and walkways. In the entrance hall, the floor was black-and-white marble, like a vast checkerboard. A curving staircase with a wrought-iron railing and banister led to cool, yawning bedrooms. In the back, there were terraced gardens leading down to a pool. Paul named the house Chisel Hall.

Although it was only a few miles from Schuyler Road, moving was an involved business. Carla's grandfather was still in poor health, looking wan. His principal activity amounted to seeing different doctors, who offered conflicting diagnoses. Bela enjoyed the attention, however, and developed a stoic attitude. Again, what amounted to a private infirmary was built for him. Paul said, "He'll outlive us all. Why should he die now? Things are finally getting interesting for him." Carla thought Paul might have a point.

Between her pregnancy and the new house, Carla stopped reading scripts and devoted herself to domestic matters. She and Paul talked to decorators, architects and gardeners. Paul insisted on converting a bedroom into a grand closet for his wife. He had the walls mirrored, like a dance studio. Two-tiered racks for dresses were hung and cedar cubicles installed. Carla tried to be pleased by the gesture, but she had already started wearing the silky jumpsuits that would become her uniform. They were an act of rebellion against all fashion tyranny. The first one had been run up by the designer on *The Third Circle*. Carla had been refining them ever since. Although the mirrored closet was filled with dresses, blouses, shoes and the like, most of it stayed in the closet, unworn and ignored.

Carla wanted to spend time with Susan, getting to know her stepdaughter, making sure she and Sophie got along. Cora said no when the Morris office and the various producers and directors called with ideas and scripts. Cora coordinated the activity, and she too was as busy as if they had been in production.

Paul thought it was a mistake for his wife to shut out Milton so completely. He wanted Sophie and the new baby to know their grandfather. The debacle at the Friars had made Paul wary of his father-in-law, but he told Carla, "The statute of limitations has run out. Invite him to dinner." Carla was surprised at how easy it was for her to forgive. Milton started coming to Chisel Hall. He was always polite to Ceil and endeared himself to Sophie and Susan, telling them stories about the gambling ships, enchanting them with tales of his daring past on the not-so-high seas.

During this pregnancy, Carla saw less of Jack. When Carla was carrying Sophie, she and Jack had remained close. Their relationship changed, of course, but she still depended on him. No matter how attached she had been to Dennis, Jack had been fundamental to her life. Now, it felt different to both of them. Part of it was simply that she was so busy. Against Jack's counsel she had accepted an offer to endorse a commercial product. Jack told her it would cheapen her in the long run. But she and Paul were spending a lot of money without any coming in, and a baby food company offered her four hundred thousand dollars to advertise their product while she was pregnant.

Even if Jack felt he was losing her, he never wavered in his devotion. He asked her to come to the bungalow for lunch and when she did, he argued against the baby food ads. It hurt her to go against his advice. It was the first time she had ever done it. It was even harder on Carla than Jack. He saw everything as a negotiation. Because she said no today didn't mean she wouldn't say yes tomorrow. He held her hand, admired her belly, and told her, "This husband of yours is shortsighted."

"How do you know it's his decision? Maybe it's mine."

"Maybe it is," he said, but his eyes said, "You would never do such a thing without being pushed."

She knew he was probably right, but Carla still appeared in a series of television commercials, in print ads and on billboards. For a while it seemed that everywhere you went there was Carla with a beatific smile on her face, pushing baby food. Even in those advertisements, which were as sentimental as their creators could make them, Carla managed a little artistic sabotage. Future Mom's glow or not, her face had a subtle libidinal aspect. It seemed to say, "Yeah, yeah, I'll have this baby. But then . . ."

Carla came to the bungalow to try to make it right with Jack. She needed Jack—she certainly had him, but because of the baby food business she felt uncertain. Even though he had been low-keyed about her rejecting his advice, she knew that along with her pregnancy, it had been hard on him. Whenever Jack saw the billboard on the Sunset Strip, with Carla—pregnant with her vast belly and glowing skin—sharing the space with a bottle of strained carrots, he would look away. In the past if she thought Jack was feeling blue or acting a little distant she would hold him, caress him, and look at him with admiration until he came around. Now, with her swollen belly, her life with Paul seemed a barrier between them in a way her other marriages never had.

Her power over Jack, the source of their enduring alliance, was erotic. It had always been that. For seventeen years, without any notable exceptions, she had only to kiss him, to touch him, and she could feel him get hard, become ardent. That was powerful for both of them. She had come to accept it in the way she accepted her beauty and her fame. Now, today, she could feel something new between them and it was unsettling.

She moved closer to him, putting an arm around him. "Who cares about some ads? It was just for the money."

"It's done," he said. She could feel the coolness. She knew it wasn't the ads as much as the fact that she had done it against his judgment. Had she not been pregnant, she would have made love to him and that might have settled it. She knew it was possible, but she was a month away from delivery and her instinct, as well as her doctor, told her not to. She looked at him with a private smile, then opened his pants, massaging him, stroking him into life. She was trying to say, "Your happiness is everything to me." He was annoyed with her and would have preferred not to respond. But Carla was still the center of his inner life. Her hands on him were persuasive. She crouched in front of him, which was no easy thing given her belly, and took him in her mouth. He still disapproved of the baby food ads, but at least for the moment, they were far from his thoughts.

Emma Loeb was born in what had become Cedars-Sinai Hospital in the spring of 1974. Emma, like Sophie before her, was healthy, happy to be in the world, and ready to take life on its own terms. Paul stayed in the delivery room, holding Carla's hand. When he held Emma, his face reflected awe and joy. Cora released a statement to the press, and the birth made news around the world. All births were a little frightening for Ceil because they made her think about the death of her first child thirty-five years earlier. She had felt the same fear when Sophie was born and it was with her again now.

Paul wanted to give a big party to celebrate his daughter's birth. Carla wasn't so sure she wanted hundreds of people traipsing through her house. She thought of big parties as events she occasionally got roped into attending. She never stayed long. She agreed to the party because it seemed important to her husband.

I brought Joan Lambert, an actress who was trying to become a screenwriter. Joan was attractive, with fabulous red hair, although not as glamorous as the crowd likely to be at Chisel Hall. We had gone to Dan Tana's for dinner before the party because Joan had said she didn't want to spend the evening either being hungry or wasting her time eating. Through our meal, she kept asking me who was going to be at the party. I was beginning to doubt the wisdom of taking her when she started to giggle. "Listen to me," she said. "Put me around a star and I turn into a fifteen-year-old. I grew up on Dr. George. This is a big deal."

"You'll be okay," I said, wondering if it was true.

Chisel Hall had a steel gate on Chalon Road. Two young men in blazers were posted there, inspecting each car before it entered. It was like driving into a studio. You gave your name and were passed in.

As we drove down the long curving driveway between rows of palms, moving downhill, then up, Joan said, "I thought old Hollywood was supposed to be dead. This is fabulous." At the house I turned the car over to a young man who saluted me, while another held the door for Joan.

When we stepped into the foyer, Joan saw some people she knew. As she and her pals started chatting, I excused myself to see if I could find our hostess. The party spilled out to the pool. As I stepped outside, onto the first of the descending terraces, I saw that the landscaping crew had been hard at work. Beds of flowers outlined the paths that led to the lawn—tall, purple agapanthus, delicate anemones, several varieties of roses, and flowering azaleas. The trees were strung with paper lanterns, enormous rice paper globes with paintings of rural Japanese scenes. The colors of the paintings filtered the light; it made everyone's skin glow.

The bash was catered by Chasen's, which meant a squad of

chefs turning out crab crêpes, as well as Chasen's standbys: chili, cheese toast and banana shortcake. There were a few hundred people there already, standing around talking.

A string quartet was playing Mozart. Cora had told me that a livelier band would be playing later. A parquet dance floor had been set down on the grass. I accepted a glass of champagne from a passing waiter. The era of white wine *über alles* had already started in Los Angeles, but Bel Air is a place where liquor has always been served, no matter what the vogue of the moment.

There were aggressively dressed people there—men in European-cut suits or Italian jackets; some of the younger men affected the English-rock-star look with tight black jeans, satin shirts and shoulder-length hair. A lot of the women were in the traditional white dresses or silky white pants. Some of the younger women, actresses mostly, were in the flashy outfits I always associated with the Sunset Strip. Most of them had long, straight hair and either impossibly high heels or leather boots. Everything they wore was tight and revealing. That meant the agents and established actors who followed them around were there as well. I kept wondering what Carla made of it all. I was enjoying looking at them when Cora Cohen slipped her arm in mine. "So?" she asked. "Does our little girl know how to throw a party, or what?"

"Cora, are you drunk?"

"I'm certainly trying. So what do you think?"

"Why do I think Carla wasn't exactly up all night polishing the silver?"

"Yeah. He sure loves a party, our new boy."

"Paul, you mean?"

"Champagne Charlie. You bring somebody?"

"I did. She's doing some business. So who's the crowd?"

"Some you know, the rest are hustlers and a bunch of M-A-Ws." I laughed at the acronym—Model-Actress-Whatever. It was a play on M-O-W, for movie-of-the-week. It had replaced starlet—a word now used only by journalists, usually the ones who still called Hollywood "Tinseltown."

I saw Paul on the other side of the pool in a little knot of producers and agents. He was listening to one of them, who was no doubt pitching an idea for Carla. Paul looked tense, determined that this evening go well. I could see his foot tapping. This marriage was the main chance for Paul Loeb, and he was going to take full advantage of it. In the moment I watched him I could see what was wrong here, why this party didn't feel right. The whole evening, with two bands and all these people determined to have a memorable time, wasn't Carla's scene at all. This was movie business as parvenu; Carla was what these people wanted. Oh, there were plenty of people around who didn't see this as a business opportunity, but a lot of the crowd was bunched up in a way that put the sweaty scent of nervous ambition in the night air. The hope of connection, of social and professional clawing, seemed to hang over everything from the string quartet to Chasen's crêpes. It was too raw for Carla; this evening took its cue from Paul Loeb.

Jack and Mona were at one of the tables, talking to a senior agent from the Morris office. At that time I'd met Jack a few times, but I didn't know him well. I thought if the opportunity presented itself, I'd reintroduce myself. I spoke to a few people, looking for anyone to talk to who wouldn't be congratulating themselves for being there.

As the evening wore on, and I still hadn't seen Carla, I got interested in the string quartet, four members of the UCLA music faculty in black tie, lost in Brahms and Mozart. They gave the party a sense of dignity and decorum—a lovely, unlikely contrast to all the hustling. By ten o'clock the older crowd was beginning to leave. The crêpe-makers from Chasen's were packing up their copper pans and putting away their Sterno. That was the cue for the string quartet to stop and for the band to start playing.

They were five young black guys called Sam and the Teaszers. They wore tuxedos with ruffled shirts. Sam did the vocals, working his way through the Aretha Franklin–James Brown repertoire. They were as enthusiastic as their audience, who bounced and shook, doing the Frug, the Swim and the Boogaloo.

On the other side of the dancers, I could see Joan was in great spirits. A little earlier she had told me an agent who had been avoiding her calls had been nice to her. She seemed to regard it as a significant moment in her life.

On my way into the house, I saw Carla. She was sitting in a white gazebo, isolated in the middle of a stretch of lawn. Night-blooming jasmine twisted through the lattice, up to the yellow, peaked roof. Because of the roof, she called it her golden gazebo. I think it was a golden place in her mind. She sat out there in the afternoons, sometimes by herself, sometimes with her kids. Tonight she was there with Jack, talking quietly, ignoring the party, seemingly unaware of the loud music and the frenzy. They looked content to be together, alone in the moonlight, surrounded by the scent of the jasmine. I would have been content just to watch them, until something caught my eye back at the pool. It was Paul, talking to yet another round of hustlers. He was engaged in his conversation, but I could see him looking past the people to the gazebo, watching his wife and Jack. I don't know how much he knew about them, but it couldn't have been easy for him. On the other side of the pool, Mona Markel was also looking at them. Who could know what she was thinking? Her face certainly gave nothing away. She was with another woman whose burnished skin was as tanned as her own. The two of them were part of the older, more established crowd, here in uneasy combination with the flashier guests. Mona and her friend were talking, but like Paul's, Mona's eyes were on Jack and Carla. A soft light in the ceiling made a little stage set out of the gazebo. The performers were Jack and Carla. Anyone who chose to glance their way was the audience. I had noticed Paul and Mona but who had noticed me? Was Carla aware she was being watched? She was always watched, so maybe she didn't care. Maybe she was sending a message to her husband: If you insist on throwing these rude, desperate parties, I'll do something equally rude and even hurtful to you. I'll spend the evening with my real lover, in full view of all the people you want to impress.

When I went inside again, people were gathered, making more polite party chatter, the kind that seemed to run through this evening and hundreds of others like it. Joan pulled me into a discussion she was having with Tink Harvey, a screenwriter who was a chum of Paul's. They'd gone to film school together a generation ago. I'd met Tink at dinner here at Chisel Hall. He was a little on the fleshy side, with a sensual sneer, a sybarite's face. Like Paul, he was about forty, charming, dapper and quite funny—itself a kind of coin in Hollywood. Because he could be bitchy, there were always rumors that he was gay or bisexual. Carla wasn't crazy about him. He'd flirted with her—which was the cause of one of the few put-downs I ever heard her make. When we were alone, she'd said of Tink, "He could be in drag for either sex."

"Mr. Burton, I presume," he said, as I shook his hand. "A man with sense enough to bring Joan Lambert to the ball."

"Do I hear flattery?" Joan asked. "About time."

"More where that came from, my dear," Tink said. It sounded

like a practiced line, but it seemed to please Joan. Tink's wit struck me as more compulsive than funny. It was his way of establishing his presence, marking territory, the way a dog pisses on the ground. "So," he said. "What new indignities in the scriptwriting game?"

"I haven't found any new ones—just a continuing drive on the part of the studios to perfect the old ones." Now he's got me doing it, I thought—trying to sparkle with screenwriter babble.

"Perhaps I can be your white knight, too," he said.

"What does that mean?" I asked, knowing the answer.

"I can tell you," Joan said. "Tink and I've been talking about a wonderful story about two women bank robbers and a cop they're both in love with. I was just pointing out how ideal I'd be to write it."

"Hiring writers now, are you?" I asked.

"If they have interesting ideas or fabulous red hair."

"When did that start?" I asked. He's become a producer. That's got to mean he's found a way to do it on Carla's name, I thought.

"Paul and I have formed a production company. I mean it, Gabe. You're always welcome to pitch. I'd love to take you to lunch and hear what's on your mind."

"I thought you were taking me to lunch," Joan said, practically fluttering her eyes.

"Absolutely," he said, putting a hand on the small of her back. "Paul and I are looking for imaginative ideas. We're going to be a writers' company. Ideas are what count with us. The steak, not the sizzle. A minimum of studio interference. You'd be comfortable with us, Gabe."

All I could think was Tink and Paul had bandied Carla's name about at a studio and walked away with a production deal. I wondered how much Carla knew about it. Tink had never been a candidate for sainthood. As a producer the guy would be an absolute monster. "Congratulations," I said. "I'll give it some thought."

"We're buying a couple books you might be right for."

"Can I get you another drink, Joan?"

"No," she said. "I thought I'd just stay here and see if Tink can top himself."

I excused myself to go back outside. As I wandered away from the house, Sam and the Teaszers and the intrepid dancers were still at it. I was enjoying the night air out near the gazebo.

Jack and Carla were gone now, but I saw a junior agent I recognized from the Morris office and one of the M-A-Ws. They had unscrewed the light bulb in the gazebo so the stage set was in shadows. When I got closer I could see why. They were sitting on the floor of the gazebo, snorting what I assumed was cocaine. She was wearing a low-cut turquoise leather dress that had ridden up past her knee-high boots and settled around her hips. Mr. Agent was holding a tiny coke spoon to her nose; his other hand was lodged between her legs. If they saw me, they didn't care. All I could think was, welcome to the world and the new Hollywood, Emma Loeb.

I finally got to talk to Carla that evening, back in the house. She was wearing one of her jumpsuits. This one was dark blue. In honor of the evening she'd added diamond earrings and a small gold necklace. She enjoyed dressing so simply in the midst of all this overreaching stylishness. She put her arm through mine, as Cora had done earlier, and asked if I was having a good time.

"Sure. What's not to like?"

"I guess that's true," she said, trying to convince herself. "Everybody likes a party."

"Except you?"

"No. It's fine. Paul enjoys it. I heard you brought someone. Where is she?"

I was tempted to point out the hottest-looking M-A-W in the room, but when Joan saw me talking with Carla, she came over to be introduced. Carla had a wicked look in her eye, and I knew she was contemplating mischief. She acted like a co-conspirator with me in a campaign to impress Joan. "You be good to this man," Carla said to her. "If he's not happy, I'll hear about it." That might not sound like much to the world at large, but if you can think of all Hollywood as a version of a Renaissance court, full of tyrants and flatterers, where cunning prevails and favors are power, then any word from the sovereign is considered magic and discussed endlessly. Carla wasn't the only ruler, but she was certainly the sovereign of the moment. The slightest bit of instruction from her to someone as anxious to please as Joan, well, let me put it this way: Joan was now convinced she was spending the evening with a man in a position to help her get anything she might want. Had I cared to use it, it was a hell of an advantage. I kissed Carla on the cheek and told her we were about to leave.

"Already?" she asked. "I didn't even get to talk to you. Can we have lunch next week?"

"Of course."

"I'm not sure of my schedule. Cora'll call you." Then she turned to Joan, who was doing her best to keep her jaw from hanging open, and said, "Bye, Joan. Hope I get to see you again."

As we were leaving, Carla's grandfather Bela turned up. He was wearing a seersucker suit that spilled over his narrow shoulders. He had grown so frail that he looked as if he might fall over and impale himself on his walking stick. A nurse was helping him. The former *luftmensch* of Boyle Heights was making a tour of the party, a promenade. He went from group to group, nodding, shaking hands, and welcoming people as if he were the host. While he was circulating, I could hear children squealing, and I glanced up toward the sound. Sophie and Susan in their pajamas were squatting at the top of the staircase, watching it all. Then I saw Ceil was with them. Grandma was on the stairs, too, happy to act like a ten-year-old, watching the adults at play. Ceil finally had what she wanted. She lived in a big house with children where everything was provided for her. After forty-five years, Ceil had managed to re-create the orphanage of her own childhood.

22.

When we met for lunch at Ma Maison a few days later, I expected Carla to ask what had happened with Joan after the party. But by the time we were seated, after we'd run the gamut of people who wanted a word with her, she had apparently forgotten all about it. Yet she seemed to know my mood, or maybe it was more obvious than I thought. "Something wrong?" she asked.

"Screenwriter blues, I guess."

"Should I try to get you a fancy gig—a big picture?"

I smiled at her notion of how easy it was, even for her. "I don't think I could manage to go to a movie today, let alone write one. But thanks. I figure I'm ready to take some serious time off."

"Why?" she asked.

"People keep me sending me scripts to rewrite."

"Of course they do. You're brilliant at it."

"Maybe. Bobby Shepherd sent me one. It's about this psychiatrist and his beautiful patient. They run off together. They figure shrinking her isn't helping either of them. So they go to Tangier. Or maybe it was Algiers."

"This supposed to be a comedy?"

"The very problem. Bobby thinks it's high drama. It's not bad, a little confused. I've seen worse."

"Hell," she said, "I've probably been in worse."

"I know what you mean. Anyway, Bobby's assumption is that I can straighten it out."

"So what happens?" she asked, always ready to listen to a story, even this one.

"Once they're in the casbah or somewhere, they get mixed up with a bunch of mythological creatures, most of whom seem to be goats or bitch goddesses. And one weird sleazeball who keeps turning up trying to sell them the secret of the universe."

"Gabe, so far you couldn't make it worse."

"Wait. I read it carefully. I took notes. My usual drill. But each time I turned the pages, no matter how hard I tried, all I could think was this thing is dead right for Bob Hope, Bing Crosby and Dorothy Lamour."

She started to laugh. "Bing and Lamour are the shrink and the patient, right?"

"Yeah. Hope's the sleazy mystic. We change the title to *The Road to Mental Health*. See why I need some time off?"

"Okay. You win. Want me to help?"

"I'd like to talk to Jack Markel about finding something else for myself."

"Working on my book's not enough?"

"It would be in addition."

"Okay. He'll have an idea or something."

"Does he know about you and me?"

"Gabe, Jack knows everything about me."

"Then he should write the book with you."

"Hah! He knows it's going to get written one way or another. He wants to make sure he comes off okay."

I figured any help Jack might give me would be contingent on my helping Carla with her memoirs. Either she told him not to try to cram a deal like that down my throat, or more likely, he assumed if he helped me, I would consider myself obligated. Whatever the case, he called and asked me to lunch—the Vine Street Derby, an older bit of Hollywood than Ma Maison. If nothing else my personal drama got me into some interesting restaurants. Jack was gracious, interested in why I felt I wanted out of screenwriting. It wasn't a business question, but a philosophical one. I skipped the Hope-Crosby business, but I did tell him all the reasons screenwriters always haul out—no control over my work, I was sick of being at the mercy of producers and studio executives who based their judgments on what their children or maids said. I was tired of being regarded as a mercenary hack and held in contempt for doing what I had been hired to do. I assumed he'd heard it all before.

He listened as I ran down my list. "It's true, all that you say. I think it's because once a screenplay exists—if it's any good—it looks easy. If a script looks strained, it doesn't work."

"Yeah," I said, seeing his point. "Then people wonder why it costs so much. I always tell them, 'Think it's easy? Get a hundred and twenty-five sheets of blank paper and see what you can do.' "

"Does it help?"

"Nope." If Jack had any idea that Tink Harvey and Paul Loeb's venture played a part in my decision to get out, he didn't say. For all I knew, he'd set up that deal.

"Let's think about it," he said. "Above the line, there's acting, directing and producing. Am I right to assume you're not an actor?"

"That's right. And I'm probably the only screenwriter in town who doesn't want to direct."

"You want to produce?"

"I want to do something that isn't dependent on other people's capricious judgments."

"Ever think about completion bonds?" he asked, as if it were the likeliest of occupations.

"The insurance on the money?"

"It's a very good business."

"How would I learn?"

"If you want to pursue it, I might be able to help. Bondsmen aren't crazy about telling their procedures to possible competition, but I think I can convince one to sit down with you. You'll need an underwriter. Lloyd's does it. I can help. You'll need customers. When Carla's pictures aren't directly financed by a major, they require bonds. We've spread it around. She's never paid much attention. It could be worked out."

"You make it sound easy."

"Gabe, all the years I've been around the picture business have taught me one certainty: Getting the job is always harder than doing it."

I was to spend a few weeks in the offices of the Pacific Assurance Company. Its president was Mort Brady, and I was to listen in on his phone conversations, read contracts and memoranda, and see if I could learn how he did it. Mort was about Jack's age, a stylish fellow who always wore a polka-dot bow tie. I found him direct and easy to learn from.

There was something a little unsettling about sitting on an extension phone listening to Mort shmooze with producers. Because he was good at what he did, it looked like he did very little. After I'd been there a few weeks, Mort said, "You can do this. It isn't brain surgery. Why open your own office? Put a desk in here. With Markel behind you, you'll have business. I'll pay you a draw against what you earn. In a few months, if you're bringing in enough, we'll make it a partnership. I'm talking about equity."

No new bondsman ever got a better offer. Mort was a practical guy. If Jack was my patron, the deals would follow. It meant an active pipeline to Jack Markel for Pacific Assurance. That never hurt anybody.

In my new life as a guarantor, the only one of my Hollywood chums I saw was Carla. She kept saying, "What have I started?" I think she expected me to give it all up and go back to scripts. I didn't know how happy I was in my new life, but I knew I didn't miss screenwriting. She still mentioned her memoirs from time to time but she wasn't insistent. I asked if I couldn't defer a decision until I learned more about my new business. I didn't want to take on two new tasks at once. That was fine with her.

Soon I was working on the bond for *Thinning Out*, a picture of Carla's that Paul and Tink were planning. It was a comedy about diets that Tink had written. I thought it was a ghastly script; a terrible mistake for Carla to be doing. When I told Mort what I thought of the venture, he told me to keep my mouth shut. The last thing he needed was a partner with aesthetic opinions about our customers. The most attractive thing about *Thinning Out* for Carla was that it was to shoot in Los Angeles on a soundstage and on locations around town. It meant she could live at Chisel Hall and spend time with her kids. A lot of it took place at a health club. Carla was to play a slender enough woman who believed she was overweight. Tink's point seemed to be that we should all learn to accept ourselves as we are. His second point was a lot of footage of women in leotards.

When she wasn't working, Carla was busy with her kids and with Paul's latest acquisition, a yacht. Paul had named it the *Tête-à-Tate*. Carla invited me to go for a cruise with them for a weekend, through the Channel Islands and into Santa Barbara. Cora and the two older girls were going.

The boat, which was quite stately, was white with a lot of varnished teak; ninety feet long and run by two big Daimler-Benz turbo diesels. There were six cabins, including a stateroom with a Jacuzzi. The saloon, as Paul was always careful to call it, had soft leather sofas and a black lacquer bar. The aft deck, where we ate dinner, was shaded by a blue-and-white striped canopy. Carla kept the boat because her family was happy on board. She knew that yachting weekends weren't typical American life, but the presence of her children made her feel like a mom and that made her feel good.

The captain of the *Tête-à-Tate,* Buddy DeSantis, worked for Carla and Paul full-time, tending the boat and standing ready to launch on short notice. DeSantis was about thirty, a Santa Cruz dropout and a surfer.

When we were three hours out, I began feeling the tension between Carla and Paul. They had retreated to their cabin. I could hear them arguing about *Thinning Out,* a script for which Carla had no more regard than I did. She wanted to put off the start date and have some work done on the script. I heard Paul yell back to her, "You're turning a go-picture into a development deal."

"The only place that thing's going is into the toilet," she shouted back. "It's just too dumb."

"Then why did three studios bid on it?"

"They'll make anything with a star in it," she yelled back with exasperation in her voice. "Who cares what a studio thinks? All those guys care about are some play-dates next year. You're supposed to know about this."

As I was listening—it was a big boat, but not so big that an argument that loud could be private—I heard the crux of the problem with their professional alliance, if not their marriage. Paul, successful as he had been, was used to spending his time trying to persuade studios to back him. It was what almost everyone in Hollywood had to do. But Carla was always the pursued, never a pursuer. That a studio wanted to back a picture seemed unremarkable to her—that's what studios did. I couldn't help thinking that Paul Loeb had better get it sorted out and he had better do it fast.

Sophie and Susan had heard the argument, too. They were huddled on the deck with Cora. They had the frightened look of children who only want to be safe. Susan knew by hard experience and Sophie by instinct that if their parents' marriage failed, they would be the ones to suffer. Cora was trying to comfort them. "Just grown-up stuff," she said, brushing Sophie's hair out of her eyes. "About a movie." Susan, who had seen more of the world and arguing adults, wasn't buying it.

The plan had been to go to Santa Rosa Island, to visit the ranch there and see the horses and maybe the wild pigs. But the tension between Paul and Carla was getting worse, so by the time we were off Oxnard, we decided to have a look at Anacapa, which was closer. Going to the nearer island didn't ease the tension, but the girls, in the way of children, either chose to ignore it or just got used to it.

As we came around the northern tip of the island, in the direction of Cathedral Cove, we decided to go ashore to explore the rocks and have a picnic. Buddy and Ubaldo, the Mexican sailor who was his crew, lowered the ship's dinghy, and we chugged into the inlet carrying a bottle of Taittinger champagne and a basket of sandwiches and salads. Anacapa is really three uninhabited islands made up of craggy gray cliffs created by wind and surf. Paul steered the little boat through large rock formations, created eons ago by the Pacific winds and the ocean itself. It was a series of rock arches and lagoons that seemed ghostly still, even though the waves of the ocean were only a few hundred feet away.

When we found an inlet where we could go ashore, we draped our shoes around our necks, rolled up our cuffs, and dragged the dinghy through the surf and onto the beach. Paul carried Susan while I managed Sophie. For the moment at least, the tension between Paul and Carla had eased. Cora found a rocky ledge where she left the picnic basket. We went for a hike, walking single file, scrambling over the rocks. Susan was determined to walk on her own, but Carla had taken Sophie. They moved on ahead, to the top of some boulders where they could look out on a part of the island that couldn't be seen from where the *Tête-à-Tate* was anchored. She held Sophie's hand and both of them were very still as they looked down. Paul called to her, asking what it was, but she didn't answer.

When we got to the top we could see that she was looking out onto a tide pool where a herd of harbor seals, maybe two hundred, were stretched out on the black volcanic sand and on the rocks, the sun reflecting off their lush coats. Carla was staring at them, enchanted by their swollen roundness. Even the bulls had a feminine curve to them. They were gathered to begin their mating ritual.

"It's a seals' singles bar," Paul said. Cora scowled at him, but Carla was too entranced to notice. With Sophie riding on her hip, she said, "I want to get closer," and started toward the seals. Paul wasn't sure how the creatures would react, but he knew his wife well enough not to bother trying to stop her. He started to come with her, but she shook her head and handed Sophie to him. "You stay with Daddy," she said. The tide was out and the seals seemed to be napping, or perhaps just waiting for their collective libido to ignite. The sandpipers, gulls and scrub jays that flocked on the black sand, eating seal droppings and leftovers, fluttered away as Carla descended the rocks.

The seals themselves seemed indifferent to her presence. Paul, perhaps made nervous by the possibility of an experience more mystical than rational, made a barking sound. Cora scowled at him and said, "Be quiet!"

Paul glared at her, angry enough to fire her. I think he was on the edge of it when it probably occurred to him that Carla would divorce him before she'd lose Cora. He didn't like being told off, even this mildly, in front of his kids. When he barked it had caused a few of the seals to bark back, and a few of them to rise up and make harsh, unfriendly noises. Paul comforted Sophie, who had started to whimper. Susan moved away from her father and came to stand just behind Cora and me, clinging to Cora's leg.

Below us, in the tide pool, Carla seemed to be hearing only the seals. It drew her deeper into their midst. She looked serene and certainly not threatened as she kept edging toward the center of the herd. She stood as still as she could, inhaling their scent, trying to look into their sad, bulbous eyes, willing them to be quiet. As she calmed herself they seemed to calm down, too. The barking stopped and they lay back again, apparently accepting her presence. She gazed at them, moving her eyes from one to another, as if she, now accepted by them, was deciding if she would return the favor.

On a cropping of rock near where she was standing, two young bull pups began making threatening gestures, not at Carla, but rather each other, as if they were performing, hoping for Carla's approval. She watched as they played out what she knew intuitively was a rehearsal for the mating rituals that would come later. The pups gouged each other's necks, piercing the other's skin with incisors that were already sharp. Carla was drawn to them, to their innocence and the way they played their part, without any self-consciousness or even, she imagined, awareness of what they were doing. When one would sink a tooth into the other's flesh, the victor would bark in triumph, but the sound was still squeaky, the voice of an adolescent. It looked as if the dominant one were showing off, perhaps even squeaking for Carla. It seemed to me that for a moment or two, Carla was at peace, at one with her world and the world of these animals, satisfied to stand among them. She was glowing and her radiance seemed to affect the seals. There was a stillness over it all that was positively eerie. I could certainly feel it. I could see the kids felt it, too. Cora smiled but Paul looked unchanged, as if he were planning his next wisecrack. Carla reached down and touched a young cow, who didn't bark or react at all. Carla stroked her, enjoying the wet, greasy fur under her hand.

Paul's voice broke her reverie as he called out, "Little Georgine selects a future fur coat." I thought Cora was going to slug him. Until he said that, I had been sure Paul was feeling some pride at his wife's ability to stand among the seals and not disturb them. Even if he refused to acknowledge it, he was fascinated by her control of these animals. Carla certainly heard him, because it ended her visit. She came back up to where we were standing. She didn't say anything, just scooped up Sophie again, and headed back over the rocks to where we had left our lunch, letting the rest of us follow.

We never did get to Santa Barbara. The next morning we went for a swim and returned to Los Angeles. Sophie's sunburn was the excuse, but the reason for going back was that Paul had gotten on Carla's nerves. She didn't want to be cooped up with him on the boat.

After that troubled weekend, Carla began shooting *Thinning Out*, which turned out to be an enormous hit. In it Carla had a bit of dialogue that became famous. After her character had dieted and exercised ferociously and lost a minuscule amount of weight, she looked at herself in a three-sided mirror and said, "Look how I look." Carla said it with such incredulousness that you couldn't help but laugh. It seemed to sum up the whole movie. Here was this woman who had labored mightily to bring forth so little—but then instead of being angry or disappointed, she convinced herself it was terrific. Audiences laughed and the line became a kind of tag. Whenever something didn't go quite right, but you wanted to put a good face on it, "Look how I look" did the trick. If a joke didn't go over, comedians saved themselves and got laughs by saying it. Teenagers who wanted to sound sophisticated used it. The line and Carla sort of merged in the public consciousness. For a while it was like her theme song.

Since I had hated the script, and had told Mort so, I assumed he would kid me about the film's success. But he remembered it differently. The popularity of the picture overwhelmed his memory. In his mind, he and I had discussed the script, and I, as a onetime screenwriter, had told him how promising it was. Only Carla and I knew we both thought it was inane before it began. No matter how big a hit it had become, we both still felt that way.

Paul felt they were on a roll. When Carla refused to even consider a sequel, he ranted at her, reminding her that because of him and his foresight and judgment she now had the biggest hit of her career. His smugness wasn't quite the way to her heart.

She didn't walk out on him, not exactly anyway, but she started considering scripts submitted by other producers. It hurt Paul's feelings but he knew enough not to try to intervene except through persuasion. As Cora pointed out, "What could he do? Tell the Morris office not to send her scripts?" He didn't think Carla should appear only in pictures he and Tink produced, but he did think that given that they were married and he had produced *Thinning Out*, he ought to be in first position. Carla refused to discuss it.

Sidney Shepherd had been after her to do *Changing Partners*, the story of an older woman who falls in love with a younger man. Although Carla was not yet forty, the story of a woman who felt herself aging and who had a troubled marriage seemed right to her. When Paul found the script on Carla's chair in the gazebo at Chisel Hall, he read the first sixty pages and then started mocking it, reading speeches aloud, declaring it ludicrous and hopelessly passé. Cora told him, "I can't think of a better way to get her to do that script than telling her she shouldn't. You're acting like you're on Sidney Shepherd's payroll."

Carla had begun spending more time with Jack again at the bungalow. He was about to turn seventy, an age when a man is bound to take stock. Mona had breast cancer which had required a mastectomy. Her pain had moved Jack, had made him feel closer to his wife than he had in years, and he had been spending more time with her. Mona's illness and the fact that Carla was raising three children had changed her relationship with Jack. He still felt ardent with Carla and their time together was romantic, but it was also more reflective. He looked strong and virile as ever to her, and in a funny way she thought he looked as he did when she first met him, when he was in his forties. It wasn't true, of course, and Carla knew that. In her mind, there were two Jacks—the one she met at the Hollywood Bowl with Igor Stravinsky, all those years ago, the one who had pursued and loved her the way no other man ever had or could; and the aging gentleman who was a private combination of fatherly strength and lover's ardor, who advised her in professional matters and whose very presence made her feel secure.

As she looked around the bungalow, this place where she had spent the most passionate hours of her life, she saw that it, unlike Jack and herself, had not changed with time. Instead of getting older, as they had, the bungalow had been kept polished and painted by the hotel. The furniture always seemed new. If it was never quite stylish, it still always seemed fresh. She wondered when the hotel did all the work. Since Chisel Hall, she had been aware of the difficulties of running a house and keeping it in repair. She had never seen a handyman in the bungalow, never even noticed a paintbrush.

Jack held her hand as they sat on the sofa while she explained the difficulty at home about which picture she would choose to do next. Jack saw at once the real issues involved. "Your husband wants your vote. Hit or not, he needs to show the studios he can deliver your services. He'll be hurt if you do Sidney's picture first."

"You mean his career?"

"Of course. His feelings, too. You can see that, can't you? He'll see it as an insult that makes him look foolish."

"I don't want to do that. I really don't. But you know, I don't care if *Thinning Out* is the biggest smash of all time. It's a wretched, dumb movie and I'm ashamed of it."

"Carla, Carla," he said, holding her in his arms, kissing her forehead. "Don't you think you're being just a little contrary because you're mad at your husband?"

"The movie stinks. When people go around repeating that line it turns my stomach. I mean that. I get sick thinking about it."

"How's Sidney's script? Is it good?"

"It's okay. *Changing Partners.* I would play a woman who's worried about aging—which is less of a stretch than I wish."

"You're not aging."

"Ever hear of entropy? Dennis used to talk about it."

"Now you're thinking about Dennis?"

"Not Dennis, entropy. Besides, I always like my last husband best."

Jack laughed at that and said, "You're so much funnier than you know. *Thinning Out* was no accident. There are two non-personal things wrong with Sidney's picture. It doubles Toronto for L.A.—not a sign of a first-class venture."

"Just the interiors."

"Until they start shooting the exteriors up there, too. It doesn't matter. It'll get you away for a while."

"What else?"

"The studio could change hands in the middle of production—for sure before the picture's in the theaters."

"I'm more worried about Paul," she said.

"He can tell people you'll do his next. Do Sidney's picture. Go to Toronto."

He kissed her again and held her, needing her against him. They were content to sit like that for a few minutes, in an easy embrace, each feeling the other's warmth. Carla could feel the rhythm and the pulse of his heart. She began to match her own breathing to it, finding comfort, as if they were dancing and he was leading. It made her remember the night at the Beverly Hilton after the Oscars when they had danced together and not given a damn who saw them or what anyone thought.

As she lost herself in memory, her mind finally got free of her domestic problems and questions of scripts, and roamed back over the years. She thought of her old Thunderbird, how Jack had given it to her to commemorate their first time together in the Thunderbird Hotel, and how she had driven it so long. She remembered how he looked when he had turned fifty, so powerful to her, so male and permanent; how he had known exactly what to do when her father had gotten into so much trouble. It was Jack who had called to tell her about it, so it would be his voice she heard when she had to listen to the awful news. She thought of how they had endured when she lived in New York with Dennis, reading all those endless books. Even then he was always there. She would have been happy to stay like that, matching her breathing to his, letting her mind drift back through the years of their life together. She wondered if memory wasn't better even than the thing itself. Sometimes it felt that way. That was what acting was all about—conjuring emotion from memory, reliving it, holding a mirror up to desire. No matter what hard turns her life had taken, her performances had always been more real and more valuable to her than life itself. She turned her face to his, kissed him tenderly, and said, "I love you, Jack, I really do."

"And I love you. I always have, I always will." He kissed her, then looked at her face, studying it as he had done so many times before, looking for the mystery he always found there.

three

The Prodigy of Bluff

23.

While Carla's body was being brought back to Los Angeles, on Monday morning, Mort Brady and I met with the Shepherds in Century City. The funeral was to be Wednesday, with burial in Westwood Memorial Park. None of that stopped Sidney and Bobby from getting to what was on their minds—the completion bond.

"I expect you guys to call your underwriter and explain the facts of life," Sidney said, about to abandon *Changing Partners*. Sidney fancied himself a showman of the old school, along the lines of Zanuck or Goldwyn. In the days before the Shepherds worked in these offices, and actually owned a film lot, Sidney always called his studio the store. Thirty years in the business, and Sidney never learned to read a script. But he could cut a tough deal. "Without her there's no picture. We can't do the last two weeks. This is an act of God," he said, quoting the boilerplate language from the contract that he felt would let him off the hook.

"Lloyd's might not see it that way," I said.

"Persuade them."

Mort knew I wanted to try to finish the movie. He thought I was letting personal feelings get in the way of what he saw as a simple business decision. He was right about part of it—my feelings about Carla were more important to me than the completion bond business. To my surprise, I found I had an unexpected ally in Bobby Shepherd. Apparently Frank Wheat had been calling Bobby, telling him how the picture could be finished and released. When Bobby defended that option, his father just glared. "We have an obligation here," Bobby said, ignoring his father. Bobby, who had become a lawyer, had a sense of scripts. "The public's going to want to see her last picture," he said. "We're the ones who have it; let's exploit it."

"Act of God or not," Mort said, "Lloyd's will blame us if they have to pay. We'll lose our underwriter." Now this wasn't exactly true—possible, but not definite. I couldn't quite see what Mort was up to, so I kept my mouth shut.

"The hell with Lloyd's," Sidney said. "Do the right thing and you'll have a contract with us rich enough for other underwriters to come running." These two old birds were hatching a bribe. Play ball on this, Sidney was saying, and we'll throw business your way. Maybe because the whole thing made me sick, what I found myself thinking about was not Sidney's offer, which I now realized was what Mort had been waiting for all along, but that the content, shape and fate of a movie was being decided and the director was in no way involved. The media and the people these men called "the talent" might think of Hollywood as a sort of directocracy, but here, in Century City, where it counts, only money has a voice.

Back in our office Mort told me he couldn't believe I was hesitating. "Your end of what was on the table could be, personally, a quarter-million a year."

"He made that pretty clear, Mort."

"You're saying no to that? Let me give you some advice, Gabe. You want to make a monument to Carla Tate, well, God bless. But don't sign away your commercial future to do it."

"Why throw the picture away? If it can't be finished, that's one thing. That's what the bond's for. Her last picture's worth more in the theaters than not."

"That's a theory. Our obligation is to our customer."

"Let me think about it," I said, which is what I always say when I've already made up my mind but need time to figure how best to go about getting what I want. We both knew if there were any way for me to see that *Changing Partners* was finished, I'd do it. It would mean the end of my partnership with Mort and the enduring enmity of Sidney Shepherd. The wild card was Bobby. He'd probably be my ally, and since he and I were the same generation, in the long run that relationship was the more important one.

While I was mulling this over, Mort called Lloyd's and told them that in all likelihood they'd have to pay. They instructed him to begin proceedings to take possession of the negative. That doesn't mean physically—the negative was in a vault at the lab and would stay there—but ownership would shift from the Shepherds to Pacific Assurance, as agents for Lloyd's. If Lloyd's paid, then it would be in their interest to finish the film and recoup some money from it. Sidney would then probably try to get Lloyd's to hire his company to do the work—he'd give up his profit position, but get his cash back and take a fee from Lloyd's. You could be sure he'd finish it badly under those circumstances. If he was forced to spend his own money, with only an insurance claim for the time he was shut down, he'd do a better job because he'd keep the profits.

The funeral service was held at the Wilshire Boulevard Temple. Carla hadn't been a member of a temple, or of anything other than the Screen Actors Guild or the Academy, that I was ever aware of. She wouldn't have minded; she might even have been amused. This place, which was sometimes called the above-the-line shul, was modeled after the Pantheon and seats fifteen hundred. The biblical murals on the walls of the sanctuary were painted by the Warner Bros. art department.

A crowd had gathered out front. They weren't trying to get in—that was by numbered invitation. They were orderly enough—subdued, really. Some of them had come to see the celebrities, but others were there because they wanted to feel some emotion. Real feeling was definitely in the air out there, certainly as much as I could feel inside. They wanted a last sense of her.

The senior rabbi, Edgar Magnin, clergyman to the movie business, was in his eighties at the time but he still looked like a giant redwood. As he was going about his rabbinical duties, I saw Frank Wheat come into the temple with Lila Bledsoe on his arm. Lila was wearing a black dress, which was respectful, but it also happened to set off her white skin to great advantage. She was so young and hot that somebody had to be sleeping with her. Of course, it was the director. They both looked a little nervous, with probably not too many synagogues in either of their pasts.

Rabbi Magnin rose to the occasion. He didn't pretend he knew Carla better than he did, or that she was more religious than she was, as the rabbis of my own childhood would have done. He didn't make fatuous claims for either Carla or God. He talked about her artistry and the terrible sadness of her death. Then he began recounting her career, not just giving a biographical sketch of the woman, but analyzing her performances, both as a child and as an adult. Of her childhood, he said: "She worked on instinct, a prodigy of bluff, the tiny mistress of her own only partly understood secrets, of passions, dreams and nightmares. She was able to do what pleased adults without herself fully understanding just what it was she was doing. She had a concentrated imagination, a rich, uncritical talent."

Edgar Magnin was a remarkable man in many ways, but I had never thought of him as a film critic. Then he started talking about her as an adult. "It was her talent, her abilities and skills that made her great, of course. But there was also a matter of physical beauty, allure. The exterior—skin deep and all that—was important. But there was something deeper about her beauty. Her presence itself was compelling. When Carla was there, she was absolutely there. And that was the case all her short life. Always our golden girl." The man saw her life whole, from its humble beginnings to its messy conclusion. He said it all in the rolling voice that had been filling that vast sanctuary since the thirties. It made me weep. I was not alone.

Westwood Memorial Park is an unlikely oasis in what has become a wildly built-up part of the city. When the cemetery was first used this part of town still had bean fields. Now it's between some stucco bungalows and a movie theater, in the shadows of hulking office buildings. The changes had all come during Carla's lifetime. Monroe is in a vault in this little cemetery.

A vast, comforting pepper tree had grown up in the center of the graveyard. Groman's Mortuary had set up white wooden chairs and a sweeping canopy, redundant under its branches. I was sort of patrolling the back edge of the crowd, too restless to sit, but unable to leave. There were fewer people here than at the temple, but still enough of a crowd that a security force had been set up.

After Carla's coffin had been lowered into the ground, and after Milton had fainted, Rabbi Magnin was reciting the Kaddish, the ancient prayer for the dead. I couldn't hear it all because Frank Wheat, with Lila Bledsoe still on his arm, had pulled me aside. He introduced me to Lila, who of course had absolutely no memory of having met me in Toronto seven weeks before. Frank asked her to leave us alone for a few minutes. She wasn't crazy about being dismissed, but she wandered off in the direction of Monroe's tomb.

"What are they going to do?" he asked.

"Sidney wants to file a claim and say good-bye. He doesn't think it can be finished."

"But it can," Frank said excitedly. "I've thought it through. It can be done." Then he began outlining the problems as he saw them. "There's that love scene to go. I can fake it with body parts—specific shots of Bill Meserve, and we get a model to double Carla in the skin shots. Cut right into the center, no chitchat, just boom and up on them fucking. It'll look like a perfume commercial, but it'll be okay. I'll show a lot of rustling sheets. The critics'll call it high style."

"No close-ups?"

"I can reshoot some of the negative of the other close-ups. Change the angle. It'll work, Gabe. The big thing is to get somebody first-rate to write new continuity."

That dirt was being heaped on Carla's coffin even as he spoke didn't seem to bother him. He made some noises about finishing the picture being the best tribute to her—which was becoming the anthem of all involved, with each person speaking to his own interests in the name of honoring Carla's memory. Frank's scheme amounted to hiring a very expensive writer to reshape the end of the movie. The only way that could be done, expensive writer or not, was to put the focus on Lila's character, she being alive and available. Frank didn't mention that. Maybe he didn't remember I used to be a screenwriter. Or maybe he figured that the less he talked about Lila and the more he talked about Carla the likelier he would be to get to finish his movie. I could see a couple things with more clarity than comfort: that he was right, that was the way to finish the movie; and that Carla's fear that Lila was the future, and therefore a danger to her, was more prescient than she imagined. The picture could be finished by making it Lila's. And it was all to be done over Carla's dead body.

Jack was at the funeral, without Mona. He had nodded to me, but we hadn't spoken. That night he called, ready to talk about who should write the new ending. "Dick Schraft did the production polish," I said. "He knows the script pretty well. This is a different situation, though."

Jack asked if I thought Arcady Metzler would be of value.

Arcady Metzler was generally considered the best rewrite man in Hollywood. Arcady wanted to direct now, and didn't get involved with projects in which that wasn't a possibility. The other part of the Arcady Metzler problem was that he had retreated into his house in Malibu, where he was said to consume large amounts of cocaine. I mentioned that to Jack, who didn't sound surprised. Even if Arcady were *compos* and available, his fee would be in the neighborhood of two hundred grand. "What about Sidney and Bobby?" I asked.

"I'll talk to them. I'll speak to Metzler's agents. Then I want you to talk to him. I'll tell Frank Wheat you're going to function as de facto producer. Lloyd's will think you're protecting the money. Wheat leads with his dick. We're not doing this for his girlfriend's career. You stay close to these people."

"Why me?"

"Don't pretend to be naive. Look to the future," he said, as if he could read my thoughts. "It's better for you, for everybody. Finish the picture."

As I was considering the odds against Arcady Metzler being available, let alone interested in a task of this sort, he called and asked if I'd come out to the beach to talk it over. That meant Jack had already dealt his hand. Arcady was a famous character in the movie business. He was in his late forties and had been doing rewrites for years. He had written several pictures of his own as well, and a few had been hits, but it was as a script doctor that he was in demand. He was an eccentric who kept dropping out of the business, then coming back determined to direct.

As I drove out to Malibu I thought about his skill. He could take a hundred and fifty confused script pages and in a few weeks turn them into something like the Platonic ideal of a script. Arcady was a sort of fallen intellectual, a scholar who had gotten detoured in the sun. He had been working toward a Ph.D. in history at Harvard. Before he wrote his dissertation, he had taken some time off to travel. When he got to L.A. he must have liked it, because he never went back to Cambridge. When I was doing rewriting myself, Arcady had occasionally thrown work my way. I wasn't bad at it, but the producers always made it clear that I was their second choice. The only reason they had gambled on me was that Arcady Metzler had suggested it. I used to try to thank him when that happened. He always said, "Let's hear how grateful you are when those thugs are through with you."

The Colony, where Arcady lived, is the most social part of Malibu, a collection of beach houses along the spit of sand where Malibu, as a haven for the well-to-do of Hollywood, began. Originally people leased land, put up shacks, and lazed away the weekends there. The shacks are long gone, but the idea of rebuilding them remains. People are forever buying a small place, tearing it down, and putting up a grander one. Since there's only room for about a hundred and fifty houses, and every year more and more people want to live there, the price of real estate just keeps going up. All this was on my mind as the guard in his little Mediterranean guardhouse passed me through.

Arcady's door was open. The living room was decorated with white canvas-covered sofas and chairs and about thirty large pillows, each covered in what was once part of an expensive rug—Kilims mostly. The living room opened onto a patio that looked out over the sand to the ocean beyond. All the houses in the Colony were arranged like that, but each time I saw those patios, the sand and then the Pacific, I was reminded anew how pleasant it can be to be rich in Hollywood.

Arcady was on the patio reading *The New Republic*. He was short and squat, built along the lines of a fireplug. His eyes were dreamy, as if they were watching some private movie. I always thought at least part of him was still in Widener Library, lost in the eighteenth century. His companions of the moment were a pair of nubile nymphs taking the sun. Visions of a ménage flooded my mind. Then he introduced them. One was his daughter, the other his girlfriend. They both looked about twenty. I could swear they were both named Laura. Ménage indeed. Arcady's life was stranger than my pedestrian fantasies.

"Gabriel Burton," he announced. "A fellow who has lately been chewing on the nature of risk and chance in the lives of movie stars. In his own, too, I'd bet." Before I could even try to spar, he turned to the pair of Lauras and said, "He's in a business where you have to pay for death."

"We're trying to avoid paying," I said.

"By finishing the movie. A nice conundrum. Much too complex for the movies, right, Mr. Bondsman?" He immediately began a little soliloquy on scripts. "Why use a good story for a script? Good means complex. Pictures botch that every time. More than one tone, a given in an interesting novel, is a disaster in a script. If the director doesn't muddle it, then the studio will—they who live in fear the public might actually not be stupid." Just a typical Arcady Metzler diatribe. How could I not like the guy? I didn't even try to answer. I just applauded, which seemed to satisfy him. We left the Lauras and went for a stroll along the beach. The Colony was always crowded on the weekends, but now in the middle of the week, it seemed Arcady, his spaniel mutt and I had the million-dollar sand to ourselves. The sun was setting. Directors call it the magic hour—when everything at Malibu is bathed in a reflected red light. The rocks, the sand, the sea itself, were all glowing red.

As we walked, Arcady kept asking me questions about the situation at Shepherd-International. "Sidney and Bobby—that's real," he said. "Not some bullshit movie."

"I guess. It's pretty simple, though. Sidney wants out, Bobby wants to try to finish it."

"Then that lines Sidney up against Markel. Sidney's doomed."

"Maybe."

"I envy you, Gabe. You're right in the middle of all this. It's sure more compelling than what I do." He wanted to ask questions about the chicanery around the completion bond. He would have preferred to ignore the script problems and just talk about the deal, making subtle inquiries. "Following the money—the only trail worth the hike" is the way he put it. I asked if he couldn't force himself to address the script for a few minutes.

"Yeah, sure," he said, but then he began to talk about Carla. "I always had a sort of long-distance crush on her," he said. "I guess everybody did."

"That was her business," I managed.

"Whenever something like this happens, all the professional thumb-suckers say, 'It's the end of an era.' For once, they're right. This really is. She's a generation removed from the golden age, but still, Carla's from the Hollywood that was. From when the country could worship a child and make her an adult at seven. Some might say, then turn her back into a seven-year-old as an adult." All that just poured out of him. The man had been thinking about Carla, no doubt about it.

"You really are a historian, aren't you?" I said.

"Historian *manqué*, now. The Hollywood that Carla was?

Some of it's around, but it's going fast. The studios are all going to be like Paramount—part of big conglomerates. It's the end, Gabe. Not just of Carla. *Fin de siècle, fin du monde.*" Then, as suddenly as he had started, he shifted gears again. "Yeah, yeah," he said, as if I had complained he was getting off the subject. "I read the cutting continuity. I talked to the ever-gracious Frank Wheat."

"He called you?"

"Pushing his girlfriend."

"What do you think of that—putting the focus on Lila?"

"I don't see any other way. It'll be a weird movie, but the audience'll know about Carla. They'll feel like they're a part of the rewrite. You could do it yourself."

"Have you seen any of the film yet?"

"No. I hear Carla's great and Lila's good."

"That's about right."

"I should look at the assembly," he said. Then perhaps thinking it sounded as if he didn't care to, he added, "I'll look at all the footage if you think it would be valuable." I could hear a screenwriter's deference to a producer. It happened even with a distinguished screenwriter and an absolutely untried producer. "It'll come down to writing three, four scenes and some transitions. It'll be a little abrupt. I think the real trouble is, Frankie boy's going to have a major looping problem."

He meant that on any picture a lot of the dialogue has to be rerecorded. The actors come to the studio and watch their image on a screen and redo any lines that were muffled in the original take or have some problem the mixer can't solve. It's a routine procedure, but as Arcady was pointing out, it requires that you have the actors.

"What are you going to do about that?" he asked.

"Use every track we've got and if there's a crisis, there's a woman who does a club act of impersonations. She does a great Carla."

"Perfect. A comedy club geek has the last word on Carla Tate."

"It's not the last word. Think of it as a helping voice. Can I ask you why you're doing it?"

"Markel's going to help me with the financing of a project of mine."

"You mean he's getting you a gig directing?"

"Right. So when did you become a producer?"

"It's a one-shot deal, Arcady."

"You're the right guy for it. Funny thing," he said, fumbling in his pocket, "that this should turn out to be her last picture."

"Why funny?"

"Ironic I mean. It's about aging. The only thing on this earth she never got to do. You want some lunch? Laura's making a salad."

I didn't ask which Laura. I had to get back to town. I could see what he was taking out of his pocket.

"Toot up," he said. "If you're going to hang out in hell, might as well get warm by the fire."

"No thanks."

"Guess you're not really a producer after all," he said, snorting a tiny spoonful.

"Why is that?"

"Real producers either want to get in on it because it's free, or they want to stop me from committing a public felony." His eyes didn't look as if they were in Cambridge anymore. I suspected he had shifted from the intricacies of the movie—both the deal and the script—to whichever Laura made him happiest.

"Can I ask you one question about it? You snort that stuff around your daughter?"

"It's her dope. I gave it to her for introducing me to Laura."

I laughed, asked him when I might expect pages, and drove back to town. On the way, I found myself considering the nature of insurance and what Arcady had called risk and chance. If Carla had been more prudent, perhaps she'd be alive. But then she wouldn't have been Carla. I, to my regret, was the man who had sold her the guarantee.

Sidney Shepherd had a fit when he learned Jack was moving ahead to finish the movie and that he had interceded with Lloyd's on behalf of Pacific Assurance. Sidney called Lloyd's and said this was all my doing and how dare they listen to an insurance salesman rather than to him. He told them that if they tried to complete this movie, they were going to learn some expensive lessons.

I felt certain I was on the right side. If I could claim any tactical wisdom in all this, it was that my own interests had aligned me with Jack rather than Sidney. Jack moved fast. He lined himself up with Bobby Shepherd and they began acquiring stock and proxies. Within a week they had the votes on the Shepherd-International board to name Sidney the Founding Chairman and C.E.O. Emeritus. In other words, fired and shoved upstairs. Bobby was made C.E.O. Son had toppled father. It was all anybody in Hollywood could talk about. The trades wrote about nothing else. Jack's name was never mentioned.

Once Bobby was promoted, my reign as temporary producer came to an end. This was Bobby's chance to be out on the front lines, and he wasn't going to let anybody else do the job. With the revised script in hand, the filming itself was like an afterthought. It was too expensive to go back to Toronto for so little time. What was required was done on L.A. streets and on a stage. Arcady had written a big scene that could be shot in a tight angle. Frank Wheat settled in with the editor, Henry Sisto, to make a film out of all the footage. That would take a few months and there was no way to hurry it. When the editing had begun, Jack Markel invited me to lunch at the Hillcrest Country Club.

Hillcrest had been established in the twenties by the Los Angeles Jewish gentry in response to the various Gentile clubs that would have nothing to do with them. The result, during the club's beginnings, was a conservative, straitlaced society that did its best to ape its oppressors. No movie people were admitted. All that changed during the Depression and again after the war. These days, producers, studio executives and the more reputable agents had lunch there, played golf with their clients and customers, and in the evenings brought their wives to dinner.

I met Jack in the men's dining room. There's always a lot of table-hopping at a place like this, but on this day, all the show-business *machers* seemed to recognize that a lunch between Jack Markel and me was private. It was hard for me to get used to the idea that these people knew my business. I think they thought of me as a sidekick of Jack's in demolishing Sidney Shepherd. When we sat down I thought I felt the room become oddly quiet. The reason quickly became apparent: Sidney was there. When he saw Jack, he rose from his table and walked out. Everyone reacts differently to a moment like that. Most of the room was watching Sidney; my own instinct was to watch Jack. His face remained still, impassive. Not a tic, not a blink. Sidney practically slammed down his chair as he left. Jack waited a few moments, until the room calmed down, ignoring the fuss, refusing to get drawn into it. He simply asked what I thought of the new footage. I knew he got nightly reports from Frank Wheat, but he was just checking.

"It'll work. Frank's very clever with this sort of thing."

"When we release it, we should make a virtue out of all that's gone into it. Tell the public that the picture had to be redesigned to account for circumstances. It'll make people interested."

"I'm sure you're right, Jack." I was waiting for what would come. Jack certainly didn't invite me here to discuss the marketing campaign. Then it came, straight and simple.

"I want to know what happened on that boat," he said.

I knew what he meant. I'd puzzled over the question myself. "You've probably heard the same rumors I have."

"I don't know. Have I?" he asked.

"That Paul and Tink Harvey were lovers and Carla walked in on them. That Carla and Tink were lovers. That all three of them were on drugs." He just nodded as I recounted the gossip. Jack had held power for too long and was by inclination too cynical about human nature to discount anything, no matter how apparently unlikely. I knew one thing more about him, from having dealt with him over the last weeks. He wouldn't rest until he either knew the truth about Carla's death or was convinced that it was unknowable. It was a separate issue from finishing *Changing Partners*. That was for Carla. Resolving this question was for himself. He was turning to me rather than, say, a private detective, for the same reason he had turned to me to help finish the movie. Carla's interests were of fundamental importance to me. He was willing to bet that if I found out something scabrous about her, I would tell him, but not the media. As usual, in matters of business and psychology, he was right.

"Complete the puzzle, Gabe. Speak to anybody you need to. If somebody's hesitant to talk, let me know, and if pressure can be brought, I'll do it. There's no price for a task like this. Of course I'll cover your costs for whatever comes up. But the reason to do it is so you and I can sleep at night. You understand."

"What do you think I'll find?"

"Do I think you'll find a crime? I don't know that."

"If I do?"

"You mean will I turn some goons loose?"

"I'm sorry. I guess that is what I meant."

"It's okay," Jack said, smiling. "With my reputation, people always think something like that. Believe it or not, I don't know any goons."

That wasn't exactly true. He might not take them to lunch at

Hillcrest, but I knew damn well he knew where to find them and how to use them. What he had given me was a lawyer's answer. It sounded like a denial, but he hadn't said he wouldn't adjudicate the matter privately.

First I talked with Buddy DeSantis, the yacht captain; his crew; then to Cora, of course; to the Santa Barbara coroner; to some people Carla had spoken to in a restaurant on Saturday night; to Tink Harvey and eventually to Paul Loeb. He was the only one who hesitated in any serious way. At first I thought it was because he was planning his own version of the events for a book or a movie. Possibly not. No matter how opportunistic this marriage might have been, Paul was genuinely grieving and trying to keep his family together. He thanked me for working to finish the movie. Then he said if there was anything of Carla's, some small memento that I might like, to tell him and he'd see that I got it. I couldn't think what I wanted beyond my memories, but it was a generous offer and I liked him for it. I drew bits and pieces from all of them until I was able to piece together a chronology of what had happened that weekend, to give to Jack.

24.

When *Changing Partners* returned to Los Angeles, Carla had a few days before shooting resumed. She and Paul planned to spend the weekend with their kids and Tink Harvey, cruising up to Santa Barbara on the *Tête-à-Tate*. Paul had stayed in Los Angeles Friday night to have dinner with a studio executive. Carla and Tink had gone ahead. Paul was to drive up Saturday morning with the children.

Four hours out, Carla was reading scripts on the aft deck, trying to enjoy the sun without getting a tan that wouldn't match the film already shot in the Canadian locations. Buddy DeSantis came to tell her about the weather and water conditions, a ritual that always amused her because she never had the slightest idea what he was talking about. When Tink saw Buddy with Carla, he strolled out onto the deck. Tink had been giving Carla a wide berth, but now he was halfway through a pitcher of Bloody Marys, and couldn't resist an opportunity to mock what he thought of as Buddy's nautical pretensions. Tink had found that if he called the ship's cabins bedrooms, it would set Buddy's teeth on edge. The engine room had become the basement. The bow and the stern were the pointy end and the blunt end.

"We should be in S.B. about six," Buddy said. "We're making eleven knots." He glanced over at Tink, girding himself for the wisecrack he knew was on its way.

"Never trust these stinkpots," Tink said in a sincere voice. "A man wants a halyard and a couple of sheets in the wind. Am I right?" Buddy was baffled by Tink. He never knew how to take him, which was part of Tink's pleasure. If Buddy'd had the sense to look irritated, Tink might have considered it victory enough and stopped. As it was, he couldn't stop wallowing in mangled nautical lingo. "If you don't mind drinking while you drive, I'll pour you one."

"Maybe later," Buddy said, forcing a smile.

"That's the trouble with life at sea," Tink said, sounding sympathetic. "Can't relax for a minute. Fire up the barbecue, shoot a few hoops with the kids, then boom, you've got to go swab a deck."

"Tink, cool it," Carla said, as Buddy, his face frozen, nodded and backed away.

"Why do you do that?" Carla asked. "He doesn't get it and he never will."

"It amuses me. Admit it, it amuses you, too."

"So what? It upsets Buddy. It's cruel."

"In your husband's absence, I'm the understudy. Just handling domestic duties and trying to keep you smiling."

Carla thought she heard a hint of a pass in the crack about being Paul's understudy, which didn't appeal to her at all; a little of Tink Harvey went a long way with her. She decided that not only did she not want to go ashore with him for dinner, but she wanted to reward Buddy for his stoicism in the face of Tink's mockery. When she thought Tink could hear, she told Buddy, "I'd like you to take me ashore for dinner. It'll be just the two of us." Buddy, who had never had a meal with Carla *à deux,* stammered out his pleasure. Tink heard the invitation and understood he was being left behind. He poured himself another drink.

Buddy anchored the *Tête-à-Tate* outside the Santa Barbara breakwall, because she was too big to fit in one of the slips. He left her in Ubaldo's hands. Tink was getting drunker on board as Buddy and Carla were going ashore in the rubber dinghy. Buddy arranged himself at the rudder, hoping some of his pals might see them together. "Shall we try the Club?" he asked.

When her face looked blank, he added, "Santa Barbara Yacht Club. I'm sure they'd let us in."

"How about Brophy's Clam Bar?" she said, mentioning a dive on the pier. He looked so disappointed that Carla told him to pick a place. He brought the dinghy about and headed across the harbor toward Stearns Wharf.

They went up the waterside ladder into the Harbor Restaurant. Entering through the back door meant you had arrived by boat and were entitled to be fawned over by the help. A movie star coming up the waterside ladder short-circuited the staff.

Carla was happy to sit in a captain's chair sipping vodka and watching the boats in the harbor, but Buddy was determined to take advantage of his time with her. He wanted to let her know he was more than the fellow who captained her yacht and managed the boat's affairs. Carla half expected him to tell her he really wanted to direct, but he seemed pleased to go on about the tricky currents between the harbor and the Channel Islands. Every now and then she would look up and admire his weathered face.

As the room filled, Carla could sense what was going on. The manager or whoever was running the place was admitting people into her presence—probably selling tickets. As Buddy went on about the treacherous ways of the currents, she could see the manager, a ferret in a Hawaiian shirt, trying to catch her attention. "I don't want to eat here," she said, abruptly. She was up and walking out as Buddy hurried after her.

On the wharf, it was as if a message had gone out. People had gathered to stare. Cameras appeared; Instamatic flashes blinking, shutters clicking. It was a sound she was used to, had come to think of as part of the natural soundscape—all those cameras, making blurry photos to be displayed or handed around, proof they had seen her. The more worldly ones whispered, "Don't look . . . don't stare . . . There's Carla Tate . . ." Occasionally people asked for an autograph or stepped close to say hello. On the one hand, Carla enjoyed the awe these people felt and she pursued it, was addicted to it. On the other, she resented it and felt oppressed. Her wish, insofar as she thought about it, was to be able to turn it on or off at will. Tonight, when she just wanted to walk on the wharf, she would have preferred anonymity. Another night, she might wish for all these people to beg for a smile.

At Cabrillo Boulevard, where the wharf begins, Buddy asked if she wanted to go to the Biltmore Hotel for dinner. That was the last thing Carla wanted. She had a vision of well-to-do vacationers gawking at her. She glanced across the boulevard at Castagnola's Lobster House. "There," she said. "I want a lobster."

Maybe it was the earnest way Buddy chose the bottle of Orvieto, but once they were seated, Carla's mood changed and she began asking him personal questions. As he was going on about his childhood sailing lessons, Carla was thinking about her daughters and the fun they would have together on the boat, when she was seized with a warm desire to call her husband.

"How's it going?" Paul asked. "The Tinkster on his good behavior?"

"Hah! What a maniac."

"Where are you?"

"Some restaurant. I ditched him. I'm not going back on board till you get here."

"Buddy with you?"

"Yeah. He thinks he's on a date or something. When are you coming?"

"In the morning. Have him book you a room at the Biltmore. I'll try to get up there early. When you get checked in, call me."

"Is everybody excited about coming?"

"That's not working out. Sophie wants to go to a party and Emma's got a sore throat. She shouldn't come."

"She was fine. When did it start?"

"This afternoon. Susan changed her mind, too."

"I'm coming home then. I'm going to rent a car."

"She's okay. Susan played with her. I talked to the doctor. It'll take twenty-four hours. Carmen's there."

"How'd she get it?"

"She's four years old. It's been known to happen."

"Can't you even take care of her for one night?"

"I've been taking care of her for two months," he said sharply. Then, thinking better of it, said, "Go back to the boat or check into a hotel. Whatever. If she's better, I'll bring her. If Susan changes her mind, I'll bring her, too."

After she hung up, Carla didn't want to stay at Castagnola's anymore. She left her lobster uneaten and she and Buddy wandered over to Rocky Galanti's, a college bar on the waterfront with caricatures of the patrons painted on the walls. Local bands played in the back room and students danced and got drunk on pitchers of draft beer. The saloon was on the ground floor of the Californian Hotel, a dive that by virtue of its seventy-five-year history had been declared a landmark. Carla and Buddy sat at the long wooden bar knocking back brandies, while college boys gawked. One particularly attractive specimen, a big blond, in madras Bermuda shorts and penny loafers without socks, lingered for so long that Buddy was about to tell him to move on, when Carla looked up at him and he asked her to dance.

"Love to, sailor," she said.

Carla danced with him as the band played "Proud Mary." His pals marveled at their friend's good fortune. He told Carla his name was Rick and he was in heaven. "Then you must be a saint," Carla said. "But Rick's no name for a saint. I'm going to declare you Saint Ambrose." He beamed as Carla jumped about and shook herself in his astonished face. Carla could measure her heat and calibrate her power over men precisely. Part of that skill was her ability to appear to lose sight of it and cut loose and dance. In her heart, deeper than Ambrose could see, she was in absolute control. As they danced, Ambrose began to touch her, reaching for her and stroking her hair, until as suddenly as she had started, she decided she didn't feel like dancing any longer.

Later, while her young suitor was standing by in case Carla wanted to dance again, she turned to Buddy and said, "Let's stay here tonight."

"In this place?"

"Just do it. Get me a room. Get yourself one. I'll worry about the rest of it tomorrow."

Their rooms were adjacent and Carla just fell on her bed, too drunk to take off her clothes. A few minutes later, Buddy knocked. "Are you okay?" he asked. "Do you need anything?"

She told him she was fine, and to wake her in the morning. As Buddy went back to his room, disappointed, he heard someone in the hall. He peered out and saw Ambrose, carrying a brandy bottle, knocking on Carla's door. "Now what?" she called.

"It's me. Rick . . . Ambrose. How you doing?"

Carla opened the door and looked him over. He was attractive in an inane fraternity boy way, but if Carla wanted anything, it was a shower, not a one-night stand with this jerk. "Forget it," she said. "Go home." But Ambrose was not about to be put off so easily. Carla tried to push the door shut on him, but Ambrose was moving into the room.

"Come on," he growled, "let's dance some more."

Before Carla could react, Buddy was in the hall with an arm on the kid's shoulder. "Fun's over, pal," he said. "Let's go." The boy looked from Carla to Buddy, trying to decide his best move.

Carla smiled at him and said, "Some other time, maybe." When he hesitated, Buddy kicked his foot out of the door and Ambrose backed off. After a moment, Carla and Buddy could hear young men laughing. A few of the boy's friends, the ones who had probably bribed the clerk to tell them Carla's room number, were lurking nearby, taking bets on how successful their friend would be. Buddy knew enough just to say good night and return to his room.

Paul arrived at noon on Saturday, without the children. Aside from a few harmless cracks about his wife's date with Buddy DeSantis, Paul was in good spirits, glad to see Tink and looking forward to the sun. He assured Carla that Emma was doing fine. He had told Carmen to feed her all the ice cream she wanted.

That evening, as the *Tête-à-Tate* sat outside the harbor breakwall, Carla showered and changed for dinner. "I don't see how she could get sick," Carla said, still thinking about their daughter. "She was fine."

"It's a sore throat. No one caused it." He knew that the combination of the long weeks in Canada, Tink's rudeness to Buddy, and Emma's sore throat was likely to make Carla on edge. As she dressed, she grew silent again, concentrating on selecting another of her jumpsuits. She chose khaki from the several that she kept on the boat. As she stepped into it, Paul admired his wife's figure. She was thirty-nine, had given birth twice, but what little weight she had put on seemed to suit her. Sometimes, late at night, if she couldn't sleep, Paul would see her studying her hips, which had spread a bit in recent years. Nonetheless her beauty still amazed him. "We can call from the restaurant," he said, assuming Emma's condition was the reason for Carla's silence. "I booked a table at the Biltmore. Okay?"

"Sure. Poor Buddy. That's where he wanted to go last night. I made him take me to some chowder place. I suppose Tink has to come."

"Absolutely. He is what he is. Enjoy it. A lot of people think he's one of the funniest men they know. You two have a tough time coming up here?"

"The man is loaded and, for all I know, on drugs."

"Very possibly," Paul said.

The stately Biltmore, with red tile roof, white stucco walls, and well-clipped rolling lawns, was one of the oldest hotels in Southern California. As late as the 1960s, the Biltmore wouldn't rent rooms to Jews, and if a man's hair touched his collar, he was refused entry. The main dining room, called La Marina, was more polished in its reaction to celebrities than the Harbor Restaurant on Stearns Wharf. The maître d', whose name, Paul remembered, was Thomas, greeted them warmly and assured them he had reserved a good, quiet table. The place might have been a little suburban for Carla's taste, but Thomas seemed to know by instinct just how much of a fuss to make. It was enough to relax her.

Carla wanted to call home before she sat down, and Thomas offered the phone in his office where she could have privacy. He escorted her to his cubicle behind the bar, and waited outside while she spoke. Emma was already asleep, but Carmen told Carla the child was feeling better, her sore throat all but gone. "Did you look? Hold her tongue down with a spoon and look right down there?" Carla asked.

"Jes," Carmen said, still unable to pronounce an English *Y* fifteen years after leaving Mexico. "Only a little red. She's asleeping now." When Carla was through, Thomas took her back to the table and held her chair.

The dining room faced the ocean, its large glass panels looking over the hotel grounds to the breakwall, where the *Tête-à-Tate* was visible in the distance, riding high in the water. Carla, Paul and Tink ordered vodkas on ice. Thomas sent a waiter over to the table with a platter of *panzanella*—chunks of bread and tomato, soaked in olive oil.

A few tables away was a family of eight, three generations. The senior member of their group, a tall, white-haired, well-tanned, patrician gentleman, raised his glass in a toast to Carla. He did it sweetly, without pretense. Probably the grandfather, Carla thought. The men in the family wore navy blazers and the women had identical white pleated skirts and silk blouses in different colors. They certainly didn't look like autograph hounds. Among them was a little girl of about seven with long, straight blond hair. Carla found the child adorable. Thomas came back to the table to ask Paul, on behalf of the large family, if he and Carla would accept a bottle of champagne. Thomas said that the older man, Mr. Purnoy, was a businessman and a member of the school board. He and Mrs. Purnoy were celebrating their anniversary. Paul started to say no, which was what he always did in these situations, but the offer pleased Carla so much that she said, "How sweet. Of course we will." As she approached to thank them, the men rose. Carla heard their polite remarks, but she couldn't take her eyes off the little girl, whose name was Babette. Carla stroked the child's hair and asked if she might braid it. Babette sat still and silent, basking in the attention, as Carla removed the bobby pins and carefully wove one thick plait. When Carla was done, she twisted and piled the braid on Babette's head, securing it with the bobby pins, and gave the child a kiss.

As Carla was about to return to her own table, she saw Thomas greeting two couples at the door. It was Jack and Mona Markel and a couple Carla didn't recognize. By the time Carla noticed Jack he had already seen her. He walked over, kissed her on the cheek, and said "Hello, darling. Who are you with?" Carla gestured toward her table, and saw Paul already coming toward them. Jack shook Paul's hand and introduced his guests. "You know Mona," he said. "And this is Cal and Luanne Snyder."

"Why don't you come have a drink?" Paul offered. Cal Snyder smiled but waited for Jack to decide. Cal was a lawyer who represented several movie stars. He was in his early forties, with a relaxed New Orleans accent. A Hollywood lawyer with movie-star clients was a powerful man, the sort who one day might run a studio, perhaps had already been offered such a job. That Snyder deferred to Jack was a sign of Markel's position. It wasn't lost on Paul Loeb. Luanne, with her soft features and loose, flowing skirt, looked like a fleshy Southern belle. She seemed a little drunk. "We'd love to," Jack said.

The table was round and large enough to accommodate four additional chairs. Jack sat next to Carla. As he did she turned toward him slightly, away from her husband. Her movement was tiny, only a few degrees, done as subtly and as naturally as a screen performance. Paul shifted uncomfortably in his own chair. Paul knew his wife and Jack had once been lovers. He believed the relationship was now only a professional one. What Paul also knew was that Jack Markel was one of the few people who was Carla's peer and equal, who commanded her unqualified respect. She was the epitome of public beauty, he the apotheosis of secret power. It was impossible not to think of them as a pair. It put Paul on the sidelines and it was hard on him.

Cal Snyder seemed to sense the tension. "We're up for the horse auction tomorrow," Cal said, turning to the safety of small talk. "The Arabians. Luanne's determined to have herself an Arabian horse."

"It's true," Luanne said in a honeyed voice. "I believe I'd lie down and die for an Arabian of my very own."

"As Arabs go, I prefer Lawrence," Tink said. Paul laughed, but the others, who had no taste for campy humor, only smiled politely.

"Are you staying at the hotel?" Paul asked, directing the question to Mona.

"Yes," Jack said.

With a husband who played his cards as closely as Jack did, Mona had learned years ago to say little in situations where she wasn't certain of the relationships. Tink Harvey, who understood the source of the tension at the table, pretended not to notice.

"Did you ever get to enjoy Toronto?" Jack asked, polite and poker-faced.

"It was okay," Carla said. "I'm glad to be home." As she said it, a hint of a pout appeared on her face. Paul recognized that look. It used to appear when she put her hand on his knee under the table. He coughed uncomfortably, realizing Carla's hands were not visible.

"Did you have much to do with the Shepherds?" Cal asked.

"Bobby came up to tell me how great it all was."

"Did you believe him?" Cal asked, with a grin.

"I just asked Jack what to do."

"And what did he tell you?" Cal asked in his droll, down-home voice.

"Jack always tells me the same thing—do good work and if they give me a hard time, let him know."

"Sounds like wise counsel," Cal said. "Acting is everything. We run around chasing phone calls and money, but without acting, what it's all for, don't you think?"

"I thought the script was everything," Tink said. "Or was that last week?" Everyone laughed and the conversation continued, but under it there was a tension generated by Carla's nearness to Jack. Luanne glanced over at Paul, to see how he was reacting to the unspoken drama, which suggested she knew about Carla and Jack. Whenever she caught Paul's eye, she smiled and all but fluttered her lashes. When Jack noticed it, he finished his mineral water and said, "We'll leave you to your dinner."

"Stay." Carla said, unnerved that Jack would leave. "Come back to the boat. Come out tomorrow."

Paul didn't look pleased with his wife's invitations. Mona watched Paul's face and said, a little too quickly, "We have the auction." When the four of them rose to go to their own table, Mona took Jack's arm, pulled him close, and let him guide her across the room. It was a gesture that was at once both possessive and dependent. Carla felt as if Mona were declaring victory.

When they were gone, Carla looked abandoned, then angry. Her emotions were on her face, clear and readable. Carla had long ago made peace with Jack's marriage. She didn't want to be Mona—she believed that her own relationship with Jack had endured precisely because they weren't married. But hearing about the auction and watching them act like the older married couple they were was hard on Carla. Sitting next to Jack, then not being able to go off with him when she was feeling tense from her time with Paul and Tink, and disappointed at not having her daughters with her, and most of all, seeing Paul and Jack together—a pairing that in Carla's eyes made Paul come in a distant second—disturbed her terribly. She declared the meal finished even though they hadn't eaten. When she left the room with her husband and Tink following, little Babette smiled brightly and got up to kiss her good-bye. But Carla didn't notice the child, and walked right past her.

At the *Tête-à-Tate*, Ubaldo climbed down the ladder and secured the dinghy, then offered his hand to Carla as she climbed up. In his annoyance, Paul considered sleeping in the saloon but then followed Carla into their cabin. Paul rarely started arguments with his wife. It was the price, he realized soon after they were married, of having a rich and famous spouse if you yourself were not, and aspired to be both. "You knew he was going to be there, didn't you?"

"I didn't even know where we were going. You made the arrangements."

"When we got there, you made a call. Then Don Corleone shows up."

"I called Emma!"

"Then you called him. You knew he was staying in the hotel. I'm going to have a drink." When Paul left, Carla stretched out on the bed, in the hope of getting some sleep. Her head was starting to hurt, and because it was Saturday night there was loud music playing in the harbor. The noise made her head feel worse. She went out on deck, where she found her husband and Tink smoking a joint.

"Little of what made Maui famous?" Tink asked, offering the joint.

"That's why you didn't want the kids here," Carla snapped.

"The kids aren't here because they didn't want to come. So knock it off," Paul answered.

"Well, I don't like drugs."

"I'll put it away," Tink said, about to snuff it out.

"Give me that," she said, taking it from him. Paul thought she was going to throw it overboard, and perhaps that was her intention, but instead, she took a long hit, hoping to calm herself.

"Carla Tate," Tink said, laughing. "The conflicted movie star–narc, a new hyphenate, strikes a blow against drugs."

"Shut up, Tink. I'm sick of your cracks. They're rude and desperate. I'm going to sleep," she said, and left. Carla's anger and her words made Tink's face flush red.

Paul and Tink stayed in the saloon, getting high, reminiscing about their student days, pointedly ignoring the subject of Jack Markel, whose departure they both knew had set off Carla's foul mood.

Carla tossed on the bed, her head spinning from the marijuana, vodka and wine. The music from the boats in the harbor seemed to get louder and her sense of irritation grew until she came back to the saloon. "I can't sleep. My head hurts. There's too much noise."

"Want me to make you a cup of tea?" Paul asked, in an attempt at reconciliation.

"I don't want to stay here."

"Oh? Back to the Biltmore, I suppose?"

"Just move this boat somewhere else. Anacapa."

"Get some sleep. You need it."

"I'll do it myself." She started to leave to wake Buddy.

"I'll do it," Paul said. "Maybe it will be quieter out there." When Paul left the saloon, Tink, still angry from Carla's insult and unsure of the balance of the situation, offered her a joint again. She ignored him and went back to her cabin without a word.

Buddy pushed the *Tête-à-Tate* to seventeen knots so the trip to Anacapa could be made in an hour and a half, and he could get back to sleep. The activity calmed Carla, but by then Paul was in a dark mood because of his wife's refusal to accept his offer of tea. He followed her into the cabin, still thinking about Jack Markel. "He's so fucking old."

"So what? Get off it, okay? I hate this."

"You never see him anymore," Paul said, not bothering to cover the sarcasm in his voice and unable to let go of the fight.

"You think that was some secret rendezvous? With his wife and those other people?"

"You fawned over him. You can pretend you didn't, but you did. You knew he was up here. Why lie?"

"I don't know his schedule and I'm not responsible for what you imagine about every man I ever knew," Carla said, growing weary of the argument.

"I just want to know about you and Jack Markel now. I have a right to know."

"I was glad to see him. So what? He's a lot easier to take than that maniac out there," she said, nodding toward the saloon and Tink Harvey.

"Kid yourself all you want," Paul answered, "but don't try to kid me. We are not talking about an old school chum of yours. It's entirely different and if you don't know it, I'm telling you now."

"Thanks for the lesson. Will there be a test?"

"Carla, you have an amazing ability to turn into an asshole sometimes. This is definitely one of the times."

"What?" she screamed. "What did you say?"

"Take it easy," Paul said, worried he'd gone too far.

"You don't treat me like that. I don't want to be here with you. I don't want to be anywhere with you."

"Now you go on the offense. A sure sign you're in the wrong. I can't imagine where you picked up that little tactic. Pure Markel. Cut the shit and go to sleep."

If there had been a grenade, she would have pulled the pin. Instead, she grabbed a brass ashtray and aimed it at her husband. He sidestepped it, but then she began throwing whatever was at hand, a pair of wineglasses, a saucer and a copy of *Vogue*. The magazine hit Paul's Adam's apple. It made him choke but that gave Carla no satisfaction. She grabbed a nearly empty champagne bottle and threatened him with it, swinging it like a club, the pale liquid splashing out. She might have hit him with it, but it flew out of her hand and sailed across the room, bouncing off the bulkhead.

"Jesus!" he said, gasping for breath. "How can I talk to you?"

She charged at him, out of control, kicking his shins, clawing at his face. "I hate you. You make me sick."

Paul grabbed her wrists and squeezed them together. He tried to contain his anger, but his voice came out in a hiss. "Just cool it, Carla. Stop right now."

"You stop it," she snarled. "I don't have to listen to you. You're pathetic. Your jealousy's pathetic."

"Don't say things like that," he said, releasing her. "I don't want to have this fight."

When they heard the anchor drop, Carla glanced out and saw they were near Cathedral Cove, where they had docked a few weeks earlier. "I want off this boat. Right now."

"We'll go back to Santa Barbara then, I don't care."

"I want to go see the seals."

"Fine. Camp out on the beach with God's creatures."

"Maybe I will. Maybe I'll go to Santa Barbara! Maybe I'll do both." She yelled so loud that it hurt her throat.

"Going to see Mr. Big, right?"

"He doesn't call me an asshole."

"Because you don't act like one when he's around."

"I'm going to the seals. I'd rather sleep with them."

"If you want to go play with the seals, go right ahead. Maybe they'll make you happy, because I sure as hell can't."

She wasn't listening anymore. She had left the cabin, heading for the aft deck where the dinghy was stowed. "If you must go," Paul called after her, "let me get Buddy or Ubaldo to lower the damn thing and go with you."

"I'll do it myself! I don't need your help!" she screamed. It was loud enough so that Buddy, Ubaldo and Tink were aware of it. But each of them had been around Carla's rages enough to know to stay out of sight.

After my lunch with Jack at Hillcrest, and after I had talked to everyone I could about Carla's last weekend, I went out to the California Yacht Club at Marina del Rey to have a look at the *Tête-à-Tate*. She was sitting there, big enough to require an end slip, just gently rocking in the breeze. Journalists had been sniffing around in the past days without much luck, but Cora had arranged for me to go aboard. A guard kept his eye on me, but gave me the run of the boat. I don't know what I expected—clues maybe, like in a detective movie. As I paced the deck a few things rumbled through my head. The first was that I didn't have the faintest idea what I was looking for. The second was that I knew exactly. It was clues all right, but not in the usual sense. I was looking for a sign of Carla, her spoor really, something that would tell me what had happened here. After I had walked around the decks, glanced in the engine room and the galley, I went into the main cabin. I opened Carla's closets. Several of her silk jumpsuits were still hanging there. I stared at them, touched them, trying to find her presence, to sense her. Although I didn't feel anything I could identify, something must have been touched off by her clothes, because I found myself heading for the stern. There was a metal ladder that went over the side. It was for getting in and out of the dinghy that had been stowed there. I left my shoes on deck, rolled up my trousers, and let myself over the side. There were scratches on the hull, a lot of them. In one ghastly moment of insight, I knew if the coroner had looked under Carla's fingernails, he would have found paint from the hull. As I stood there, clinging to that little metal ladder with the water lapping at my bare feet, I had a picture of Carla scratching at the side of the *Tête-à-Tate*, trying to climb back on board. I could see it, a clear image of her desperation. I wanted to reach out to her, give her my hand and help her to safety. It made me tremble, but if I was right, and I had no doubt that I was, it cleared up one thing. It meant that even if she had gone overboard on purpose, which is to say if even for a moment she had tried to kill herself, she had changed her mind. She had wanted to get back on board, to save herself. There was comfort in that, not much, but some; a man in grief grabs at whatever he can.

That shred of evidence did something strange to me. It released my grief. Until that moment I had been contained, maddeningly methodical about everything, determined to do what needed to be done. Here, on the side of the yacht, stretching to run my fingers over the scratches in the hull, touching those tiny grooves where her fingernails had tried so hard to get a grip, made me let go of everything. It wasn't just tears or sobs. My body convulsed, as I felt all the pent-up agony of these last weeks pour through and out of me. A moment of great clarity came over me and I knew what had happened. I could see her last moments on the boat and in the water.

• • •

Carla had started for Buddy's cabin, to tell him to turn the boat around again and take it back to the Santa Barbara harbor, but then she thought, no, it really was the seals that she wanted. They had made her feel peaceful, if only for a few moments, and that's what she needed now. Buddy's down jacket was hanging near the galley. Instead of looking for him and asking for help with the dinghy, she grabbed the jacket and pulled it over her jumpsuit. She went straight to the stern without looking into the saloon, where Tink was still drinking and smoking a joint.

The dinghy was lashed to the ship with lines that extended onto the deck, so the little boat could be hauled aboard if necessary. Although Carla had never released the dinghy herself, she had seen Ubaldo do it dozens of times. She climbed over the deck and let herself down the ladder. When she was next to the dinghy she untied the lines that held it secure. As she did, she also mistakenly freed the safety line that tethered the little boat to the *Tête-à-Tate*. When it settled into the water, it floated freely, not attached to anything. She didn't realize she should have left the safety line in place until she was in the dinghy. She could see that it was going to float away if she didn't move quickly. It was still close enough that a jump from the ladder was possible. Maybe at another time she could have managed. But then again, at another time, when she wasn't as angry at Paul or when she hadn't had quite as much to drink or perhaps hadn't seen Jack with his wife, she would have had the sense not even to try. But she jumped and managed to hit the edge of the dinghy, which pushed it away from her as she fell into the water. It wasn't yet a matter of concern beyond the insult to her dignity. The water here was calm and her husband and the others were on board.

While the dinghy bobbed in the water, Carla paddled the few feet back to the boat to grab onto the ladder. On her first try she couldn't reach the bottom rung. It didn't seem far, just far enough to be out of easy reach. She stretched for it and managed only to touch the hull of the *Tête-à-Tate*. She grabbed for the boat, scratching at it, unable to grip it, only to scrape her fingernails along the wood, digging grooves in the paint and sliding back into the water. When she was unable to reach the ladder she called out for the first time. She just yelled "Help!" as loudly as she could a few times. Although she was asking for help, she wasn't waiting for it. The dinghy was still near enough that although she felt rattled and certainly stupid for getting herself into this dilemma, she felt more inconvenienced than frightened. What little had happened had happened so quickly it seemed only seconds earlier that she had been standing on the deck. As she thrashed her way through the water, she slapped at the side of the dinghy, trying to pull it to her. The sides were inflated rubber tubes and they offered no help. She dug her fingernails into the rubber, scratching at it just as she had done on the side of the boat. As she wrestled with the dinghy, she lost her grip, and for a brief moment, a harbinger of what was to come, Carla went under into the cold water, slapping at the dinghy, trying to hold it fast, but only managing to push it away. For a moment or two of dark terror, she flailed about, underwater, beneath the dinghy. When she resurfaced, her lungs had started to take in water. She was terrified but exhilarated that she had surfaced. It gave her confidence. The dinghy itself was floating, its outboard engine still in the air, tilted upright, but out of reach. She knew she was at risk here, but it still seemed manageable. She called out again, crying her husband's name, yelling and trying to remain steady.

What she hadn't anticipated was the weight of the waterlogged down jacket and the fierceness of the currents that sweep through the Channel Islands. Sailors know about the currents and Buddy had taken them into account when he anchored the *Tête-à-Tate*, keeping her out of the wind's way. Splashing about in the water, trying to board the dinghy, Carla had pushed it into the current. It was an inflatable rubber boat, just a balloon on the water, at the mercy of the currents and the winds. She yelled again to the boat, but now the wind was stronger than her lungs. She could see she was being swept away, but she could also see she was headed toward the mainland, in the direction of Oxnard. As she tried to keep her grip on the rubber dinghy, she turned to look back at the ship, and to make another try at calling for help. As she shouted she saw Tink on the aft deck, near the stern. He was looking out to sea, looking, she hoped, at her. She called out, "Tink, down here! Tink!" She could see him looking around as if he'd heard her voice. Except for the wind, and his stoned condition, he would have heard her. He had only to glance over the stern and he would see the dinghy was gone. But instead he stood there for a few more seconds, with glazed eyes, then turned away. When Carla yelled, she loosened her grip and swallowed more seawater.

Carla was still thinking more clearly than not. She knew the trip from Anacapa to the harbor at Oxnard in the dinghy, using the outboard motor, would take a few hours. The current felt fast. Even if she couldn't climb into the dinghy, she was certain she could hold on to it. But the currents around the Channel Islands aren't consistent. They change all the time. Several hundred yards from the *Tête-à-Tate* the currents shifted again, and Carla began being pushed north, parallel to the shore, but not toward it. It was a starry night and the visibility was good, but as the yacht receded and the shore grew no closer, Carla began to get scared. She didn't know the term hypothermia, but she knew the water was cold and her arms and legs were getting numb rather than just more tired. For a moment she considered abandoning the dinghy and trying to swim; that such a thought might make even momentary sense frightened her and made her wonder if her judgment was impaired. Instead, she gathered her mental strength, even as her physical strength was ebbing, and began paddling toward land, kicking her legs out behind her, pushing on the dinghy the way her children had done with a paddleboard in the pool when they were learning to swim. She decided to take control of the little boat and push it, rather than let it drag her wherever it might. She would kick and push it to the shore no matter what the current's inclination. It seemed to work and Carla took heart at her ability to change the dinghy's course by physical strength, courage and will. She had never given up on anything in her life, had never considered giving up, and now, as always, it was working. She would use the dinghy to stay afloat and use the power in her legs to guide it.

Miles from where the *Tête-à-Tate* was anchored, the land juts out into the water at a place called Rincon Point. It's a famous surfer's beach, north of Carpenteria, not far from the highway. Carla could see the cliffs and the rocks of the Point in the distance. It might not be the harbor, but it was land and it would do. There was still more distance to the Point than she had already traveled. She was tired and scared, but she knew she had enough strength to get there. But the reason the Point is good for surfing is that the currents and streams meet there, swirl about and create the eddies and vast waves that attract surfers from around the world who come to test themselves. With the Rincon rocks still far ahead, but in her view, the dinghy began to come about, forming circles in the water. The rocks would appear, then disappear as the waves washed over her, and the optimism she felt only a moment earlier slipped away as the hypothermia numbed her hands. Carla tried to clutch the dinghy, as she was enveloped by the white, salty foam that rose in airy sheets. It seemed to have no density. It was like thrashing about in feathers. As she rose and broke through what she thought was the surface, she gasped for breath, thinking she was free. She took welcome air into her lungs, but there was foam too, and her lungs filled with water. The more she tried to breathe, the more foamy water she swallowed.

She made another try to board the dinghy, scratching at the round rubber tube, reaching above the foam that is as dangerous as a gun, grasping for a grip that would not come. In the water that was taking her, she saw her children as if they were with her, but beyond her reach. Above them, she saw Jack's face, hovering over the girls, protecting them. She clung to the faces for comfort, even as she knew what the vision meant. Then, shifting in the mist, she saw elusive glimpses of the living and the gone, of time present and past. Cora, calling to her and looking inward; Ma Leeper and Skeeter; herself as Barbara Farrell; little Bobby Dryer followed by Brandon Holt in his Dr. George costume riding Lewis the horse, through a green field that was the Metro lot of long ago. Then Milton with Ceil, holding hands, looking impossibly young and full of hope, reaching for her. She wanted to ask them for forgiveness and understanding, to tell them none of it mattered, that she wanted to love them. She didn't think that exactly in words, any more than the images before her were real pictures, but rather a swirl of feeling that flowed through her. Above them all was still Jack, his dark eyes looking down into the water, keeping them all safe and willing her to be calm, giving her peace. About a mile from Rincon Point her body temperature dropped so low that Jack's face dissolved into a white light that filled her heart, and then diminished to a tiny point until she lost consciousness and slipped beneath the dinghy.

25.

Shepherd-International, in what I liked to think of as the Bobby Shepherd era, managed to get *Changing Partners* into the theaters less than six months after Carla's funeral. There wasn't a premiere in the old sense. No one held those anymore. Like Carla herself, black-tie opening nights with giddy crowds and scores of reporters and photographers were part of a Hollywood that is receding now, disappearing really. Because Bobby didn't trust the movie, his marketing department opened it in nine hundred theaters at once and crossed their fingers. It did well enough. The critics stumbled over each other with long articles summing up Carla's career. Some were quite astute, but I don't think any of them did a better job than Edgar Magnin had at her funeral. She would have loved that. Her view would have been that the world probably didn't need another rabbi, but it sure as hell didn't need any more film critics. Only in Carla's hometown could both occupations be combined in one guy.

Arcady Metzler was declared a hero, and articles were written about him, too. The press got the idea that he had been solely responsible for saving the movie. *Esquire* did a profile of him that announced we were living in "the age of the rewrite." Arcady thought it was hilarious. One of the Lauras gave him a T-shirt emblazoned with the words "Media Hero." He wore it everywhere for a while. Lila was the other winner. Audiences responded to her and she got a lot of studio offers. Because she was the last actress to work with Carla, articles were written calling her Carla's successor. Cora told her how to handle it. Lila made sure to tell all the interviewers that she had learned so much from Carla, was flattered by the comparison, and hoped someday to deserve it. They lapped it up exactly as Cora had said they would.

After the picture opened, Bobby put Jack on the board of Shepherd-International. Jack had accumulated so much stock and so many proxies during the fight with Sidney that the idea seemed only natural. It was the most public position Jack had ever held. Board members don't set day-to-day policy, but Bobby didn't make a serious move that he didn't discuss with Jack. One of their first actions together was to set up Arcady's picture. He was to direct.

When Arcady's situation was settled, Jack took me to lunch at Hillcrest again and asked, "What are your plans?" He sounded like my father.

"I think the completion bond business and I are finished, if that's what you mean." I guessed he wanted to help because he knew Carla would have wanted it. She wasn't the sort who would have ever said to Jack, If anything happens to me, take care of Gabe. She didn't think that way, and besides, she never thought anything would happen to her. "I really don't have any plans, Jack. I'm not feeling very ambitious."

"You know we're doing Arcady's picture?"

"Yeah. He deserves the shot."

"You should produce it."

"Just like that?"

"If he deserves a shot, as you put it, then so do you."

"Have you mentioned this to him?"

"Arcady'd be lucky to have you."

That meant that one of the conditions of the deal was that Jack got to name the producer. I didn't think it was necessary for me to mention that I understood that. Instead, I said, "Carla once told me her definition of a producer. She said it was a guy who knows a writer." We both laughed—at the joke and at the idea of her telling it. Remembering Carla laughing put the real subject of this lunch on the table. It wasn't my future.

"I miss her," he said. It wasn't much of a remark, but Jack never talked about his feelings, certainly not to me.

"I know," I said. "All the time."

"From the time I was in my fifties, it was on my mind that I'd go first. It was only logical. I figured she'd have a good thirty years without me. I used to think about how she would think about me when I was gone. I planned for it. There was a letter for her, telling her what to do—how to handle everything. I'd made all the arrangements."

We were quiet for a moment. I could see that letter, and could picture Carla reading it. I wondered if it bothered Jack to be saying these things to me. He was such a negotiator, it was possible that in his mind, ignoring the fact that I had been her lover, too, was the price of his offer to make me a producer. He must have sensed my discomfort, because he spoke to it, as if he'd been reading my mind.

"I lived through three marriages with her. I think I know about all the men. Helping you is a way to remember her. Make this transition, Gabe. For yourself and your future."

When I nodded, we both smiled. We knew our scheming and planning together would have pleased her. I couldn't help thinking that I had set out to understand her so that my own life might go forward. Now here was Carla, through Jack, helping me find my ambition again.

So Arcady Metzler, M.H. (for media hero), and I went into business. We cast Lila Bledsoe, hired Cora Cohen to look after her, and I began a new part of my life. As Jack once pointed out, like so much else in Hollywood, producing movies isn't all that difficult, it's getting yourself in the position to do it that's tough. I made the transition, as Jack called it, and it made my life full. But still, late at night when I was alone and couldn't sleep, in the hours when a man finds out what's really on his mind, I would see her, always the same way, thrashing about in the cold dark water, struggling and pushing against the current, her arms outstretched, rising up through the foam, asking for the help I could not give her.